WINTER'S LEGION

(DAUGHTER OF WINTER, BOOK 4)

CORINA DOUGLAS

Burning Legacies Publishing

Also by Corina Douglas

Daughter of Winter Series:

Daughter of Winter (Book 1)

Winter's Mantle (Book 2)

Winter's Shield (Book 3)

Winter's Legion (Book 4)

Winter's Vengeance (Book 5)

Winter's Reign (Book 6)

*Winter's Legacy (Book 7)

Complements to the Daughter of Winter Series:

Winter's Companion

Rising from the Ashes

The Morrigan: Wings of War

Cernunnos & the Winged Changeling

Dagda: A New Dawn

Winter Solstice

The Morrigan Trilogy:

*Badb (Book 1)

Cursed Heir Series:

Cold Moon (Prequel)

*Hunter's Moon (Book 1)

(* = releasing soon)

Publishing by *Burning Legacies Publishing Limited*

Editing by Joy Sephton from *Justemagine*

Cover design art by Maria at *Artscandare*

ISBN: 978-1-067-07598-9 (ebook)

ISBN: 978-0-473-53719-7 (paperback)

ISBN: 978-1-067-07595-8 (hardback)

TRIGGER WARNINGS

Daughter of Winter follows the myths and legends behind the great winter goddess, Cailleach Bheur. Inside, you'll find two parallel stories at play—one in the present day, and the other in third century BC, Ancient Scotland. This series is very dear to my heart and covers a lot of ground, both in the present and the past, boasting word counts of up to 160,000 words as the series progresses. Complements to this series offer an in-depth look at additional characters including Dagda, Morrígan, and Cernunnos, and other series are being created as a result.

Before reading, please be aware this series is a DARK fantasy romance series, and that as the series progresses, a lot of trauma unfolds. Thus, there are a number of warnings applicable to this series <u>as a whole</u>, including:

- *Pagan rituals*
- *Bully romance*
- *Emotional and physical trauma*
- *Unsavoury dialogue*

- *Child/baby harm*
- *Sexual abuse*
- *Torture*
- *Violence and gore*
- *Each book in the series ends on a cliff-hanger, and*
- *In terms of spice levels, the romance between the two main characters in the past storyline turns steamy in book 2, but in the present storyline, it is slow burn and doesn't turn steamy until book 4. All spicy scenes are open door.*

If any of the above is not to your reading pleasure, please reconsider reading this series. However, if this type of story sounds like your jam, welcome aboard—I truly hope you enjoy the ride!

See you on the Other side,

Corina x

PRONUNCIATION GUIDE

Just like there are numerous versions of the Celtic myths themselves, there are various ways to pronounce the names below depending on which dialect you choose to follow (Scottish, Irish, or Welsh). It is important to note that I have not stayed true to any one dialect in this pronunciation guide; rather, I have chosen the pronunciation that best reflects how I perceived the characters in my head. And as I am English speaking (with a New Zealand accent!), keep this in mind when reading my English phonetic below.

However, for those that crave to know how these words *should* sound, you can access a free pronunciation guide to most of the words in this book—as said by a native Scottish highlands voice actor—by visiting this link: https://BookHip. com/FKVQQNW

People:

Arawn — aah-ronne

Brydie — bri-dee

Cailleach Bheur — car-lee-arch vere

Drust — drus-tt

Talorgan — tell-lore-gone

Tritus — try-tis

Gauls — goals

Cernunnos — ker-noo-noss

Morrígan — more-a-gin

Dagda — darg-dah

Brighid — bree-ach

Falin — fah-lyn

Girom — g-rome

Sedia — see-dee-a

Tuatha Dé Danann — too-huh day dan-in

Nuada — new-ah-dah

Cerridwen — care-re-dwen

Carman — car-men

Dub, Dain, Dothur — doob, dane, doth-er

Eachna — ee-arch-na

Airmid — air-midt

Lorcan — lore-kin

Mahon — maa-hin

Padriac — pard-rick

Uren — ew-rin

Lonc — lonc-hh

Brude — brewed

EVENTS:

Samhain — sow-win

Yule — you-ll

PLACES:

Aviemore — a-vee-maw

Cairngorms — ken-gawmz

Mothachail — moth-a-chail

Ben Macdui — ben mic-doo-e

Beinn na Caillich — been nah kay-lick

Ben Cruachan — ben crew-ah-chan

Cliffs of Moher — cliffs of more

Gulf of Corryvreckan — gulf of kor-ri-vrak-gin

The Cuillins — the cool-ins

Glamaig — gla-may-ge

Glenn Caillich — glenn kaylick

Glen Sligachan — glenn sleek-ik-hin

Isle of Skye — isle of sky

Kyle of Lochalsh — ky-l of lock-alsh

Sgùrr Alasdair — sker-alas-ter

Slieve na Calliagh — sleeve nah car-li-ah

Faerie — fair-ry

Hag's Cairn — hargs karne

Hag's Head — hargs head

Inverie, Mallaig — inver-ee, ma-laig

CREATURES

Cù-Sìth — coo-she

Siren — sigh-rin

Sluagh — slew-agh

Banshee — bann-she

Dullahan — doo-la-han

Wulver — wowl-ver

MISC

Carlin stone — car-lin stone

Shieling — she-ling

Tarn — tarrne

Druidry — drew-id-dree

Druid — drew-id

PART TWO

CHAPTER 1

TALORGAN

"What? Did you just say that you lost them?" Talorgan spat.

Falin snarled menacingly, his reptilian eyes latching onto the dark druid with a voracious hunger. His guttural voice was layered with the weight of age. "Am I speaking another language, druid?" the dragon rumbled. "Or are you having trouble understanding what my response means? I said, the Winter Goddess and the child escaped."

Unmindful of the threat the dragon posed, Talorgan ground his teeth together and grated, "How?"

"They had help from another of your kind."

Talorgan froze. "Another druid?" He hadn't reckoned on the aid of an outsider, a third player in this game of cat and mouse. Who had come to the Winter Goddess's aid? Why had they also taken the child? Did they know of the sin committed by its birth?

Falin growled, "Is that not what I said?"

As soon as the words left his mouth, the dragon released a stream of fire directly above Talorgan's head. The heat and embers of the torrent singed his skin. It was a reminder the dragon's patience was thin; he would tolerate impudence no longer. And Talorgan knew that if Falin saw what he'd done to his enemy, now hidden in the brush behind them, the dragon's wrath would be unparalleled.

Holding firm to his confidence in the bond the Dark God had orchestrated between him and this dragon, Talorgan held up a hand and allowed his own anger to match that of Falin's. He would not give into fear, nor would he cower to a being who was now his equal—no matter how powerful that being was. "I will not apologize for questioning that which cannot be possible, Falin. I had heard you were all-powerful, a beast of such magnitude that nothing could best your intelligence, your strength, or your speed. Were those descriptions wrong? Have I been bonded to a dragon who is not only stupid, but slow as well?"

The dragon elicited a snarl and clawed the ground. It was the only warning Talorgan had before Falin reared back and inhaled, his ebony scales turning a deep bloodred. Knowing what that signaled, Talorgan didn't have time to think, he merely reacted. Throwing his hands out, he screamed, "Halt!"

Not trusting that his command would stop Falin, he released his power as well. Red and black smoke loosed from his palms and slammed into the dragon's gaping maw. Falin's jaws snapped shut, a spout of smoke escaping from the dragon's nostrils as his power choked the fire that had been about to rain down upon his head.

Talorgan held his gaze and felt his insides curl. There was hatred there—an intense, soul-searing hatred born of the dragon's knowledge that he, Talorgan, had the power to bring him to heel.

Talorgan hadn't been certain of the exact level of power he'd been gifted by the Dark God, because he hadn't tested it until now. But this reaction confirmed Arawn had delivered on his promise—that Falin was his to command should he be able to call the beast to heel.

That confidence was suddenly shattered when Falin opened his mouth again and let loose a torrent of such raging fire that Talorgan felt his skin burn even from his respectful distance. The campfire to his left sputtered, the flames almost extinguishing.

"Do not push me, druid!" Falin roared from his massive, serrated jaws. "Regardless of the bond that connects my life to yours, I will not hesitate to crush you from existence."

Ignoring his erratic heartbeat, Talorgan forced himself to reply cynically, "Even at the cost of your own? Would you barter the end of your existence for mine?"

The dragon snarled again, and there was no denying the black rage in his tone. He'd pushed the beast as far as he dared. To prod him again would result in Falin ending his life—no matter if it ended his own as well.

Arawn had played a clever game, tying them to one another. Their relationship was a double-edged sword—a relationship that would either end in unparalleled power or their combined death.

Talorgan wasn't surprised by his Dark God's 'gift.' In the short time he'd come to know Arawn, this was not unexpected. Arawn took great pleasure in hurting others, in turning their emotions upside down and exposing both their secrets and their desires. He turned this into sport—entertainment for his immortal existence. This reminder was enough for Talorgan to turn his mind to the task at hand, for his one true desire had escaped—Cailleach, the Winter Goddess whom the gods had chosen for his own, and whom another man had defiled.

He clenched his fists to stop the instinctive urge to storm

over to the dead Gaul and spit on his lifeless body. That would only show Falin he'd killed that which the dragon had been promised, and it would not help his case with the beast whatsoever. No, he had to tread carefully through this quagmire of lies, because he still needed Falin's aid to reclaim Cailleach...which meant he needed to offer the dragon an olive branch.

Releasing a breath, Talorgan ground out reluctantly, "I apologize for my insolence. I am consumed with rage because I have lost everything I desire. This path I am upon is due to the woman who escaped your clutches, and I am telling myself she would not be worthy if she was so easily caught. A chase it will have to be then."

The dragon snorted, his features still tight with wrath and a gnawing frustration that couldn't be hidden. "Let us hope this bond between us will not be tested by your desires any further, druid, or this will be a short-lived relationship indeed."

Talorgan knew as he looked upon Falin's large, ancient face that a normal man would have been reduced to frozen terror with that delivery, even going so far as to soil his pants. A dark edge of fear still licked his spine in the presence of the beast, but the more bravado and false confidence he exuded, the easier it became to push that fear aside. Holding firm to this position, he pressed, "Do you have any idea where they went?"

Falin snorted, his muzzle peeling back to show razor-sharp teeth. "The portal was only large enough to accommodate the two of them, and as soon as the druid stepped through, he closed it. I saw nothing that would herald their location."

Talorgan clenched his jaw. Was there no clue to her whereabouts? The beast before him was reticent with his choice of words; questioning him was like squeezing water from a stone. He lifted a hand and rubbed it down the side of his face and felt the sticky smear of blood. It was a reminder of the actions he'd performed in a mad craze only minutes before the dragon's return. He wiped his hand along his robe, and the touch of that fabric brought a new question to his mind, the answer to which surely the dragon would know. "Did you see the color of this druid's robes?"

Falin didn't blink, those reptilian eyes never moving from Talorgan's form. The constant attention had him off-balance, although he would do nothing to show this beast how he felt. Being weak in the eyes of this immortal creature would not bode well for an equal balance of power between them.

"Falin?" he prompted. "Did you see the color of his robes?"

The dragon snorted, a puff of black smoke escaping his nostrils to float up into the still night air. "His robes were the color of the forest."

Green. The admission made Talorgan's heart skip a beat. It could only be one man. One druid who had once been his master in every sense of the word. Girom. The Master of Herbs was the only one who had taken an interest in Talorgan's activities over the last two years, the only one to question if his motives were true—and if he still followed the light.

Talorgan still remembered the look in his mentor's eyes as he'd blatantly lied, "Yes, master. I still adhere to the light." He swore the man had seen right through him, to his innermost memories, where his secret meeting with Arawn during bull sleep was emblazoned across his soul.

But even after that clue, he had failed to realize his old

master was watching him—him, and it appeared, his Winter Goddess. Whom he had now *taken.*

Rage coursed through him again, his body stiffening.

The dragon eyed him, those reptilian eyes not missing the anger now flooding his senses. Calm. He needed to remain calm. *This is not the end,* he reminded himself. *This is merely the beginning; a setback easily overcome. Remember what you have won tonight. Remember the victory.*

He turned his head to look at where Tritus's body lay—or what was left of it. He'd tried his hardest to control his rage. To ensure his nemesis ended life slowly, painfully, and with the knowledge of all he'd lost. He'd hoped, before the man passed, to hold the body of the Gaul's dead babe in front of him before dealing that killing blow. He'd wanted to relish the pain that would be etched on Tritus's face, to know that a thousand sharp blades had pierced the Gaul's soul.

He had also hoped to have Cailleach by his side. To have taken her mouth and her body while Tritus lay there, bound and tied, incapable of stopping his wandering hands and lips as he laid claim to the Winter Goddess in every way possible.

He'd imagined entering her sex. Imagined implanting his seed in her womb on a final soul-searing thrust that would cause Cailleach to cry out with ultimate pleasure.... Yes, he'd had many dreams of how those last moments of Tritus's life would play out. But all that had been taken away by the bastard's provocations!

Tritus had pushed him too far. Taunting him and insinuating that the goddess would never accept him. Never love him. He'd boasted that he—a Gaul from another land who followed different gods—had managed to enslave her with ease, claiming that she'd fallen into his arms with the innate knowledge they were meant to be together. That his soul was entwined with hers since the very beginning of time. And when the bastard had started to talk about the baby that grew in her womb—the baby that was soon to be born—Talorgan had had enough.

The rage that had feathered in his belly had spread throughout his body in a vicious, uncontrollable wave. His plans had been obliterated by the fear that what the Gaul said was true. Talorgan barely remembered muttering the words that came out of his mouth, or the clenching of his hands. He'd held them together so tightly, and the action, along with his enchantment, had heralded the final moments of Tritus's life, choking the very breath from the Gaul's body.

His nemesis had died a swift death, his life gone in the mere blink of an eye. It happened so fast that Talorgan had stood in shock for a few moments, and it wasn't until he heard the echo of Falin's roar reverberating across the mountains that he broke from his trance. He knew what that sound heralded. It had been an announcement that the dragon had been thwarted, that he had failed not only to capture the Winter Goddess, but also in taking the life of her child. The message, along with the Gaul's life ending so abruptly, had caused Talorgan to go mad.

The moments that followed were a blur of animalistic, all-consuming hatred. A hatred so profound that he'd lost all sense of self. And when he'd calmed down enough to become conscious of the here and now, Talorgan had found himself gripping his runic knife in one hand and his body wholly enrobed in blood. His eyes unerringly traveled to Tritus, and the evidence of his actions had become crystal clear. The man was unrecognizable, his face and body a ruined mess of slashes and gaping wounds, entrails and organs haphazardly thrown around the campfire, mixed with the brambles Tritus had called upon only moments before. But what had stopped Talorgan in his tracks and made his heart clench in a painful vice was that, upon the only part of the man's body that hadn't been sullied, there were two black horns curling out of his dark head.

Horns that hadn't been there before—ever.

Talorgan had fixed his gaze on those horns, a sickening realization flooding through him, for there was no mistaking the bloodline they divulged. There was only one god that claimed that right—Cernunnos, the Wild God of the Forest.

Questions raced through his mind as to who this Gaul had been. Had Tritus been the son of Cernunnos? Had Cailleach claimed a lover worthy of her bloodline? But then, why was the man not all-powerful? Why had he, a mere druid, been able to best Tritus if he was indeed a god? If Tritus had been the spawn of the gods, Tritus should have easily won their skirmish. If that were true, it should have been *him* who lay upon the ground, his soul fled and bodily remains in ruin. Because that truth hadn't eventuated, it wasn't possible Tritus had been the son of the gods, unless... he could only claim half of that birthright.

The thought had stopped him cold, because with it came the unmistakable burn of searing truth. It explained the abilities Tritus had held—his ability to see past the veil of Cailleach's true form, and the reason why he had captured the goddess' attention.

The knowledge that another of his gods had spawned a devil—a mixing of the bloodlines between mortal and immortal—was enough to harden Talorgan's heart one step further and acknowledge that Arawn was the only one whom he could trust. The Dark God held true to his nature, ruling his people with an iron fist; there was no misunderstanding between what he could do and would do. Arawn was as he appeared, true and without artifice, and it was this surety that caused Talorgan to fully accept his new path—the path on which he was always meant to be.

But all these revelations didn't stop what he craved. They didn't stop him wanting that which was still denied him—Cailleach. With a burning vengeance in his chest, Talorgan had stood over the remains of his nemesis and promised himself he would not only claim the Winter Goddess with his last breath, but he would also end the evidence of her tryst with Tritus by killing their child. The only satisfaction he had in admitting these goals to himself was knowing he had the power to do so. After all, he now had a dragon of unimaginable power, and his bargain with Arawn had also gifted him immeasurable strength and an immortal life.

Time was therefore not of consequence in fulfilling his desire; however, time was something he did not want to give his enemies. For no doubt, Cailleach and Girom had spread news of his demise and how he had unleashed Arawn. He knew there would be an uprising against him. He would need to build an army, and quickly. Time, in that regard, was not on his side.

Falin, clearly sick of waiting on his reply, interrupted his thoughts with a snarl. "Are we done here, druid? I wish to feed. My hunt was unsuccessful, and I hunger for sustenance. Where is the man you promised me? The man who smells like more than a mortal?"

The dragon's words sent a chill chasing down Talorgan's spine. Had Falin smelt the Gaul's lineage on him? Is that why he'd wanted Tritus as payment for capturing the Winter Goddess? To a dragon, was a half-mortal and a half-god a delicacy, just as a child would be?

Talorgan hid his shudder and was thankful of the runes he'd quickly laid around what remained of Tritus's body before the dragon returned. They were effectively shielding the sight and smell of the man's death from the beast. Talorgan hadn't been certain they would work, but given Falin's question, it was clear they had, and it gave him the courage to lie. "My enemy escaped."

Falin looked at him with an intense hunger, as if he desired his life in payment for forfeiting Tritus's.

It was true he had promised Falin the Gaul as payment for his task, but as he hadn't brought Cailleach back, that payment was no longer due. It was time to remind him of that. "I trust you are not going to chastise me for letting him escape, especially when you failed at your own task. Given you haven't brought me the Winter Goddess, your payment is forfeit."

Falin spread his wings to their furthest extent, blocking the moon's light, and ground out, "Do not play games with me, druid. You will not like the end result."

Talorgan inclined his head. "I promise you I have not lied. However, given the state he was in when he escaped, I have no doubt he will not be alive for much longer."

The dragon looked around the campsite, taking note of the debris, which included a large number of brambles and dead bugs. He raised his snout and sniffed the air. His lips peeled back from his maw as he rumbled, "The smells here are off. There is too much in the way of magic to determine that which is real." His golden eyes, dissected by slitted red pupils, narrowed on Talorgan. "I am no stranger to subterfuge, and if I find you have lied to me, our bond will end."

"Of course," Talorgan replied smoothly, bowing his head. "And I expect absolute honesty from you in return. Again, I am sorry the man escaped, but you have no right to claim him given your own failure."

At this, Falin released a menacing snarl, but Talorgan didn't give him the satisfaction of a flinch as he added, "Given that we have no leads on the Winter Goddess's whereabouts, I have no further need of you tonight. It is best you return to the Underworld and eat your fill. I have much to plan and put into action, and I will progress more effectively without your presence tailing mine. The world is not yet ready to know of your existence, Falin, but know this, your time will come, and I promise you it will come soon. Arawn's plans are of benefit to us all, and your aid furthers his cause as well as mine. Take the rest you deserve while you can, Falin. When dawn breaks, I will call upon your services once again, and it would be in your best interests to be ready."

The dragon considered him with a precision that caused the hairs on the back of Talorgan's neck to rise. "And what would those interests be, druid? For I will not waste my time and efforts on empty promises. I know I am forced to comply with your commands, but know this—if those commands do not result in any benefit of my own, the threat of death is not powerful enough to bind me to this parasitic relationship. I will meet it head on. At least in the Afterlife I will be able to eat and drink my fill without the onus of other...*requirements*."

Talorgan felt the warning as it was meant to be—a reminder that his grip on this dragon's reins were tenuous at best. But he masked those thoughts from his face as he replied smoothly, "I promise you that when I next call upon your services, Falin, there will be a feast of such proportions that you will not hunger for days after."

And that promise was not a lie. For war was coming, that he knew with certainty.

CHAPTER 2

BRYDIE

PRESENT DAY, SCOTLAND

The oppressive silence stretched as we left the settlement of Broadford behind and began the steep, treacherous climb back up the mountain to the shieling. The weather had changed since the morning's drive down to the village, the rare blue sky now replaced with threatening rain clouds; a reminder that winter was trying to hold on with everything it could before relenting to the coming spring.

Gage's voice cut the silence, his tone brusque, the memory of what he'd just done still hovering between us. "As soon as we get back, we'll be packing our bags and tidying up. We need to leave the place clean. I don't want anyone to happen upon the shieling by chance and find evidence of our stay. McKenzie, can you tackle your room and the kitchen? Give Aidan something to do as well; he'll be upset we're moving again."

McKenzie nodded, her features tight.

The car tires crunched loudly as the snow chains scrabbled for purchase, and I clutched at the door handle, my knuckles white. Since having the truth revealed behind my parents' death and understanding that I'd also been in the vehicle when it went over the bridge into the river had made my phobia worse.

"Brydie." Gage's demand broke through my fear, and I lifted my eyes to catch his cerulean gaze in the rearview mirror. "I'll leave you to clean our room while I scout the road. I want to make sure no one has followed us. Logan, you and Ian sort out the rest of the house."

Gage's demand was a ploy. I knew he was distracting me from my irrational fear, and because he expected a response, I nodded. His eyes bored into mine, and in that gaze, which was complemented by our internal connection, I felt a shared understanding. Gage knew I was still reeling from the confrontation with the young man at the Claymore. Garret had been about to kill me or capture me, it mattered not, but thanks to an ingrained reaction, I'd been the one who became the monster—the hunter instead of the hunted.

I remembered that vicious urge to mete out justice, to obliterate Garret into nothing. That urge had been so strong my jaw still ached from clenching my teeth together. The incident had been a test of my power. A test that Gage said I'd passed...but I felt I'd failed.

I remembered his words at the restaurant: *"Carrying power is a curse as well as a blessing...and you passed the test, Brydie. You fought the shadow of your power."*

Right then, I'd understood what having power truly meant. Understood that with a single thought, I had the ability to nurture life or destroy it. Gage was the one to pull me away from the edge. I hadn't recognized how far I'd fallen or how far I'd come in taking Garret's life. But Gage had. He'd recognized the death I hungered for, and if I hadn't relinquished control to my bodyguard, Garret would be dead, his blood on my hands.

The interrogation that followed had been a blur, as had the silent, weighted walk back to the vehicle with Logan and McKenzie. As we waited for Gage to return, none of us keen to sit in the vehicle, they didn't say a word about my instinctive reaction. Time had slowed to a crawl, and I'd impatiently began to pace up and down the street. McKenzie and Logan watched me warily as they stood by the vehicle, Logan's eyes hooded but alert, McKenzie's weighing.

Gage wasn't long, less than ten minutes, and I knew by the tightness in his face and the white brackets around his mouth what it was he'd had to do.

My voice was hoarse. "Is he alive?"

Gage didn't hesitate to respond, it was almost as if he'd been expecting the question, and I suppose he had given he could feel my anxiety. "Yes. Talorgan didn't have control of him for long. He was lucky."

Lucky. It was a poor choice of words, because Garret hadn't been lucky that Talorgan had gotten hold of him. Just as Talorgan had managed to take control of James, my ex-fiancé, back in New Zealand. James was *lucky* too—even though Gage had had to stab him in the back in order to break his connection to Talorgan. Lucky? I didn't think so. Even so, my Guardian had done what he'd needed to, carrying out everything his role entailed in order to save me...except this time, I knew he'd been saving me from myself.

Swallowing hard, I pushed the thought away. Later. There would be time to consider all of this later, when we had relocated and the threat of Talorgan had passed. Still, I felt wild relief that against all odds Garret had survived, and it was all thanks to Gage.

The object of my thoughts cut me another weighing look through the rearview mirror. Concern arrowed down our shared line, flavored with the shadow of woodsmoke and forged steel. My breath caught at his show of emotion. Emotion that told me he cared.

Every move he made, every action, every comment, every emotion shared down our internal line was another confirmation that he was more than who he pretended to be. That the cold, aloof shell he held around himself was just a guise, a means of protection. He was an enigma, a puzzle I had yet to solve, and from the gentle probing I'd given his twin brother, I knew Logan would not tell me anything. Any revelations of Gage's past would have to come from the man himself. But since Gage put up walls everywhere I turned—even denying the strength of the powerful attraction that simmered between us—it was clear my Guardian wanted nothing more from me than the relationship we already shared.

The car went over another bump, and I froze once again, my hand still clenching the door handle. Trapped. I felt trapped. I closed my eyes and breathed deeply, trying to focus on anything but the car ride. A question arose that I'd pushed away earlier and I blurted, "You mentioned before that Callum has found the fifth descendant. Do any of you know who that is?"

Silence. I looked at Gage. His body and shoulders were tight as he navigated a sharp bend in the road.

It was McKenzie who answered. "Yes."

I cut her a glance when nothing else was forthcoming, and she avoided my gaze to look out the window at the passing vista of snow-capped rocks. Unease pooled in my stomach. For the last few weeks, Gage and McKenzie had been keeping something from me. Was it this?

"Who is it?" I pushed. "Is it a member of our clan?"

Logan, who was sitting in the driver's seat in front of me, shot his twin brother a glance. It was telling, for through their twin bond, Logan could feel Gage's emotions just as I could. I honed into our connection and identified reluctance and a twinge of anxiety coming from my Guardian. This didn't give me confidence.

"Gage?" I disregarded the voice inside my head that told me to leave it alone—the voice of the old Brydie, the Brydie who had been ignorant of her legacy and hidden away in New Zealand some four months before, and demanded, "Tell me."

Gage's hands clenched on the wheel as he replied, "I'm not sure."

"You're not sure? What the hell does that mean?"

His jaw tightened. "It's complicated and not suited for a discussion here and now."

"When, then?" I pushed. There was something in his tone, and along with McKenzie's odd behavior, I wasn't going to let this go.

His next words were low. "Soon. When we get to the shieling, I'll tell you everything."

McKenzie shifted in the seat beside me, and I captured her and Gage's shared gaze in the mirror again. I wanted to scream. Why was now not a good time? Was it because I'd lost control at the Claymore and whatever they had to share had the potential to make me lose control? No. No, I couldn't think that way.

I reached out and touched McKenzie's arm gently. "Should I be worried?" I asked her softly.

Her lips tightened, but she shook her head. "No, Gage has done everything I would have done."

Knowing there was nothing else to learn until Gage was ready to tell me, I turned away from her and went back to looking out of the window as we continued to climb up the snow-clad mountain. I took note of the landmarks, confirming with relief that in another twenty minutes we would be back at the shieling and I'd be out of this bloody contraption.

"Where are we headed next?" Logan asked. "We'll need a new base before we work on retrieving the descendant."

"I haven't had a chance to think on that yet," Gage admitted. "You got any ideas, brother?"

Logan ran a hand through his close-cropped short hair. He was Gage's identical twin but without the rough edges. Where Gage was hard and brusque, Logan was refined and smooth. Gage's hair was overlong and he usually dressed all in black, but Logan's hair was shorter, his clothing tailored. He was also the more amicable of the two, carrying a genuine, easy-going warmth about him. "It's coming into spring," he mused. "The tourists will be flocking to all of the usual haunts. You chose Beinn na Caillich because no one would think to come here in winter. What about the Gulf of Corryvreckan? The spring tempest will soon be rising; most won't risk its power."

Gage made a sound of agreement. "There's tremendous power there. It's possible we could use it to enter the Institute and mask our return."

"But where would we stay?" McKenzie asked. "The Corryvreckan whirlpool is a narrow strait in the middle of two islands."

"There's a shieling on the west coast of the mainland," Gage said. "Less than a kilometer from the water's edge. It's camouflaged against the hillside and only accessible through private land."

"That sounds plausible," she agreed.

But then I remembered what Callum had at his disposal. "Will the power of the whirlpool be enough to combat the Dagda's cauldron, though?"

Logan swiveled in his seat to look at McKenzie. "Is the Dagda's cauldron as powerful as they say?"

McKenzie's voice was quiet, but the undertone of fear was audible. "Yes. I have seen it in my visions—and Callum wielding its power."

I hid a shiver. The leader of our druidic clan was one of the most dangerous men I had ever met, even without the cauldron in his possession.

"Tell us what you saw, McKenzie," Gage said.

McKenzie's hands curled into tight fists, and my belly clenched again. The red-haired Dream Walker was not a woman to show fear. She was fierce; a fighter. I reached out and placed a hand over hers, squeezing it gently. Her eyes darted to mine as she shared, "I saw him holding the cauldron. He was scrying, watching our movements."

Gage swore as he thrust the truck into low gear as we climbed past a ravine to our left. I felt the air becoming thin and knew we were close to the shieling, even if we could not see more than a few meters of the track ahead of us. Everything was white due to the blanket of ever-present low fog that hung over the mountains.

Logan asked, "And you think Callum can see us, even with the glamour?"

McKenzie's face was white. "Yes. He holds one of the four treasures of the Tuatha Dé Danann in his possession. It's as old as the gods themselves and carries unimaginable power."

This time I couldn't stop the shudder that raked down my spine. It was said the four treasures had come from a land not of this world, and that with the four treasures also came their people, the Tuatha Dé Danann. I'd met Callum and his guards; I'd felt their power. Collectively, they were strong, but with a treasure such as the cauldron, they would be damn near invincible. My heart raced at the predicament we were in, aware that not only did I have to face Talorgan at Samhain as prophecy required, but also Callum, the leader of our druidic clan—a man who had fallen to the darkness and dragged a good number of our people down with him.

McKenzie's voice cut through my churning thoughts. "I vote that we head to Ireland. It's an unpredictable move that could gain us the time we need to recoup, both before and after we infiltrate the Institute."

"Where in Ireland?" Gage asked.

"How about Slieve na Calliagh?" she suggested.

I'd heard the term before, from stories my father had shared with me as a child. "The megalithic tombs in County Meath? It's said Hag's Cairn is tied to Cailleach, that she dropped large rocks on her way past the mounds."

McKenzie nodded. "Yes, but there is also an equinox stone there. It's illuminated at the dawn of spring, so there's power there on two fronts." Her gaze turned to mine. "How did you know about it?"

"My father. He used to tell me stories during my childhood."

Gage growled, "Andrew carried more secrets than we knew. We underestimated him."

I stiffened. "He did what he thought best."

Even though my father didn't tell me of my legacy or what it was I might one day become, he had subconsciously prepared me for the journey I was now on. I recalled again those last moments with him—memories that had recently resurfaced through my visitation with the Winter Goddess. We'd learned my father held druidic power—not much, but a touch of water magic. Enough to save me that fateful evening when our car had gone over the bridge and into the river.

This revelation had shocked Gage. Andrew was supposed to have been Dormant. Who had pulled me from the river that night remained a mystery. We assumed that same person had also returned me to my home in Hamilton. I knew this plagued my Guardian. It confirmed there was another player in the game—someone whom we weren't sure was on our side or Talorgan's.

Logan cleared his throat. "Would the cauldron's power reach Ireland?"

"I'd say it's more than possible," Gage confirmed.

"Then how would we escape its reach? By entering another world?" Logan snorted at his own joke.

But Gage froze. "There is such a place," he admitted quietly.

McKenzie understood almost immediately what Gage was referring to. "Surely you're not talking about The Rowan Tree? They moved their people to another world twelve years ago. I heard it can only be accessed by a portal."

The Rowan Tree? I'd heard that term before; Ian had told me they were our people's cousins.

"They're the obvious choice," Gage returned. "It's also where the cauldron was first found and most likely where it was stolen from."

I could hear the frown in Logan's voice as he asked, "How would we get there?"

"The portal remains open as some of their people still interact in this world, and Lorcan, their leader, needs the intel. As much as The Rowan Tree like to keep to themselves, they know they're risking their own necks if they isolate themselves completely from everyone else."

"And is he to be trusted, or is he of the same ilk as Callum?" I asked, gut churning at the memory of Callum. I couldn't take it if he was.

"Lorcan is not Callum," Gage replied firmly, "and he can be trusted—to an extent."

Logan tapped a finger to his chin. "Hmm, well, this feels like the right path. I've been seeing an image in my mind since we left the Claymore, one I can't shake."

McKenzie's voice was sharp. "A vision?"

He shrugged. "No, it's not like a movie playing out, but more of an image."

"What kind of image?"

"A tree with red berries. I've just come to realize it's a Rowan tree."

McKenzie narrowed her eyes at Logan. "You claim to have no druidic magic, yet you are receptive to other forces. The Rowan tree is symbolic for many reasons. It's the tree of life, symbolizing courage, wisdom, and protection, all of which we are searching for right now. I think Logan's just confirmed our next step."

I turned to McKenzie and asked, "Is there a chance The Rowan Tree will turn us away?"

"I'm not sure, but it will be worth reminding them that if Talorgan wins this war, his reach will extend to their world soon enough."

She was right, and I didn't need the shared connection with my Guardian to tell me he was worried. It was in the way he clenched his jaw, how his hands once again tightened on the wheel. I knew he was reminded that his brother, if not all of us, may not make it to the end of October.

My mouth was suddenly bone dry at the thought my life could very well be reduced to the next eight months. That stark truth caused my heart to pound, and not wholly with anguish that I may not live to a ripe old age, but also with a fear that what I truly desired would slip through my fingers.

My gaze shifted to the back of my Guardian's head, fixating on the long strands of ebony hair curling at his nape. I suddenly ached to run my fingers through those glossy strands. My imagination needed no further encouragement, and images were soon rolling through my mind of us together, naked and entangled. My mouth dried when I felt Gage's intense scrutiny again. I avoided his eyes in the mirror; I didn't need to see what I knew would be in them because I could feel it along our shared line—censure, and a hard denial.

With that brutal reminder, the burning images fled, chased away by the cold, stark knowledge that my Guardian would never allow us to become more than a mentor and his protégé.

CHAPTER 3
GAGE
PRESENT DAY, SCOTLAND

I shoved the vehicle into park and turned off the engine in front of the shieling. McKenzie and Logan immediately jumped out and entered the stone cottage, their figures hunched over as they fought the chill, lashing wind that had arisen during the last fifty meters of our climb. When Brydie didn't exit the vehicle, I unclipped my seatbelt and turned to face her.

"You want to do it here?" I asked, knowing full well she was waiting on my confession as to who the fifth descendant was.

She nodded, her face set in determined lines. "I'm not leaving until you tell me."

I wasn't ready. I didn't think I'd ever be ready. This secret had hounded me for as long as I'd known her, and with a sinking feeling, I knew Ian had been right all those months ago—I should have told Brydie who it was as soon as I'd realized. But I hadn't, and here we were; the time for truth had reared its ugly head. "There was a reason why we didn't share it with you—"

"Enough, Gage. Just spit it out!"

Fine. At her demanding tone, I growled, "Chloe is the fifth descendant."

Brydie blinked. Her voice when it came was small, almost breathless. "What?"

Feeling the back of my neck tingle in warning, I repeated, "Chloe is the fifth descendant."

Her eyes widened to their furthest reach, the silver in her irises swirling with disbelief. Her face blanched. "Chloe? *My* Chloe?"

I nodded.

"What? How...how do you know that? When did you find out?"

"The day she left New Zealand."

I could see her calculating that it had been almost four months since then. "And you've known all this time?"

"Yes."

For a moment there was absolute silence, and I knew it was the calm before a storm right before she cried, "Why didn't you tell me? Why have you kept this from me? Didn't you think I had a right to know? She's my best friend, for fuck's sake!"

"We couldn't have you distracted. What good would you be worrying about her while trying to come into your legacy? Besides, she was in no danger."

Brydie stilled. "No danger?" The lines around her mouth became more pronounced as she ground out, "You said Callum has the fifth descendant. How do you know she's *not* in danger? What else did McKenzie see?"

The air between us quivered, and I could feel the telltale tickle of her power snapping at the back of my neck. Brydie was hovering on the edge of losing control; her emotions escalating. My voice was soft, soothing, and I tried to send as much reassurance down our shared line as possible as I said, "McKenzie tells me that she's alive—"

"Alive?" Her voice was livid, her usually pallid face hosting bright spots of color. "How fucking bad is it for you to say that she's still alive?"

I knew then that whatever I said wasn't going to mollify her. Still, I tried again. "I don't know how bad she is. All I know is that McKenzie saw her in the dungeons."

"The dungeons?" The temperature suddenly dropped, a chill permeating the vehicle.

My breath showed as a puff of white as I carefully replied, "We have no idea how long she's been there. Given McKenzie's vision only came this morning, it's safe to assume she was recently taken."

Brydie laughed, the tone dark and dangerous, and in her silver eyes raged violence. "Assumptions are not truth, Gage. Be very careful what you assume. And you are talking about Callum—a man who holds the Dagda's cauldron."

She was right. Callum could use the cauldron to do whatever he desired to Chloe, even bend her to his will.

Brydie was watching me closely. "Do you have nothing else to say?" she growled.

"I didn't think an apology was—"

"You fucking bastard!"

It was the only warning I got before her hands glowed, and a fist came flying into my nose. My head flew backward, blood immediately spurting. I instantly curbed my instinctive reaction to defend myself. I deserved this punishment. I deserved her wrath. The hurt I could feel down our shared line was crippling, and I was all too mindful of the fact that it was due to my actions—my decisions.

There was also an awareness that Brydie was on the cusp of losing all control, and it was my job to ensure she stayed on the right side of the line—no matter if she ended up hating me more than she already did.

I roughly sketched a rune with my fingers. A wall sprang up between us, deflecting not just her second blow but returning the power that surged from her palms. It ricocheted into her face, her ash-blonde hair billowing behind her.

Her lips peeled back in a snarl. With her silver eyes swirling with unimaginable power and her blonde hair trailing behind her, it hit me that she looked more like her ancestor than she knew. "You fucking coward!" she sneered.

"I'm sorry, but whether you are willing to listen to me or not, I did this to protect you," I said through the barrier, feeling my chest squeeze with her overwhelming feelings of pain and anger. I felt as though she'd punched me right in the heart. "And I promise you that we'll work on retrieving Chloe as soon as we've relocated—as soon as you're safe."

"You did this to protect me? Stop making excuses!" Her voice was scathing. She narrowed her eyes, the extent of her hatred implicit, and her next words were as cold as winter, deliberate, conveying everything that raged inside her. "You've destroyed my trust. How dare you keep this from me? I fucking hate you for it!"

She wrenched the door open and shot out of the vehicle; but rather than head into the safety and security of the shieling, she turned and blindly fled up the mountain, her magic swirling around her palms.

I simply watched her, filled with self-loathing as her form was swallowed by the squalling wind and driving rain.

AFTER HEALING my nose and removing all trace of the blood from the vehicle and my clothes, I entered the shieling. As soon as I closed the door, I became aware of how silent it was inside the building, the shrieking of the rising wind muffled by the stone exterior. The back of my neck still tingled; a sharp irritation that proclaimed loud and clear that the emotions my protégé was currently feeling were being channeled in the weather. There was a storm brewing, one that would soon be centered upon us. It was fitting, for it matched the turbulent violence rioting in my chest.

After Brydie had disappeared, I'd reduced the power of our internal connection, temporarily compressing the filaments that conveyed our emotions. I was too much of a coward to accept them for what they were. I already felt low, ashamed of my actions; because if Logan had been the fifth descendant then I would have wanted to know. I would have *killed* to know. And after watching Brydie and Chloe back in New Zealand, I knew that although Brydie didn't have any siblings, Chloe had claimed that bond.

A throat cleared in the oppressive silence, and I looked up to see McKenzie, Logan, and Ian hovering near the doorway that led to the kitchen. Their faces were tense, expressions carefully neutral, their demeanor conveying the storm brewing outside hadn't gone unnoticed.

Ian was the one to break the silence. "How did it go?"

I waved a hand out the window. "As expected. She fucking hates me."

McKenzie grimaced, but Ian shrugged my response off. "I doubt that, man. What she's feeling now is betrayal. In time, she'll come to see why you withheld the truth from her."

I looked at him sharply, wanting to lash out. "Speaking from experience, are you?"

He flinched. "Be very careful what you say, Gage."

I was fucking beyond being careful, not when hurt also raged in my own chest. "Fine, we'll dodge what everyone knows."

"Gage," McKenzie broke in warningly. "Just calm down."

I cut her a swift glance. "Don't worry, I'm fucking calm. But we"—I gestured at Ian—"have unfinished business. Are you saying that you agree with my directive now? That after all your protestations, you think I now took the right path by not telling her that her best friend was the fifth descendant?"

Ian's face was bleak, and the words, when they came, appeared torn from him as he snarled, "Yes, damn you, you were right. Is that what you want to hear?"

Even said in anger, his admission floored me, especially after all his arguments to the contrary. I narrowed my gaze on his face. "Why the sudden change of heart, Ian?"

He looked away, past my shoulder, as he muttered, "I was clouded by my own emotions. You weren't. You could see what needed to be done. And, damn you, you were right —she needed to come into her legacy first, without any distractions."

"Even if that distraction was her best friend?" I pressed, needing to hear it, needing a win.

"Yes," he snarled. "Especially if she'd known her best friend was one of us! It's obvious what she would have done. She feels too much just to let it go. She wouldn't have progressed, wouldn't have come into her legacy. Hell, she might not even be alive. So, yes, damn you, you were fucking right. Happy now?"

I shook my head. "No, I'm not happy."

"I agree with Ian," McKenzie said softly. "Even though Brydie's hurting right now, it was the right thing to do. Sometimes we need to make a hard choice. This was one of those times, Gage, and I still think it was the right one. My conscience is clear, and I stand by my support of your decision."

I cut my gaze to Logan. He was just as much in the dark as Brydie had been. But it was clear that McKenzie and Ian had filled him in while we were in the car. My brother always had an opinion and one he never had any trouble sharing, even if he knew it would hurt me. Logan wasn't touched by this prophecy, but his view was one I valued more than the others. He'd been with me right from the start, through all the battles I'd fought in life. He also knew me better than anyone and never hesitated to tell me what he thought.

Logan didn't let me down. "I know what it's like to desire something you can't have—to want to save someone you love." His gaze was unwavering, and I withheld a flinch, aware he was talking about a moment in our past where I'd pushed him away. "That said, I think you should have revealed the truth to her a lot earlier. Did you ever consider using Chloe as motivation to progress?" He paused, and then shrugged. "Maybe she would have come into her legacy sooner, maybe not. There's no way of knowing, but given who and what Brydie is, I feel you made the right choice. She was vulnerable without her power. You also need to remember that you're touched by prophecy. Fate would have guided you along the way, and knowing you, I'm aware you're not one to make rash decisions. I trust your judgement, Gage, so I think you did what you needed to, and in time, Brydie will too."

As if to prove a point, the glass in the windowpanes rattled as the wind howled with a menace and a draft of icy wind whipped around the room. The hair whispered at the back of my neck, and I felt the wrath in those icy tendrils. "It's clear Brydie doesn't see it that way."

Logan gave me a small half-smile, but there was no humor in his eyes.

My heart pounded as I smelled his fear conveyed in the sharp tang of sweat. I blinked, then discreetly inhaled, confirming it wasn't just his fear I could smell but all of them. It took me but a moment to realize it wasn't me they were afraid of—it was Brydie.

She was more than the naive girl I'd found in New Zealand four months ago; she was now a Daughter of Winter, carrying a cloak of power that hovered over her shoulders like a second skin. The level of that power was yet to be seen, but given what we'd witnessed at the Claymore, it was clear she would be different to all the other Daughters before her because her first instinct had been to attack. To respond to the threat, rather than find a way to diffuse it.

Brydie hadn't given Garret a chance, going straight for the kill. Her response wasn't a shock, not when I shared an affinity toward that same instinctive reaction, and especially not when she'd relinquished control to me when asked. But clearly, she had scared McKenzie and Logan, and going by Ian's face, him too.

Regardless of what they felt, I had to get Brydie back. She was vulnerable, and the storm she was creating was a calling card to Talorgan's sycophants. After what had happened at the Claymore, we needed to leave, and quickly. My sixth sense was screaming that we were playing with fire the longer we delayed, but knowing that my actions were what had caused this response meant it wouldn't be me who would calm her down. I needed a volunteer.

I stared at each of them in turn, instantly dismissing Ian. The tension between him and Brydie was still there, her rejection a sore point between them. I moved to assess my brother, but given he had no magic to protect himself with, I decided on McKenzie. I held her gaze. "One of us needs to get Brydie. This unprecedented storm will draw attention we don't need. She won't want to see me, not after the blow I've just dealt. You're the best choice to calm her down, but only if you're willing to take the role. I won't force you."

McKenzie was nodding before I'd even finished. "I'll go, but I will need you to keep Aidan calm."

I instantly nodded. "Where is he?"

"In our bedroom, packing," McKenzie confirmed. "Jack's with him." She raised her fingers and waved them. "I've muffled the sound. Given what happened at the estate, if he gets wind that Talorgan has found us, I'll lose him to fear again."

I ground my jaw at the reminder that the estate was in ruins. "I agree. The kid has already dealt with enough." I considered McKenzie's attire. "I suggest you tell him you need to head outside for some mountain herbs before we leave. Change into warmer clothes while you're there; you'll need them."

McKenzie nodded and left the room.

Ian asked, "McKenzie mentioned there was a threat at the Claymore, that Brydie's reaction was unpredictable. What did she mean by that?"

I looked at Logan, who gave his head a little shake, confirming they hadn't told Ian the full story. "She attacked one of Talorgan's acolytes."

Ian raised a brow. "How is that unpredictable?"

"There was no hesitation; she didn't question the man."

Logan's gaze held understanding. He was aware I walked that line myself, but Ian's face was bleak as he asked, "She went for the kill?"

I nodded.

"If she reacts that way, how can we trust her around others?" he said. "Her power is just beginning. You said it yourself that you haven't felt the depth of her well yet. How much power does she hold? What happens if her instincts are wrong and she makes a fatal flaw? We—"

"Stop!" I snarled, my harsh tone a mirror of the raging storm outside. "Brydie denied that urge, Ian. She retained control of her power—she conceded it to me! To have withdrawn herself in the heat of the moment means she remained in control. You have nothing to fear." I pointed to the storm outside. "That is nothing to be afraid of either. That is a mere reaction. Besides, it's not aimed at you, but me. She's hurt and she's raging. Brydie could have aimed everything she's feeling at me, or at the shieling itself. Christ, she could have killed me if she'd put her mind to it. But she didn't, Ian. She held on."

I lowered my hand, and my voice became softer, less abrasive. "Do not be afraid of her, and don't paint that picture of her either, because if you want the future you desire and the retribution you're owed, then you'll do well to remember this conversation, because it won't be the last time she behaves this way. Her response is instinctual, and Brydie attacks those who are a threat, not those who aren't." I stared at him, a fierceness burning in my chest as I added, "And none of us needs division. Not within this unit."

Because regardless of the fact that Brydie had hit me in the nose for the news I'd delivered, I knew she could have punched through my protective shield if she'd wanted to. But she hadn't, she'd held it together by voluntarily leaving the vehicle to release her anger elsewhere. I was proud of who she'd become—who she was still becoming.

Ian's lips thinned into a line. Behind his spectacles, his eyes burned with emotion. Yes, I'd put him in his place again. Yes, I'd reminded him of what was at stake again, but it was very clear his anxiety wasn't about my response; it was about the image he'd held of Brydie—the image that was now crumbling behind the truth of who and what she'd become. I, on the other hand, had always known who it was she would one day become—a Daughter of Winter, Cailleach's descendant in every way. A woman with power. And if we were to succeed against Talorgan, she would be a woman who wasn't afraid to use it.

Ian must have seen what was in my face for he held up a hand and took a step toward me, but just as he was about to open his mouth, McKenzie re-entered the room, layered in a ski jacket, woolen hat, and gloves.

Turning away from Ian, I reached out for her as she walked past me for the door. "Take off your gloves when you get close to her," I said to her. "Don't gamble on full compliance."

Her green eyes widened, and a tinge of fear swirled in their depths.

"It's the only element of surprise you'll have," I said firmly. "Don't be afraid to use what little fire magic you have to defend yourself. She will handle it, I assure you."

Her face blanched, but she nodded.

I reminded her, "You don't have to go if you don't want to. I won't force you."

McKenzie shook her head, her red hair a vibrant stain of

color in stark contrast to her fair skin. "No, you're the worst choice. Leave her with me."

I stared at her a moment longer, testing that affirmation, and when I saw firm confidence settle over her features, I released her. "If you aren't back within the hour, I'll come looking."

"Just watch Aidan."

"We will."

She gave me a fleeting smile before turning to open the front door and leaving on an icy blast of wind and snow.

The interlude with McKenzie had given me time to rein in my anger toward Ian. I reminded myself that we didn't need a division in our ranks and that whatever Ian felt for Brydie right now wasn't my concern. It was his. I needed to focus on getting us out of here, and more importantly, getting Brydie to safety. Because once we arrived in Ireland, I knew she would be hell bent on rescuing Chloe.

Turning to the men, I said firmly, "I need you to wipe all evidence of our visit from this place. As soon as the women return, we're leaving."

"Where are we going?" asked Ian.

"The Rowan Tree is our best bet. There's also the possibility of tapping into the pending spring equinox at Slieve na Calliagh."

Ian almost seemed to do a double take. He lifted a hand to push his glasses back up the bridge of his nose. "We're going to Ireland? Why there? Surely we don't have to leave Scotland?"

"McKenzie and Logan both felt this was the path we should take, and I respect McKenzie's visions and my brother's intuition enough to realize we shouldn't ignore them. And even though it didn't come under consideration at the time, visiting The Rowan Tree will allow us to find out more about the Dagda's cauldron and what threat Callum poses."

Ian looked between me and Logan. "You trust his intuition? Even though he has no druidic power?"

Fire boiled in my blood, my gift straining to release the emotions I'd been tethering over the last hour. "You're walking a fine line, Ian. I know you're reeling with all the changes, but if you ever disrespect my brother or his abilities again, the balance we share will be permanently unsettled. And I'll guarantee that if you care to analyze exactly whom and what you are angry at, you'll come to understand it's not my brother but me that you're pissed at. So please, direct your anger at me in future, not Logan. Do I make myself clear?"

Ian's features twisted, a slash of red high on his cheekbones. The silence between us lengthened.

Logan broke it, stepping forward with his hands raised. "No, this is my fault. I'm sorry, Ian. It's clear I took your place in the decision. I recognize I'm not one of the descendants, and I apologize for stepping out of turn."

My brother's concession seemed to mollify Ian somewhat, and at the same time, illustrate how petty he was behaving.

Ian sighed, his body visibly releasing tension. "No, you were right. Ireland is a good choice. I don't know what's wrong with me." He held out a hand to Logan. "I'm sorry for my behavior."

Logan didn't hesitate, reaching one hand out with a grin to clasp his hand while clapping his other on his back. "Nothing to be sorry for, man. It's understandable given everything going on. But since you got your panties in a twist and we've been ordered to clean this joint, you've drawn the short straw on toilet cleaning duty."

Ian grimaced but gave a stilted nod. "I guess I deserved that." He then turned to face me, and his face was tight as he admitted, "You were right. I had Brydie on a pedestal. I'm sorry; I shouldn't have taken that out on you."

Knowing he was hurting, that whatever hope of a future he'd held onto with Brydie had now been surely crushed, I offered him an olive branch. "No need to apologize. Let's just stick together, and if you ever have a problem with me again, I suggest you come and see me directly."

He nodded, and I felt that we were good, or as good as we could get given the circumstances. But then he said, "In that case, I would like to get Ingrid out of the Institute, and I would welcome this group's support in doing so."

Ingrid was his sister, and I recalled Callum had claimed during our altercation at Aviemore that she was whom he had recently taken for his wife. I considered Ian, noting his drawn features. This meant a lot to him. "Is it true, then?"

Ian's jaw clenched. "Yes. While you were away this morning, my source confirmed she married Callum a month ago."

"Then I will help you retrieve her as soon as we can attend to it, but I can't promise that won't be until after we get Chloe back."

His relief was evident. "Thank you." And without saying another word, Ian bowed his head and left the room.

I watched him leave, feeling the anguish he was carrying. Being Callum's wife would not be easy for Ingrid, and I suspected Ian, and his parents, would suffer for this circumstance just as much as she would.

I turned back to Logan, who was waiting patiently. "I'll need you to sweep the room Brydie and I were sharing while you keep an eye on Aidan," I said.

He raised a brow. "Why? Are you going after McKenzie now?"

"No, I'm fairly certain she'll succeed in bringing Brydie back. But after what happened at the Claymore, we're sitting ducks. I'm heading back down the mountain to take watch on the road. Brydie's storm may be generating unwanted attention, and I'm not relaxing my guard until we've left this place behind."

CHAPTER 4
CAILLEACH
3RD CENTURY BC, ANCIENT SCOTLAND

Cailleach held true to her anger; it would aid her through the coming discussion. She had to be strong for this confrontation, for confrontation it was. Broken inside, all matter of emotion twisted and fierce, there was nothing she wanted more on this earth than revenge.

Tritus had been killed, murdered by Talorgan, and the path to blame was a tangled one. The druid had been aided by Arawn, because he desired something that was outside of his reach—her; and he had fallen to the promise inherent in her dark brother's power in order to get what he wanted.

Cailleach was angry she'd offered retribution to Talorgan; that she'd been benevolent two years prior when she should have sought justice, swift and sure with his death. The knowledge was painfully bittersweet, because in the end, it was her lover who had granted Talorgan his freedom and his life. Tritus, cognizant of the feelings of his best friend, Drust, who was also the druid's twin brother, had saved Talorgan's life by pleading for the punishment to be meted out in the form of a service. Her lover's sentence had been thoughtful and just, if not the clean cut of death she preferred. And biting down his pride, Talorgan had taken the olive branch that was offered.

Cailleach now recognized that incident as the pivotal event that had begun their journey down this route. She understood now with a clarity that only hindsight can bring that things might have been different if they had been aware of the consequences of that decision. Both her and Tritus had been unaware of Talorgan's infatuation with her, of his lustful longings as she bathed at the tarn, his vengeful plans to claim her as his own. They'd lived in bliss, cocooned from the world, and what she'd come to know as true happiness. Her time with Tritus, together with his love, was a blessing she had never thought she'd experience.

Although...it had been overshadowed by a warning. One she had never forgotten. And, going by the sudden prickling in the still night air, she knew the crux of that warning was now here....

As soon as the thought had formed in her mind, the universe answered. There came a sudden shifting between the worlds, and the space before her was rent in two by a violent deluge of heat and flame.

The blaze burned with an unearthly intensity that had Cailleach stumbling backward, her feet sliding on the loose shingle of the mountain. The heat was in complete antithesis to her own magic; fire to her ice, and it was so intense that she felt as if her skin would slough right off the bone.

The light of the flames was blinding, a riot of orange, red, and gold. The colors violently coalesced before morphing into a gigantic bird that instantly commanded her attention and her fear.

The Phoenix. Also known as The Custodian of Creation —or her father.

The Custodian of Creation hovered above her, his flapping wings spreading a myriad of embers and twinkling fireflies into the air. His blazing gaze found hers, the irises lit with an incandescent red flame.

Cailleach stilled her quaking heart and called upon her fledgling power that had been regenerating since the baby's birth. She claimed just enough to shield her body from the heat and forced herself to stand there.

Although he was eternal, the Phoenix was not one to waste time. His voice roared through her mind in an otherworldly tone. The sound was both feminine and masculine, at once a sweeping symphony as well as a discordant melody, and although the words were not said aloud, they commanded a respect that had her dropping to her knees.

"My child, have you called me to make claim to the boon I offered you nigh on a year ago?"

Cailleach swallowed against her suddenly dry throat. For all her bravado, she hadn't prepared herself for this encounter, and in fact couldn't have. The power play between them would forever be skewed. The Phoenix was the only being in the universe with sufficient power to destroy her—to destroy all the gods—and that cold, hard truth was like an old wound that never healed, something she was always conscious of but had no choice but to endure.

Pushing past her parched fear, she responded, "Yes." Then, unable to hide the anger and the anguish screaming inside her, she lashed out, "And in hindsight, I can now see that your so-called boon was offered in recognition of the loss I would have to suffer—the loss you did not tell me would be borne by my lover!"

The Phoenix cocked his head to the side, those sharp

eyes narrowing on her face. His gaze burned like the pain of a hot poker lancing directly into her mind. Cailleach felt as though he was ripping her soul asunder, twisting it inside and out as if to determine all her secrets. A detached part of her brain understood this was what it would have felt like for Tritus and all the other minds she had raped in the past when they had been subjected to her scrutiny.

It was an effort to hold the Phoenix's gaze, but hold it she did, the anguish in her heart demanding that she confront the being who had not honestly shared how her time with her lover would end.

"What are you saying, my child? That it was unfair of me to tell you the truth of what you faced? Or are you upset that you did not pay the price in his place? After all, that was the outcome you believed was coming, is it not?"

His words cut her to the quick. It was true, she had always believed she would pay the ultimate cost, not Tritus. He hadn't deserved to die; they'd only just found each other. Not to mention the legacy they'd unveiled around his bloodline, discovering he was half-mortal and half-god, the scion of a powerful druid and her brother, Cernunnos.

"Yes, that was the outcome I envisaged, especially because you did not lead me to believe otherwise," she bit out haltingly.

The Phoenix's tone was quietly demanding. *"Explain, child."*

It was a tangled path, one Cailleach felt she had been cleverly led down. Almost as if she'd stood upon the edge of a lake and, not wanting to get her dress wet, had been encouraged to jump on a series of skipping stones in a haphazard line that looked innocent and sporadic enough, but was in fact a series of cleverly-placed steps that she must take to get to this point.

Had the Phoenix orchestrated all of it? Even so far as the tryst between Cernunnos and his druidic lover, whose union would not only create Tritus, but also cement her role as the new custodian of winter? Had he also known Talorgan would one day awaken Arawn, selling his soul in return for a power that would place their world in jeopardy? After all, the Phoenix saw everything—forward, backward, and the present.

Cailleach shivered at the ramifications. She held power in her own right, but the Phoenix far eclipsed that of any one of her siblings, even Arawn. However, their father had always seemed to stand slightly apart, never siding with any one of his children. Offering boons where necessary, yes, and often on a whim but with no apparent reason. But now, Cailleach wondered if they weren't all chance but rather ingredients of an aged brew that he had been concocting for his immortal palate.

Hurt and anger speared her chest. There was no denying these thoughts held an element of truth. How could anyone, even an all-powerful being, stay autonomous when they also felt a level of emotion—even if it was just anger or mild disdain?

Her emotions escalated; it was impossible to stay neutral in the face of the Phoenix. Cailleach had experienced too much loss to deny the pain she carried like an open wound, and besides, she had a child to protect against all odds. But first, she felt recklessly driven to penetrate the cold, removed exterior of this magnificent being, to illustrate the horror of what she was really going through, and she chose to break the weighted silence with words that had been holed up inside her since her wall of shock had broken.

"I feel like a pawn, utilized for a means to an end. At the same time, I feel broken, having been gifted with a love that could bring the world to a halt, only to have it ripped away from me. I do not understand why you would want me to experience such joy only to plunge me into the depths of such agony."

The Phoenix considered her for a moment. *"I forget the minds of my children are still clouded by their desires. No matter the level of power you all wield, neutrality is still something each of you struggle with, some more than others. But you have forced me to see something I had not considered—that I did not account for how emotionally affected you would be in the face of this loss."*

Cailleach felt her mouth drop open. "Is that all you have to say?" she screamed, no longer cognizant of who and what she spoke to. "To compensate for the loss I have suffered, you comment on my failing to remain neutral? To not feel?" She jumped to her feet with no thought for her safety, fear driving her urgency. "Tell me what is coming! You see all paths. I need to know—will Talorgan and my dark brother win this war? Will I be chained to a life of misery next to that druid's side?"

The Phoenix's plumage suddenly flared—an overwhelming conflagration of heat and fiery wrath. *"Silence!"*

The harsh intonation of his voice shredded her composure, the rage dissipating in a flurry of stark terror at the sudden awareness that she had pushed her father too far. Cailleach raised her arms to cover her scorching face, again stumbling back as the Phoenix roared, *"No matter what has befallen you, insolence will not be tolerated! You were aware of the ramifications of your decision. Did I not warn you of this outcome? That your time together would be short-lived? Did you not agree to that time, no matter how little it would be, regardless of the consequences?"*

His voice was overwhelmingly authoritarian, and his

flaming body shimmered, the flames crackling with a vibrant ferocity across his feathers. Burning sparks snapped in front of her face, singeing her hair and her dress.

Aware that she must recover and counteract the level of disrespect she had handed out, she raised one hand to beseech her father. It was then Cailleach heard the wail of her child, mournful and forlorn from inside the shieling behind her. It reminded her of why she had called upon the Phoenix, of the boon she now bargained for with her insolent words. That knowledge was like a dousing of ice over her ravaged nerves.

She had been a fool! Her actions could very well have destroyed the only chance she had for her child. Hard guilt speared her chest, and with it a renewed determination that she would not fail her daughter; she would not fail Tritus. She had lost enough.

Cailleach again dropped to her knees on the stony shingle and bowed her head in deference to the Custodian of Creation. Deciding that honesty was her only bargaining chip in the face of his wrath, and knowing full well he could raze her to the ground if the whim took him, she held onto hope as she said with as much emotion as she could muster, "I apologize, Father. I am hurt and not myself. Please excuse my insolence."

The Phoenix's plumage did not waver, its intensity remaining in the face of her apology. Cailleach did not dare lift her head. She was aware she stood upon a knife's edge, aware that anger, along with fear, still ruled her expression. The silence stretched, heavy and weighted, and Cailleach heard her infant daughter wail even louder.

Whether it was the sound of her child or the fact that she didn't lift her head in response, the Phoenix's flare suddenly died to a whisper, and his voice was sharp in the night air. *"I recognize that loss, my child, and even though I do not understand it, I can see and feel what your lover's absence has done to you. For that, I will allow you that one transgression. You have been forewarned."*

Feeling her heart beat erratically in her chest at the level of her relief, Cailleach could do nothing except incline her head and respond simply, "Thank you, Father."

"Now, what is the boon, my child? Time is pivotal. The worlds are stirring; change is occurring. Claim your due now, for we must make haste."

Cailleach, her heart thundering in her chest, finally lifted her head to look upon the Phoenix's powerful visage. After what had just happened, her confidence now wavered. Reminding herself that she was all-powerful, a queen among even the gods, she held fast to her will and shared with a courage she didn't know she had, "I ask that you protect my child and those of her line. I ask that you restrict the movements of my dark brother and his disciples—that you scour them from this earth so they can never again hurt me or mine again. And I ask that you reunite me with Tritus. I wish to leave this plane and rejoin him in the Other."

The Phoenix opened his wickedly curved beak and screeched. It was a sound so piercingly shrill that it caused Cailleach's heart to trip, and a feeling of strong foreboding followed. It was a sound she knew to her very soul—it was the sound that heralded her death.

CHAPTER 5
THE PHOENIX
3RD CENTURY BC, ANCIENT SCOTLAND

He recoiled at the insolent words of his child. How dare she? How dare she use his gift as a tool to bargain for more?

These questions broke through his momentary shock, and he could not stop the visceral reaction that flared through his veins. Could not halt the need to seek final, swift, and vengeful retribution. He had warned her, had told her in no uncertain terms that he would not warrant another transgression. And this—this was a blatant transgression, because she hadn't asked for one boon, but three! Three!

His plumage came alight in a blazing inferno, and he flung back his head to shout his outrage, calling forth the power that slumbered within. It surged forward eagerly, crying out to be used. He inhaled it greedily, sucking in the potent energy that could destroy life. Facing his daughter, he lowered his head and released the final kiss of death.

The flame shot forth and speared his daughter in the chest. No matter what sins she had committed tonight, he would watch her final moments, to etch the details of this circumstance forever onto his memory so it would never happen again.

He felt a twinge of regret that one of his children would die at his own hand and recognized it was his own failing that had caused her death. It was obvious he hadn't succeeded in teaching them control—control over their human desires, and control over their emotions.

Cailleach was flung backward, her body hitting the loose shingle and sliding a few feet down the mountain. But instead of disintegrating into ash, his power winked out, as if it were a candle flame snuffed by a draught. And there, alone on the shingle, lay his daughter, wholly alive.

The Phoenix froze; even his flaming plumage became still. The deafening silence was broken by a choking, gasping cough. His daughter's hacking sounds were punctuated by movement, her body turning onto its side to curl into a ball as she held protective hands over her chest.

Her movements thrust him into motion. He flung his wings out to their widest wingspan, and with a few mighty strokes, he was hovering above her. She'd managed to come to her knees, one hand still clutching her chest—at the same place he'd fired his death arrow.

"Why are you still alive?"

The words were stilted, rough and abrasive even to his own ears, but they also conveyed the level of his shock. No one had survived his fateful touch before—no one. He had been created for one reason and one reason alone. He was an eternal sentinel, rising again and again, ensuring a constant balance was maintained over the land, only interfering if a catastrophe threatened to skew the balance of nature. He stood on the cusp of life and death, the line between good and evil, and he commanded a level of respect for such power. He alone could end his children's lives, and once that decision was made, nothing could deflect it...until now.

Cailleach looked up, her face bone-white, her moonlight hair a tangled mess of stones and dust. Her silver eyes were swirling with both shock and fear as she gasped out, "I have no idea."

The Phoenix cocked his head to the side, his mind racing. *"Stand up."*

Cailleach pushed herself slowly to her feet, one hand still clutched to her chest.

"Lower your hand."

As her hand fell away, the Phoenix caught sight of a glowing stone against her chest. A stone he recognized, and one he felt he knew. The incandescence from his blazing plumage hit the smoky amber stone, refracting the gem in a myriad of light. His breath caught at the significance of what that stone was and where it had come from...the Stone of Destiny.

He felt the tingle of its power to his core, innately understanding that it was made from the same matter he was. He hadn't seen the stone or the other three objects of power in an eon. They were weapons created by his hands; tools he'd urged into existence to lead his children and their descendants to maintain a balance in this world. He remembered giving them to the Tuatha Dé Danann just after he'd created them.

The Phoenix had seen many things in his life, and indeed, many paths. He knew those four treasures would prove imperative not only to his children, but also to him, as a reminder that whoever wielded them was of consequence.

Fragments of memories hit him then, releasing one after the other, as if seeing the stone had released a dam of evidence. He recalled moments where he'd manipulated others: his son, Cernunnos; his other son, Dagda; his daughter, Morrígan; and also Cailleach's lover, Tritus. All of these careful manipulations had been done to maintain the balance.

And it appeared this child in front of him wore a sliver of one of those treasures around her neck. It was the stone that had protected her. Regardless of its size, the pendant she wore had consumed his lethal power, saving her from certain death. It was one of four objects he couldn't destroy, and given she wore a piece of it around her neck, neither did it seem that he could destroy *her*. What was also apparent was that Cailleach's path was of absolute importance, and that whatever her requests had been, he needed to reconsider.

Conscious she stood there waiting on him, her breathing no less easy but her confusion creeping in at his lack of response, the Phoenix gave her the answers she silently demanded. *"You are fortunate, my child. Your continued existence on this earth is due to the fact that you wear the Stone of Destiny."*

Cailleach looked bewildered as she lifted a hand to clutch at the pendant. "This is from the Stone of Destiny? I thought that was a myth."

The Phoenix shook his head. *"No, my child. The stone was never myth. I grant its existence has been kept secret since its arrival on this plane, but the other weapons haven't. Your brother, Dagda, used to wield one of them, but now that he's passed over to the Other, your sister, Cerridwen, is responsible for it."*

"The cauldron? The cauldron Dagda used that is now Cerridwen's?"

"Yes. It's powers are prophetic, but it can also dispense of life or death."

Her features tightened. "Because nature requires both to be in balance."

The Phoenix inclined his head. *"Yes. All objects of power abide to this rule."*

She let go of the pendant, her face taking on a determined shine. "Why am I wearing the Stone of Destiny? Is this confirmation that Arawn will indeed arise to lay claim to this world? That what I seek of you must be fulfilled?"

This daughter is intelligent. He felt a sense of pride in this creation and understood that to lie or divert her question would do naught to persuade her, particularly when he could not inflict the retribution he normally would have. Besides, her wearing the pendant was a proclamation that it was his careful machinations that had led her to this point —that her loss was preordained and pivotal to the actions that came next. Thus, he answered with all honesty, *"The reason you wear that pendant is not to save your life, child, but to remind me that whatever message you bring is of much importance, and that my role as the Custodian of Creation is threatened by the tidings that have come to pass."*

"Does this mean you will fulfill my boon?"

The Phoenix narrowed his gaze at her insolence. *"Even though I cannot claim your death while you wear that stone, I can still cause you pain. Do not think to remain impertinent."*

She had the grace to blush and look away, and when her eyes returned to his, an apology was implicit. "I'm sorry, Father. I care for my family."

And he could feel that was so. It intrigued him. *"Give me a moment to consider."*

Turning away from his daughter, the Phoenix thought on all the careful machinations he had laid to rest. He remembered his visitation with Cernunnos; the knowledge that he would sire a child that was half-mortal, half-god—someone who would one day fulfil a need. He remembered giving Dagda the cauldron, and in return, urging him to follow his heart. This had led not only to the mercy Dagda had shown to Cernunnos's son, but also to Dagda's eventual bedding of Boann—a woman that was not his wife but with whom he had fallen in love with. This in turn had forced Cailleach to pay the price of her brother's infidelity by suffering Morrígan's wrath, and subsequently being awarded the punishing mantle of winter.

He then recalled another memory in which he'd manipulated Cernunnos's son, how he'd urged him to discover a stone in the depths of a cave—a location he'd prepared for that very moment. That man had taken the sliver he'd chipped from the main source and carried it home to fashion into a pendant for his lover—the same woman who stood here before him.

The history behind these actions was long and tangled; a careful tapestry he'd been working on since the beginning of time. There were many threads at play, making it difficult to remember which of his children were being manipulated and which weren't, but that was why he'd created the four Objects of Power. They helped balance nature while also acting as a check on his actions—a sign that proclaimed his children were touched by the hands of fate and on a careful path to bring balance to this world.

This meant Cailleach needed to continue the path she was on. But how could he grant her three boons without a tithe? He owed her one, not three. He came to a conclusion.

Turning to Cailleach, who made no move to hide her apprehension, he said, *"The first boon—protecting your daughter and her line—is freely granted; however, given I cannot always be present, this will require the act of prophecy, one which Cerridwen must wield through the cauldron. The second boon is another matter. I cannot remove my children if they have not broken any rules. Arawn only entered this world because of the failing of another—a druid whom you and your siblings created. His actions follow his nature, and he—"*

"But he will skew the balance of this world! He belongs in the Underworld!"

He felt his feathers flare, his wings flapping with a vicious backdraft that had his daughter skidding back down the shingle again. *"Silence! To interrupt my decree is to court death! I will tolerate this no longer, child. Stone or no stone, I will find someone else to follow your path, even if I have to wait generations and suffer the consequences that will befall this land with my dark son's rising."*

His daughter bowed her head, deference in her posture. "I am sorry. I am filled with loss and heartbreak. It is all I can do not to think of it. I lost everything to Arawn and his disciple; all I wish for is retribution."

"And retribution you shall have, if you allow me to finish, child! Restricting his movements will require the support of everyone involved in this tangled path. Unity is paramount, and many have been affected by my actions up to this point. Since protection of your daughter and that of her line will follow prophecy, it makes sense to address your other desires via the same path. But restricting the movement of your dark brother and his disciples will take more than simple prophecy. It will take the support of all who are involved in the threads of this tapestry."

Cailleach's face scrunched. "Tapestry?"

"I can see the future, but it is like numerous threads in a carpet. Some fray, others snap completely, and some can be mended. This means the path is never certain but is always opaque, one that can be carefully adjusted. However, to tell you

what I see only upsets the threads at play. All you need to know is that I have tugged on many strands to get to this point. In order to finish what I have started and to see the final weave of my work, those strands need to be pulled together and tied off. This means that all those whom I have touched need to give their full support to this request."

"Who?" Cailleach demanded. "Who is needed?"

The Phoenix could see the concern on her face, and because he'd watched over her for eons, he understood why the proposal would bring fear. However, unity was required, and if her requests were to be granted, a level of risk would be involved. *"You already know the answer to that, my child. Many were touched by the circumstances between you and Tritus. In order to support the prophecy, you will need the support of Dagda, Cernunnos, and Morrígan. All three played a part in making you who you are today. All three have connections that will be needed to withstand Arawn's power."*

By the look on his daughter's face, the Phoenix understood she knew the truth of what he said.

"Are you saying that the second boon will only be granted if my three siblings all give their support to my request?"

"Yes, my child. And if there is a tithe requested, you will pay it."

"A tithe?" she demanded. "Another one? Haven't I given enough already?"

The Phoenix cocked his head. *"You have given what is required, yet you asked for more than was granted. What is owed should be retribution for the insult you threw at me, but given you wear the stone, your siblings will have the right to state a tithe, if they so request."*

He could tell by the look on her face that there was only

one sibling she feared. One sibling who could very well derail her plans.

A determined look crossed her features. "Very well. And what of the third boon? With the protection of my daughter and her line, I desire to be reunited with my lover. I wish to leave this plane and rejoin Tritus in the Other."

"That, my child, is not possible. Your time here is not done. There is also the role you play. In order to pass over, winter's mantle must be awarded to another, and there is no one who could take up that position in the foreseeable future. I can promise nothing, but one of your siblings could be willing to make a deal."

Her face fell, and the Phoenix could feel the weight of her emotions, but they were fickle and a nuisance; they did nothing to change the course of her path. He was eager to weave a knot into this new tapestry so he could attend to other matters. *"Time is short, child, so I will call your siblings now. Your brothers will arrive first; Morrígan will follow. I will do all I can to explain the enormity of what is required, but what you desire must be requested by yourself and subsequently granted to you alone. I can do no more."*

"Please!" Cailleach shouted, an arm outstretched as if to halt his departure. "Morrígan will not agree to this. I know she won't. Can't you do more?"

The Phoenix shook his head as he spread his wings, his flames writhing in the cool night breeze. *"The fate of this path now lies in your hands."*

Then, with those shocking words, he winked out of existence; the only evidence of his presence being a lone red feather drifting lazily on the breeze.

CHAPTER 6
BRYDIE
PRESENT DAY, SCOTLAND

My breathing was ragged as Gage's revelation thundered in my ears.

Chloe was the fifth descendant.

Captured by The Oaken Tree.

Held captive by Callum.

Callum. The most dangerous druid we had to contend with—potentially even more dangerous than Talorgan himself. And Gage hadn't told me. No one had.

Chloe!

My heart bled anew at the loss of my friend. I wanted to go to her now; leave everyone behind. But it was a fool's errand. I didn't even know where the Institute was or how to infiltrate it, and running off on my own was a sure way to get myself killed.

I swallowed, thinking of Chloe trapped within its walls, alone and afraid. Like me, she'd been thrust into a world of druids, prophecy, and dark magic, completely unaware of the legacy she carried. But although I'd had some warning and support through the others, she'd had no one.

Why hadn't Gage gone after her back then? Why hadn't he

told me sooner? The answer came instantly: *Because you would have been left alone, unsafe and unguarded.* And it was clear Ian and McKenzie had supported his decision.

It was a betrayal that scoured me to the soul. Rage boiled anew, and my magic thrummed as I stood upon the ledge where I had learned to master my power. I was unable to see the jagged rocks below or the breathtaking peaks of the Cuillin mountain range before me. The normally breathtaking vista was a blizzard of racing winds and swirling snowflakes, a storm of neutral shades in gray, black, and white; a fitting tribute to the violence surging through my mind.

At the surge of emotion, the power within me bucked, and a blue-white arrow of power shot from my hands to spear the hovering storm clouds above. A flash of lightning followed, along with an ominous rumble, and the churning clouds pushed closer.

My mouth dropped open as I realized *I* had initiated that response...or rather, my legacy had. I could feel it sharp awareness, its hovering stillness. Like a predator watching its prey. Its essence hovered like a shadow, weighted and persistent. Even hurting, part of me remained aware that if my legacy was given full reign, I would be in danger of succumbing to the madness inside me. That, with one slip of the reins, I would unravel into something different... something *other.*

I'd believed I had mastered its power. But I'd been wrong. So wrong. My legacy had merely been waiting for another opportunity to take over. And it appeared that moment was now—when my brittle control had been shattered with the news that my best friend was being held prisoner at the Institute.

A sob escaped my lips, and I was barely aware of my

actions as another burst of surging power shot from my hands and into the storm above. I jumped when the sky boomed directly above me and slipped on the ice, my shoulder smashing onto the rocky ledge. My scream was swallowed by the shrieking wind, my vision reduced to a few feet ahead of me as an eddy of dense snowflakes erupted from the burgeoning storm clouds overhead.

As the wet snow seeped into my jeans and woolen jumper, I could do nothing but lie there, panting through the pain. I suddenly craved the calming presence of my Guardian. Deep down, I knew he had kept who and what Chloe was a secret from me because he'd feared for my safety. His path was entwined with my own, and he was called to it whether he liked it or not. I also knew his reason for withholding the truth about Chloe was sound, because I would have done everything I could to get her back, regardless of the consequences. And now...after knowing the power Talorgan and Callum carried, it would have been a death sentence—and Gage had known it.

Damn him!

Angry at myself now, I cradled the arm of my injured shoulder and gingerly pushed back to my feet, lifting my head to face the storm now raging with unleashed violence upon the mountain range I stood upon. It was a storm of my own making because I had lost control.

It was time to take it back.

I screamed to the brooding sky, "You do not control me. I control you!"

The wind whistled like a shrieking woman, its icy fingers lashing against my skin and unraveling my long, blonde braid to riot in a writhing mass around my head. I ignored my legacy's response, instead concentrating on my breathing as I fought to control my thoughts and emotions.

In and out. In and out. Eyes unseeing, stance frozen, I blocked it all out, releasing the anger, the hurt, the fear, the denial; purging it all until I was empty of every emotion that held me captive.

I didn't know how long I stood there or that the storm was slowly abating until a voice, snatched by the wind, penetrated. I blinked, coming back to the present, and carefully turned around on the ledge. The warm scent of cinnamon apples alerted me as to who it was that came.

McKenzie emerged a moment later, her face bone-white, her bright red hair swirling in the wind. For a moment I felt lost, deflated. I'd assumed Gage would follow me. Instead, he'd sent McKenzie, someone neutral. *Clever.*

Her words came again, and I heard them clearly this time, the wind now reduced to a wail. "Come down from the ledge, Brydie."

Resistance churned in my gut. "No. I have no desire to listen to what you have to say."

McKenzie cocked her head to the side as she pulled the lapels of her ski jacket around her body. "Would you risk our location, then? Talorgan and those he's wrested control over will be watching us, and this storm you've created will not go unnoticed."

Her words were a splash of clarity after the incident with Garret only an hour prior. A chill chased down my spine; I'd forgotten that prevalent risk. She was right—my storm was a calling card, and if someone had noticed, regardless of the storm or the perilous drive up the mountain on the cusp of spring, they would come. Coerced by Talorgan, they would be forced to obey...and they would lose their lives for it, whether I claimed them or the mountain did.

Yet, McKenzie had no right to discipline me for my actions. The storm was a gut reaction to the news Gage had shared—a reaction they must have known was coming! McKenzie had also known Chloe was the fifth descendant. That meant she had held this information from me just as much as Gage had. With that in mind, I growled, "Let them come."

Her eyes widened, those emerald irises darkening to the color of dark moss, and this time when she responded, it was anger that laced her words, the tone no longer careful but filled with her own budding power. "You would risk Aidan?"

The name was a douse of cold water. Aidan, her nine-year-old son, was an innocent in all of this. He was still reeling from the attack that had been aimed at me and had watched his childhood home be razed to the ground by a fire I now recalled had been lit by Callum...the very man who held Chloe prisoner. I returned with a wave of renewed anger, "You risked Chloe!"

I regretted the words as soon as they left my lips. I didn't want to risk Aidan, and I didn't want to push McKenzie, but I was unable to control the anger that was once again building in my chest.

McKenzie's features tightened, and her hands clenched at her sides. They were gloveless, the skin of her fingers a bright red against the white snow. The show of power was unmistakable, and shock coursed through me. *McKenzie had fire magic?*

Before I could ask her how that was possible, fire flew from her hands. I reacted instinctively, releasing a burst of my own power to instantly snuff her flames. "Was that meant to stop me?" I snarled. I'd carefully buffered the strength of my attack so that it ricocheted off her answering fire, splintering outward in a storm of hail and snow.

I gritted my teeth as I stared at her, holding my position.

Her face was tight, grim and determined...but in those green eyes, I could see real fear. I faltered and immediately felt my anger fade. McKenzie didn't deserve my wrath or my guilt. I took a step toward her, hands raised in supplication as regret churned in my gut. But she misinterpreted my response as another attack and released a second stream of fire. Blinded by the bright light, I tried to raise a shield, but my feet slipped on the icy rocks underneath.

As soon as I hit the ground, she was there, standing above me, her coat and bright red hair billowing in the wind. Her lips were peeled back into a feral snarl as she quickly wove a rune in the air. Her actions afforded me a chance to retaliate. I didn't, aware that one more move from me would be the end of my relationship with her—potentially the end of everything, the prophecy included.

I smelt her cinnamon apple scent flood my senses just as my hands became strangely heavy. It felt as if they were manacled by invisible chains. I flexed my fingers, testing the strength of my magic, but there was no response, no blue-white light. My power had gone.

I gasped. "What have you done?"

She met my gaze, unflinching, her pale face set in grim determination. "I have caged your power as payment for the risks you were willing to take with your childish outburst."

I stiffened. "Childish? You call my reaction to the truth being withheld about my best friend, childish? You call allowing her to fall into the hands of Callum and all that it entails, childish?" I raised my hands, now useless conduits, and cried, "Why couldn't we have gone after her? Why didn't you tell me sooner? Why keep it from me?"

"Because of how you'd respond," she bit back. "Look at you! Look at how you're behaving. Your emotions have overruled all sense of reason, and now that you have come into your power, you are uncontrollable." Her face was scathing as she held my gaze. "Can you control what you're feeling right now, Brydie? Can you control the magic in your veins? No! That much is obvious. And because of that, you're a danger not only to yourself, but to all of us around you. Pull yourself together. This won't get Chloe back!"

Her words were piercing because they held the weight of truth. I hadn't even taken a moment to think about why they had kept Chloe's position a secret from me; I'd merely reacted. But looking at McKenzie, and knowing Gage had held not only her support, but also Ian's and possibly Logan's, clearly, there was a valid reason for it, whether I'd wanted to hear it or not.

I swallowed. When had I become such a blind fool? An internal thrum of power answered, and it was a blatant reminder of how much it took from me...how much it was changing me. My legacy was a double-edged sword. Power came with recriminations—a balance. And it appeared that balance was exacted with heightened senses and heightened emotions. Their combined betrayal hurt, more than I cared to admit. But ultimately, I was aware I was more upset that *he* had personally withheld this news from me. Not everybody else, just him. Gage. My Guardian.

I'd come to trust him. To believe in him. To open myself to the possibilities of my role and his own. That delicate bridge between us had been severed by his betrayal, and it stung, more than I'd believed. But it was time to pull myself together. Chloe needed me. They all did.

I released a breath and looked beyond the ledge. The storm had dissipated, the clouds above now plump and soft, the wind back to a tolerable level. The village of Broadford could once again be glimpsed between the low cloud. The snow-capped mountains sparkled in the weak afternoon light, the storm of before a distant memory, remnant of the freshly powdered snow.

My voice was small. "I'm sorry. I've made a mess of everything. I was just so upset. I hope you know I would never intentionally endanger any of us, especially Aidan. "

With her face drawn and a depth of sadness lurking in her eyes, McKenzie came forward and placed a hand on my arm. "I know. And for what it's worth, I probably would have reacted the same if I was in your shoes."

Something eased in my chest at her words, and I asked her quietly, "Does that mean you'll help me retrieve her?"

"I'll do everything in my power to help you get her back."

"Thank you," I whispered.

She gave me a small smile and turned away to look down the mountain. The path was clear and serene, in stark contrast to what it had looked like an hour ago. "We should head back. Gage will be a caged lion until we return."

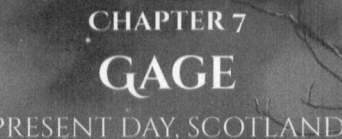

CHAPTER 7
GAGE
PRESENT DAY, SCOTLAND

The wind screamed past me as another flurry of snowflakes slid down the back of my neck. It was freezing out here, bone-cold and frigid. There was no denying the storm was due to the woman currently releasing her rage to the heavens above. My protégé, the woman I was meant to protect.

And here I was, watching the goddamned road.

A coward, unwilling to face her.

I ground my jaw as guilt slithered in my gut and peered to my left, then my right, searching the blizzard for any sign of movement. There was nothing. Not a creature stirred, even the birds having fled. The storm was a clear indication of how Brydie was feeling, and I knew I'd made the right choice in sending McKenzie. There was no way Brydie would listen to me; I would only drive her further over the brink.

The wind shrieked again, and another flurry of ice crystals fell, coating my hair and eyelashes. I felt their wet touch seep through my long strands and lifted a hand to brush them away, only to end up pushing the hair into my eyes. I damn well needed to cut it. Except there wasn't time for those needs. Not when the prophecy was drawing to a close, not when I had a Daughter of Winter to protect and now a descendant to rescue. *I'll just shave it off. McKenzie will help me.*

But it wasn't her whom I envisioned running her fingers through my hair, nor was it her face leaning down toward mine. My body instinctively reacted as I now imagined Brydie leaning forward to brush her lips over my own, her hands clenching my hair tightly. In my mind, I took everything she offered with a voracious hunger that couldn't be sated with just one kiss.

The vision was destroyed when the wind shrieked again, throwing a gust so strong it sent me back a step. I blinked, seeing the road in front of me obscured by snow and ice once more. The interruption was a reminder that the images in my mind were a dream that would go unrecognized given the woman responsible for this storm was presently enraged at my actions. It was doubtful she'd ever forgive me.

I lifted a hand to pinch the bridge of my nose, feeling the tenderness of the bone. It had hurt like hell when Brydie punched me. I'd relished the pain, knew I deserved it. Resetting the bone had felt wrong as I'd watched her run away up the mountain. I was surprised I'd gotten off so lightly. I deserved more. Much more.

Sighing, I dropped my hand and peered once more into the storm.

Nothing moved.

Then my neck burned, a vicious red-hot thrust of pain.

I froze, my eyes narrowing against the blizzard as I looked down the road we'd come. Nothing approached. I slowly turned in a circle, stepping away from the protective overhang I'd been sheltering under and exposed my body to the storm as I sent my senses out wide.

I inhaled, and a range of scents flooded my senses, no obvious direction to any of them. I inhaled again, this time closing my eyes as I turned full circle, ignoring everything but the notes on the air. My neck throbbed insistently, in tune with the rampant beat of my heart.

It was faint, almost non-existent, but I knew that smell. I'd been raised to fear it: acrid smoke and burning flesh.

Fuck! He was here! But where?

My heart lurched in my chest, my thoughts instantly going to Brydie, who was currently unaware and lost to her rage. A sitting target on the mountain. I spent a few precious seconds trying to locate the direction of the scent, but the blizzard was a savage riot. I was unable to confirm which direction it came from.

It didn't matter, not when the only place I needed to be was next to my protégé.

Locking onto her location with my senses, I turned and ran. My neck screamed with urgency as I raced through the storm, grimly tunneling down to the core of my power.

Don't be too late. Don't be too late.

CHAPTER 8
BRYDIE
PRESENT DAY, SCOTLAND

McKenzie led the way down the mountain. My hands felt wooden and physically heavy but no longer burned with an aching need to release my power; that urge had gone once I'd calmed down.

A natural soft gray mist had fallen, reducing our vision to a few feet. It was quiet, eerie, with not even a breath of wind stirring, but there was a sense of tranquility, very much like the calm after a storm.

McKenzie suddenly slowed and held up a gloved hand. "Stop."

I halted. "What is it?"

"Shh!"

Her frame was tense, her other hand curled at her side. I looked around, but all I could see was gray mist. I turned back to McKenzie, who was slowly pulling off her gloves. A prickle of awareness stabbed insistently at my lower back, and I felt a vibration against my chest. I knew without reaching inside my sweater that my pendant would be lit with an amber fire. Heart pounding, I opened my senses and was immediately hit with a presence—menacing and full of animosity.

An icy chill settled over my skin. I hadn't felt the cold until that point—not once—but now it swept through my body with a viciousness that cut me to the bone. It was a different kind of coldness, dark and deadly, carrying a wealth of sinister emotion. My teeth chattered, and I felt sweat slide down my spine, only to freeze moments later against my skin. There was an instinctual knowledge that whatever was out there held immeasurable power.

And I was helpless, my magic and hands bound.

I inhaled sharply, trying to goddamn *think*. When the cold air hit the back of my throat, I gagged. But it wasn't the cold that made me choke, it was the taste—acrid smoke and burning flesh.

I coughed, my hands scrabbling at my throat in a useless attempt to get rid of the taste. McKenzie hissed in warning, her emerald eyes wide with terror. I instantly quietened, taking small shallow breaths as she turned slowly, searching the area around us. I followed suit, narrowing my eyes against the gray mist but still unable to see anything.

McKenzie suddenly thrust both of her hands forward, down the path ahead. "Stop right there!" she cried.

For a moment, there was silence, not even the wind whispered; then there came a wheezing chuckle. It echoed in the mist surrounding us, and I swiveled, trying to determine where it came from. A stray breeze blew between us, and the mist suddenly evaporated, revealing a middle-aged man in hiking boots who stood not ten feet on the path ahead of us.

He looked seasoned, like an expert climber, yet ill-prepared with no sign of a pack on his back. His words were low, a dark taunt. "Or what will you do to me, Dream

Walker? You have limited powers that are not suited to confrontation."

My skin whispered with abhorrence. McKenzie's tension slithered across the back of my neck, and I could hear the filaments in her voice straining as she demanded, "Who are you?"

"I think you already know the answer to that question, Dream Walker."

She blanched. "Talorgan."

He sketched a jerky bow, the movements of his body not quite coordinated as he flicked a hand at his form. "In presence, although not in the flesh."

McKenzie's features were tight. "People are not chattel!"

Talorgan lifted a brow. "If they insist on being weak minded, I would be a fool not to take the opportunity afforded me. Besides, they agree to the manipulation."

"Because you blackmail them!" she spat.

He shrugged. "Everyone desires something. This man was no different."

"And what is it you desire?" McKenzie asked.

He laughed again, a dry, wracking laugh forced between chapped lips. "You know what it is I desire, for she is standing right behind you." His gaze shifted to mine then, piercing me with a hard stare.

The brown eyes staring back at me weren't fully human; there was a deep, unquenchable thirst for violence lurking within their depths.

When I didn't respond, Talorgan cocked his head to the side. "I find this whole arrangement interesting. Did you not see me coming, Dream Walker?"

McKenzie took a step back, now within touching distance. Her voice was stilted as she ignored his question with one of her own. "How did you escape the confines of the Nether? St. Brighid's Day was days ago."

A wicked smile graced his lips. It looked garish, as if forced upon the man's features in an arrangement that wasn't natural. "It appears my new partnership with my latest sycophant is bringing a host of benefits. He is a gifted Dream Walker, and given his other gifts, I no longer need to wait for the veils between the worlds to become thin."

"Callum." McKenzie's response was barely a whisper, but he still heard her.

His smile widened. "The druid is a rare find. I'm certain he carries more darkness in his heart than I ever did." Talorgan paused, his dark eyes considering her as he asked, "Why is it that you have not attacked me?"

McKenzie made a strangled noise, and I knew it was because she'd suddenly remembered what it was she had done in trapping my magic. Given her power was no use in a fight, we were sitting ducks. My throat went bone dry at the position we were in.

At our lack of response, Talorgan's sharp gaze swept between us, and the smirk slipped off his face. "Are we going to play a game then, is that it?"

I clamped my lips together and refused to answer him. The bluff was all we had.

He closed his eyes and inhaled. "Ahh." His eyes flew open, and he dropped his gaze pointedly to my hands. "I can sense what you have done to her, Dream Walker. The rune is unmistakable, and given the recent storm which led me up here, I can guess as to why she was subdued." Talorgan turned back to me, his eyes narrowed. "But what I don't understand, descendant, is why you let her. Are you not a Daughter of Winter? A woman with unimaginable power?" The last words were sneered, a mocking tribute.

I clenched my hands at the insinuation that I was less than what I was meant to be, and my magic responded, internally rioting with the insult. "I did what I needed to."

Talorgan threw his head back and laughed, the tone harsh and grating. "Ahh, so you chose the high road." He swept his gaze over my body and spat upon the snow in a show of contempt. "You are weak! Why would you deny your power? Do you think these people would think highly of you? That you'd be accepted? You have no need of them, not when you could rule them all."

The words were curated with dark promise, and in spite of myself, I felt a surge of excitement as I imagined being able to let go of the power that writhed inside me, to give it free rein and do with it as I would, without any checks or hesitation. But after today, I was more than aware there was darkness in that path, cruel and deadly, and that if I gave into that urge, I would no longer be who I was. Instead, I would be a carbon copy of the man before me.

"I will not follow you," I returned with as much vehemence as I could muster. "There is emptiness in your path. You crave that which you cannot have. Were Arawn's gifts not enough for you? I'd wager you still hunger for that which you originally lost."

He snarled and took a menacing step toward me, deliberately, slowly, his eyes never leaving mine. My arms prickled, the hairs rising as I forced myself to stand my ground, conscious there was less than ten meters between us. *I know these paths,* I reminded myself. *I know this mountain. He's in a body he is unfamiliar with.* A body that was clearly fighting him.

Talorgan's lips lifted into a mirthless smile when I didn't retreat, and there was almost a tinge of respect in his tone as he replied, "You are playing with fire, descendant. But your fire pleases me. There is no question of your lineage, not when you didn't run just now, not when you smell of her."

"I am not Cailleach."

His nostrils flared. "No, you are not," he growled, lips peeling back from his teeth. "You are the scion of that Gaul bastard as well!"

He took another step closer, and this time his left leg spasmed with the movement. His features twisted queerly, as if he were in pain. With horror, I realized that it wasn't Talorgan who was in pain but the man who he possessed. Was the person inside still conscious of everything that was happening? Was he silently screaming out for help? I felt sick to my stomach at the thought of being trapped like that, at being forced to do things against my will.

Talorgan didn't seem to notice the predicament his vessel was in. His focus was single-minded, his scrutiny unnerving as he eyed my form. "You look just as she did. The hair, the eyes, the body."

My clothes, wet from the storm, were plastered against my skin, leaving nothing to the imagination. His eyes lowered, running down my throat to linger on my breasts, my stomach, the vee between my thighs, and finally, my legs, visibly drinking his fill of my body. He added huskily, "You are her child in every way."

His concession was a punch to the gut. Talorgan took another step closer, his intense gaze now swirling with hunger.

"Stop!" McKenzie cried aloud, moving sideways to stand between us with her hand raised. A shimmer of raw fire swirled around her palm.

Talorgan stared at her for a beat before a low, dark laugh escaped his lips. "You think you can stop me with that pathetic morsel of fire magic, Dream Walker? I think not, and I tire of this interlude." All mirth vanished as his face ground into hard angles. "It is time to test my new nemesis, and I will relish this attack for as long as I can sustain it."

Talorgan raised his hands, but before he had a chance to call upon his power, McKenzie released a wild cry as her flames lanced Talorgan's chest. His clothing came instantaneously ablaze. But Talorgan didn't cry out. Not one sound came from his mouth. And although his clothing was aflame, he neither took the time to stop and put it out, nor acknowledge it.

I gasped. Horror eclipsed my fear, because it was obvious this druid was not just immortal but able to possess others without feeling their pain. But what of the man inside the vessel? Was he experiencing the burn of McKenzie's fire?

McKenzie reached out to grab my arm, her fingers biting into my flesh. "We have to run! Now!" She yanked on my arm, pulling me back the way we'd come.

"No, it's a dead end," I managed to gasp out.

"We have no choice! Hurry!"

Fear propelled me forward as I turned and followed her. Behind us, I could hear Talorgan, a low chuckle escaping his lips as he called out, "I thought you weren't a coward."

My heart lurched at the taunt, but I didn't respond, too intent on carving a safe path through the wealth of rocks under the fresh snow, their surface slippery with ice. My next step proved just how treacherous it was when my ankle twisted and rolled to the side. I cried out, landing on my knees in the snow.

Talorgan's voice came again, but this time it sounded forced and slightly pained. "You can't run and you can't hide. There is only one way down this mountain."

The hairs on the back of my neck rose, and I couldn't

help but look behind me. He had fallen behind a few meters, but he still doggedly came toward us. The fire had swallowed his jacket, his hair was now ablaze, and blood was running out of his nose, but still he continued walking.

I turned away, intent on getting to my feet. McKenzie reached down to help me, but then she glanced back behind us, and her features twisted with such horror that I couldn't help looking back myself.

This time I saw what was really in front of me. This wasn't Talorgan, but Talorgan in a man's body, and what I saw was a man who was struggling. Although he hadn't made a sound, the man's movements were jerky, desperate, his features twisted into what could only be described as an internal cry of pain. His eyes, though, they were all Talorgan, bent on the chase ahead.

McKenzie tugged on my arm again, her face parchment white. "Come on!" she screamed.

I turned back to forge ahead, only to find we were within a few feet of my training ledge, the storm having cleared to illustrate endless blue sky and brooding peaks on the horizon. Past that rocky ledge was nothing but a steep drop, the jagged rocks lifted in supplication to the sky. Death was this way, over that ledge. Death was what we would find.

I caught McKenzie's gaze; she'd realized the same. Her eyes were wide, the white's almost eclipsing her emerald irises, but in her gaze was an understanding—that this would be our final stand. We turned as one to face our nemesis, and I could feel her body trembling beside mine.

"I'm sorry," she forced out on a jagged breath. "I shouldn't have chained your magic. This is all my fault."

No, it wasn't. I was the one who had run away. I was the one who had called upon the storm, proclaiming my location to one and all. This was all on me, and as I opened my mouth to say just that, a blurred figure came into focus behind Talorgan. It was a man, running, his ebony hair trailing in the breeze behind him.

Gage!

Before I could cry out, his hands lifted. The coil of his power hit the advancing man squarely in the back. Talorgan was thrust forward, the force of Gage's attack causing him to stumble, and he teetered as fire now blazed over his back as well as down his front.

Still eerily quiet, Talorgan regained his feet and turned to face his attacker. Although Gage had ceased running, he did not stop his purposeful advance, his features hardened into a wall of stone as he strode forward. "You have no place here—it is not your time," my Guardian snarled.

Talorgan stretched his burned and bleeding lips into a triumphant smile. "Is that so? Then why am I here? Does it scare you, druid, to know that the rules have changed? That I can now come and go as I will?"

Gage's face paled, but he held firm. "It matters not. Not when you can't do anything; not when you can't use your power."

At Gage's revelation, I realized Talorgan hadn't attacked us because he couldn't—which meant his vessel held no druidic power!

Talorgan laughed. "Oh, I beg to differ. I've achieved what I set out to achieve. I've met Cailleach's descendant—the one you all thought to hide from me. Pointless in the end, really. And it matters not whether the veils are thin or not. I no longer have to bide my time in order to visit." His burned mouth lifted in a cruel, garish smile. "My new partnership is bringing a host of benefits I am excited to explore."

My Guardian's face hardened. "Regardless of whether you are chained to the Nether or not, it's obvious you hold limited power outside of your real form. I'd call it a wasted win." Gage's eyes ran over the ravaged body of Talorgan's vessel. "In fact, I'd say you don't have much time left on this plane at all."

Just as the words left Gage's lips, Talorgan's legs gave out, and he fell to his knees in the snow. Even then, Talorgan made no move to bank the fire ravaging his vessel's body. The smell of burnt hair and human skin wafted on the breeze, adding another layer to the putrid signature Talorgan carried. I was horrified to see there was no inch of his clothing uncovered by flames—he was a live, burning fireball.

On his knees, Talorgan forced out on a rasp, "You think you are so clever, but you do not see what is right in front of you. I do not fear the reckoning to come, druid. You will not beat me. Your support is dwindling. Your people are turning away from the light, drawn to the power of my Dark God." He suddenly grinned, the vision raw and grotesque as his swirling brown eyes remained unmolested in his bleeding, ravaged face. "The future has been cast. It is inevitable. Your time will come, and I will celebrate your fall—the last of my brother's line."

Shock stole my breath, and I cut my gaze to Gage, seeing his face blanch, his next step faltering. His mouth opened, his cerulean eyes swirling with confusion. I made a sound in my throat, lifting a hand in his direction as I felt his pain and confusion. His gaze flickered to mine, capturing my gaze for a beat before his features tightened with keen determination.

He turned back to Talorgan, his hands now clenching into fists as he began to mutter under his breath with unwavering focus.

In return, Talorgan laughed, the sound a ragged gasp,

and even though his voice had weakened, it was no less chilling, for it was confidence that reined in that tone, a sense of formidable strength and power. "You can send me away," he forced out, panting now with exertion, "but I'll be back. And whether it be next time or the one after, one of these moments will be your last." He shifted his gaze to mine, his eyes piercing. "And you, my lady—you will face me alone," he added on a dark promise.

My blood chilled. I couldn't look away from him. Talorgan's confidence never waned and his stare never wavered, even as Gage, his features bleak, opened his clenched fists and shouted, "Be gone!"

Without breaking our stare, Talorgan winked, then he closed his eyes. And when they opened, the man in front of me suddenly screamed in a new voice filled with unending agony, "Help me!"

For a second, I simply stared at the man, then I cried out as I realized Talorgan had gone and the man before me was here and in pain. But before I could take two steps, McKenzie had my arm in a vice. "No!" she bit out. "He may still be tainted."

I pointed a shaking finger at the man, who was now writhing in the snow, his screams piercing. "Look at him! Talorgan is gone. He needs us."

I wrenched out of her grasp and raced forward, but as I drew near, I could see there was nothing I could do. There was nothing anyone could do. His clothing was gone, melted to his charred skin, his features unrecognizable.

Ignoring the smell and the horror, I dropped to my knees beside him and lifted my hands. But as soon as I raised them, I remembered I could do nothing with my power locked away, not even relieve him from the pain.

My head whipped toward my Guardian. "Help him!" I implored. "You have the gift of healing—help him!"

Gage's face was like stone. While holding my gaze, he slowly shook his head, his words weighted with a sense of finality. "He is beyond my help. The Afterlife already awaits."

"What? No!" I gestured at the man's trembling chest, still slowly rising and falling. "He still breathes, Gage. There's a chance. Please help him!"

Something flickered in his eyes; it looked like a reflection of his pain. "I cannot. The fire has already taken him."

"No, he—" Still in denial, I looked down at the victim of Talorgan's machinations...only to find Gage was right. The man was no longer breathing.

He had gone.

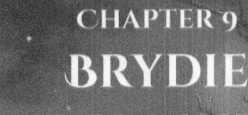

CHAPTER 9
BRYDIE
PRESENT DAY, SCOTLAND

I numbly watched Gage send Talorgan's latest victim to the Other. I wondered if he'd had a family; a partner or children who were waiting on his return.

The start of our brisk hike back to the shieling was silent, all of us quietly paying homage to the man who had just lost his life. The breeze had died off, and the weather was hushed and still. The snow crunched loudly under our boots, and a gray mist once again shrouded the mountain range, the view of Broadford Village lost to a sea of low cloud. I broke the silence to ask, "How did Talorgan possess him? He made it sound as though there was a bargain made."

Gage didn't break his stride. "There was. Talorgan would have made him an offer, something he desired, and in return, asked for his consent."

"That's it?"

Gage shot me a look over his shoulder. "It doesn't have to be explicit. Consent is consent."

I stopped. "That isn't consent. That's betrayal and misinformation!"

Gage didn't disagree. "Yes. And after an agreement was made, an opening would have been formed between them, one Talorgan would have taken full advantage of."

His face was a smooth mask, but he didn't fool me. I could feel his anger—and his anguish—that he'd once again had to take a life. "But how did that happen if Talorgan is in the Nether?" I pressed.

"He told us how," McKenzie interjected. "He said he had a Dream Walker."

Gage's voice was hard. "Callum."

Christ! Everywhere we turned, he was a thorn in our side, aiding Talorgan when he was bound to help us. I couldn't understand it. How could he lead his people knowingly into tyranny? "But how did Talorgan succeed in gaining full possession? He was physically in his body."

"That level of acceptance requires time," McKenzie responded. "Talorgan would have been in contact with him numerous times."

I frowned. "So, Garret was still Garret because Talorgan had only touched him once or twice?"

"Yes," Gage confirmed. "And it's also the reason he's still alive."

Or was when Gage had left him.

"Going by his clothing and lack of a backpack, that man was unprepared for the trek up this mountain," McKenzie mused. "But he would have been a local, someone who knew the risks in a storm. Talorgan's hold would have been strong to force him up here in that blizzard."

I stopped walking as the truth of that statement hit me. It was my fault the man died. My fault Talorgan had possessed him. My fault he'd been forced to walk up this mountain so ill-prepared—all because of the storm I'd created. A calling card that had shouted 'come and get me.'

"Brydie?" asked McKenzie, her face pinched in a frown as she and Gage came to a stop in front of me. "What is it?"

"Whether or not Talorgan possessed him, I was the one who killed him," I confessed in a hoarse voice. "You were right—his death is on my hands. If I hadn't generated that storm, if I'd controlled my reaction on hearing about Chloe, he would still be alive."

McKenzie laid a hand on my arm. "No, Brydie, it's more complicated than that. Haven't you been listening? A deal would have been made. It wouldn't have been the first time Talorgan coerced him."

That may be so, but she'd shouted the truth an hour ago —she'd screamed how selfish I was being by using my magic on the mountain, the risk it would entail; that such an unnatural storm would gain the attention of our enemy.

...And now another innocent had died. I shook her hand off, my chest tight with the knowledge I was responsible for yet another life. The first were my parents; the second, James; the third, the gardener at the estate; and then today, Garret, and now this man. Unknown, unnamed, but another victim, nonetheless.

Gage had said both James and Garret were alive when he'd left them, but what did that mean? Had they died soon after? The only way to remove Talorgan was to stab the victim, shocking the body and the mind to enable a loophole to eradicate his spirit. I remembered the knife Gage held in his hand, the runic symbols a dark scar on the ancient blade. He kept it hidden at his lower back, just under the waistband of his jeans. What did it feel like to carry that weight? Not it's physical weight but its emotional and psychological weight? How many times had he had to use it?

...Too many if he always carried it.

Gage had told me once that a victim's survival depended on how far Talorgan had insinuated himself into their minds. But I wondered now that if they survived the stabbing, would those people ever be the same? Would they return to who they'd been before Talorgan possessed them? I didn't see my ex-fiancé after he'd attacked me, because Gage had whisked me away to Scotland that very night. That had been four months ago. James would have healed by now, physically at least, but what about mentally? Would he still be the same man? Or was he someone different, carrying a taint of the darkness that once tempted him?

I felt Gage's scrutiny and looked up. His eyes were hooded, and the connection between us was carefully blank, as if he was shielding his emotions. He didn't fool me. He knew exactly what I was feeling, most likely exactly what I was thinking, and I waited for his condemnation, tensing as I anticipated the blow. But he surprised me, neither accepting my self-recrimination nor denying it as he said, "We're all human, Brydie. That's what makes us who we are. To deny an emotional response is to tell us not to breathe. There's times when we need that release, and carrying magic only amplifies that need. We become dangerous if we don't let our emotional responses out. But there are ways to do it safely, ways to control it. I have failed to show you how to do that, so it's my fault that man died, not yours."

"Your fault?" Oh no, he wasn't going to carry this weight. This was mine alone. "I don't think so, Gage. Up there, I didn't give a damn if I put everyone at risk. Ask her!" I flung a hand out at McKenzie.

Her face was pale, but she didn't say a word.

Gage didn't even look at McKenzie, his eyes steadfast on my own. "I'm not giving you an excuse, Brydie, but his death is my fault, not yours. I'm your mentor. I should have taught you techniques for emotional release, ways to manage your anger safely without putting others at risk. Hell, I know how dangerous that is more than most...and I should have told you about Chloe from the start."

I swallowed. Those reasons still didn't excuse what I had done, though. I pushed that churning thought away to ask the last question burning inside me. A question that could grant a modicum of absolution. "Was there any hope for that man, whether we attacked Talorgan or not?"

Holding my gaze, Gage shook his head. "Not after full possession. As soon as Talorgan was granted entry that deeply into his soul, his life was over. Mortals can't accommodate everything Talorgan is. The weight of his power is too much for the mind."

I considered that for a moment, then asked, "What if the vessel were a druid? Or someone with a sixth sense?"

"I've never met a druid who agreed to such possession, nor heard of it happening. It's possible one of us could host him longer, but I suspect we'd still have a shelf life."

My blood chilled at the thought of Talorgan taking one of us, of taking me. Swallowing hard, I continued walking down the mountain.

LOGAN WAS WAITING for us on our return. When he lifted a hand in greeting, there was a flurry of movement from the vehicle. A slim figure emerged and began to run toward us, a small dog in tow. Moments later, Aidan threw himself at McKenzie.

"Hi, son," she murmured into his hair, hugging him tightly. Jack came to a halt beside him and sat on his heels and looked up at them both, tongue lolling from the side of his mouth.

Aidan pulled back. "Mom, why did you take so long? I was so worried, especially when there was a storm."

"Shh, Aidan, it's fine. The storm abated and I have what I need." She patted the side of her coat pocket.

He frowned. "But I thought you had all you needed from your visit to town this morning?"

McKenzie smiled and turned him gently toward the car. "I'll have you know that not all shops stock what I need."

"What were you missing then?"

McKenzie shook her head. "Nothing for you to worry about, love."

Aidan looked unconvinced but obediently followed his mom to the vehicle. Jack followed dutifully behind, his paws leaving footprints in the fresh snow.

Logan slowly approached, his gaze watchful.

"All sorted?" Gage asked his twin.

"Yes, the shieling is clean."

"Good, it's time to head out then. Jump into the vehicle. I'll just do a last sweep before we leave. I'm sure Ian's grumbling about how cold it is down there."

Logan nodded at Gage before asking me quietly, "You alright, Brydie?"

I swallowed at his concern. "You heard about Chloe?"

He nodded, eyes somber. "I'm sorry."

Gage looked away, his jaw set, and I could feel the tension coming from his frame even without our internal connection.

Without looking at my Guardian, I said to Logan, "I can't leave Chloe with Callum a moment longer than necessary. As soon as we resettle, I'm going after her with or without anyone's help."

"That's unnecessary," Gage growled. "We'll all be working together to retrieve her. Chloe is as much a part of this group as anyone."

"You're not going to tell me to stay behind," I snapped.

"Can I stop you?" he returned.

Something eased in my chest then, and I willed myself not to show any emotion. Not after what had happened on the mountain, not after what had happened in the car. "Thank you," I said quietly.

"You must realize that because Callum not only has the Dagda's cauldron, but is also in league with Talorgan, that there is a need to do this right, Brydie," Gage said softly. "We can't just go and get her. There are a series of steps we need to go through, the first being finding sanctuary with The Rowan Tree. We need to present our case in person, and if our cousins offer refuge, only then will we be able to work on a plan to infiltrate the Institute. It won't be an easy mission by any means, and we'll need help on the inside."

I knew what he was saying. He also knew how I felt about that help. "Do you still trust Alison? Because I don't, and I will not barter my best friend's life on her motives."

Gage considered me. "If you feel you can't work with Alison, Chloe's retrieval will be delayed. Our only other contacts at this stage are Oona, Briana, Conall, or Mark, and they'll wonder why I haven't gone through Alison first, and will no doubt tell her of our plans anyway. If Callum has Chloe, we don't have time to establish a relationship with anyone else. Are you willing to risk leaving Chloe there for a few months while we find another ally?" He crossed his arms over his chest and stared at me with that unrelenting cerulean gaze.

I bit the inside of my lip, holding back a curse. He'd neatly put me in a corner, and he was damn well right—we didn't have time to find another sympathizer within The Oaken Tree, not with the threat of Samhain looming. And aside from what Alison felt for me, and I for her, it was clear she had Gage and McKenzie's trust, and I trusted them both, even when their actions were not agreeable with my own.

I released a breath. "Fine, we'll use Alison."

Gage simply replied, "So be it."

Logan, who'd been silent up to this point, cleared his throat and stepped between us, placing an arm around my shoulders. "Good. Well, given that's decided, we should get going. The sooner we get to Ireland, the sooner we'll have refuge. Shall we?" He gestured at the vehicle.

Gage jerked his head at the shieling. "I'll be along after I've swept the building."

Logan lifted his chin at his brother and turned me toward the vehicle, but I hesitated. "Wait." I had words left unsaid, words I needed to voice.

Turning to Gage, I forced them out, ignoring the hurt that once again surged in my chest. "I understand why you kept Chloe's identity a secret from me. And you were right— I would have reacted just as I had now. I would have run away to find her...and ended up putting everyone at risk. I'm sorry."

Gage's eyes burned with an emotion I couldn't read as he said quietly, "No, you wouldn't have, because I would have stopped you."

I inhaled sharply. "That would only have caused animosity between us—"

"More than what there already is?" he said sharply.

My lips lifted in a ghost of a smile. "True. But regardless, you were right; my training wouldn't have progressed. There was no way I would have been able to concentrate, and there was a high possibility I would have never embraced my legacy."

He stilled, but I could feel the intensity of his gaze as it roamed over my features. "Thank you."

The words were simple, but they were honest. My breath hitched as he took a step closer, one hand lifting. But then he blinked, and his hand fell back to his side. I gave him a sad smile and turned to walk toward the vehicle.

A second later, Logan fell in beside me. "You surprised him, you know."

I couldn't look at him, my chest felt too tight. "I didn't see surprise on his face."

"You misunderstood."

I stopped in front of the vehicle, one hand resting on the door handle, still unable to look Logan in the eye. "What do you mean? His reaction was clear enough."

"No. I meant that you surprised him with your response about Chloe. He wasn't expecting you to be so forgiving."

"You don't think I'm reasonable?" I shot back, lifting my gaze to his.

He held up both of his hands. "I didn't say that. But I know you have more insight than I do. I think I would have been pissed for a lot longer, and for that, I respect you more than you know."

"But?" Because I knew there was a but.

"But you can't read my brother. Not like I can. Couldn't you feel that he wanted to hug you then?"

I looked back at Gage, who was just now entering the shieling. As if feeling my gaze, he turned, his blue eyes searching mine before he turned away. "You're wrong. I can read him very well. We are connected, after all."

Logan snorted. "Well, one of you isn't listening to the other, then. Because all I felt from Gage right then was longing. And what you thought you saw was the opposite to what he felt."

I looked back at Logan, my mouth opening, but he didn't give me a chance to respond, adding, "He likes you, Brydie, more than he's willing to admit."

I snapped my mouth shut, feeling my pulse race with hope. I stared into the eyes of Gage's twin, so like him in looks but so opposite in personality, and thought that if Gage were even a bit like Logan, that hope could take wing. But Gage wasn't Logan, and that hope died with my next breath.

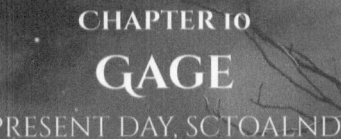

We picked Ian up on our way down the mountain. Brydie didn't even look at him when he entered the vehicle, her gaze trained on the snow outside. Her demeanor worried me. I knew what rune McKenzie had used on her, and its effect wouldn't be pleasant. Holding that constant simmer of power at bay would create a huge amount of tension, which wasn't what Brydie needed in an already tension-filled position. But there was nothing I could do except keep an eye on her and ride out the storm.

Aidan, for all our careful machinations, had been aware something was afoot. His first words as I'd slid behind the wheel were, "Where are we going?"

I told him the truth. "Ireland. We're visiting your cousins."

"But I don't have any cousins."

"They're distant cousins, love," his mother had murmured. "Their clan is called The Rowan Tree."

He frowned and absently patted the Jack Russell on his lap but didn't ask any further questions.

Brydie, however, had asked in a wooden voice, "Who are The Rowan Tree?"

Aware Aidan would pick up on the tension between me and my charge, I flicked a look at McKenzie, who, catching my silent request to respond, turned to Brydie and said, "There are two clans in Ireland, each distinguished by geographic location. The Alder Tree resides in northern Ireland, and The Rowan Tree resides in Southern Ireland. But The Rowan Tree is unique; it has a few differences to the other clans." McKenzie gave Brydie a half-smile as she revealed, "They're fae."

"Fae?"

"Yes, they're Morrígan's people."

I caught the look on Brydie's face as she put two and two together. "The Morrígan of the Tuatha Dé Danann is their war goddess?"

McKenzie nodded. "Yes, but she was more than just a renowned warrior. She was also their Sovereign Goddess and responsible for choosing who would lead their people."

Brydie raised a brow. "So the legends are true, then?"

"Up to a point. The Tuatha only lasted in this world for a few centuries. Morrígan fled before the rise of Christianity sometime in the third century, but she left her legacy with the people that remained." McKenzie wrapped an arm around Aidan's shoulders as he leaned into her and added, "The Rowan Tree aren't druids like we are. They have different gifts to ours, but we refer to them as our cousins because we look at the world similarly. We all hold to the ideal of maintaining the balance and that nature provides symmetry."

Logan turned around to face her from the front seat next to me. I caught the look of curiosity sparkling in his eyes and remembered he'd never met the fae. Since I inherited the gifts that came with the role of being the Daughter's Guardian, he had forged a different path, turning his back on our heritage.

"And do they walk among us, with mortals and druids alike?" he asked.

McKenzie nodded.

"Do they...look different to us?"

She smiled. "Yes."

Aidan tipped his head back to watch his mother's face. "Are they just like in the books, with pointed ears and wings, Mom?"

She laughed. "As a matter of fact, yes. Although, they use glamor to conceal their true form. If you were to meet them on the street, they would appear just like you and me. The only differences are that they would typically be a little taller and hold a certain type of magnetism."

Aidan's brow furrowed. "Magnetism? Do you mean they're attractive?"

I hid a smile as McKenzie blinked down at her son. "Yes, darling. It means they hold a certain allure."

He nodded, his face serious. "So the books really are true then."

Ian let loose a low laugh from the back.

McKenzie patted her son's head, her face settling into an expression of maternal pride. My chest tightened as I thought of my own son, Saul. He was of a similar age to Aidan, but he'd been living in the States since Catriona had left Scotland just before he was born. I still remembered the evening she'd stood at my door, the rain pounding on the pavement outside as she told me in no uncertain terms that she was leaving and I would have nothing more to do with our son. I wasn't to visit, nor would I be welcome in his life.

She'd stayed true to her word. I never heard when she'd

gone into labor, or that my son had been born. Yet Catriona had still had the audacity to ask for financial support a month later. I'd complied with her demands, of course, and unbeknownst to her, had kept tabs on my boy as soon as I knew of his birth. A report arrived every fortnight.

Listening to McKenzie talk to Aidan just now, I wondered if Catriona had taught Saul about our heritage. Wondered if she had read him stories about the myths and legends of the Celtic gods. She wasn't a druid herself, but she had been born in Scotland and knew all the old stories. But after receiving recent reports, I didn't hold out much hope. From the sound of things, Catriona was living true to form. Having a child hadn't stopped her, and I knew all too well how my monthly donations of financial support were furthering her selfish needs.

Saul was nearly ten, an age that defined whether he would inherit my legacy, along with the power the role of Guardian entailed. I gripped the steering wheel as anxiety roiled in my gut. My son would not navigate that all on his own. The timing was far from perfect with the Daughter of Winter in my care and Samhain fast approaching, but there was no denying it was time to extract him. As soon as we were settled with The Rowan Tree and had retrieved Chloe from the Institute, it was time for my son to learn who he really was.

"Do the fae hold the same powers as we do?" Logan now asked, bringing me back to the conversation in the vehicle.

McKenzie shook her head. "Morrígan's people hold power that is different to ours. It is not of this world."

Ian broke in from the back, "Which is a good thing they're on our side as they are also tied to Cailleach's prophecy."

Brydie frowned. "You've mentioned before that one of

the fae may have saved me following the car crash with my parents. Do you think that person came from The Rowan Tree?"

I held her eyes in the rearview mirror. "That's what I hope we're going to find out." I didn't like leaving loose ends untied. It was imperative we find out who this other player was and whether they were friend or foe.

Brydie looked away. I ignored the tight feeling in my chest and reminded myself that whatever she felt about me didn't affect how I fulfilled my role...if only my traitorous heart would listen.

"And you think we'll be safe with the fae?" Logan pressed. "Is their world removed from the attention of Talorgan and Callum?"

McKenzie hissed, and I glanced in the mirror at Aidan. The kid was hunched in his seat, Jack sitting alert on his knee.

Realizing his mistake, Logan immediately apologized. "Sorry, I didn't mean—"

"Just leave it," McKenzie said sharply. "We should turn our mind to booking our ferry to Ireland. I don't want to be delayed at the docks for six hours." She turned to her son, Jack now clenched tightly in his arms. She murmured softly to him, conveying the conversation was well and truly over as she sought to distract Aidan from what he'd seen and heard these last few months.

The boy's reactions were a reminder we all carried scars, most of which were invisible. I swept another glance at my protégé, seeing her lips tighten as she looked through the window at the passing landscape, and acknowledged that some of them were permanently lined across our heart.

SOME NINE HOURS later on the brink of dawn, we took the ferry from Holyhead to Ireland. I hadn't been willing to risk the less popular crossing at Bootle, preferring to lose ourselves in the crowds that flocked to the more popular destination. There was safety in numbers.

I hadn't relinquished the wheel during the drive. My compulsion to ensure our safety was one that couldn't be ignored. Ian had asked if I needed relieving once, and I'd been clipped in my response, whereas Logan had known not to ask at all. My brother could feel my need to take control like a burning ache of desire. I'd said in no uncertain terms that I was fine and that they should all get some sleep.

They'd followed my barked command and, somewhere along the way, I'd felt the filaments of my internal connection with Brydie fully reopen as the rune McKenzie had imposed on her magic finally wore off. The accompanying relief was a double-edged sword, because it meant I couldn't feign my emotional distance any longer.

McKenzie assured me during a gas stop that she hadn't foreseen any troubles on our journey, but I wasn't convinced. Not after Talorgan had managed to approach us on Beinn na Caillich without prior warning. The thought still caused a chill to chase down my spine, and this latest development axed any sort of peace I may have found between now and Samhain.

I'd craved the ending to this godforsaken prophecy for a very long time, but over the last few months, that desire had changed. Brydie had grown in both her power and her position. She showed promise that she could handle most threats thrown at her, but there were still moments where she was vulnerable. Moments she wasn't prepared for...as illustrated yesterday, both at the Claymore and on Beinn na Caillich.

While they slept, I spent those silent hours mulling over various training exercises we could use to test her level of control. The situations were all unpleasant, and she would hate me for it, but they were necessary. Power came with consequence, and as her Guardian, I was aware of its burden all too well. Our emotions were a conflagration; they could help or hinder our actions, and consequences could be devastating. As I knew only too well.

After burning down the family home, I'd tried to protect myself by pushing Logan away. Reuben had shown me how fucking stupid I'd been in believing I could outrun my emotions. My former mentor had been relentless in his pursuit to make me understand I was useless without Logan's love and support. A liability rather than an asset. I'd been lucky. Lucky Logan had forgiven me for pushing him away those nine long years. Lucky he'd accepted me back into his life when I'd finally reached out to him at Rueben's urging. Lucky, because if we hadn't reconnected, I didn't think I'd still be alive...or on this side of the druidic code.

Accepting Logan back into my life had brought a measure of control, along with happiness. It had also brought fear. Fear that he would be harmed or used against me. But that burden was one that had to be carried. That's what love was, I'd soon come to realize. It made you vulnerable, but the journey wasn't worth living without it. Over the years, Logan had been joined by Saul and Ian, soon followed by McKenzie and Aidan...and against all my actions to prevent otherwise, Brydie had joined that list too.

But it's more than that, a voice whispered in my head. *You desire her as well. More than you deserve.*

As if on cue, Brydie moaned in her sleep, a soft sound full of distress. I froze, wondering if even in sleep she could feel my angst along our internal connection; the need I felt for her. Hands clenching the wheel, I waited until she resettled against the headrest and fell back into a deep slumber.

I exhaled, admitting to myself it was time to stop hiding from the truth. It was pointless anyway. Logan knew exactly how I felt about Brydie, possibly better than I did. And even though she hadn't fully comprehended what she could feel from me herself, my mixed responses were only upsetting the balance between us. And that couldn't happen, not any longer. Because, going by her reaction to the news about Chloe, this would only push her to lose control again. I could live with her hatred of me, I could live with the blame, but what I couldn't live with was her failures, especially if I were the cause of them.

Acid burned at the back of my throat, because now I'd acknowledged the problem, I had to fucking address it. The only question was when.

CHAPTER 11
CAILLEACH

Nothing could have prepared Cailleach for that meeting with her brothers.

The Phoenix had made good on his word, for with his departure, as the lone feather reached the shingle at her feet, two forms immediately begun to waver into existence.

Tears immediately pricked at her eyes. She blinked them away, and in that moment, her brothers' features became sharp and defined. Her brothers shared only one trait, their dark hair—but there the similarities ended. Dagda's hair was straight, whereas Cernunnos's was lush and curly, and a set of majestic brown antlers rose from the crown of his head. Dagda was dressed in a standard tunic with pants and leather boots, but her wild brother was bare chested. The silver torc around his neck was his only adornment, and plain, rustic breeches stretched across his muscled legs.

Her brothers' gazes latched first on each other, both of their jaws dropping, before they became aware of her presence in the shadows. It was Dagda, always the spokesperson, who broke the stunned silence. "Cailleach? Is that you?"

She nodded, unable to speak past the tears choking the back of her throat. Under her breath, she offered a sharp command, and the clouds that had covered the moon since her altercation with the Phoenix scudded away to offer a semblance of light. The moonlight landed on Dagda's face, and she witnessed his surprise turn quickly into apprehension as he realized he was no longer in the Other.

"What have you done, sister?" he demanded. "Why am I back in this world?"

"And I?" Cernunnos growled.

His gravelly voice was just as she remembered. Her wild brother had preferred the solace of the forest and the creatures who inhabited it, so much so that he barely conversed with his siblings or his mortal subjects. But whenever he had, he did not waste words; always honest and direct.

Cailleach swallowed hard and stepped forward to break away from the cloak of shadows at her back. Raising her chin, she said simply, "Because I need you."

Dagda raised a brow, and his gaze raked her form from head to toe. "You are no longer the crone but who you once were. You...met your fate." He paused, his gaze narrowing over her features with a scrutiny that left her feeling vulnerable. Dagda always had a way of seeing right to her soul, to the emotions she tried so hard to hide. "But your body language, your tone, it tells another story. What has happened, Cal? Did you not find your fated mate?"

Cailleach flinched, reminded of why she was there and of who had orchestrated her fateful meeting with Tritus. She forced the emotions away in an effort to concentrate on the task at hand. She needed the support of both Cernunnos and Dagda to ensure the prophecy was strong enough to contain their dark brother and his followers. "Yes,

I did. Although, he is now gone." She swallowed and continued, "I know of your machinations, brother. I know how you tried to offer me solace in the role that was thrust upon me."

Dagda's features remained carefully neutral. "I did it to repay the debt I owed you. I did it to offer you a chance at happiness."

Cailleach nodded, her heart heavy. "I know, Dagda. I know." She looked at Cernunnos then, capturing her wild brother's emerald gaze as she murmured, "I find it fitting that Cernunnos's son was the key to that knowledge. He saw through the curse Morrígan laid over me and was the first to see me for who I really am—the woman behind the crone."

She could still remember the memory she had raped from Tritus's mind that fateful day some two years past—the truth behind the story of his birth. His mother had sacrificed her life to save his, and because of Dagda's machinations, it was Tritus's bloodline—the bloodline of her wild brother—that had allowed Tritus to see behind the guise of the hideous crone.

Cernunnos had gone deathly still, and his features were a frozen mask as he asked slowly, "What are you talking about, sister? What son?"

Cailleach felt her chest tighten at her brother's question. Had he not known his lover was pregnant when he passed over to the Other? *Oh no....* Acutely aware of the loss she was about to induce, Cailleach said softly, "Brenna was with child when you died, Cernunnos."

His face went slack, his emerald eyes twin blades of shock and grief. "I had a son?" he whispered, as though repeating this truth to himself would cement all that it carried. "And, Brenna? What happened to my love?"

Not able to bear the hope on her brother's face,

Cailleach looked away as she admitted, "She died in order to protect your child."

Dagda made a sound then, his voice gentle. "Her actions brought honor to you, brother. She was magnificent."

Cailleach raised her head to look at Cernunnos. The grief on his face was a honed blade as he ever so slowly rounded on his brother. "Tell me," he ground out in a gravel-hewn voice, "of how you would know of the fate of my lover, Dagda? And how you would know of a prophecy that involved my son, who is now also dead?"

Dagda's form wavered, becoming slightly opaque, and Cailleach caught his throat bob up and down. They were both aware of the power their wild brother wielded. He was a veritable king of the forest, the oldest of all of them. And not only did Cernunnos hold power like a living, breathing cloak, but he held both the physical strength and the lethal intelligence to make him one of their deadliest siblings.

As the silence lengthened, Cernunnos growled a warning, more beast than man.

Dagda didn't need further prompting. "Isn't it obvious, Cernunnos? I was the one who initiated the prophecy."

"Prophecy? What godforsaken prophecy, Dagda? What prophecy involved *my* son?"

Dagda looked at Cailleach. "Not just your son, Cernunnos, but also your sister."

Cernunnos's face mottled. "Cease these games! Spit out the truth. Do not hide behind words; I would know what has befallen my blood—NOW!"

Cailleach took a step back even though she was not on the receiving end of her brother's wrath. Part of her felt pity for Dagda, especially as she knew he had done the best he could for Cernunnos's family. There had been no easy choices, not when Brenna had birthed their son in her village, subjecting the knowledge of the child's ancestry to the druid who helped deliver their babe. But the child's horned existence had traveled like wildfire, and Brenna had been left with only one choice—to do her utmost to save the life of their child before it was taken with hers. Given the position Cailleach was now similarly in, she understood there was no easy path ahead of her, no matter which one she chose.

Dagda cleared his throat, his hands raised in front of him to ward off Cernunnos's prowling approach. "Alright, brother. I will be as succinct as possible. I orchestrated a prophecy that would not only ensure your son's survival, but one that would also grant a modicum of happiness to our sister. I did this for many reasons. The first being that I owed a debt to Cal. The second is that Brenna called upon me as soon as your child was born. She asked me to protect the babe before the druids could kill him."

"Why would someone try to kill an innocent babe?" Cernunnos roared. "Couldn't you hide him? Given Brenna's blood, he was still mortal."

Dagda shook his head. "No, not when he was also a half-god."

"What do you mean?"

Pity and a deep sadness welled within Dagda's eyes. "The sin you and Brenna committed by lying together was immediately obvious, Cernunnos, especially because the child bore your features." Dagda's eyes lifted, pointedly resting on the large, curling bones protruding from his dark curls.

Cernunnos's eyes widened, and his voice was thick. "The child resembled me?"

Dagda nodded. "Not only in looks, but also in power.

Even as a babe, I could feel he carried a legacy, one that could rival my own children."

Hearing Dagda discuss her murdered lover was almost too much for Cailleach to bear. She bit her lip to withhold her cry of distress, tasting the blood that welled upon her tongue. Her wild brother needed this moment. Given what she'd seen in Tritus's buried memories, she knew Cernunnos loved Brenna with everything he had. Her brother had risked all that he was and the kingdom he ruled for a short dalliance with her. The irony of their situations was not lost on Cailleach, because she'd risked the same, and the loss hurt, more than she could have imagined.

Cernunnos, his features now composed, asked softly, "What happened to him?"

Cailleach couldn't understand how Cernunnos could remain so collected, not when the mere thought of Tritus caused her heart to bleed.

"Brenna asked me to protect him by hiding his heritage from others," Dagda responded just as quietly, as if aware his words would create wounds that couldn't be healed. "I saw her request as an opportunity. Morrígan had reason to believe I had strayed from our marriage bed." He swallowed. "Even though I had, Cailleach protected my honor by discrediting her claim in front of Morrígan's court. But my wife knew it was a cover-up, and it spiked her ire. Given Cailleach's public proclamation, Morrígan tried to save face by punishing me through our sister."

"Are you telling me this is how Cailleach became the Goddess of Winter?" Cernunnos demanded.

Dagda nodded. "Yes, and she threw in a cruel penalty with that decree. Morrígan demanded Cailleach become all that the role entails by personifying death and destruction itself."

Cernunnos lifted a brow, his eyes flitting between them. "And what did that make her? She looks no different to me."

Dagda's smile was sad as he said quietly, "A hag of such irrefutable appearance that she would wield power and control by a mere glance."

Cernunnos looked to Cailleach again, eyes roving down her form as he snarled, "As I said, she looks no different to me. What are these lies, brother?"

Cailleach broke in, her voice desperate. "It is true, Cernunnos. The veil of the crone isn't visible to our family, but I swear everyone else sees the crone...that is, until Dagda softened Morrígan's decree by allowing one man to see past the veil."

Cernunnos became preternaturally still as he whispered, "My son."

It wasn't a question, but Cailleach answered it anyway. "Yes. Dagda cemented this action through prophecy, marking Tritus as my fated mate. But Dagda gave me more than that, for I not only gained a lover, but also a partner with whom to rule over winter."

"Tritus had these skills?"

Cailleach nodded, her heart squeezing at the memory of their time together. "Your son held skills that were similar to yours. He was able to nurture the forest and regenerate it for the needs of all its inhabitants. He balanced the storms I wielded."

Cernunnos smiled then. It was fragile, filled with pride yet edged with profound loss. "My son favored his mother then. Brenna had an incredible gift for seeing the good in others." He bowed his head, and Cailleach knew it was in homage to the woman and the son he'd lost.

"I am sorry, Cernunnos," she whispered, feeling that ache intensify in her chest.

His head lifted, and his green eyes pierced right into her soul. Pain, sharp and haunting, raked across Cernunnos's face, and his words were thick and forced. "I knew it. I knew she wouldn't voluntarily leave this plane, even if I was waiting for her. I would expect nothing less from the woman I fell in love with." He swallowed and turned away.

The admission caused grief to ride up like a wave, clogging her throat with tears. Cernunnos had just admitted he hadn't found Brenna in the Other, and even though she may have forgotten him in this world, it was obvious he hadn't forgotten her. Being a mortal, had Brenna been reborn in the Other as someone else, completely ignorant of her past. It was true then, that when crossing over, only the gods remembered their previous lives. But...did this mean she would never meet Tritus again?

The question filled her with panic. If this were true, the loss she now experienced was unfathomable, for that one morsel of hope was all that was propelling her forward, all that was driving her to see this prophecy enacted. She had to see Tritus again, she had to!

...Then she remembered Arawn and Talorgan, and the price they had to exact. No, this prophecy wasn't just for the protection of their daughter, or for her chance to meet Tritus in the Other, it was to also prevent her dark brother and his disciples from destroying this world. Should she share this with her brothers? And what of the other truth they had skirted around? The truth that it was Dagda whose hand had ended Brenna's life; that their brother had demanded her life as the tithe for protecting their son? As she hesitated over the decision, a noise shattered the still air.

It was the unmistakable wail of a baby's cry.

Cailleach's heart clenched at the sound, and her breasts immediately tightened, aching with an awareness that the child needed feeding. She had ignored the cries before when the Phoenix was here; she couldn't ignore them again. Just as she turned to attend her daughter, Cernunnos demanded, "What is that noise? Is that a child?"

Dagda had also stilled, his eyes narrowing on her face. "Hold, sister. Why are we here? You told us you needed us. Does it have something to do with that child?"

Cailleach could not look away from their scrutiny. Besides, it was time. "It has everything to do with it," she confessed. "Please, just wait here. I will return to you both as soon as I'm able."

Dagda's mouth dropped. "*Your* child? To whom?"

Cailleach looked at Cernunnos and wasn't surprised when she saw the sudden realization on his face. Cernunnos knew why he was here, why they'd come full circle. A hint of a smile crossed his face as he said, "To my son."

CAILLEACH FED and ministered to her daughter as quickly as she could, aware that her brothers were waiting for an explanation outside. There was also the irrepressible knowledge that her time was severely limited. She knew Talorgan, and even her brother, Arawn, would not whittle away an opportunity to extend the ground they'd already taken. They were coming for her, and soon. She had a day at most to see her plans through, a mere cycle of the sun and moon.

As her child suckled, she ruminated on what the green druid might be doing and where he'd gone. She wondered what part he played in all this. He had saved both her and her daughter's lives. Was he an ally, then?

He'd told her he was off to get help when he left the shieling before the new dawn had risen. What that help would be, she had no idea, but given she was sequestered in his home and he hadn't killed her child, she had to trust he was on her side. Because a side was needed. A division had occurred between her and her dark brother. A division that would only mean one thing—that war was coming.

The child broke from her breast, and it was the natural release of a baby that had drunk her fill. Cailleach adjusted her gown, lifted the child to her shoulder, and gently rubbed her back. It was strange how she innately knew what to do. Ever since she knew herself to be with child, she had agonized over her ability to be a good mother, but after the initial shock of Tritus's death had passed and she acknowledged the child's existence, she couldn't deny that the act of mothering had come with a natural ease. It was also a surprise to find she enjoyed the role. These quiet moments spent feeding were a balm to her ravaged soul, for here lay a piece of Tritus, his legacy continued in their daughter.

When Cailleach heard her daughter give a soft burp, she carefully laid her in the crook of her arm where she could gaze upon her sweet face in the gentle glow of the fire that was for the child's benefit rather than her own. As the Goddess of Winter, she did not feel the cold, and neither would her child when she came of age to exhibit power.

Her daughter's eyes were closed, and Cailleach felt sad that she could no longer look into those green eyes that were so like her father's...and so like those of the grandfather who stood outside the shieling. She laid a hand over a small, pink cheek and stared at the child's snub nose before running a hand over the light down covering the top of her head. If it weren't for the soft texture under her fingertips, Cailleach wouldn't have known if her daughter even had hair. But this afternoon, in the light of day, when she'd held her for the first time, she'd seen the bright, pearlescent glint of hair upon her daughter's head. It was confirmation the child would have her hair—a magnificent mane of pale moonlight.

A noise came from the other side of the room, a soft swish of the hide being lifted. Cailleach snarled, her eyes snapping to the doorway even as her arms tightened around her precious bundle. Her daughter gave a soft murmur of discontent as Cernunnos entered.

"Sister," he said in greeting. "I would like to meet my grandchild. Will you allow it?"

Cailleach froze. His simple words were layered with a myriad of emotions that conveyed all that he had lost, but also all that he hoped to gain from a connection with her child. She didn't need time to contemplate her response. Conceding to his request would, in a small way, buffer the loss of his lover and their son, and she couldn't deny him. "Of course, I would be honored for you to meet her."

She rose from her chair by the fire as Cernunnos bowed his head in thanks and came toward her. He looked large and powerful, his legs corded with muscle, his chest liberally sprinkled with hair. Cailleach had often imagined that, along with his sheer size and the majestic horns on his head, the hair on his chest was in fact fur, in recognition of his rightful place as the ruler of his kingdom. However, one day when she'd given into her urge and asked to touch it, she'd found it was just as coarse and wiry as that of her other brothers, even that of his son.

Cernunnos came to a stop in front of her, his confidence instantly vanishing as he looked upon the soft, sleeping baby in her arms. Her heart melted.

"It's alright, Cernunnos, she will not be disturbed by your touch. She is fed and warm and will welcome your embrace."

Cailleach held the baby out to her brother and watched with a lump in her throat as Cernunnos tentatively transferred the baby into the crook of his own arm. He looked down at the child, and Cailleach did not miss the tender look that crossed his face as he asked, "She? I have a granddaughter?"

Cailleach nodded. "Tritus was right all this time. He'd often tease me we were going to have a daughter, but I didn't believe him."

Cernunnos looked up, his gaze piercing. "Teased? He teased you, sister?"

Cailleach nodded, her lips twisting ruefully. "Yes, and often." Then she looked away as she felt a soft flush rise up her cheeks, for talking about Tritus's teasing only made her remember how those moments usually ended—entangled with each other, lost in the pleasure of their bodies and the beating of their hearts.

"Ahh, I recognize the look on your face," Cernunnos murmured. "And I am glad for it. That is the way it is meant to be between lovers." His eyes twinkled as he shared, "I found Brenna insufferable at times, and she I, but those moments were temporary, short-lived by the passion, loyalty, and love that fueled our bond."

Cailleach nodded, understanding yet again that she and her brother shared more than just a sibling bond.

Cernunnos looked back down at his granddaughter. "And what do I call my grandchild? Does she have a name?"

Cailleach cleared her throat, her daughter's name having been chosen at that moment when she'd recognized Tritus still lived within their child. "I have named her Gra."

"Love? You have given her the name, 'Love'?"

"Yes, in recognition of the emotion she brings to me as well as the connection to her father."

She saw compassion in his gaze. "It is a fitting name, sister," he said tenderly, once more casting his gaze upon his granddaughter.

A soft silence fell between them. After a while, Cernunnos dropped a tender kiss on the child's forehead and held her out to Cailleach. "Thank you for letting me hold this blood of my blood. She is truly beautiful, and I can feel her soul connected to mine through my son."

Cailleach blinked away tears. "I believe she got the best of both of us, just as you believe in whom Tritus became."

Cernunnos nodded sadly.

Feeling his pain, Cailleach shared, "I can honestly say, brother, that he was my everything. Tritus possessed not only integrity, honesty, and courage, but also humility. You would have been proud to call him your son."

Cernunnos smiled, a misty, wavering smile. "Thank you."

She nodded, and as he turned to leave the room, she lay Gra back inside the wooden crib by the fire. Laying a blanket over the tiny, precious child, she whispered, "I'll be back soon, Gra. Sleep easy," before exiting the shieling after her wild brother.

Outside, they found Dagda sitting on a rock nearby, his head in his hands. Cailleach knew he'd heard everything. Their hearing was exceptional, especially in this still, mountain air.

At the crunch of their feet on the loose shingle, Dagda stood and looked at them both, remorse on his face. "I am sorry, Cal, for the loss you have suffered. I am sorry if my machinations brought you grief." He then turned to their brother. "And you, Cernunnos, I am sorry that it was I who dealt the final kiss to your lover. Brenna was a strong woman and one I admired greatly. Please know I did not enjoy delivering the tithe owed in return for her request."

Cailleach and Cernunnos both stopped in front of him and said as one, "We forgive you, Dagda."

Dagda's mouth dropped open, and he looked between them, lost. "What? Where is your anger?"

Cailleach turned to look at Cernunnos, sharing a secret smile that only they could understand before Cernunnos shared, "You have no idea what you gave us, do you, Dagda? The happiness that we experienced?"

"But I killed your lover!" he exclaimed.

"I suspected you dealt the final blow, but I also know you didn't do it willingly, and if I know Brenna, she would have understood the ramifications of her request before making it. I've no doubt your actions gave her peace—an opportunity to enter the afterlife with the knowledge that our son would have a chance to live. I appreciate that time was short-lived, but our life is not ruled by the movement of the sun and the moon. Life is measured in the moments we share and the moments we enjoy. I know you may not understand what I am referring to, but my time with Brenna, though shortened to the span of one-and-a-half years, was worth more to me than the eons spent alone before that. I truly lived during my time with her, Dagda, and I know she did, too, mortal or not."

Dagda's face was awed, grateful. He replied softly, "She went with honor, brother. So much honor. It is a moment that will forever be etched upon my memory." He turned to Cailleach. "And what of you, sister? Do you truly accept my apology?"

Cailleach did not hesitate. "I do not think you

understand the gift you gave me, Dagda. Like Cernunnos, I am appreciative of the time I had with Tritus, and I am aware that nothing will ever compare to those moments spent with him. He was my everything. Without him, I feel I am missing something vital—that I am only half of whom I'm meant to be. That recognition is a curse as well as a gift, because I now have an awareness of what I am missing in my life." She clenched her hands together, her heart twisting with loss. "I suppose I should blame you for placing me in this mess, but I find I can't. What Cernunnos said, what he shared with Brenna, it is true—that time and those memories are worth more to me than anything. I feel as if I have truly lived, brother, and for that I thank you."

Dagda looked slightly shocked at her response. For a moment, all he could do was glance between them as if waiting on another response, as if what they'd shared was a mere interlude to the real one about to fall. As they returned his stare with firm honesty, Cailleach saw the moment Dagda began to understand they did indeed speak the truth.

"In that case, I am happy to have been of service to you both," he finally said. "And part of me hopes that I will have the opportunity to experience happiness such as you both have."

Cailleach tilted her head as she considered him. "What happened to Boann? I thought that what you shared was love?"

He smiled faintly. "I think what I felt with her pales in comparison to what you have just shared."

Cailleach gave him a gentle smile. "Then I wish you luck in finding your own happiness, brother."

He nodded, and she knew this moment had soothed his fears, that they'd addressed the questions that plagued his conscience. She could understand that now, given she herself was the puppet master rather than the puppet. She could also understand the level of guilt and the weight of responsibility involved in initiating a prophecy. It was a path that would forever be her responsibility, because whatever the consequences from now onward, she alone would be the one to carry them.

Cernunnos broke the poignant silence. "I think it is time you shared why we are here, Cal. Our presence is clearly a gift from the Phoenix. We all know that no god comes back to this world after they have left it. Whatever it is must be important enough to have the Phoenix's support. The time has come to share those reasons."

He was right. There was no going backward, only forward, and time was of the essence. Already, the last star in the night sky had winked into existence.

"The time we have spent together to this point has not been wasted," she began. "It lays the foundation for why we are gathered here. We know we are subject to the whims of the All Father. As the Custodian of Creation, he sees not only what is coming but also what has come to pass. What I have to say affects our future.

"The Phoenix approached me after I first met Tritus. He warned me that my time with him would end in an atrocity that would result in catastrophic change and asked that I end my relationship with him then and there. I didn't, aware, even then, that what I felt for Tritus and what we had together was worth more than any lifetime. I fought for more time with Tritus, however short that would be."

Cernunnos shifted, his hands raking through the curls on his head. "This sounds very familiar, for the same happened to me."

His admission confirmed her own suspicions. "I had suspected as much. Since that meeting with the Phoenix, I have had lots of time to contemplate why my relationship with Tritus would pique our father's interest. He does not usually waste his time on petty squabbles, and every path returns to the beginning. It is always an endless circle."

"What are you talking about, Cal?" Dagda demanded. "Speak plainly."

"Sorry, Dagda. What I'm trying to say is that the Phoenix can see a myriad of paths, each leading in different futures. But he can also see backward, to the paths that inevitably led us down these routes. He sought me out because he had seen something in our future—an anomaly that upset the balance of nature. Whatever it was, was clearly dependent on whatever happened between Tritus and me. When I argued that I would not let Tritus go, even with the knowledge that our world might then end, he acquiesced. But he left with a warning that our time would be limited; marked by a profound loss that would outweigh the gain. But for the loss to come, he offered me a boon."

Cernunnos stilled, and it was enough for Cailleach to understand that he, too, had experienced something similar. It was another confirmation their paths had been entwined since the world began, their entanglement set in the stars. Not only did they share blood, but they also shared responsibilities—both of them having taken upon the role of Winter's Mantle, both of them having experienced a love that was a sin, yet the most otherworldly, glorious relationship anyone could have.

"And I assume we are here because you require something from us both?" Dagda asked.

"Yes." Cailleach twisted her hands together as she wondered how best to drop the bombshell that their dark brother had escaped his underworld cage.

"Well, what is it, Cal?" Dagda prompted.

Cailleach released a breath. "There was one who was jealous of our union, one who desired me for his own. In order to win me over, this man—this druid—called out to our dark brother. Arawn answered and offered him aid in return for the gift of his soul."

Cernunnos snarled, the sound so animalistic the hairs on Cailleach's arms rose. "What sin is this?" he roared. "His actions will rend the veil between our worlds!"

"Exactly," Cailleach whispered. "But this druid—Talorgan—he did not stop there. He was given immortality and bonded to Falin, one of Arawn's dragons. With this aid in hand, Talorgan approached us not more than two days ago, with the intention of not only taking me by force, but also murdering Tritus and our child."

Cernunnos growled low and deep, and his hands clenched tightly into fists.

Cailleach felt guilty for the words she forced out next. "I ran at Tritus's urging. He wanted me to run, to keep our child safe. He knew I couldn't help him, that my powers were restricted while I was pregnant, so he made a stand in order to save us."

Cailleach's breath caught in her throat, grief encapsulating her once again. She still couldn't fathom what Tritus had done, the life he'd sacrificed to give her and Gra a chance to escape. The reminder of their final kiss was soul searing, and she lifted her hand to her lips, imagining the pressure of his touch.

Cernunnos asked between clenched teeth, "What happened to him?"

Swallowing hard, Cailleach forced herself to finish it, to share those last horrendous moments. "Talorgan called upon Falin to find me, then he turned on Tritus. I ran, but Gra chose that moment to come. Just before the labor pains hit, I heard the sound of Falin approaching. I was soon lost to the act of childbirth, and she arrived not long after. At the exact moment she was born, I felt my internal connection with Tritus sever." Biting her lip to hold in an instinctive cry of grief, she turned away from their scrutiny and added softly, "Like the circle of time, with the birthing of our daughter, his life passed into the Other."

There was a moment of respectful silence. Cailleach could almost read what was going through Cernunnos's head. She knew he held a deep-rooted respect and sense of pride for what his son had done, while at the same time, the grief of his loss would be piercing him like a dull blade.

"And then, sister?" Dagda asked softly. "It is clear you escaped Falin. How was that so?"

Cailleach pressed her lips together at the memory. Shame still crippled her at how she had forgotten about her daughter, leaving the poor child bereft and alone on the forest floor as a predator came for them. "Another druid arrived," she finally shared. "Someone I've not met before. All I recall is that he wore a green robe. He sent me through a portal to this shieling here on this mountain. Then he went back for Gra. I...I don't recall much of what happened. I was lost by the knowledge that Tritus had gone, but I do know we just barely escaped the dragon's wrath."

Cernunnos looked around sharply. "And where is this druid? Can he be trusted?"

"He's gone. He left at dawn this morning. I'm ashamed to say I didn't acknowledge or thank him for his actions. Without him, Gra and I would both be dead."

Cernunnos ran a hand over his head, mussing the dark curls surrounding his horns. It was a gesture Cailleach had missed without knowing it, a gesture his son had replicated. Her brother felt his emotions keenly, more than most of them, and now, as she looked at him, she realized it wasn't a weakness but in fact a strength that only added to his primal allure.

"I think we can assume this druid is on your side, especially given your enemies have not found you since his departure." He drew a breath, looking sidelong at Dagda as he added, "But you'll need to determine that for yourself as we do not have the time to investigate." He gestured at his body which still wavered, turning slightly opaque. "The Phoenix has only granted our presence here until daybreak. Once the dawn crests, we will return to the Other."

Cailleach felt loss hit her anew. This moment spent with her brothers would be too short if she did not reach an agreement. "Your time here will be longer if you agree to help me."

Cernunnos's gaze sharpened. "Knowing what you've told us, it is clear the Phoenix's reason for calling us here is due to the threat Arawn poses. We all know our brother's nature. He will not hesitate to take everything this world offers, and given the fickleness of our followers, more than just Talorgan will heed his call. No doubt more have already joined him, enticed by power and greed."

"It is true," she said slowly. "The heart of this threat is Arawn. The Phoenix foretold his coming many years ago. He's been preparing for this event for a very long time, manipulating not only my path, but also yours."

Dagda grunted. "So I've been feeling guilt for actions I never really conceived or agreed to?"

Cernunnos shook his head. "No, you've got it wrong. Those were still our actions, still our choices. Father's persuasion is gentle at times, just a nudge, while at others it's a sharp stab that can't be ignored. Either way, we always have a choice—we choose to follow a coercion or we don't."

Cailleach interrupted quietly, "Just as you have a choice now, brothers. I have used my boon with the Phoenix to protect my child. I have asked that Gra be protected, and that of her children's children." She blew out a breath. "But I also asked for two more boons: to remove Arawn and his disciples from this world, and to join Tritus in the Other."

Dagda looked aghast, his mouth dropping open. "What? I am surprised you are still standing! Our father does not tolerate such greedy insolence. He has not been known to offer boons lightly, if at all."

Cailleach bowed her head, a little ashamed. "I know. It was a risk, but I was past feeling anything other than desperation. Besides, I did not escape his wrath. He attacked me, and I thought I'd breathed my last moment on this world...but I didn't disintegrate to ash and wink from existence. The pendant saved me."

"Pendant?" Cernunnos asked.

Cailleach lifted the amber gemstone from around her neck. "This. Your son gave it to me as a token of his love. I'm positive he had no idea of its true significance. The Phoenix told me it was cut from the Stone of Destiny. That wearing it was a reminder of my importance and the actions I would undertake. It seemed to convince Father my request was important."

Her brothers looked even more shocked.

Cernunnos was the first to break the silence. "The Stone of Destiny is real? We've all seen the spear, the sword, and the cauldron, but the stone has never been seen or found by anyone. We've thought it a myth since time began."

Cailleach shook her head. "Apparently it wasn't, and your son was the one who found it. He cut a sliver from it and fashioned the piece into this pendant as a gift for me."

"Circles within circles," Dagda murmured.

Cailleach agreed, for it was now obvious how the threads had all been tied together.

"So, what do you need us for? What decision do we have to make?" Cernunnos asked. "It's evident we would support the removal of Arawn and his disciples from this plane."

Cailleach released a breath of relief. "Thank you."

Dagda looked at her strangely. "There's something else, though, isn't there?"

A grimace crossed her lips. "Yes. The Phoenix claims my three requests can only be resolved through prophecy, and for that to happen, I would need the support of three of my siblings."

"Three?" Dagda asked.

"You, Cernunnos, and Morrígan."

Dagda's face was suddenly stripped of all color. "Morrígan? She has not forgiven you for the lie you told."

"I know," Cailleach admitted softly. "But I have to try. If she does not agree, the Phoenix will not support the instigation of the prophecy. He said I would need the support of all the races. Not only were you three chosen to complete the circle, but each of you have a tie to the others we share this world with. Morrígan serves the fae, you serve the druids, and Cernunnos serves the animals and the dwarves. I'll need each of them in order to ensure this prophecy is powerful enough to send Arawn and his disciples back to the Underground."

"This is no easy task, Cal," Dagda said softly.

"Do you think I don't know that?" she cried, throwing her hands up into the air. "She hates me! She's the one who thrust the mantle of winter upon me. The one who demanded I become a crone, feared and alone. But as I found the exact opposite to what she wanted of me, she won't want to support my request, not when I didn't suffer as she thought I would."

"That's not quite true," Cernunnos said quietly. "Everyone wants something, and Morrígan is no different. We just need to figure out what that is."

Dagda's face was grim as he reminded them, "Before sunrise."

CHAPTER 12

BRYDIE

G age turned off the vehicle mid-afternoon. Ahead, a wealth of dark blue ocean stretched endlessly to the west, and to the north was a jagged line of cliffs that I would know anywhere—The Cliffs of Moher.

The cliffs were all I'd dreamed them to be, their sheer rocky sides black and alluring, at once dangerous but also otherworldly. The waves broke against the walls in an endless symphony, creating continuous scouring and erosion, and I ached to get out of the car so I could smell the sea breeze and take a closer look. There was power here.

It had been a long, tension-filled drive, with a three-hour break spent on the ferry from Holyhead to Dublin. I'd managed to catch some sleep and awoken to find my magic had returned. But even with the short nap, I was still tired. It reminded me of my last long-haul trip—where Gage had drugged and then taken me from New Zealand to London against my will. I'd woken up on the plane when we were close to landing at Heathrow. I remembered the emotions well, the feeling of absolute terror, shock, and fear. Back then, I'd had no idea of how far Gage would go to protect me. No idea of the emotions he kept hidden under a layer of cool reserve. There were no pretenses now, though.

The object of my thoughts turned to face us, tension around his eyes. He looked exhausted. "We're a bit early. The sun needs to hit Hag's Head before we can obtain entry."

"Hag's Head?"

He waved a hand at the outcrop perched on the cliff in front of us. "Can you see the woman looking out to sea?"

I could see no one.

"Look at the rock, Brydie," Logan suggested from his seat next to Gage.

I squinted my eyes against the sun's reflection and focused on the rocky formation in front of us. It took me a moment to realize what Gage was referring to. The rock had been shaped into the side profile of a woman's head, looking out to sea, a sense of sorrow to the image. "I see her."

"When the setting sun hits her face, the doorway will be revealed. Only then will we be able to enter The Rowan Tree."

I blinked at him. "How exactly? Do you mean the door is through that rock?"

McKenzie loosed a low laugh. "Not quite. We'll be going through a portal. The sun on the rock is merely a signal that confirms the time it will be open."

"Cool!" Aidan exclaimed, bouncing in excitement, and Jack let out a short bark of encouragement from his lap.

I looked back at the line of cliffs. "If we have some time, can I take a short walk along the cliffs?"

Gage's response was immediate. "No."

Logan swiveled to his brother. "Come on, Gage, we all need some breathing room. We've been traveling for hours. Besides, there's no one around." He indicated the vacant pathway running along the cliffs. There was what looked like a visitor center in the distance, but it was a fair ways north of our position.

Gage's jaw was tight, but he released a sigh. "Fine. I think my legs would appreciate a stretch."

"You think?" Ian shot from the back seat. "Try sitting back here for the last twelve hours."

"No one forced you back there, man," Logan returned with a grin. "Quit moaning. You had three hours on the ferry to walk around. You should have used it wisely rather than browse the net."

Ian glared back at him, and I hid a smile as McKenzie said, "This is disturbing; you two are still acting like a married couple. There's only so much of this I can take. Come on, Aidan, let's check out the cliffs."

McKenzie pushed open her door as I did the same to mine. My heart was racing at the thought of meeting more of my people. Even though my life was a far cry from what it had once been, a large part of me still remained that introverted young woman Gage had found in New Zealand. I was just better at hiding it now.

I'd thought my path was laid out before me—my career, where I would settle. I hadn't had many friends, but I'd had Chloe. It was going to be a quiet life, without many ripples in an otherwise mundane routine...until my life had dramatically changed these last four months. Now I was now on a timeline, hounded by an immortal intent on killing me. An altercation I could neither run away from nor deny.

I stopped at the cliff's edge, and took in the vista before me. It didn't disappoint. The cliffs had an age-old charm, a careful balance between cruelty and beauty; a natural illustration of light and dark. I felt a sense of peace here but also a sense of significance that life was precious. The cliffs were a demarcation between life and death. Beyond that edge was eternal darkness. No one would survive a fall.

As I looked upon their symbolism, I felt his eyes on me, and I couldn't stop myself from turning to meet his gaze. Gage's features were neutral, but his eyes swirled with an intensity that belied his causal stance.

"Come away from the edge. The wind gusts are strong here and many have been caught unawares," he said gruffly.

I looked down at the barrier. It was flimsy, a basic rope held between a row of standards. A small sign warning of wind gusts was planted not far from where I stood. As if to punctuate his statement, a sharp blast of wind hit me, and I stumbled a few feet closer to that edge.

Gage hissed and moved toward me.

I raised my own hand, holding him back. "I'm fine."

Face tight, he jerked his chin, motioning me to come toward him. For some reason, the request made me nervous. There was something in his carefully contrived expression, something he was hiding. I tested the filaments of our internal bond. He felt neutral, as if he was holding his emotions in check, as if he'd placed a wall between us to block the path of his thoughts. I swallowed. How the hell had he done that? Was it payback for what I'd done back at Beinn na Caillich?

Sorrow punched me in the gut. *What was happening to us?* Swallowing, I held his gaze as I walked toward him. Logan, standing to Gage's left some ten feet away, must have felt something from his brother for he sent me a sidelong glance. Noting my intent, he turned and walked away from us, his lips pursed as he whistled a casual tune. The wind carried it away from my ears, the sound drowned by the waves as I stopped just in front of my Guardian.

"You're shielding your emotions from me?"

His face tightened. "I have my reasons."

I felt my throat lock at his guarded response. "Is this because of Chloe?"

"No. This is about me."

Confused, I searched his face, but it was clear he wasn't going to elaborate. "Why did you call me over?"

There was a momentary pause before he said quietly, "I wanted to say I'm sorry about Chloe."

Not only could I now feel it, but I could see it on his face. Guilt was what assuaged me at this confession. "I know."

He blinked, staring at me intently. "That's it? Don't tell me you're ready to forgive me that easily?"

I looked away, searching the trail along the cliffs, and spotted McKenzie and Aidan walking hand in hand back toward the car. Ian was beside them, his face animated as he said something to Aidan. I said slowly, "I realized on the mountain that you didn't intentionally hold the information back to hurt me. I admit that took me a while to figure out, but I do understood you've done everything you could to watch over her." I turned back to face him then, feeling something shift in our internal bond. But his eyes were still unreadable as I added, "I think I'm more upset that it's Callum who has her. We don't know what his intentions are toward her. I'm worried about her, Gage."

His jaw clenched. "It's no secret we underestimated him. I'm still surprised McKenzie didn't have a warning in her visions. There was no way of knowing if her disappearance was sinister or not, but it was important to progress your lessons and embrace your legacy. I had to make a choice, Brydie. I chose you. In every path, I would choose you."

Because he had no choice. Regardless of the paths before him, prophecy would innately make him protect me over all others. It was a curse as well as a blessing, especially when it was a decision that affected you or another you loved. Swallowing hard, I said quietly, "I do. I understand now. I can see why you were drawn to protect and aid me, but you still had a choice to tell me what you knew— especially after I'd come into my magic. There was no excuses then, Gage. Why, Gage?"

A muscle feathered in his jaw as he stared back at me. "Because I'd just found out about Callum; what he now has in his possession and who he's aligned himself with. It also became imperative that on unlocking your power, you learned to control it. It wasn't my intention to forget Chloe at that point, I just had other things to address first. I genuinely did not see sharing that news with you as a priority, not when it would make you unfocused or cause you to lose control at the wrong time." He turned his whole body to face me and took a step closer. "I am touched by prophecy, Brydie. My actions are guided by fate. The Daughter of Winter will always be my priority—*you* will always be my priority."

I couldn't look away. His tone, his words, his face—not to mention the emotions now once again coming down our shared line—it all screamed that Gage hadn't intentionally forgotten Chloe, he'd merely been manipulated by the role he was required to fulfil. It didn't ease the feeling of betrayal clawing up my throat but it did remind me of how entrapped we all were. Our lives weren't our own. Our time wasn't our own. "I understand," I said quietly. "And for what it's worth, I'm sorry for how I behaved. I'm sorry I hurt you."

He never broke our gaze. "I deserved it. You were right to lash out at me."

I shook my head, chest aching. "No, I wasn't." I desperately wanted to reach out and touch him, but I felt too brittle and unable to take his rejection right now. "Let's just focus on getting her back."

As if he'd heard my silent call, Gage reached out and grabbed my arm. A parody of emotions surged from his touch. My eyes cut back to his, shock capturing my breath.

Gage's eyes burned as he said with sincere promise, "As soon as we're settled with The Rowan Tree, we'll get her back. I promise."

Words eluded me. His presence was dangerous, but his touch even more so. It clouded my mind, driving a new urge to the forefront—not Chloe's safety, but my own. I leaned toward him—

"It's time!"

Ian's shout cut through the moment, and I whirled to find him standing by that strange rock formation. The late afternoon sun was now slanting across the woman's face. And to the left, inland from the rock, came a high-pitched whine. As I watched, the air shimmered, then coalesced into a whirling portal from which a black hooded figure emerged.

"Come on!" Ian urged, gesturing at us to hurry.

I turned back to Gage, aware our moment was lost. He knew it, too, for his eyes conveyed an apology as he tugged on my arm and said, "Come on, it's time to meet the fae."

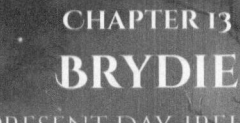

CHAPTER 13
BRYDIE
PRESENT DAY, IRELAND

G age led me toward the portal; Ian, Logan, McKenzie, and Aidan following our path. As we got closer, I saw the figure in black was a woman, her robe billowing behind her with the combined force of the rising winds and the nearly translucent portal.

The woman's gaze remained trained on Gage, as if aware of who and where the threat would come from. Her stance was confident, deliberate, and in one hand she clutched a wickedly curved dagger.

Gage's grip on my hand tightened as he stopped a few feet from the woman. "Eachna. It's been a while."

Eachna inclined her head, a stray lock of curly black hair whipping about her face. Her sable eyes were narrowed on Gage. "Indeed. Duane told me there were druids waiting outside. I couldn't help but come and investigate; we've had no word of expected arrivals."

It was a carefully worded turn of phrase that indicated they'd been expecting trouble.

"I'm sorry we sent no prior warning. We didn't want

word to fall into the wrong hands," he returned smoothly. "We come asking for sanctuary; a few months at most."

Eachna looked between us carefully. Her gaze alighted on McKenzie and Aidan, then Logan and Ian, who had his laptop bag over his shoulder, before turning to me. "There are a few here I don't recognize," she replied, pointedly staring at me. "But given this woman's eyes and the color of her hair, I'm surprised you need sanctuary. Cailleach's descendant is safest in her own domain. Why are you not at the estate in Scotland?"

"It's gone," he replied shortly. "Burnt down by the leader of The Oaken Tree."

Eachna's hand visibly tightened around her dagger. Shock coated her tone. "The leader of The Oaken Tree burned down the estate?"

"Yes." Gage cocked his head to the side as he searched her face. "Have things changed that much that you have lost touch with this world? I'm surprised the fae didn't feel the consequences of that night."

Eachna bared her teeth, and my blood chilled at the sight of her sharp canines. "What are you alluding to, druid? We've noticed nothing of consequence on this world."

The change in address didn't go unnoticed. "Nothing of consequence?" he repeated coldly. "Talorgan is coming, Eachna. His power has spread to other sycophants, one of which is the leader of our clan."

Eachna froze, an eerie stillness settling over her body. *A natural predator,* a voice whispered in my head.

Her words when they came were slow, deliberate. "Fergus has turned away from the light?"

"No, not Fergus; he's dead."

Eachna's eyes visibly widened. "Who replaced him?"

"Callum. He is now the leader of The Oaken Tree."

Eachna's lips thinned. "This does not bode well."

"Indeed, but that's not the worst of it. Callum also has the Dagda's cauldron."

She gasped and looked swiftly at each of us, seeing the expressions on the faces of Logan, Ian, and McKenzie, all confirming Gage's message.

"It's time to call in your people's debt, Eachna," he now said firmly. "The fae need to stand with us."

She snarled, "Our people owe yours no allegiance. That tie was broken long ago by our Sovereign Goddess."

"Are you saying you no longer recognize the agreement made between Morrígan and Cailleach?" Gage said tightly. "The one that ties your people to helping Cailleach's direct descendant?"

Eachna, her eyes flickering with heat, said between her teeth, "I will allow you entry into Faerie. However, let me make it clear that the act of *allowing* you entry into our realm is not an agreement to support your cause. That is not my decision to make."

"Whose is it, then?" Gage demanded.

Eachna smiled, and it was a cold thing. "Lorcan's. He will have the final say as to whether or not we will provide the aid you require."

Gage considered Eachna, and I didn't move as his hand tightened around mine. "From what I know of Lorcan, he is a man of his word. I look forward to a frank discussion with him."

Eachna smirked. "Good, because he would not allow you otherwise." She cut her eyes between me and Gage again, then pointedly looked down at our clasped hands. "And I can see that you have a lot to share." With that, she turned on her heel to face the portal and threw over her shoulder, "Follow me, and be quick about it."

I felt my stomach dip as I looked at the oscillating hole Eachna had just disappeared through. My voice was thin as I admitted to Gage, "I've never been through a portal."

"There's nothing to it. Just put one foot in front of the other."

"That's it?"

His lips lifted. "Not quite. There will be a sense of vertigo, possibly some nausea, but it will soon pass. Just keep moving." He squeezed my hand and then let it go. "Come on, it won't stay open long."

As he turned toward the portal, I felt the loss of his touch. We were entering fae territory, and although McKenzie had said The Rowan Tree were our cousins, this initial meeting with Eachna did not bode well. But we had to start somewhere, starting with stepping through that portal. Taking a deep breath, I pushed aside my misgivings and followed my Guardian. One step, two, and then I was walking upon soft dewy grass under a starry, moonlit night, the others exiting the portal behind me.

The full moon bathed our surroundings in a soft ethereal light. I turned in a circle and saw we were now standing in a glade, a small stream tinkling musically to our left while tall trees stood sentinel. A carpet of lush grass, rich with purple and white wildflowers lay under my feet, and upon the air was a light breeze and what looked like thousands of tiny lights bobbing around us. Fireflies.

"Wow! Way cool," Aidan exclaimed from behind me, Jack swiveling his head from left to right at the twinkling fireflies.

"Isn't it just?" Ian murmured.

"Our people prefer the natural world before it was touched," Eachna shared, standing a few feet ahead. "It's one of the reasons we left the world above."

"And where are we exactly?" Logan said, echoing my thoughts.

"In a world closely related to yours, but on a different plane."

Aidan's eyes bugged out. "You mean like the Nether or the Other?"

Eachna eyes softened as she gave the boy a small smile. "Yes, very similar." She turned back to Gage. "I'll let Lorcan know you've arrived. Stay here; no one will disturb you." Inclining her head, she swiftly disappeared into the foliage.

I looked at Gage. "You didn't mention the relationship between our clans was strained."

A muscle ticked in his jaw. "I didn't know it had become this bad. It's been over ten years since I visited The Rowan Tree."

Ian pushed his glasses up the bridge of his nose. "What of their leader? Is he reasonable?"

Gage ran a hand through his hair, the ebony strands lifting in the soft breeze. "I knew him. We were initiates together."

"But is he reasonable?" repeated Logan.

Gage shrugged. "He was charismatic. He would suit his role."

"Let's hope he understands the threat hovering over us all," McKenzie murmured.

"Good, because I would appreciate your honesty," said a deep baritone.

I whirled to see a man standing in bare feet a few feet away. He had a pair of tight leather breeches on and was bare-chested, with long, dark, chocolate brown hair cresting his shoulders. His body was sculpted and lean, with not an ounce of wasted flesh. As I stared at him, I felt the first stirrings of desire. Flushed, I forced my gaze to his face. His dark green eyes held a rich vibrancy as he carefully observed us, but it was his peaked ears that caught my attention. They were sharp and distinctive, marking who and what he was—fae.

Gage stepped forward, a hand offered in greeting. "Lorcan. It's good to see you again."

The leader of The Rowan Tree received him with a tight hand clasp. "Well met, Gage. It's been nigh on ten years since we last saw each other. You look as though you've matured somewhat since then." He gave a fleeting smile as he let Gage's hand go and ran his gaze over the rest of us. "You've picked up quite an interesting crew."

"We share a common bond. It's the reason we're here."

"Yes, I can feel it, even if Eachna hadn't shared who and what you have brought here. But first things first, and that's proper introductions." Lorcan turned to McKenzie first, his gaze appreciative. "I haven't seen a Dream Walker in a while. Welcome to our home, my lady. Please, call me Lorcan."

McKenzie blushed, a red stain high on her cheekbones as she accepted his hand. "Thank you. My name is McKenzie."

"A lovely name for a beautiful rose."

The blush on McKenzie's face spread even further, and for the first time ever, I saw her composure slip. She released Lorcan's hand and reached for her son, pulling him close. "This is my son, Aidan."

Lorcan dropped his gaze to the boy, his lips tipping into a genuine smile as he reached out a hand and laid it on the boy's shoulder. "Aidan. In Irish, your name means born of fire. A strapping name for a fine lad." He cocked his head to the ground and asked, "And who is your companion?"

Aidan's pride was apparent as he bent down to pick up the Jack Russell at his feet. "This is Jack. He's my dog."

"Well, welcome to Jack too, then." Lorcan gave the animal a quick pat on its head.

McKenzie nudged her son, who replied, "Thank you, sir."

Sending him a slight nod, Lorcan moved onto Ian. A frown creased his brow as he looked the tall scholar up and down. "A Lore Keeper? The last time I saw one of you was just before Morrígan sent us away."

Ian's lips twisted into a grimace as he accepted Lorcan's hand. "Partly true, sir. I don't hold an active position anymore. I lost the role a few years ago when I left the clan and no longer have access to one of the Lore Books."

Lorcan eyed him. "And is this dismissal from The Oaken Tree going to cause problems during your stay here?"

Ian lifted a shoulder, releasing Lorcan's hand. "I doubt it; I'm of no consequence to our clan. I am surprised, though, that you haven't seen any of us for a while. I thought one of our Lore Keepers worked closely with your people to help preserve Morrígan's history?"

Lorcan waved a dismissive hand. "We have no need of a Lore Keeper. Being long-lived means there is no pressing need to record events."

There was something in Lorcan's response that didn't sit well, and as my gaze drifted to Gage's face, it was clear he hadn't missed it either.

"True," Ian returned. "But somewhere along the line, you'll have to address the need."

"Thank you; I appreciate your opinion on the matter," Lorcan replied, his smile more teeth than warmth. "And I must admit I'm intrigued by your story. You'll have to tell me about it during your stay."

Ian inclined his head.

Lorcan turned to Logan next, who had already stepped

forward and had a hand held out in greeting. "I'm Logan. Long story short, I'm no one special"—he jerked his thumb at Gage—"apart from the fact that I'm this guy's brother. Nice to meet you."

Lorcan took his proffered hand, clasping it tightly. "Welcome, Logan. But you're wrong about that—you're more than this man's brother. You're touched by prophecy just as much as everyone here."

Logan narrowed his eyes as he pulled back from the fae leader. "You're right. I'm here to make sure my brother does nothing stupid."

"Hmm."

Logan opened his mouth but didn't get a chance to reply as Lorcan turned those green, all-seeing eyes of his onto mine. My core throbbed in response. Flustered, I took a step back. Lorcan wasn't perturbed, his eyes intent as he advanced. His sudden closeness had my blood thrumming. I desperately looked away, only to catch Gage's ever watchful gaze. His features were drawn, his nostrils flaring. It took me a moment to understand that he could smell my desire, and that had my cheeks instantly flaming.

Lorcan's voice was like smooth honey, and its draw pulled my gaze back to his face. "You need no introduction, not with that hair and those gray eyes of your mother."

His words cut through the film of lust. "My mother?"

Lorcan smiled, and with the exception of his canines, revealed a row of strong, straight teeth. "Your first mother, child. Cailleach."

I trembled, and my voice was harsher than I'd intended. "She is not my mother." I could still remember the Winter Goddess pushing me into the tarn behind the estate, along with that terrifying feeling of drowning as she'd sent me back to my body.

Lorcan's smile only widened. "She is your blood mother, child. The people of The Oaken Tree are all her children. Just as everything here is Morrígan's." He gestured at the surrounding glade and then held out his hand. "Come. Let us not debate the actions of our gods. Instead, let us formally greet each other. Tell me your name."

"Brydie," I said, accepting his hand. His strong fingers tightened around mine, and I felt calluses on the pads of his fingers—a leader who earned his title. A tingle ran down my arm, arrowing straight between my legs. What was with my reaction to this man? Why did he elicit such a response? Then I recalled all the previous handshakes he'd gone through—the men's' wince of discomfort and McKenzie's blush. Did he have similar power to Cailleach? Could he read my mind like she could? Unease prickled in my belly at being such easy prey.

I released his hand and stepped back once more, needing to put space between us. "Nice to meet you."

Gage's voice was sharp. "Now that you've satisfied your curiosity about us, did we pass the test? Will you offer hospitality to your cousins?"

Lorcan didn't even look abashed at being caught out. "Distant cousins," he corrected in a mild voice. "And yes, you passed the test. With news of Talorgan rising, I had to be sure. My people are well protected here. We do not need anyone infiltrating our home and destroying the peace we have worked so hard to establish."

"Even though you are tied by an ancient pact to help Cailleach's descendant?" Gage shot back.

"There was no question of aid in that quarter," Lorcan said sharply, the mask slipping. "Morrígan gave her word to Cailleach, and we follow her decree without question. But if my test had ended differently, that aid may have come in a different form, yes, and not one which involved staying here with my people."

With those words, he confirmed he used his power to determine if we had been touched by Talorgan. The revelation was refreshing. I inclined my head. "Thank you for being honest."

His expression was approving as he returned smoothly, "Of course; the fae cannot lie."

The response gave me pause, but I wasn't naïve. Words could be twisted, omitted, or carefully contrived in such a way that the truth could become opaque, and Lorcan and his people would remain untrustworthy until proven otherwise. I simply inclined my head.

Lorcan sent me a sly smile before turning to face the group. "Well, with everything said and done, I have the pleasure of formally inviting you into our home." He raised his arms above his head and, with a flourish, he snapped his fingers. "Welcome to Faerie."

The glade around us instantly shimmered. In one moment it was empty, in the next, we were standing in the middle of a crowd of fae.

CHAPTER 14
BRYDIE
PRESENT DAY, IRELAND

My heart stopped at the faces staring back at us. Some were filled with curiosity, some with censure, but most with hate. Without having it confirmed, I knew they'd been here the whole time, glamoured behind a cunning veil, listening and watching as we interacted with Lorcan.

Lorcan addressed his people, turning in a slow circle as he announced, "Join me in welcoming Cailleach's descendant and her party to Faerie. As you will have heard, these druids all passed the test, and the threat of Talorgan does not encroach on our domain. I encourage you to make them feel welcome and show them what true fae hospitality is. It has been at least a decade since we welcomed one of our cousins into our home."

Turning back to us, he said in a low voice, "I'm aware you have things to share, but I'm conscious you've had a long journey, and the fae are not inhospitable. I give you leave to get settled in for the next few hours before joining me for the evening meal. After that, we will discuss the coming threat and what it is you need from me and my people." Lorcan then motioned to a short, brown-haired woman in the crowd. "Airmid."

The woman stepped forward. "Yes?" Her voice was soft, lilting, and as sweet as she appeared.

"Please show our guests to their rooms. Offer them the east lodgings."

Surprise flickered across her features as she inclined her head and turned to face us. "Follow me," she said to us, before weaving a path through the crowd of fae.

I fell into step behind Gage and tried not to linger on the faces staring back at me. The fae were beautiful. Each face, each item of clothing, was of absolute perfection; unmarred, perfect beauty—a trait no doubt inherited from their Sovereign Goddess.

The depth of the crowd was greater than I had thought. Close to five hundred fae had gathered in the forest, and as we left Lorcan behind, I observed a number of them were perched in the trees above, their bows loosely drawn and trained on us. These fae looked at us carefully, their gazes unfriendly, their distinctive ears flat against their heads. Going by their leather attire and the weapons strapped to various parts of their bodies, I knew them for what they were. Warriors.

As we walked under a large tree, I heard one above hiss in warning, a stream of soft expletives following. Walking directly in front of me, Gage tensed, but his gait didn't falter as we followed Airmid. Taking his cue, I looked straight ahead, trying to ignore the archers in the trees and the threat they posed. I didn't need to look behind me to know McKenzie would be doing her best to shield Aidan from the condemnation in their eyes.

As we cleared the last of the fae and the noise of the crowd reduced to a faint murmur, I heard Logan say under his breath just behind me, "Well, that was an occurrence I would not like to repeat. Lorcan's touch was crippling. How is it that you women didn't feel the pain we men did?"

"What do you mean?" I asked, turning to face him.

Logan raised a brow. "You didn't look pained when he shook your hand. Rather, you looked like you...wanted him to touch you."

My face flamed. I was mortified Logan had seen that—did that mean everyone had seen that? I stumbled, my foot tripping over a root. Always attuned to me, Gage whipped around and grabbed my arm, steadying me.

Face still flaming, I murmured a thank you and shook my arm free.

His mouth tightened, his eyes burning with words unsaid as he eyed me. He didn't need to say them, not when I could feel jealousy firing down our shared line. I opened my mouth to try and explain that I couldn't help what I'd felt when Lorcan touched me—Christ, even when he'd looked at me! Tried to explain that I'd been coerced to feel that which I didn't voluntarily feel, but Gage released my arm as though it burned and swiftly turned back to face Airmid, who had stopped just ahead of us.

"Everything alright?" she called out.

"Yes, sorry, I just stumbled. Please, continue."

She gave me a quiet smile and resumed walking, the five of us following.

I became aware of the lively chatter of birds twittering in the trees around us. As if on cue, a starling flew past, its wings iridescent with purple and green plumage in the warm afternoon light. A trio of blackbirds and a grackle followed. Their movements made me pause, and I became cognizant that we were indeed somewhere else, the weather here being calmer, warmer, closer to summer than spring.

I was suddenly feeling exhausted, the last twenty-four hours catching up with me. I looked over my shoulder to see how Aidan was coping. Jack was still clutched tightly in his arms, tongue lolling from the side of his mouth. It would do Aidan good to rest here, even temporarily. There was a feeling of peace and security in this world; whatever storm awaited us did not hover here.

We rounded the dense thicket of trees, and I got my first view of our new home. It wasn't the cabin I'd been expecting, the most obvious difference being that it wasn't on the ground, but rather secured high in the trees. It was the stuff of childhood dreams—a veritable tree house, but on a much grander scale.

The trees appeared to lend themselves to the development, their thick trunks and long branches intertwining like a lovers caress to support the large wooden cabin among its boughs. Along the walls and over the roof was a mass of green foliage, a mix of what appeared to be ivy, hydrangea, climbing roses, star jasmine, passionflower, and clematis armandii—all climbing evergreens that flourished in the shade.

My steps quickened as we walked closer. This was a dream made real. I couldn't take my eyes off the colorful roses, their petals bright against the various shades of dappled green foliage.

As we stopped at the base of the tree, I tried not to think about what my garden back in New Zealand must now look like. I couldn't bear to think of all those plants I'd lovingly cultivated now tangled with weeds.

Airmid gestured to the wooden ladder nestled against the trunk of the largest tree. It was cleverly designed, having been carved into the tree itself. "Access is obtained here. I trust that your lodgings will be suitable, however, if you require anything further, please don't hesitate to contact me."

"And how would we do that?" McKenzie asked.

Airmid laughed softly. "My apologies. It has been a while since we had visitors. The best way to reach me is by talking to one of the birds. They'll contact me immediately if something is amiss."

McKenzie raised her brows. "You can communicate with the birds?"

Airmid paused, her eyes widening and her lips curving into an O of surprise. "You can't?"

Ignoring her question, Gage replied smoothly, "I'm sure everything will be more than satisfactory, Airmid, thank you. If we need anything further, one of us will find you at dinner tonight."

Noting the dismissal, Airmid smiled at us all. "Of course, I will leave you to your rest. In a few hours, I will come back and escort you to dinner."

The small woman turned and headed back down the path, vanishing into the thicket of trees.

Aidan didn't waste any time scrambling for the ladder, his dog still nestled in the crook of an arm.

McKenzie scolded him, "Not so fast, Aidan. Let me take Jack." She shot Gage a glance. "Assuming it's okay to head on up?"

At Gage's nod, Aidan squealed. "Awesome! I'm getting first dibs on a room. Can we sleep at the top, Mom?"

A smile broke across McKenzie's face, and I knew it for what it was—relief that her son was once again behaving as any normal boy his age would. "Sure, honey. Just take it slowly—and no running."

"Cool!" Aidan passed over Jack to his mother and soon vanished, scooting up the ladder and onto the wooden platform above, his footsteps muffled overhead. McKenzie climbed up a few rungs and passed Jack up into Aidan's outstretched hands before continuing on.

"You're next, Brydie," Ian said from beside me. "Ladies first."

Surprised that he'd directly addressed me, I stared at him, conscious there was so much left unsaid between us. Our last proper conversation at Beinn na Caillich had been weeks ago now, but it was still present between us every time we met each other's gazes. The loss of his friendship still hurt, but I deserved it after stringing him along.

I thanked Ian with a tentative smile and began the climb up the ladder, Gage following close behind.

As I cleared the platform, I couldn't help gasping at what greeted me. On the floor above, I could hear excited squeals and pounding feet, Aidan already having forgotten his promise to his mother. The distraction did nothing to take away from the architectural wonder of the building. I corrected my earlier assumption that this was a tree house. It was so much more than that, tastefully modernized with effortless luxury.

The deck before me was generous, boasting tree branches growing overhead as shade sails, and numerous potted plants were cleverly located on the deck, offering areas of privacy adjacent to overstuffed outdoor furniture. There was also a table and chairs for outdoor dining. And the view! The deck was flooded in late afternoon sunlight; the trees around the house cleverly grown with their branches pulled back in a curved concave, effectively opening the canopy to the blue sky above. And all around us, beyond the deck, was the forest, an abundance of trees offering a private sanctuary. Up here, I could smell pine and wildflowers, the air fresh and moist with new and old growth.

This tree house, and our recent meeting with the fae, all added to the surreal feeling that we were removed from reality, that the shadow of Talorgan had just been a dream. For a moment, I entertained the thought of remaining here, of never returning to the world above. But that dream lasted only a second. With so many lives at stake, it wasn't an option. And I could never forget Chloe. Chloe, who was still held captive by The Oaken Tree. Chloe, who was a part of this prophecy and also my best friend. Guilt was a knife thrust in my chest, and the beauty of our lodgings suddenly faded to reveal what they really were—a place to hide from the world.

I turned my back on that gorgeous view and entered the house. The dark brown décor should have cast a gloom over the living area, but strategically placed lamps cast a soft amber light, creating a soothing ambience. I barely glanced at the overstuffed couches or the inviting platters of fresh fruit, cheese, and crackers that awaited on the kitchen bench. All I wanted was my own space and to get away from everyone else. As I continued on down a hallway, Ian and Logan stopped behind me to partake of the snacks in the kitchen.

I could feel my Guardian watching me from the living room and there was an urgency to get away. A host of conflicting emotions had been firing down our shared line over the last twelve hours of travel. From concern to fear to anxiety to jealousy; each of them a mirror to the feelings that had churned in my gut. I knew he'd been reliving those moments on Beinn na Caillich, the actions he'd had to execute, especially after Talorgan's host had faltered under the weight of darkness carried by the immortal druid.

No, not a host, I reminded myself, *but a man. Someone unsuspecting, someone innocent.* Part of me knew this sense of removal was a defense mechanism, a tactic to buffer the truth of the actions I had witnessed—actions that I would one day have to undertake. Bile rose at the back of my throat, and I bit my lip, appalled by my lack of humanity. Who was I becoming? Was I turning into the same type of monster we fought? I couldn't deny something had changed inside me since that incident with Garret at the Claymore. I was no longer innocent, no longer naïve, and I was suddenly desperate to get away from everyone and stop pretending I was okay. I kept my gaze straight ahead and blindly walked away.

The house was larger than I had thought, the hallway turning in a circle around what I assumed was the trunk of the main tree, and I wondered if I would end up back at the kitchen. A few moments later, I came to a dead end, right in front of a closed door. I reached out and turned the knob. It was unlocked. Pushing it open, I could see it was a bedroom, and I stepped inside, closing the door firmly behind me.

The room was spaciously appointed, with not just a bed and ensuite but also a kitchen and living area. What caught my eye wasn't the luxurious modern amenities but the large open balcony to my right which faced into the forest beyond. I opened the sliding glass door and walked onto the wooden deck. The balcony was enclosed on either side with a natural trellis that was bursting with climbing evergreens. It gave a sense of privacy to the space and made me feel as if I was alone. Perfect.

Walking to the edge of the wooden barrier, I looked out at the dense grove of trees. The sun shone down on my head, its rays of light piercing the foliage and turning the leaves a bright, golden green. Birds of various plumage sang and twittered, their sweet song trilling upon the late afternoon air.

There was peace here and harmony. That which I craved. I stood there for a few moments, silently taking it in and willing my bones to relax. It wasn't until I felt exhaustion begin to once again drag me down that I turned back to my room. The large, king size bed looked inviting and was strategically placed just beside the glass door, affording a generous view of the forest. To the right was the kitchen, and upon the counter there was a bottle of red wine and a selection of chocolates. The fae definitely knew how to show hospitality.

I hadn't tasted wine in months, let alone chocolate, but its allure wasn't enough to win out over rest. The bed called to me, and I succumbed to my exhaustion, reaching up to undo my long braid and reclining upon the feather soft mattress. As soon as my head touched the pillow, I was out.

CHAPTER 15
GAGE
PRESENT DAY, IRELAND

I exited the ladder onto the platform of our lodgings and had to admit I was impressed. The fae had a range of skills they excelled at, architecture and construction among them. I could remember my last visit, ten years ago. The lodgings I'd stayed at then had been a lot simpler compared to what we were offered now but still a feat of architecture.

I looked out to the forest, aware that although there was only one point of entry and exit, we were still vulnerable. The ladder was a pretext of security. I knew the fae, knew what they were capable of, Lorcan in particular. I lifted my gaze, and using all my senses, I perused the trees. I wasn't surprised when I smelt their scent—at least four of them, no doubt sent by Lorcan to watch and observe his 'guests.'

Lorcan wasn't naïve, and in some ways he was as cruel as Callum, but I knew where his caution sprang from. I narrowed my eyes and felt my vision sharpen, now able to pierce the canopies and thick foliage. It didn't take long to catch movement, and I followed my senses until I marked the position of each of the fae sentries. They carried bows, loosely strung, their gazes bluntly meeting mine as I found them, their sight clearly as defined. Holding tight to my anger, I sent each of them a sharp nod before turning to enter the building.

Ian and Logan were arguing in the kitchen as they partook of the snacks on the counter. Logan held up a beer as he called out, "Gage, come join us. We're arguing the merits of football."

I recognized this moment for what it was—they'd fallen into a sense of false security. Didn't they understand we still had a mission to accomplish? I shook my head as I looked around the room. "Not now. Where's Brydie?"

Ian pointed down the hallway leading off the living area. "Off to find a room."

That familiar scent of pine trees with a sharp hint of frost lingered in the air as I walked down the twisting hallway. I wasn't surprised she'd chosen the room at the back of the house where the hallway terminated. I'd felt those emotions twisting inside her: the guilt, the fear, the desire. What Lorcan's presence and his touch had done to her burned inside me, penetrating the tightly controlled façade I worked so hard to keep in place. It was another confirmation that despite all my attempts otherwise, I had been ensnared. Like so many descendants before me, I was inexplicably drawn to the Daughter of Winter like a moth to a goddamn flame.

I silently stood outside her door, listening intently. I couldn't sense any movement or hear any sound. The internal line we shared had gone quiet in the only way it could while one of us was at rest. I knew she was safe here. Under the agreement Morrígan and Cailleach had made many years past, Lorcan wouldn't permit any threat to our party...yet I couldn't deny the urge to check on her.

I grasped the door handle and tested it gently. Locked.

My jaw clenched. There was no denying who the barred door was meant to keep out, but I wouldn't be perturbed. Murmuring under my breath, I sketched a rune on the air and felt the internal mechanism in the lock slide back. The door opened without a sound.

Brydie was splayed on the bed, her face angled toward the vista of trees visible through the glass doors that led to the balcony. I softly shut the door and moved toward the bed. Part of me was aware I had done what I needed to in ensuring she was safe, but I was unable to stop myself. My pulse pounded in my ears as I took in her face, her nose, slightly uptilted, and those red lips that looked so lush and inviting. My gaze ran helplessly down her body, lingering on her high breasts, and my groin strained against the zipper of my jeans. Her nipples peaked through her shirt, as if aware of my attention even in sleep.

I shifted, feeling more than an intruder as I ran my eyes over her flat stomach and muscled legs, recognizing the changes I had wrought. Brydie no longer had the soft body of a young woman but one hardened by regular training. This new form suited her, the power within her body a match to the power that writhed within her veins. She had become what she was meant to be: a Daughter of Winter, and the respect I held for her determination and grit was profound in that moment.

She'd unraveled her usual braid, and her long, pale blonde hair splayed invitingly across the pillow. I leaned over the bed, a hand involuntarily reaching out to touch it. Her hair felt silky smooth, and I leaned closer and inhaled. This close, her scent was ripe and full, a frosted pine-filled breeze that was sharp and fresh. My groin strained again, my eyes hungrily devouring her lips.

There came a flicker of movement outside on the

balcony, a flutter of ebony wings swooping past the window in an almost invisible glide.

I froze, looking out to the balcony. My muscles locked with tension when I realized it wasn't the fae guards that stared back at me but a crow. Its dark plumage was camouflaged in the shade of a tree, and startling intelligence lingered in its sharp eyes. Eyes that weren't the usual brown but a dark, rich emerald. Eyes that I recognized with chilling accuracy. Eyes that were focused too intently on mine.

Lorcan.

I'd heard the rumors that claimed he was a direct descendant of the Sovereign Goddess. The rumors also claimed he could shape shift into Morrígan's form. It appeared both were true.

The crow's beady eyes were trained on mine, and the understanding in them was clear. Holding my gaze, the crow tipped its head back and cawed. It was a sound of triumph, for the crow knew what it was that I feared...what I craved.

Then, with a flutter of its wings, it was gone.

CHAPTER 16
CAILLEACH
3RD CENTURY BC, ANCIENT SCOTLAND

KRA-KRAAA!

Morrígan's coming was heralded by the clarion call of a crow and a sinuous black smoke that smothered the sable bird in a dark cloud. The smoke cleared to reveal a woman, naked, tall, and slender, with feminine curves and glossy black hair trailing down her back.

Morrígan stared back at them, her green eyes blazing from within a face that could stop a thousand suns. "What is the meaning of this summons?" she demanded. "And from my siblings and husband, no less."

Cailleach tried to maintain a neutral visage as she captured her sister's eyes. That momentary connection was brief, but it seared her to her soul, because she could still feel animosity there and a deep-rooted hatred. Cailleach refused to look away and fervently hoped Gra did not wake again during this pivotal exchange.

Dagda cleared his throat. They had decided he would be the spokesperson. "It is lovely to see you again, wife. Would you do us the honor of dressing so that we may refrain from ogling your desirable body and give you the respect you deserve?"

Morrígan looked pointedly down her slim, white, naked form, then lifted a hand to her mouth in shocked jest. "You'll have to excuse me, I was in the middle of something when the Phoenix called."

Cailleach knew exactly what that something was. Her sister's throaty voice alone could entice both men and women to her bed.

"We apologize for the inconvenience."

Morrígan smiled, her sensuous lips etched with coy pleasure. "You haven't lost your glib tongue in the Other, husband. Besides, I would have thought you missed me and my temptress's body. I assume there aren't many in the Other with such offerings as mine?" She cupped a naked breast in one hand, squeezing the tip so her nipple budded and thrust forward in blatant offering.

Cailleach felt anger, lightning quick, hit her in the chest. Morrígan's taunts sickened her. Her words and actions were always filled with insecurity, yet at the same time a demand for homage. It was always this way with Morrígan, and she was once again reminded of why she had lied for Dagda when he lay with Boann all those years before.

"No one compares to you, Morrígan," Dagda returned smoothly, and Cailleach could not understand how there was not even a hint of derision in his tone. "Especially after what we shared before the second Fomorian attack. But I am worried that we will not be able to continue a conversation with you looking so distracting. Would you mind robing so we can discuss why you were called here?"

Morrígan ignored him, instead, looking at each of them in turn. "This trio intrigues me. Two brothers, returned from the Other, and a sister who has no loyalty to me and mine.

Why would the Phoenix summon me here? Father was his usual ambiguous self and said you would explain."

Dagda's voice was firm. "And we can, Morrígan, but after you robe."

Her eyes narrowed on Dagda's, and her rosebud lips thinned. The silence between them lengthened, until Morrígan pouted, "Oh fine! You were always one to ruin my fun."

She suddenly whirled, a circle of darkness camouflaging her form. This time, when the smoke cleared, she wore a flimsy black shift with thin straps, and over her shoulders lay a long, ebony feathered cloak that shimmered under the moonlight as if it were a bird in flight.

Morrígan gestured at her clothing. "Happy?"

When Dagda nodded, she demanded, "Now tell me why am I here. And more importantly, why have you and Cernunnos escaped from the Other?"

"We have a deal to make."

Morrígan snorted. "A deal? With you three? I don't make deals with those who dislike me." Her gaze was pointed as it momentarily cut to Cailleach. "Besides, what deal can a dead man make, husband? There is nothing I want from the Other—not until my time has come and I am forced to tread that world."

Dagda, now tired of her teasing, ground out, "Our marriage was dissolved on my death, Morrígan. I wear the ruby no more." He lifted his left hand.

Morrígan's smile faltered as she caught sight of Dagda's naked fingers, but her voice was full of bravado as she replied, "My mistake. How remiss of me. I should have said my *dead ex-husband*. How is the Other, by the way? I'd heard that the next world is not as lush as this one."

Cernunnos frowned, glancing between their brother

and Morrígan. Cailleach knew he was perplexed at their relationship. Anyone could see it was filled with insecurities, hurt, and anger; vastly different to the relationship she and Tritus, and no doubt, Cernunnos and Brenna, had shared.

Dagda shrugged in response to Morrígan's question. "It is no different, although I have the free will to do as I please."

Morrígan stiffened, her features tightening as she forced out between stiff lips, "As do I." She looked pointedly at his crotch as she added, "In fact, I was just enjoying one of life's pleasures. Do they still allow you to take your pleasure in the Other, Dagda?"

Dagda's eyes narrowed. "Stop it, Morrígan! I don't want to play this game, not when our time is limited. Don't you know by now that your actions are wasted? What we had here—what we felt—was not real, so don't pretend it was otherwise."

Her dark eyes narrowed. "Even that time when we faced the Fomorians a second time? Even that time when you told me you loved me?" she growled softly, her eyes flashing with a myriad of emotions. "That was mere days before your death, Dagda! Was it all a lie? A ruse to transfer power so we could destroy our enemies?"

Cailleach could see the raw hurt swirling in her green depths, and she felt a whisper of unease travel over her skin. Had they erred in allowing Dagda to be the spokesperson here? There was clearly still a wealth of emotion entangled between these two.

She opened her mouth to intercede, but Cernunnos beat her to it. He took a step toward Morrígan. The dark-haired woman immediately cut her eyes to his, no longer desirable and innocent, but a well-trained warrior assessing the threat he posed. As a war goddess, Morrígan held immeasurable power, and her link to the Tuatha Dé Danann made her even more powerful than most of the other gods, for the fae had a different kind of magic, more *other* than that offered by this world. But even though they lived longer than mortals, they were not immortal and could still die at the hands of others.

The Tuatha Dé Danann had come from the stars, another of the Phoenix's creations. Morrígan had been born among them and was the most powerful of her people. As such, she'd been awarded the role of Sovereign Goddess following that of her mother, which meant she had the final say in who would rule her people. Those worthy of becoming the king or queen of the fae were only awarded the role if they had Morrígan's blessing—a blessing that was filled with desire and sexual release. Because those who wore the crown and all it entailed could only do so after Morrígan had bedded them—and survived to tell the tale.

With his hands raised in front of him, Cernunnos said, "Morrígan, it has been a while since I laid eyes upon you. You are mature and flush with power. The girl I remember is clearly no more."

Morrígan blinked. "I'm not sure if that is a compliment or not, Cernunnos."

"Definitely a compliment, sister," he returned in as smooth a voice as he could convey given his guttural tone. "I recall our childhood spent tumbling down hills. Those memories of innocence still give me great pleasure."

His tone was genuine and Morrígan clearly felt that, for she replied simply, "So do I."

Cailleach felt the tension between them ratchet down a notch and withheld an audible sigh of relief.

Cernunnos, as if aware he had the advantage, pushed, "We do not want to argue with you, Morrígan, and we do not want to upset you. Whatever history you hold with Dagda is not something we want or need to bring up."

"Good." She looked pointedly at Dagda. "Because it has no place here."

Cernunnos inclined his head.

"Why am I here?" Morrígan demanded again.

Cailleach caught Cernunnos's questing gaze and saw the permission he was asking for—given her volatile history with Morrígan, he thought it best to share what had happened between her, Arawn, and Talorgan. She gave him a quick nod, and Cernunnos wasted no time in telling their sister about the actions that had led to this point.

"Arawn is free to come and go on this plane as he pleases?" asked Morrígan.

Cernunnos growled, his anger at their brother's actions shattering his normally controlled shell. "Yes, there is nothing to stop him since he received the druid's soul. It has effectively anchored him to this world again."

Morrígan snarled in return, her beautiful face twisting into a mask of anger. "Stupid mortals! How can you stand to receive fealty from these imbeciles?"

Dagda, who had been silent up to this point, grit his teeth and said in a low voice, "Be careful, Morrígan. Those are my people you are insulting."

She shrugged. "I am entitled to my opinions."

"Not if we are trying to keep the peace."

She sneered, "What peace, husband?" She gestured between them disdainfully. "There is no peace here."

"*Ex*-husband," Dagda reinforced in return.

Morrígan glared at him, her hands clenching at her sides. Cailleach saw a curl of dark magic escape from her palm, hungering for release. She gestured at Dagda to halt his ribbing; they needed Morrígan's support.

Dagda's jaw angled stubbornly, but at her firm stare, he forced out, "I'm sorry, Morrígan. That was uncalled for."

"It was," Morrígan responded tightly. Turning her back on her ex-husband, she faced Cernunnos. "I grow tired of this and wish to return to my home. You have explained about Arawn. Clearly, you have a plan to eradicate him. Given that I have been called here against my will and the Phoenix is also involved, why would you need me? Is this just a courtesy call to warn me of the war coming? Because I've already decided I will take my people and enter Faerie until this tides over. I have no place in this war, and I've begun to like the new world we have created far better than the machinations that revolve in this one." Her gaze was pointedly aimed at Cailleach.

Before she could retort, Cernunnos said softly, "I wouldn't recommend you run, Morrígan. This war will affect us all, whether we are in this world or not. You remember our dark brother, surely? He will not be content with conquering one world alone. He will come after Faerie next. It is in your best interests to fight with us, and fight now."

"You think this is my war? Oh no, this was not my doing, and I refuse to accept responsibility for it." With unleashed violence, she lifted pointed a finger at Cailleach. "This is her doing!" She then pointed at Dagda. "And his! If they had not interfered and dallied outside of their roles, this wouldn't have happened."

"No!" Cailleach cried, unable to hold back any longer. "That's not true. The Phoenix told me he saw this coming eons ago. He made it sound as if Arawn's rising would have happened regardless. Our father put mechanisms in place to prevent Arawn's rule overtaking this world. The pendant I wear, my meeting with Tritus"—she glanced at Dagda and added softly —"Dagda's sin...it is all related."

Morrígan hissed, "Dagda's sin? So, you do admit to it, then? After all these years, I am finally granted the respect I'm owed with the truth?"

Her face was livid. Her cloak of ebony feathers rippled eerily under the light of the full moon as if they would take flight, and her green eyes were flashing with emotion, hurt and rage vying for equal attention. Her words were layered with the weight of a thousand oceans as she said, "You have hurt me more than you know. For that, I cannot forgive you."

Silence fell, heavy and poignant. Cailleach knew she wouldn't gain Morrígan's forgiveness, but she had to try—guilty or not—for the sake of the prophecy. Morrígan was hurting, and given that it was related to matters of the heart, Cailleach understood the feeling well as she'd just lost Tritus. She also understood that even though Dagda hadn't died, Morrígan had still lost him. Her stomach knotted at her sister's loss and the visceral hurt she must suffer in his presence every time she saw him.

Sympathy swelling within her chest, she said quietly, "I forgive you, Morrígan. I understand why you lashed out at me as you did. Although I do not agree with your actions, I can understand them. To love someone who does not feel the same in return is a death itself."

Morrígan sneered, "*You* forgive *me*? And whose unrequited love is it that I pine for?" She flicked her gaze at Dagda, who had gone preternaturally still. Her emerald eyes were hard as they raked his form. "Let us get this straight, sister, here and now—I did not love Dagda; I never have!"

Cailleach flinched at the level of hurt in Morrígan's voice, acutely conscious that Morrígan wasn't even aware of it. Had her sister denied her true emotions all this time?

What had happened to her? Why was she so filled with anger and resentment? It was obvious contradicting the statement would only do more damage.

Her heart breaking for her sister, she inclined her head and said with a heavy heart, "I'm sorry, Morrígan. For all that you have gone through, I'm sorry."

The words appeared unprecedented for Morrígan stiffened, as if some part of her understood that Cailleach knew what it was she felt. Then her face twisted, her unblemished, pale skin marred by harsh lines. "I do not want or need your sympathy. Don't you see that I have everything I need? Haven't you been listening? I no longer need this world and its inhabitants." She swept her arms around the area with disdain. "I have the fae. They are my people, more powerful and intelligent than any of these mortals you call druids. Do not be sorry for me, because they provide all the love I require. And from what I have seen"—she gestured at the three of them—"you are all broken, having lost those *you* love."

Cailleach swallowed hard. There was nothing she could say to rebut that naked statement. It was true—she had lost Tritus, just as Cernunnos and Dagda had also lost their own lovers. But how could she argue with Morrígan that having felt love in its true sense, and having that same love returned for however long it lasted, was still living—still more than whatever it was Morrígan experienced now or in the future?

She couldn't. That much was obvious. She sent a fervent wish that her dark sister would find the love she deserved soon and said aloud instead, "You're right. Love is a steppingstone in this journey we are now upon. It is also why you have been called here. After all, you love your people, and now Arawn threatens whatever peace you currently shelter them with, whether it be in this world or in Faerie. Because of that, are you willing to listen further to what Cernunnos has to say?"

Morrígan stared at them all, her features tight. Cailleach had the feeling her sister balanced upon a fine edge, as if one mis-step or the wrong word would cause her to shatter. It was another insight into how Morrígan felt. For it was very obvious she felt deeply, potentially more than they ever could.

Cailleach's heart squeezed at the hurt this woman carried in conjunction with her role. Would Morrígan ever have the chance to feel real love, especially when she was tasked to be the Sovereign Goddess of her people? How could any lover let her sleep with others willingly, whether they were to be crowned or not? Cailleach knew she would never have let Tritus sleep with others—man or woman—for he was hers, and she was his, and no one and nothing could have come between them.

In the deafening silence, Morrígan said slowly, "I was summoned by Father. That alone tells me that what you have to say is of utmost importance, and indeed, what I have heard so far does make me fear for my people and our lands. It would be remiss of me to ignore whatever Cernunnos has to share." She turned to him, waving one hand in a gesture to continue. "So please, explain."

Cernunnos's gaze was soft, in sharp contradiction to the guttural tones of his voice. "There isn't much left to tell except that Cailleach has asked Father if we can address the threat Arawn poses through prophecy."

"What?" Morrígan looked between them. "Why are we talking about prophecy? I thought we were here to talk of war and strategy."

"Because we do not have the power to stop him. A war

between Cailleach and whatever siblings and their people she can muster will be short-lived. Arawn has had months, if not years, to prepare for this occurrence. As soon as he gained Talorgan's soul, he would have put his plan in motion. I've no doubt his dark army is already assembling."

Morrígan looked between them, as if to confirm whether Cernunnos was jesting. "But prophecy is unpredictable. It never runs a direct path. There are many twists involved, including numerous possible outcomes. Arawn may still rise, no matter what prophecy we put in place. Is that a risk you are willing to take?"

Dagda cut in sharply, "It is what Father agreed to."

Morrígan's eyes widened. "But he is not one to support prophecy! And if this is so important, why does he not banish our dark brother? He has the power. As the Phoenix, he can eliminate Arawn at any moment."

Cailleach shook her head. "Father will not do that because Arawn has broken no rules. Talorgan gave his soul willingly. Whether Arawn bartered with him or not is of no consequence. What is important is that Talorgan approached him free of mind and free of will. He was never coerced to awaken Arawn—he sought him out unprovoked. If Arawn operated within the realm of his jurisdiction, Father cannot remove him."

Morrígan swore, her feathered cloak ruffling. "This is a right mess. How was this not prevented?"

"Placing blame will not get us out of this," Dagda said. "But unity will."

Cernunnos nodded. "Yes, and Father has decided that prophecy will be able to deal with this matter, provided we all give our full support."

Morrígan's brows rose. "Excuse me?"

Cernunnos's eyes narrowed at her incredulous tone. "It

is true, sister. If you, me, and Dagda give our full support to this prophecy, then Father believes Arawn will return to the Underworld."

Morrígan looked between them, her eyes round. Then she crowed, "Are you telling me that I hold the power to decide whether we support Cailleach, or whether we allow Arawn to take this world and kill whoever he pleases?"

Cernunnos gritted out, "Yes."

Morrígan's amusement vanished as she turned to Cailleach. "Alright, then let me make this very clear—I have no problem sacrificing a child that shouldn't have been allowed to exist."

Unable to hold herself in check anymore, Cailleach stormed forward. She came within touching distance of her sister and stabbed a finger at Morrígan's chest. "There will be no sacrifice! Never threaten my daughter again! This one warning is all I will give you. The next one will be your last breath."

Morrígan snarled, her gorgeous face twisting in rage. "Is that so, sister? Then I welcome the threat. I have grown tired of late; the fae have become a malleable lot, but you will be a great diversion. Shall we put on a show here? Let's confirm once and for all who holds the most power between us."

"Ladies!" shouted Cernunnos, firmly pushing himself between them, a hand lifted to halt each woman. "Now is not the time to cause dissention. With Arawn here, we must show unity. There is a war coming, one we must win."

His words hit Cailleach where she needed them the most, eroding the red hot haze of anger that had arisen at Morrígan's threat against her child. *Remember Gra,* she reminded herself. *Keeping the peace with Morrígan will give her a chance to live.*

Swallowing her anger, Cailleach ground out, "Our wild

brother is right; we need to work together. Arawn is the biggest threat here. I will not apologize for my behavior because my child means everything to me, but that does not mean we cannot work together. Don't you agree, sister? Come, let us settle what needs to be done."

Morrígan smiled coldly, her blood-red lips a rich slash of color in contrast to her pale skin and sable hair. "How very mature of you, but don't go expecting an apology from me. And be careful how you word things. There is no settling happening just yet. I would first like to know more about what this prophecy will entail, and even then, I will need to carefully consider if my support should be freely given."

Cailleach's heart pounded furiously. Was what she had feared coming to fruition? Would Morrígan refuse her support? The Phoenix's gamble might not pay off. She flicked her gaze to Cernunnos, knowing he could see the panic there.

Her brother addressed Morrígan. "Of course, it's only fitting that you know what you are agreeing to, and we understand your hesitation for we also had a choice in the matter. Cailleach has requested two boons from the Phoenix, both of which he will support through prophecy—but only if we also give our support.

"Her first request is that Arawn and his disciples be sent back Underground. Dagda and I have agreed, because this world will perish under Arawn's rule. He and his people do not understand fealty. They don't understand compassion or sacrifice. All they live for is blood, death, and chaos. This world will die, and I will not see that happen, not when we have the chance to return to it, and not when we have subjects who do not deserve to be sacrificed."

Morrígan's face blanched. Her voice was reed thin. "I understand the threat Arawn poses. I also know he can, and will, follow us back to Faerie. Even though I broached it before, my people do not desire to move there just yet. The seat of our power is still growing, and it would be foolish to return now, not when threats like these can follow us back and destroy what we seek to protect. In that regard, my support for this request is therefore given."

Dagda blew out an audible breath, and Cernunnos followed her concession up quickly with, "Thank you, Morrígan. Your support is deeply appreciated."

She waved a hand at the words and looked at Cailleach. With lips pursed, she considered her sister. "Now, what is her second request? What does our dear sister want? Another lover?"

Cailleach could not bear to be quiet any longer. She opened her mouth to retort, but Cernunnos cut her off once again.

"No," he growled in a low voice. "She wishes to be reunited with my son in the Other."

Morrígan stilled, and her eyes cut back to the Wild God of the Forest. "*Your* son?"

"Yes. His name was Tritus. He died protecting Cailleach and their child not a day past."

Morrígan's face paled even further. "I don't recall you having a son, Cernunnos. Whose child was it? Not that whore of a druid, I assume, or else your son would never have lived to meet our dear sister."

Cernunnos's features darkened, his chest muscles rippling with his restrained anger. "Brenna was no whore, Morrígan, and given your role, I thought you would understand that. Let me speak plainly—like Cailleach with her child; I, too, will allow no transgressions against Brenna or my son! Is that understood?"

Morrígan considered him, her stance proud and

unforgiving. Cailleach thought she wouldn't agree, but then she lifted a languid hand and waved it in front of her face. "Of course, I tire of this game anyway. It is as you said before, brother; I miss those days we could simply tumble down the hill." She looked past them, her eyes unseeing of the gleaming mountain vista now shrouded in moonlight. Her words, when they came, were almost absent. "I wish I did not have a race of fae to manage, or the responsibilities I do now. The fae are a fickle, headstrong bunch. We clash as much as we agree."

Cernunnos didn't hesitate to respond, taking the olive branch she offered. "You are well-matched, sister. They would only follow someone with strength and intelligence. Take the complement as it is due. No one ever said that being a leader is easy."

"No." She cut her gaze back to Cernunnos. "You were always wise. Even when your emotions ran high." She paused before conceding quietly, "I have missed you."

He inclined his head with a slight smile. "And I you, Morrígan."

Feeling the intruder but knowing they needed Morrígan's support, Cailleach cleared her throat and asked, "So, does this mean you give your support to both of my requests? That you approve of setting a prophecy in motion which will return Arawn and his disciples to their world, and also that I be sent to the Other to be reunited with Tritus when this is accomplished?"

Morrígan studied her. As the silence stretched between them, Cailleach felt the spot between her shoulder blades tingle. It was an omen that didn't bode well.

"Morrígan?" prompted Cernunnos into the weighted silence.

Morrígan lifted her lips into a smile. "Yes, I have decided.

I agree to both requests if a tithe is paid. These requests require payment. Our sister cannot be allowed to make decisions without checks; the skew of power between us would be unbalanced, and I can't have that."

Cailleach felt her blood run cold. "And what tithe did you have in mind?"

Morrígan speared her with a cynical, calculating gaze as she said succinctly, "*Tithes*, sister dear, not tithe. You did ask for two requests after all, and besides, the Phoenix has granted you a boon already. Given it's the safety of your child, I cannot ask for the antithesis, but I make it known here and now that I would ask for your child's life if I could. Therefore, of the two boons you have asked my support for, I propose two tithes. The first being that you fulfil your role of Winter Goddess as the crone until such a time as your followers are no more. The second being that when your time has come to leave this world, you will wait in the Nether until the prophecy surrounding your child has come to an end. Only then will you transfer to the Other."

Cailleach heard a high-pitched ringing in her ears, and for a moment, could do nothing except stand there in shock, staring at her sister. Moments later, the significance of those demands came crashing upon her.

"What? NO!" Cailleach cried, flinging her arms out in a wild gesture. She screeched, her voice fracturing, "Do you have any idea of what you're asking? As the crone, I would not be able to look after my daughter! I wouldn't be able to feed her, let alone clothe her. What would become of her? Who would protect her?"

"Your child will live," Morrígan sneered. "You were granted a boon from the Phoenix. He will ensure she survives."

Cailleach's heart stopped. It didn't matter if she lived,

because if she must revert to being the crone, she would still not get the chance to mother her daughter. And Morrígan knew it.

Cailleach's voice was a rasp. "But what of Tritus? He is my everything. How could you be so cruel as to let me dwell in the Nether, unable to be reunited with him? To have to wait until the prophecy is fulfilled could take eons. You know the mortals don't remember us as we remember them, Morrígan! The longer I am separated from him, the more likely it is he will forget me..." Her voice broke completely then, and she bit her tongue hard to stop the wail threatening to release from her very heart.

Morrígan's face was almost soft in the moonlight as she glanced at Dagda. "I know," she said simply.

Dagda's face blanched, understanding rippling across his features.

Morrígan turned back to Cailleach. "You have felt and experienced that which I haven't—real love. You have been given the greatest gift, and yet you ask for more. For that, I resent you. For that, I am angry. And for that, you will pay. These tithes are the asking price of my support. I will relent no further."

Cailleach felt as if her world was crashing down. She had gambled everything she held dear, fought with everything she had to convince not only the Phoenix, but also her siblings, to keep not just her child safe but to also be reunited with Tritus. And now Morrígan, in one fell swoop, would take all that away. She would never see Gra grow old, never know her daughter's touch as she grew from toddler to young woman, and then into an adult who eventually had children of her own. And Gra...she would be denied a mother's love.

Even more devastating was that when she'd lost all her

followers, Morrígan was asking that she be sent to the Nether until the prophecy had been fulfilled. This request had unknown ramifications—she could wait there for eons before all the threads came together. Prophecy was unpredictable; time was of no consequence, and all the while, Tritus would be in the Other, reborn. Every day without her was another day he would make his new life, another day he would grow older, another day to forget her and what they had shared in this world, another day to make memories that were not also hers...possibly even sharing them with another.

But Morrígan had left her with no choice. Her decree had been carefully made, and it was cruel. So very cruel. One hard glance at her sister's face was enough to confirm that Morrígan would never budge, that the tithes she requested would remain unchanged.

Cailleach looked at her brothers to find them both resigned. Cernunnos looked as though he was visibly hurting, aware of what being separated from Tritus would do to her. Dagda looked shocked, his features twisted by Morrígan's revelation and the understanding that it was his actions—or lack of them—that had led to Morrígan's demands.

Her stomach churned at the unfairness of it all. There was nothing they could do, not here, not now—nor was there an easy decision. But if Cailleach wanted to see Arawn and his disciples removed from this world, she had no choice but to agree to Morrígan's demands, for to let him run wild on this plane would mean the end of everything they held dear...even her daughter.

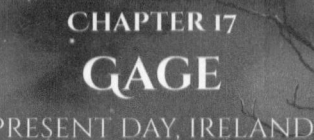

CHAPTER 17
GAGE
PRESENT DAY, IRELAND

A few hours later, Airmid's lilting voice called out the summons to dinner.

After the encounter with Lorcan, I'd exited Brydie's room to claim the one next to hers. I knew she needed the privacy, and I trusted the bond between Cailleach and Morrígan enough to know no one could threaten her safety here. Although, that clearly didn't include spying after Lorcan's visit last night.

I'd retreated to my room in the hope I would finally get some much-needed rest. But that desire was short-lived, because I gave up trying to sleep after the realization that if Lorcan—a damn stranger—could see what I felt for her, then everyone could. Fuck! It was what I'd tried so hard to prevent.

History was littered with the fall of all previous Guardians before me, tainted by the knowledge that each had fallen for his protégé. I didn't want that, didn't need it. Not when I had a son and a brother to care for. I'd also watched the train wreck of my parents' relationship, watched it dwindle to something dark and twisted as my father fell headlong into drink and my mother sought money in place of love. Those first five years of my life were a blur of uncertainty, an awareness that only Logan had my back. That feeling eased somewhat when Reuben took me under his wing. My grandfather had instinctively known what I needed, known how to direct my anger. He'd also known exactly how to train me to protect Nora, who back then was what we assumed was the last Daughter of Winter.

But even then, my relationship with Reuben had been tainted by his feelings for Nora. I'd observed his actions with both horror and derision, because he'd made numerous bad calls, all influenced by his feelings. And after watching my parents' relationship fail, after making my own bad choices with Catriona, and after observing Reuben make decisions of the heart which ended in his death, I promised myself I would not fall for my protégé. There was loss and ruin in following that route.

The last four months hadn't been easy. As soon as I met Brydie, there was an instant connection, a raging thirst that could never be slaked. It simmered under the surface of every interaction between us, a goddamn noose around my neck. That only worsened as she progressed in her training. Derision had been replaced by pride, contempt by respect, strengthening my feelings toward her until desire was now closely interwoven with a measure of affection. I'd lost the battle I'd tried so hard to fight.

Goddammit!

I had no idea what I was going to do going forward, and now wasn't the time to make rash decisions and bare all. Besides, there wasn't time—Lorcan was awaiting our presence in the dining hall. As if on cue, Airmid's call came again. Blowing out a breath, I pushed off the bed and walked to the balcony, shoving down all thoughts of my protégé, and caught sight of Airmid standing by the trees, some distance away. I lifted a hand, signaling we'd be down soon, and went to summon everyone back to the living room.

I headed for Brydie's room first, only to meet her in the corridor as she was shutting the door to her room. "Time for dinner?" she asked.

"Yes."

"Good, I'm starving."

I had no idea what to say in return, not when she looked at me with those silver eyes—so vulnerable, yet determined. Then she sidestepped my gaze to look ahead, ignoring me. Fine. It appeared this dance around each other would continue. I gestured she precede me. "Go ahead; I'll get the others. Will you let Airmid know we're coming?"

Her eyes widened, probably from the freedom I'd just bestowed on her. Ignoring the damning evidence of how overbearing I'd become, I moved on down the hallway, knowing that when we returned to the world above, the rope that held her tethered closely to my side would once again tighten.

The room McKenzie and Aidan had claimed was spacious and had a full kitchen, living area, and two bedrooms with ensuites. Aidan openly begged to stay there and eat.

"That's fine with me if your mother stays here with you, but you'll have to fend for yourself with whatever is in the pantry. We won't disrespect the fae's hospitality by bringing food back for you."

McKenzie looked at her son, who gave her a beguiling smile in return. "Please, Mom!"

"I'm sure I can rustle something up," she said.

He fist-pumped the air. "Thanks, Mom. You're the best!"

As Aidan regained his seat in front of the television, McKenzie whispered under her breath, "Thank you, Gage."

I nodded, feeling a small measure of satisfaction that I could make someone happy in this god forsaken mess.

I moved a few doors down to Ian's room and told him Airmid was waiting before heading to my brother's. Logan had chosen a room at the opposite end of the house, as far away from mine and Brydie's as he could get. The reason for this was obvious. The sibling bond we shared was a blessing and a curse, and although physical distance didn't weaken our emotional connection, the physical dissociation still went some way to establishing distance. I felt a measure of discomfort at how Logan could feel not only my desire for Brydie, but also the sexual tension so prevalent between us.

Logan answered the door, his blue eyes drowsy, his short black hair, mussed. "So soon?" he muttered. "Christ, even in fairyland I have to live by routine."

I couldn't prevent the smile his words encouraged. "Don't be fooled by the myths, Logan. The fae are a brutal bunch; they simply hide it behind a veneer of politeness and hospitality."

Logan ran his hands through his hair. "Don't worry, brother, I know a shark when I see one, and Lorcan is one of the biggest fish I've seen in the ocean for a long time."

I nodded, not surprised by my brother's intuition. He had a finely attuned sixth sense, and I trusted his impressions without question. "Get cleaned up and meet us outside."

"I'll be there in five."

True to his word, Logan appeared not soon after I met Brydie and Ian in the clearing below. Airmid didn't waste any time leading us back the way we'd come. In the last few hours, night had fallen. The path through the trees was dark and oppressive, until we heard light chatter coming from ahead. A few minutes later, we came upon a huge outdoor pavilion. It was enclosed by a pergola, cosseted by sweet, blooming roses, and an abundance of lanterns filled the area with a soft, golden light. The polished wooden deck held numerous rows of chairs and wooden tables that were decorated with vases of wildflowers, bottles of wine, glasses, plates, and cutlery. And at those tables sat the fae.

Their smooth faces were alight with animation, their clothing fine and dazzling. The women's provocative sheer dresses shone with numerous jewels and sequins. The men wore suits, their shirts crisp and clean, their hair smoothed back with not a strand out of place, and their shoes shined to perfection.

I felt instant distaste at the show of frivolity and false security they clung to. The fae had always been known for their fawning luxury, their love of comfort and elegance. It was something I'd tolerated in the past, but not now. Not when there was so much at stake. Did they not know a war raged above? That it was a war from which they could not escape? That this pretense they clung to was simply that—a mirage which concealed the truth?

As we walked closer, I sensed more than just the people in the pavilion, and I cast my eyes into the surrounding darkness. This time, I spotted them almost instantly, my senses now attuned to their patterns and location. There were guards on duty around the perimeter. Given the frivolity here, I held a measure of respect that their brown and green utilitarian uniforms were still in place. I cast my eyes upward, knowing the ground soldiers wouldn't be alone, not in this treetop haven, and spotted a few of them, looking down at us from tree limbs.

I approved of Lorcan's watch. It told me he hadn't let his

guard down, but it also portrayed a different story to the elegant luxury the fae currently exhibited. It told me that even here, a threat still hovered.

As we left the forest, the crowd hushed and turned to stare at our approach. Silence fell, but Airmid determinedly pushed on and gestured to a table for four at the edge of the pavilion. Every fae heard her say, "Please, take a seat. I hope you enjoy the dinner. At the end of the meal, I will return to escort you back."

"That won't be necessary," I replied. "I understand Lorcan wishes to see us after we have eaten. I'm sure we can find our own way back after that."

Her eyes widened slightly, but she bowed her head. "Of course. I will see you in the morning, then. Good night."

"Good night, Airmid."

The others all murmured their thanks, and we took our seats. The fae, seemingly tired of watching us, slowly turned back to their conversations. The room once again rippled with gaiety, the excitement in their voices increasing. My sensitive ears couldn't help but hear snatches of conversation.

"Oooh, I haven't seen a man like that in a long time," came a feminine drawl, the lust in her tone unmistakable.

"But he's a druid, darling. What could you find attractive about him?"

A delicious giggle. "If you can't see past the ears, Sandra, then you're a wasted cause. Aren't you in the least bit curious about what another lover, who isn't fae, can do for you?"

"Hmmm."

I grit my teeth and looked down at my hands, breathing through my nose as I tried to block out their incessant chatter. I became cognizant Logan had struck up a conversation with Brydie, the two of them falling into their usual natural rhythm. It appeared he'd replaced Ian's position as someone she could turn to—and going by the tense look on Ian's face as he fiddled with his napkin, it was clear he knew it.

More snatches of conversation came from behind me, this time more daring, as if the fae didn't care that we could hear them.

"Who is the man that looks like her Guardian? He's just divine."

A squeal and then a forced whisper, "I'd love to have him in my bed tonight."

A slap of a hand on skin. "Eyes off! He's mine," said a sharp voice.

"Stop it! You can't have all the fun," said a male in a pouty tone.

I willed myself not to smash my fist on the table and wished the goddess would grant me respite from their senseless babble. When the fuck was dinner being served? There was a jab at my ankle, and I growled under my breath, cutting my brother a scathing glare. "What the fuck was that for?"

Logan laughed. "Chill out, brother. You should be happy we're going to be fed." He leaned back with a huge smile on his face. "I know I am."

"I would if it didn't come with this senseless babble."

His grin widened. "You can understand the excitement though, especially if they've been sequestered here for the last ten years. New blood is always exciting."

There was a twinkle in his eye. He knew I was trapped. I couldn't very well start a brawl right here,. I'd be jeopardizing our safety. A fight would be disrespectful to those who'd just offered us sanctuary. Logan knew it too, the bastard. Instead of slamming my fist into his nose, I snapped, "Shut it, or you'll be sent back with no supper."

He made a wounded face and held his hands up. "Alright. Jeez, I didn't know a spot of teasing would get you so riled up." He cocked his head to the side, that goddamned twinkle still in his eye, as he said softly, "Maybe you should consider one of their offers, though. It might take the tension off."

Logan sent an imperceptible nod across the table directly to Brydie. I cut my eyes to hers and found them narrowed on my brother's face, a grimace on her lips. I could also feel her churning emotions: jealousy, anger, and surprisingly, a touch of sadness. It was the last emotion that cut through the haze of my own anger. As I turned to face him, I withheld the urge to push my chair back and grab my brother around the lapels of his shirt.

Logan's eyes widened on seeing my face, and he instantly sobered. "I'm sorry. That was childish and uncalled for." He looked between me and Brydie. "I'm just trying to ease the tension."

Squeezing my hands into fists, I growled, "As I've said before, it's none of your bloody business." I cut my gaze back to Brydie's. Again, she carefully skirted hers past mine to the fae beyond. It looked as if we were back to playing a game of avoidance, and I couldn't blame her since this tension between us was all my fault.

The voices intruded again, this time discussing Brydie.

"Is that really the Cailleach's descendant?" asked a dismissive voice. "Why the hell is she dressed like that?"

"She's a warrior, Mal, not just a woman," came a snicker.

The woman called Mal sniffed. "Still, she should have enough respect for herself and our people to come to the table appropriately dressed."

"I don't care what she's wearing. In fact, I'd prefer her without clothes. It would allow me to see her form," came a drawling male voice, his tone laced with dark promise.

My whole body tensed. I was on the verge of leaping from my chair and swinging my fists into the bastard's face.

The woman called Mal laughed wickedly, and another voice, this one sweeter and more genuine, said, "But her hair is just gorgeous! It needs no dressing up. It's the color of moonlight. Just lovely."

I couldn't help looking at my protégé again, noting how her light blonde hair, now unraveled down her back, did indeed shine like the purest moonlight. My gaze wandered over her face, lingering on her lips, and my balls tightened. I studiously forced my gaze to keep wandering, moving it onto Ian, who was now busy pouring himself a drink, a determined look on his face as if he was imagining himself anywhere but here. His attitude was the lifeline I needed, an acknowledgement of how deeply I was allowing these people to get to me. What a weak fool I had become. Following suit, I reached out to pour my own glass of red wine when a hush fell over the room.

A sharp frisson of awareness ran down my back, and I knew who it was before I saw the crow arrowing its way over everyone's heads to come to a dramatic rest on the arm of the large golden throne at the head table. The crow thrust its head back and cawed, the sound piercing in the weighted silence, before there was a blinding flash of light and Lorcan appeared in its place, resplendent in his breeches and bare, muscled chest. He sat languidly upon the throne, his only adornment a gilded crown.

He raised an ankle to lay it across one knee as he surveyed his people, and when his eyes caught mine, I again saw his understanding of what he'd seen in Brydie's room a few hours before. A small smile graced his lips before he turned back to face the room at large and announced with a regal smile, "May the goddess bless this food."

As one, the fae repeated his prayer, and the tables were suddenly laden with steaming food—platters of sizzling meat, wild rice, raw salad, vegetables gently sauteed, and a tempting array of sweets. It was a veritable feast, a reminder that the fae liked to indulge in earth's offerings...and that their magic was still in full force.

Their power had a dark, sinister twist to it, and as I watched the fae drink and eat their fill of the bounty before them, I couldn't help but feel that undercurrent of desire for illicit deeds. This wasn't unusual, not when the fae were Morrígan's people. She was a goddess of war and a woman of sexual prowess. She had never shied from brutal decisions, honesty, or truth, and her people were the same, walking a fine balance between cruelty and kindness. With their preternatural abilities and devastatingly good looks, they were lethal predators, everyone their unsuspecting prey. And Lorcan, the leader on the dais, whose eyes returned to our table again and again, was the most dangerous of all.

I decided there was no point wasting time on theories that may or may not materialize, especially when we were to meet with Lorcan very soon, so I turned my mind to the food before us, conscious I needed to restore the energy reserves I'd depleted on the drive here. I could taste a faint metallic tang at the back of my throat and knew I was close to reaching burnout after not only fending off Talorgan but ensuring we stayed safe on the journey. In effect, these next few days would be my only chance to recover before we left for the Institute, because I knew without asking that Brydie would allow no further delay, not while Chloe needed us.

As the meal came to a close, Logan murmured appreciatively and leaned back to rest his hands on his stomach. "Well, that was a far cry from the simple fare I've been forced to endure on Beinn na Caillich. Who knew the fae would know how to cook?"

"No one told you to stay on," I bluntly reminded him.

Logan raised a brow. "Are we still going to argue about this? I've told you many times before that I'm not leaving, no matter how often you point out how unwelcome I am."

I grimaced, still burning with fear at the thought of carrying Logan all the way to the end. He had it in his mind I needed him—that *he* would prevent *me* from doing something stupid. But what he didn't understand was that I had no control over my compulsions. The prophecy pushed me onward. Besides, there was nothing a man with no druidic power could do to stop me, even if he was my twin.

At my silence, Logan turned to Brydie and asked her a question. The conversation turned, with Ian joining in. Deciding I needed help if I was to sleep tonight, I reached out for the nearest bottle of wine, but as soon as my hand wrapped around the glass, a prickle hit the back of my neck. I'd had this feeling enough times before to know it wasn't a coincidence. Understanding hit me in the gut—something wasn't as it seemed.

As soon as the thought entered my subconscious, the world blurred, and the edges of the wine bottle rippled. I froze, turning all of my senses to our surroundings. I lifted my eyes to look around me, trying to detect the threat. But it wasn't a person that approached. Rather, the pavilion rippled, fresh white paint on the pillar next to me wavering, first becoming gnarled and black, then fresh and white once more. I narrowed my gaze, focusing on that pillar, and willed myself to *see*.

This time the pillar didn't flicker but remained as it really was—a series of dead, blackened brambles twisted into a mockery of a beautiful painted pavilion. My jaw aching from how tightly I held it, I looked next toward the brambles and evergreen climbers, seeing not bountiful roses with soft blooms of every shade but dead ivy, its leaves curled and brown.

I then turned to the fae, who were indeed real, but not dressed in the finery I had seen before. Rather, their clothing was tattered and worn, their hair matted and unkempt, not coiffured into an elegant bun or loose and flowing. My gaze trailed to Lorcan next, and it was there I stopped, captured by the face as still as granite. His hard green eyes proclaimed his awareness that I'd seen through the glamour. He lifted his chin, gesturing to me that it was time. I was ready.

"Gage, you should have some dessert before I take the lion's share," Logan said, interrupting my silent communication with the leader of the fae with a sharp nudge to my ribs.

I broke my gaze with Lorcan and faced my brother, noting the underlying concern in his eyes. No doubt he was aware of my sudden unease. "No need. You know I'm not the sweet tooth in the family."

"I disagree. You've had more sweet things than I've had," he returned swiftly with one of his obscene grins.

This time, Ian snorted. I didn't rise to the bait, instead, I pushed my chair back and stood. "Help yourself. I have more pressing things to attend to."

"Where are you going?" came a feminine voice.

I glanced at Brydie, surprised she'd asked. Did she feel as torn as I was when we were apart? "Lorcan and I have some unfinished business to attend to."

"I'll come with you. I'm sure he has questions about whether Nora's grandchild can stand up to her legacy."

I considered her. Had she changed her mind about freezing me out? "You don't have to. I can vouch for you."

Brydie opened her mouth to respond, but Ian cut in sharply with, "Gage is right, Brydie. Save your breath. The fae love to dance after dinner, and hell knows we need some light relief for a day or so. You should stay with us."

I stared at him, not liking his sudden intrusion. They'd been cool toward each other since that afternoon Brydie and I had shared a kiss on Beinn na Caillich...well, more than a kiss. But I was well aware that moment had been the catalyst that had caused Brydie to push Ian away—a bitter pill he had yet to swallow. I thought he'd given up on her and turned his mind to ignoring what went on between us. Why now? Had Ian forgiven her, or did he believe that with the revelation of the fifth descendant's identity and the part I'd had to play, that he had another chance with Brydie?

Ian was staring at me. His lips tipped into a half-smile, but his look was derisive. "Save the psycho analysis for later, Gage. Go and talk with Lorcan. We'll watch Brydie."

I bristled, jaw clenching, but another sharp stab in my shin prevented me from responding. Logan. I shifted my gaze to my brother and caught the minute shake of his head. *Not here.* He was right.

Releasing a breath, I turned back to Brydie and replied, "Ian's right. You should take the opportunity afforded."

Her lips thinned. "Fine."

Relieved she wasn't going to push me further, I said in parting, "I'll see you all back at our lodgings." I sent a hard glance at Logan and Ian. "I don't expect any trouble, but watch Brydie and those around her."

Ian nodded and Logan lifted his hand in a sharp salute.

As I walked away from the table I felt my protégé's gaze on my back, knowing she resented my dismissal.

Lorcan rose from his throne and started to weave his way around the seated fae, coming to a stop at the edge of the pavilion. As I approached, his eyes went past me to our table, then came back to mine. "Why did you not bring the woman?"

"She needs to rest. We've had a long journey."

Lorcan merely looked at me, his carriage granite.

I stood there, the seconds dragging between us, until I realized there was only one way this conversation could go. His stance conveyed loud and clear that we were at the mercy of the fae, and every refusal was another thorn in Lorcan's side that might cause the loss of his patience and support. Releasing a breath, I ground out, "Fine."

I turned, only to find Brydie's gaze glued to mine, almost as if she'd been waiting for the summons. I lifted a hand and beckoned. She shot out of her chair and began to weave through the crowd toward us. I didn't fail to notice the fae heads turning to watch her, or the interest in both the men's and the women's eyes. Even tired and rumpled, she was stunning, her eyes alight with silver flame, her hair a gilded shine of moonlight, not to mention the body that moved so fluidly in those jeans.

When a hand reached out and slipped over her ass, I couldn't prevent the growl that was instantly torn from my mouth. But it was a wasted reaction. Brydie whirled and slapped the hand away, bending down in front of the male's face. I didn't hear her words, but I saw how he blanched at her fierce response, the tips of his ears whitening. His hands lifted in a show of backing off and, with a cruel smile on her lips, Brydie straightened before continuing toward us.

"She's a predator in a lamb's skin."

I looked at Lorcan, my body screaming with tension. "She's off limits."

He lifted a brow, his voice mild even as his green eyes swirled with vibrant intensity. "To all the fae? Or just their leader?"

"Even their leader," I bit out through clenched teeth.

A smile, dark and sexy, lit his face. "And I suppose that only her Guardian can have her, then?"

I snarled and took a step closer, my chest almost touching his. The fae leader flared his nostrils, and his lips peeled back from his teeth, the canines lengthening in an answering show of aggression.

Finely attuned to their leader's moods, the nearby fae instantly quietened, and a sudden silence fell like a crashing wave over the tables. The only sound was Brydie's footsteps drawing ever closer.

Her voice was low but no less deadly as she came to a stop in front of us and said sharply, "Why do males persist in these pissing contests? Don't you know it's wasted on women?"

In the crowd, a few females tittered, breaking the tension that had fallen.

Lorcan shifted back onto his heels with a sardonic smile and drawled, "Well, it appears Nora's granddaughter has the backbone I was hoping she'd have. And no, us males always need something to mark our territory over. It just so happens that women are the most prized commodity over which to do it."

Brydie smiled in return, her features smoothly transforming into a pretext of congeniality, but the coldness in her eyes was in stark contrast to her next words. "The fae leader is a charmer. I would have been disappointed if you were anything less."

"Tit for tat," Lorcan murmured, and I tensed again as his eyes roved over Brydie's form. There was a knowing look in his eyes as he turned to face me, an awareness of my reaction. "It appears we don't need to stake claims anyway, druid. Your protégé can look after herself."

"Damn straight," Brydie cut in before I could. "Besides, there's a more pressing need at play, specifically our common enemies, and it would be best if we just cut to the chase now, wouldn't it?"

At her tone, Lorcan's eyes widened, and I bit my cheek to prevent the triumphant smile that threatened to spread across my face. My chest was bursting with pride. The meek, shy woman I'd met in New Zealand was no more. Instead, in her place was a woman who commanded respect, with steel in her voice and an unbreakable will.

Lorcan's jaw clenched as he turned to face his people again. As one, they quieted and expectantly turned to him. Lorcan lifted his hand and announced in a ringing voice, "I have matters to discuss with some of our guests, but please, partake of the offerings and celebrate their arrival. I will return shortly. As you were, friends."

His people murmured a farewell, and Lorcan turned to stalk into the dark forest without looking to see if we followed behind.

CHAPTER 18
GAGE

L orcan led us down a dark path until we came across another large tree, this one accommodating lodgings smaller than our own. He paused at the tree's base and turned to face us. "Welcome to my home. I promise we'll be safe here from prying eyes and ears." He gestured to the ladder built into the sturdy trunk. "After you."

I could feel the presence of the sentries in the trees as I gestured for Brydie to precede me. Without hesitation, she moved past me and up the ladder. I followed closely behind; there was no way Lorcan would be at her back.

As I cleared the platform, I found Brydie waiting on the deck, looking around at Lorcan's spacious alfresco entertainment area.

Lorcan gestured at the furniture. "Take a seat," he invited, reaching for a bottle of spirits on the table. He poured a finger into one of the short crystal tumblers and offered the glass to Brydie. "Bourbon?"

I expected her to refuse as I knew she only drank red wine, but she reached out and accepted the glass. "Thank you."

Lorcan poured his own drink and reclined on the couch next to Brydie just as I was about to take a seat. Bastard. I knew he'd purposely chosen the seat between us. As if aware of my inner turmoil, he sent me a knowing smile. "Help yourself to a bourbon."

I held back a comment as I poured myself a glass and took the armchair opposite.

"Let's cut to the chase," Lorcan began after taking a sip of his drink. "You came here because you need our aid. State the terms clearly."

Against my wishes, I felt a measure of respect at his direct approach. I gestured at Brydie. "You know who she is and what it is she is marked for—what all our party is marked for."

Lorcan nodded and flashed another smile, full of teeth. "Yes, but what are your terms?"

I gave it to him. "We require four things. We seek your people's aid in the coming war against Talorgan. We also require sanctuary. And we may need some support retrieving one of our own from The Oaken Tree." I glanced at Brydie as I added, "And there is the matter of a certain fae who may have helped the Daughter of Winter at the time of her parents' death."

Her face paled, and I felt a measure of anxiety arrow down our shared connection. I knew she hungered to find the missing link between her parents' car accident and her return to their family home. There was a good chance our deductions were true, that it was a fae who had offered that assistance, especially with the pact between Morrígan and Cailleach.

Lorcan leaned back in his chair, raising an ankle to cross it over the other knee. His hands steepled together. "Hmm. What you ask for isn't simple."

I watched him closely. "Will you deny us?"

One of his eyebrow's rose. "I didn't say that," he said mildly.

"Well, now is the time to be frank."

Lorcan's green eyes danced. "Yes, I suppose it is." He took another sip of his bourbon before saying, "The pact between Morrígan and Cailleach required us to provide aid in the coming war. It didn't mention providing aid in terms of sanctuary, not when you have numerous seats of power spread throughout Scotland, and indeed in parts of Ireland. Then there's also the question of this supposed fae who aided the Daughter of Winter a few years back." He flicked a glance at Brydie before returning his gaze to me. "Would you agree that these requests are more than what was deemed appropriate between Morrígan and Cailleach?"

I growled, "This isn't some fucking game, Lorcan! We wouldn't be here if we didn't need to."

Lorcan stared at me for a few moments and then inclined his head. "Alright. Let's take a step back. You've established what you want, but there is also something I want. Let's consider that for a moment. Agreed?"

I grit my teeth. Fucking prick was playing status games, but at least he hadn't turned on that sexual flare in which he'd held Brydie and McKenzie in thrall the last time we'd seen him. "Fine."

Lorcan smiled, a slow smirk that was full of sin. "Thank you. But first, we need to discuss what you noticed at dinner. I promise it is all interrelated. Indulge me." His sly smile was replaced by a watchful presence as he asked, "You saw through the glamour, didn't you?"

"It wasn't hard."

Lorcan's mouth thinned. "That doesn't please me. It tells me our problems worsen."

Brydie looked between us. "What glamour? What are you talking about?"

I looked at Lorcan. "Do you want to explain?"

He sighed, then gestured at the forest looming around us. "Look at the trees."

Brydie turned to face the forest, and I followed suit.

"Now, watch closely." I heard him click his fingers, and the trees instantly wavered, their images rippling until what I looked at wasn't a lush, green forest but stark, empty branches reaching eerily into the indigo sky.

Brydie gasped. "The trees...they're dying."

Lorcan's voice was soft. "Yes, just like everything else in this world. Slowly but surely, the fae are heading toward their doom."

I looked back to Lorcan. "What do you mean?"

The fae leader ran a hand through his hair, mussing the brown strands. "It's a long and complex story, but put simply, our magic has evolved. It no longer nurtures; it destroys."

I narrowed my eyes, watching every careful nuance that crossed his features. "Your people have lost balance?"

"Yes."

"Is it Talorgan?" Brydie's questioned. "Has his stain spread this far already?"

Lorcan peeled his lips back, baring those sharp canines. "It is not Talorgan," he snarled. "That druid has no power here!"

"I wouldn't be so quick to judge," I replied smoothly. "He has joined forces with Callum."

Lorcan froze, his fingers curling around his knees. "The Oaken Tree has fallen from the light?"

"Not yet, but the stain spreads with Callum at the helm."

Lorcan stroked his chin. "So we drift further apart. Cousins from a different life."

"No," I snapped, leaning forward in my seat. "The pact still stands. Morrígan made a promise to Cailleach. Regardless of what happens to The Oaken Tree, your goddess made a deal with ours. Honoring that claim is on your head."

Lorcan's voice was soft, but the threat was all the greater for the lack of a roar. "Do not think to presume, druid. Your kind have not given us anything in return, and here you are asking me for three favors, not one. It is also hard to trust you after one of your own stole one of our treasures."

The omission was the opening I'd been waiting for. "The Dagda's cauldron?"

Lorcan shifted, his eyes predatory as they ran over my form. I knew he was assessing the power and strength of an attack, readying himself for a returning launch. For a second, I considered my chances, but my neck prickled in warning. All three of us were volatile with various powers in our reach, but the one with least control was Brydie. I would not use this argument as leverage to show her abilities, or lack thereof. She was mine to protect.

Lorcan had become very still, and his eyes were watchful as the tense silence lengthened. "It's interesting you say that, because ever since the treasure was taken from our clan, our problems began."

Brydie asked sharply, "You think that the loss of the cauldron caused your people's magic to change?"

She appeared unruffled by the simmering undercurrent of animosity between us and was in fact sitting there calmly. Her reaction curbed mine, and I consciously made myself lean back in my seat. Lorcan eyed me, and I knew the same thought was crossing his mind. I hid a smirk at the fact that, yet again, Brydie was proving a point in her own way.

"Yes," Lorcan replied. "But it's more complicated than that. It was merely the start of our problems."

"Don't speak in riddles; tell us what you know," I demanded. "If we are to become allies, at the very least, we need to be honest with each other."

"So we do," he murmured softly, fingers steepling under his chin as he leaned back in his chair. He looked out to the forest as he asked quietly, "Have you heard of a women called Carman who came from Athens?"

The memory of a story hovered. "The witch with the three sons; Dub, Dian, and Dothur?"

Lorcan nodded, his eyes still far away. "Yes, but those were their second names. They were born with others in their first life."

"First life?" questioned Brydie.

Lorcan turned back to face her, his face somber. "When she arrived on our shores around 1800 BC, Carman was a single mother with a chequered past, eager to start a new life devoid of violence and the memories of her dead lover. She brought her three sons to Ireland, ready to put down new roots and live among our people. For a few seasons there was no trouble, and many appreciated her skills with plants, as she held an expansive knowledge of herbal medicine. But one season the weather destroyed the crops and a blight ran across the land, ravaging everything but Carman's own garden. She gave of her crops what she could spare after feeding her own family, but still, resentment and fear brewed, and our people rebelled, claiming she was a witch."

Lorcan's jaw tightened, and if I hadn't been watching him closely, I would have missed the telltale sign as he added, "Fear drove our people. They believed Carman was the reason their crops failed, that she was the one who brought the blight and the famine. So our people took matters into their own hands."

Brydie went still. "They killed her, didn't they?"

"Not her," Lorcan denied, "but her sons. They drove the three of them into the sea. Carman was devastated. She would not accept their fate. She went to one of our people, an outcast fae versed in the dark arts, and she enlisted his help to resurrect her sons. However, her three children weren't who they were before. Their rebirth changed them. They took great delight in destroying everything in their path. Their actions spread like wildfire throughout our land, and her sons were soon renamed for their damned actions as Dub, Dothur, and Dain."

The Irish terminology wasn't lost on me. "Darkness, Evil, and Violence," I murmured.

Lorcan nodded. "Just so."

Brydie breathed, "And Carman? What became of her?"

"The love of a mother is absolute, and after being treated as she had been, not to mention what they'd done to her sons, Carman's path was set. Her heart hardened against our people. She felt she was owed retribution, so she, together with her three sons, destroyed everything in their path in an assault on Ireland and our people."

Brydie's face was pinched. "I assume they were killed a second time?"

Lorcan's clenched his glass of bourbon. "Not quite. It took many attempts and four of our strongest people to destroy her sons. When they left this world for good, Carman was captured. She was placed in a tower in Wexford, and there she remained, cloistered for her safety and ours. It's said she screamed for days, cursing our land and our people."

"Cursing?" I questioned.

Lorcan eyed the drink in his hand, watching the amber liquid swirl as he tipped it. "For the harm we'd done to her and her sons, Carman laid a curse upon our people. She claimed there would come a time that our powers would no longer nurture. Instead, they would bring a blight upon our world. She claimed this curse would begin when we lost one of our treasures, a prize we valued with all our being."

"The Dagda's cauldron," Brydie murmured.

Lorcan nodded. "Yes; since its loss, our people have been changing, slowly but irrevocably." He sent me a sardonic look. "And now it appears we can no longer hide it."

"But what of Morrígan?" Brydie demanded. "As your Sovereign Goddess, why didn't she step in to prevent this from happening?"

Lorcan smiled, and it was a show of teeth rather than warmth. "Oh, word of the curse came to Morrígan's attention soon enough. And on investigating what had befallen Carman and her sons, our lady found that the actions of our people were sanctioned by one man only—our king."

This was a part of the story I hadn't heard, but I knew who the king had been at that time. "Bres." I wasn't surprised. The half-Fomorian had been a poor leader, unable to bind the Fomorians and the Tuatha Dé Danann as one people.

Lorcan's lip curled. "Yes. King Bres was undeserving of the sovereignty Morrígan gave him, but shortly after, she rectified that wrong by removing him from the seat of power and replacing him with her grandfather, Nuada."

"Nuada? The Tuatha Dé Danann king with the missing hand that was replaced with a silver one?" Brydie asked.

Lorcan cocked his head to the side, eyeing her. "You clearly know some, if not all, of our history, descendant of winter."

"My father is to thank for that."

The undercurrent of sorrow in her tone was unmistakable. Andrew, again, had surprised me. Conscious she was hurting, I asked Lorcan, "I'm assuming that if her curse lived on even after her death, Morrígan didn't stop it?"

Lorcan leaned back, nursing his bourbon against his thigh. "Our Sovereign Goddess is ever fair in love and war, and often the blade of truth is sharper than any sword. Morrígan admitted to our faults, taking responsibility for the persecution and murder of Carman's sons. It is said she did nothing to stop Carman's curse for she believed we deserved it."

"But she was your Sovereign Goddess!" Brydie exclaimed, her drink sloshing over the rim. I noticed she hadn't taken a sip yet. "Wasn't it her job to protect her people?"

Lorcan nodded. "And she did. Morrígan managed to make a deal with Carman in those days before the witch's death. She promised Carman that she would not withdraw the curse, that justice deserved to be served on her people for the atrocities that had occurred to both the witch and her three sons. Instead, Morrígan bartered for a loophole— a way to overcome the curse, and for reasons unknown, Carman agreed."

"And that was?" I asked with a raised brow.

Lorcan's face was like stone. "That a descendant of Morrígan and a descendant of Carman would mend the bridge."

There had been a roaring in my ears, steadily increasing with each of Lorcan's words, and I'd known what it was he was about to say before he'd said it. "You are the descendant of Morrígan," I said softly.

"Yes."

"So, you are also touched by the gods." What I'd left unsaid was that he was trapped, just as I was, but as I watched his hands clench the glass again, the knuckles white and straining, I knew he felt it.

The fae were known to have deceptive strength in their gorgeous bodies. Weapons were what they were—cunning, beautiful, sharp weapons. Their leader, the most cunning and sharpest of them all, lifted his head and stared at me directly as he said, "Yes, it appears so. As a descendant of Morrígan, I am marked by the crow herself. The curse has finally come to light, and the job of reversing its descent falls to me."

Brydie, who'd been quietly mulling over what Lorcan had shared, asked, "I thought her sons were killed? How could a descendant have survived?"

Lorcan drummed the fingers of his empty hand on his thigh. "It is said that one of her sons got a woman with child before his first death."

Brydie released a breath. "Well, at least that made the child innocent of the violence that followed." She looked at Lorcan, her eyes questioning. "But what is meant by 'mending the bridge'?"

Lorcan shrugged. "Like your own prophecy, the details are sketchy. There were no explanations given. All we know is that we have a chance to stop the blight."

Brydie's expression held compassion. "I'm sorry." Her words were simple but they conveyed a wealth of understanding.

Lorcan inclined his head, and they stared at each other for a few moments, both of them silently conveying they understood the weight the other carried. I suddenly felt like an intruder and was instantly threatened by their shared bond. My hands curled into fists and a roaring filled my ears as their shared stare continued. I opened my mouth to snarl in warning, but before I could release it, Lorcan cut his green gaze to mine.

"Be calm, druid. I am no threat to you. Our two paths are aligned but not destined to run together."

I stared at him, trying to determine whether the innuendo of the word *our* was aimed at me or Brydie, or both. I said bluntly, "Why tell us all this? I assume you need something from us to further your own cause?"

A sly smile. "Of course. Deals are the way of the world. I have already preempted what aid you require from my people, but that will be dependent on what you can provide me in return. Tit for tat."

I took a stab. "So, in return for providing us a place to stay over the coming months, you need us to find Carman's descendant?"

Lorcan nodded.

"Why can't you find this person yourself?" I gestured at his attire. "If you dressed appropriately and put a shirt on, I'm sure you could find this person without any trouble in our world."

Lorcan smirked. "I cannot. We no longer have the power to shield our fae forms in your world."

Brydie looked at his head. "But aside from the ears and canines, Eachna easily passed as human. Most of the males have long hair. It shouldn't be hard."

Lorcan shook his head. "You don't understand. Only some of us have the ability to contain who we are, and those who can do not have the skills to find Carman's descendants."

"And why is that?" I demanded.

"Because of our other skins."

Brydie blinked. "When you become the crow," she breathed.

Lorcan inclined his head. "Yes."

"And there are others who can change...skins?" she pressed.

"A few," Lorcan admitted. "Those of us who can change skins are able to retain our senses in your world but not use them, and those of us who can't, have the ability to hide our true forms. It is part of the curse."

Brydie considered him, and it wasn't hard to work out that she was trying to imagine what happened when Lorcan became the crow. The impressed look on her face set my teeth on edge, that and the desire to force Lorcan into a goddamned shirt. "Let's cut to the chase," I growled. "What is it you want us to do in return for providing us with a safe haven?"

Lorcan turned back to me, a teasing light dancing in his eyes. "I need your eyes and ears up there. The more the merrier. I'm sure that if you work together, you would have a good chance of finding Carman's descendant."

"You're assuming they live in Ireland," I returned. "What if they live in Greece? We don't have time to hunt out a descendant when we have our own tasks to fulfil, the prophecy won't allow it."

Brydie was looking between us as Lorcan took another swig of his drink then replied, "I'm not asking you to go to Greece. I understand from a trustworthy source that there is a good chance Carman's descendant still lives in Ireland."

I raised a brow. "That explains your interest in Ian and McKenzie."

He inclined his head. "Yes, fortune befell me when you turned up with them. Their skills will come in handy."

"And that's it? You just want us to keep our eyes and ears open?"

"That's it. But don't get complacent. I will expect a progress report every week that you're here."

Brydie shifted in her seat. "But what happens if we have nothing to report before Samhain? There's also the likelihood that Carman's descendant is no more."

Lorcan's face hardened. "That's not possible; Morrígan provided a loophole just as Cailleach did for you. And I refuse to believe she isn't alive—for without Carman's descendant, we are lost, and I will not accept that outcome."

I didn't doubt it, not at the look of determination crossing his features. "You're forgetting there's also Talorgan's reach to consider," I reminded him. "He's a threat to both our people. If he takes our world, there's no stopping him from taking yours next."

Lorcan's lips thinned at the ramifications of that statement. Oh yes, he'd just realized what a tangled web we had been thrust within.

His eyes were hard as he turned back to face us. "Well, I suppose that means our futures ride upon each other. Find me the descendant of Carman and I'll grant you refuge for the coming months until Samhain. Morrígan may not be here, but as her descendant, she chose me to lead our people. She would understand that as a leader, I have to make my own choices, and nothing in this world is for free. The pact between Morrígan and Cailleach will be given effect to; my people will give you aid in the coming war with

Talorgan. As to your other requests, we will follow tradition, which is a tithe for a tithe."

"What of the identity of whoever helped me that night my parents died?" Brydie pressed.

Lorcan looked at her. "That is not on the table right now," he said softly.

"But—"

"Consider my offer," Lorcan cut in firmly, "but know this —the morning's dawn will either confirm your safety or render you homeless."

I grit my teeth, my chest burning. Above ground, Talorgan was everywhere. Here, we were safe. Here, he couldn't gain entry. And if we were to infiltrate the Institute, we needed a safe base, somewhere to return with Chloe, where no one, not even Callum and his people, could find us. There was also the question of Lorcan's power. His ability to shape shift was proof enough that he held old, potent magic—that he truly was Morrígan's descendant himself. However, now wasn't the time to test those waters. Not when we could be allies instead. As such, there was nothing to debate, nothing to consider. The bastard had me and he knew it.

"Fine. We accept the tithe. In return for allowing us to stay here, we will locate the descendant of Carman."

Forcing myself not to launch at his smirking, half-naked figure, I jerked my head at Brydie to indicate we were leaving and stalked to the ladder. Lorcan's low chuckle followed me, a taunting acknowledgement that told me, regardless of my response, he knew he'd won.

CHAPTER 19

BRYDIE

PRESENT DAY, IRELAND

G age was silent the whole way back to our lodgings, likely gnawing away at the news we'd just received. What Lorcan had asked of us wasn't a heavy burden, but it added another complication to our overflowing list of tasks to attend to.

Once back at our lodgings, I was relieved to find the others weren't back from the dinner party yet. Given the day we'd had, I was eager to retire, but I wanted an update on Chloe first.

"Any word from Alison?" I asked Gage.

He nodded. "I heard from her just before we arrived at Holyhead. She'll help us get inside the Institute in return for a tithe."

"Of course, she will," I muttered, pissed that, yet again, we would owe somebody else something in return. Tithes were the druidic currency. "Why is everyone forgetting about how they're bound to help us through Cailleach's prophecy?"

"You really think that holds worth after what you've seen and heard these last few months? Callum is their leader. The prophecy and your safety is not in his best interests."

I sighed. He was right. "What is it she wants, then?"

"For us to rescue one of Callum's personal guards."

My stomach plummeted. "What?"

His features were grim as he walked over to the kitchen and poured himself a glass of water. "It won't be an easy task."

"Which guard?"

"Jake. The youngest one."

I recalled the young man with the cloying scent of smoke; a smell very similar to Talorgan's. He'd held a ball of red flame in his hands. "And you believe this task is within our reach?"

Gage's eyes remained fixed on mine. "It will have to be."

That response didn't give me a lot of confidence. "When is she expecting us to retrieve Jake? Surely not at the same time we rescue Chloe?"

Gage ran a hand through his hair, the only sign of his agitation. "She wants that, but it's not possible. We'll be lucky to leave unnoticed with Chloe as it is."

"I think that's wise. We need Chloe."

"Yes, we do, just as much as we need the support of the fae. Callum has turned our people are against us; that leaves us weak and without allies, but now Lorcan has confirmed his people's aid, there is hope. We have the beginnings of a legion."

Legion. A word that held connotations of war... "So what's the plan? When are we moving?"

He looked at me intently. I knew he was assessing my potential, whether I had it in me to cope with the rescue mission ahead. "Don't worry about me," I snapped. "I can look after my own."

His smile was faint. "Yes, you can."

The tight feeling in my chest eased somewhat as I pushed, "So, when are we leaving?"

"In three days. Alison shared Callum leaves the Institute every Thursday. That's our chance."

I nodded, hiding the pool of anxiety now causing my stomach to flip. "I assume we'll be training over the next few days then?"

He nodded. "And formulating our plan. I know of a way in, and Alison passed on enough information for me to understand where Callum's chambers are, but as you've never been to the Institute, you'll be going in blind. You'll need to memorize the layout over the next few days. There will be no room for error and no second chances. Understood?"

"Yes." I held his gaze even as I pushed down the nausea threatening to take over. "Do you still believe we can trust Alison?"

His mouth tightened at the question I was always pushing. "Yes."

"Okay." I didn't care that he was pissed; the question needed to be asked. I still didn't trust Alison, but if this was our way in, I was willing to risk anything to get Chloe back. "Well, I'm off to bed."

His gaze never wavered. "Sleep well. I'll see you at dawn."

His eyes dropped, and I felt the edge of his desire down our shared line and knew he had more than our dawn training run in mind. An answering flush raced over my skin, heat arrowing between my legs. Mortified, I averted my gaze. I didn't want to see his desire or feel his lust, not when I knew he wouldn't act upon it. The internal connection between us was demeaning enough, but I still had my pride.

Tucking that around me like a blanket, I retired to my room and locked the door.

I didn't bother turning on the lights. The golden glow of a salt lamp conveniently left on in the foyer provided enough light to change into my bed shorts and sleeping singlet. I crawled into the king size bed and curled onto my side, looking out the window into the dark trees, and willed myself to fall into the quiet oblivion.

But sleep didn't come. In the quiet of the room, the events of the last few days replayed over and over: the incident with Garret at the Claymore, the altercation with Talorgan, the man who'd died on the mountain, the horrid tasks Gage had been forced to carry out, the long journey here, meeting the fae, being tasked with finding the descendant of Carman, and now the pending mission to retrieve Chloe from the Institute. I groaned, knowing sleep wouldn't come easy tonight, no matter how exhausted I was.

I considered returning to the living room, but the thought of finding Gage still there was enough to dismiss the idea. Blowing out a frustrated sigh, I rolled onto my back, trying to ignore what it was I wanted...who it was I craved, but my thoughts couldn't be curbed.

Gage hid himself behind an impenetrable shield. I'd come to understand it was a guise to protect himself and those around him, not letting anyone else into his inner circle. What would happen if he let me in? Would that shield drop? Would he let me see who he really was? Would he give into the desire coursing between us?

An image arose, the two of us naked, my body entwined with his. That telltale flush of red was slashed across his cheekbones as he held my gaze, all that intense energy he carried focused solely on me. I imagined him moving inside me, our gazes locked as we shared those emotions physically as well as emotionally. Warmth pooled in my gut, and I flushed, unable to stop the hand now slipping inside my panties. I was wet. Slick.

A tapping came at the window, a sharp insistent peck. I shot upright in bed, my face flaming. The noise came again, and I looked outside to the balcony. It took me a while to distinguish the small black form on the arm of a chair.

A crow.

Its eyes were piercing, staring right at me with a preternatural focus. As I watched, it leaned forward and deliberately pecked at the window again, its green gaze never leaving mine. I knew exactly who it was.

Pushing out of bed, I padded silently to the door. As soon as my hand touched the door handle, there came a blinding flash of light, which was soon swallowed by a cloud of black smoke. It twisted and roiled, the smoke becoming thick and impenetrable, before suddenly dissipating in a wispy fog. In its place stood a toned, bare-chested man, his golden skin gleaming in the moonlight, his long, chocolate brown hair ruffling in the breeze.

Lorcan.

As I stared at him, I felt my breasts swell, the nipples narrowing into hard buds. I clenched my thighs together, burning with need. What the hell was wrong with me? Why did Lorcan elicit this reaction? My mind warred with my body, because this reaction was crazy—it wasn't Lorcan I wanted, it was Gage.

Lorcan silently watched me through the window, an innate knowledge in his eyes, as if he was aware of the internal battle I fought. Seeing that had my teeth clenching. I was fucking sick of the men in my life dictating what I could and couldn't do—what I felt and couldn't feel!

Not breaking Lorcan's stare, I yanked the sliding door

back. But, for all my good intentions, I couldn't prevent the husky tone of my voice as I said in greeting, "Lorcan."

His lips lifted in a charming smile. "Brydie."

The timbre of his voice was low, and it sent another arrow of desire between my legs. It was a poignant reminder this man was dangerous. For all his charm, he was a predator; a sinfully, dark, sexy predator. "Why are you here? I'd thought we'd said all we needed to say earlier."

"I have something I wish to discuss with you in private."

I considered him. Under the veneer of his usual confident, charming self, there was an undercurrent of seriousness in his gaze. I stepped aside and gestured at him to enter. "Come in."

But instead of moving, his attention never wavered from my face as he deliberately inhaled. I flushed when his lips lifted in a wicked smile, the canines now visible. Lorcan's eyes flicked to my chest, and I didn't need to look down to know my nipples were pleading for his touch—I could feel them straining against my sleep singlet. His eyes lifted back to mine, appreciation in his gaze as he replied, "I would love to, but I don't think that's wise, all things considered."

The innuendo was obvious. I stepped back from the door, my cheeks flaming as I wrapped my arms around my chest. "I'm sorry. I have no idea why I react this way around you," I said in exasperation. "Not that you're not attractive, it's just that I—"

Lorcan placed a finger over my lips. "Don't worry, you aren't going crazy, Brydie. This connection between us is my fault and something I have little control over."

"So this is one of your powers?"

He inclined his head, the long, brown strands of his hair falling across his cheek. "I am the direct descendant of Morrígan and therefore attuned to the desires of the flesh.

Our Sovereign Goddess is well known for enjoying coupling, but she didn't join with others for satiation alone —it was a means to transfer power."

I ran my eyes down his lean, muscled body and flawless features. There was no denying he was built for sex. "Are you saying my reaction to you is coerced, and it's all because the end goal will cause you to rise in power?"

Lorcan's lip curled. "I don't particularly like how you phrased that, but yes, we fae crave power, any and all forms of it, and some of us more than others."

Which meant him more than most. And given how he looked and behaved, I doubted he needed to search for volunteers to 'satiate' himself. "Arrogant of you." I gripped my arms, unwilling to drop them from my chest. I could still feel my nipples peaking, and I didn't want Lorcan to become even more conceited than he already was. "If it's a magical pull, then why can't I prevent my reaction?"

He cocked his head to the side, green eyes watchful as they rested on my face. "Are you being honest with yourself, Brydie? Do you not want to feel? We all hunger for closeness, for escape, for euphoria."

I snorted. "And you promise euphoria, is that what you're saying?"

His eyes were hooded as they traveled down my body with specific intent. "Do you doubt it? I'm well versed in what makes a woman hunger for more."

Goose pimples whispered across my skin, but I refused to rub my arms and give him the satisfaction of a response. "Maybe another time."

The glint in Lorcan's eyes told me my effort was wasted, that he knew what reaction he'd brewed. He cleared his throat and his next words were soft. "I see what is between you and your Guardian. I know he denies you even though he seeks to protect you from other's advances. Why do you allow it? And why would you turn away the attention of another?"

For a moment, I simply stared at him, shocked at his blunt questions. Then I realized he was right. Gage didn't want me. There was nothing to stop me from taking what Lorcan offered...except that when I thought of becoming close to Lorcan, of tipping my head back for his kiss, it wasn't Lorcan's face I saw above me, but Gage's.

Feeling the burn of his denial once more, I shook my head. "As much as I am flattered by your offer, Lorcan, I can't take you up on it. I can't be with someone without feeling more than a simple desire for them, and I respect you too much to not give you all of me." I laid a hand on his arm to soften my words and added, "And if we are both touched by prophecy, I would prefer we remained friends rather than lovers."

"Friends with benefits?" he countered. "They don't have to be exclusive. I am a generous lover."

Indeed. Despite myself, I felt a smile split my face. Lorcan was relentless. "Not at this time, Lorcan. But again, thank you for the offer." I stepped through the door onto the balcony and took a seat in one of the chairs, gesturing to a second one. "Do you mind telling me why you really came here? I know there's something else on your mind."

His body subtly tensed as took a seat next to me. "I came to visit you because there was something you asked for tonight. Something I didn't give you."

My heart squeezed. I knew exactly what he was referring to. "Knowledge of the fae who helped me the night my parents died."

He nodded, and a shadow of grief crossed his face. "He was my brother."

My mouth dropped open. "The fae who removed my memory, the same fae who saved me from drowning, was your brother?"

Lorcan nodded. "Yes. He was my younger brother. His name was Naal."

"Was?" I asked softly.

There was no emotion in his tone as he shared, "He died just over three years ago." At my gasp, he nodded in confirmation. "Yes, he died saving you that night your parents' vehicle went over the bridge."

I swallowed. "How?"

Lorcan looked past me into my room beyond. "After me, Naal was next in line for the throne. But he didn't want it, not the attention or the position; he was his own man, preferring solitude rather than political intrigue. When the previous Watcher came to his natural end, the position opened—"

"Watcher?"

At my question, Lorcan turned back to face me, explaining, "The position is reserved for those who choose to follow the Daughter of Winter. As the name suggests, this involves watching Cailleach's descendant."

I was floored. "Just like a Guardian?" Did Nora know she had one? What of the other Daughters? Surely Gage would have told me if he'd known.

"Not quite. The Watcher is expected to watch and observe only, not interfere. At least, that was true until Naal took the position." He ran his hands through his hair. "Naal saw the position as an escape route, a way to evade our people and way of life. He hated being sequestered away down here, especially when Carman's curse began to unfold. My younger brother preferred the reality of the world above, rather than what isn't real here. I couldn't blame him, not when I feel the same. And when our magic began to fade with the loss of the cauldron, I couldn't hold onto him any longer."

"But shouldn't Naal have been watching over Nora? Not me?"

Lorcan's features were tight. "Your father contacted me just over three years ago. He told me of your birth, and who you had become. We made a deal where he made me promise not to tell Nora. Andrew knew of the agreement between Cailleach and Morrígan, knew that one of the fae was always destined to watch over a Daughter, and he claimed that due, as was his right. But surprisingly, he asked for more—a fae who had the ability to inhibit memories, and on careful probing I understood what it was he required. At the time, Naal was with me. He carried the ability to repress memories, and when I promised your father that I would ask one of the fae to come immediately to his assistance, Naal had already decided that he would be the one to go."

My mouth dropped. I couldn't believe my father had orchestrated all of this. His actions were a tangled web that made no sense. On one hand, he'd done everything in his power to hide my legacy from me, while also doing everything in his power to protect me. I was beginning to understand I hadn't really known my father at all. "Andrew really orchestrated all of this?"

Lorcan nodded.

"And your brother agreed? Even with Nora still alive and unaware?"

His tone was heavy. "Yes. Naal understood more than anyone the need to keep those we love safe."

That short explanation conveyed a world of meaning. It told me Naal had loved and lost someone he cared about. I didn't push Lorcan for the information. It was enough to know the secret of who had helped me that night, even if it brought another shocking revelation about my father. But it also raised more questions for Lorcan. "There's something I don't understand. No matter what my father promised, weren't you obligated to tell Nora about me by way of Cailleach and Morrígan's agreement?"

It was hard not to imagine how different things could have been if he had. We may not have been able to prevent the car accident, but Nora would have taken me with her to Scotland. I would have started my training three years ago, lived with my grandmother at the estate, been under her tutelage. I could have even been able to save her from Talorgan that fateful night last Samhain; we could have fought him together.

Lorcan's jaw was hard as he ground out, "It is true; I went against the vow, but there was an incident. I had just heard a rumor that The Oaken Tree was responsible for taking the Dagda's cauldron from my people. I was not in any fit state to help my cousins out, whether we were bound by our goddess' pact or not."

"Yet you let Naal go."

Lorcan's eyes burned. "That had nothing to do with me. My brother had a will of iron. Once he'd made his mind up, there was no stopping him. He went with the dawn. It was the last time I ever saw him."

The wounded grief in his tone had me crouching in front of him. I put a hand on his arm and said softly, "For what it's worth, thank you. Your brother saved me. I've no doubt that if he hadn't been there that night, I would have drowned with my parents, or whoever was chasing us would have ended my life."

Lorcan did not hide from his grief as he met my gaze.

His words were fierce. "He believed in you, Brydie. For the two weeks he watched you, he believed in who you would become. Naal was adamant you would end the prophecy. He believed that if we helped you, there was a chance you could help us by reversing Carman's curse."

This was what had allowed us entry into their world. This was what would provide us sanctuary—a promise made between the loved ones that we had each lost—one a beloved brother, the other a beloved father. It was another bridge between me and Lorcan, this one shared through grief. I could not deny him. "I will do my best," I vowed. And I would—starting right now. "I'll talk to Gage tomorrow so he can immediately ask those loyal to our cause to keep an eye out."

His face softened, and he lifted a hand to touch my cheek. "That's all I ask."

I nodded, just stopping myself from leaning into his touch. That burning desire returned with a vengeance.

Lorcan's nostrils flared, indicating he'd smelled the change in my scent. His words had a husky undertone as he said, "And I would again encourage you to think about my previous offer. There is solace found in coupling. It would not be a chore, Brydie."

I flushed, unsure whether to be offended or not. "Thank you, but I'm firm in my decision." I held his gaze to be certain, delivering the message with my eyes as well as my words.

He held my stare until he nodded, acceptance settling over his features. "Alright. Shall we seal our pact then?"

I held out a hand.

He smiled gently. "I was thinking we'd do it the fae way. You would also gain an understanding of what is waiting for you should you change your mind about my offer."

Before I could reply, he had wrapped both of his hands around my upper arms and was leaning forward. When his lips met mine, Lorcan released a satisfied growl and crushed me against his chest, his hands moving to fist my hair. It happened so quickly, I barely had a chance to breathe. Desire coursed through me, obliterating the frustration, hurt, and anxiety. It made me realize this oblivion was what I needed, what I craved, but as my eyes closed and my lips began to move against his, I couldn't stop the images that came. Gage. His face, his smile, his touch, his goddamn scent.

My eyes flew open, and I pulled back, placing a finger firmly against Lorcan's lips. "Stop," I demanded, my chest rising and falling as I struggled to find my breath.

"Why?" he returned in that husky voice that did things to my body. His hands still gripped my hair, our bodies held tight together. "You hunger for this. We both do."

I shook my head and said with honesty, "Yes, but not with you, Lorcan."

He stiffened, and his green gaze searched mine. Whatever he found must have confirmed what I'd said, for he pulled back, dropping his hands to his sides. The loss of his touch was sudden; an aloof emptiness now lurking between us.

Lorcan's words were soft, no edge of desire gilding his tone as he said, "No matter what you believe, my offer was genuine, Brydie. I understand that you want another, but I did not lie when I said our coupling will only add to your power. That, and give you the release you need."

I pulled away from him, pushing back to my feet as I shook my head. "I wish that were true, but I am not Cailleach and you are not Morrígan, and I'd be hurting you as well as myself if I succumbed to base instinct."

Lorcan stilled, digesting my response, then released a sigh. "I understand and there is no need to apologize." He pushed to his feet and closed the gap between us, grabbing my chin between his thumb and forefinger. "I respect your decision, and I appreciate your honest response. I should lea—"

A door slammed in my room, interrupting what he was going to say, and we both whirled to see Gage standing in the doorway.

He prowled onto the balcony, a dark storm cloud of savage emotion etched upon his face. "What the fuck is going on here?"

CHAPTER 20

BRYDIE

PRESENT DAY, IRELAND

I bristled at Gage's intrusion, anger licking up my spine. "That's none of your business," I growled in return.

Gage looked at Lorcan before running his gaze blatantly down my form, and I knew he was noting the lack of physical distance between us. I shivered in the cool night air as his burning gaze took in my sleep shorts and bed singlet. As his eyes rose to meet mine, Gage ground out, "This doesn't look like nothing. I thought we'd finished our discussion earlier."

I grit my teeth. "Like I said, Gage, it's none of your business. Besides, Lorcan was just leaving."

The fae leader smiled. "Yes, it appears I am suddenly unwelcome."

I cringed at his tone but didn't berate him for the comment. I knew who Lorcan was now. The moment we'd just shared had been special. It had broken the barriers between us, providing a shared understanding of not just loss but purpose. He'd shown me a part of him that he kept hidden from others. I would maintain his trust by protecting that gift. I had few friends, and after tonight, I now classed Lorcan as one of them.

Gage lifted a brow when Lorcan didn't move and growled under his breath, "Well, it's time to leave then, Lorcan."

His hands were clenched by his side, and I could feel the maelstrom of his emotions along our shared internal line; knew just how tightly Gage was holding on to his feelings.

And so did Lorcan. With a wicked smile, the fae leader reached up and tucked a stray curl behind my ear, his hand caressing my cheek as he said in a husky whisper, "I'll see you in the morning, Brydie. Think about my offer."

Gage snarled, his body bristling. "Get out!"

I rounded on my Guardian, appalled at his lack of respect. "How dare you? You do not speak for me!"

Gage stared at me, his cerulean eyes glittering. "I'll do what I damn well please."

I slammed my hands on my hips. "You are aware of how ridiculous you sound, aren't you?"

"There is nothing ridiculous about what is going on here."

"And what exactly *is* going on here?" I returned. Then, suddenly tired of playing this game, I said, "Actually, I don't care. It's late and you're both leaving."

My Guardian's eyes burned; he didn't even flinch at my demand. "Lorcan first," he said softly.

My mouth dropped at the show of male territorialism. I glanced at Lorcan to see he, too, was bristling, any pretense of ribbing Gage now swallowed by his own male pride. I felt the burn in my chest, instantaneous and red-hot, and just contained the scream that threatened to erupt as I threw my hands between them, lashing out with my magic. A ribbon of blue-white light smashed into each of them. The men reeled backward, struck by shards of ice.

Gage clutched at his chest, one hand rubbing the area as he growled, "What the fuck, Brydie?"

Lorcan's face was livid as he stared at me accusingly, the warmth in his eyes now replaced with coldness. "You are balancing upon a fine line, descendant," he ground out softly. "There was no need to attack me."

"Don't give me reason to, then!" I spat, too angry to heed his warning. I pointed ruthlessly behind him, into the forest beyond. "Take your pissing contest outside, and get the fuck out of my room because I am going to bed."

For a moment, they both stared at me, then they looked at each other. Gage's eyes conveyed the message that Lorcan must still go first. *Christ!* I looked at Lorcan, because what I felt from Gage meant he wouldn't budge. The only way they would leave was if Lorcan capitulated first.

Lorcan glanced between us, and I watched as the anger on his face was suddenly replaced with a smirk. He gave a low bow and drawled, "It is clear that what has happened here tonight is punishment enough for you both, and as much as I'd love to stay and watch you climb out of this mess, I have duties to attend elsewhere."

Gage snarled and took a step forward.

I halted him with a raised hand. "No! Do not come any closer." Turning to the fae leader, I said firmly, "Good night, Lorcan. I look forward to continuing our discussion tomorrow." I emphasized the word discussion, and the innuendo wasn't lost on Lorcan.

"Indeed," he returned softly, "but in the meantime, think on my offer."

I felt an answering flare of anger from my Guardian, and I repeated through clenched teeth, "Good night, Lorcan."

Lorcan inclined his head, and his mocking tone was obvious as he replied, "Good night."

With that, he stepped back and snapped his fingers. A riot of black smoke began to roil at his feet, building upon itself, higher and higher. The smoke had a seductive scent, rich and sinful like dark chocolate, a fitting tribute to Lorcan's charm. This time, the change was slower, the smoke tumbling in a burgeoning mass of ebony silk until it completely submerged Lorcan. But before it covered his face, he sent Gage a slow wink, the intention wickedly obvious.

Behind me, Gage growled. In the next moment, Lorcan was gone, and from within those shadowy tendrils, a black crow arose on a victorious screech. The sleek corvid arrowed up into the night sky before swooping high above my head and silently winging its way into the forest.

At Lorcan's departure, a weighted silence fell. The moment was poignant, and not just from Lorcan's dramatic exit. I felt a sense of irony as part of me craved the freedom the fae leader held at his fingertips. But I wasn't one to prolong fate, no matter how unpleasant it could be, so I turned to face my Guardian.

His face was smooth, devoid of emotion; but the internal connection between us told a different story. "Why did you come, Gage? I wasn't in any danger."

His face tightened, and his words were almost strangled. "I didn't do this for you."

What the hell did that mean? The time for patience had gone. My interlude with Lorcan had illustrated how much I had been putting up with from Gage since our interlude on Beinn na Caillich, and it was time for change. "What is it you needed to do, Gage?" I demanded. "Did you need to stamp your claim over me? Because we've been through this. You decided that we couldn't be together, that the prophecy came first. You told me that being together might cause us both to make the wrong decision come Samhain—that the lives of others are more important to you than fleeting desire."

I slammed my hands on my hips again, trying to prevent myself from lashing out once more. Gage's cerulean gaze dropped, and my nipples instantly peaked. His face tightened, his nostrils flaring. A slash of red ran across his cheekbones and a voracious hunger arrowed down our shared line. His eyes burned into mine as he said in a low voice, "The rules haven't changed, Brydie."

His words were again contradictory to his body language, and it snapped the last thread on my patience. "Fuck the rules, Gage! This isn't a game—this is real life. You can't deny me on one hand and then tell me not to be with anyone else on the other. This isn't your decision to make, it's mine." I narrowed my eyes as I said honestly, "I've made it clear I want you. If you don't want me in return, then I am free to look for somebody else. And you have no say in the matter."

He glared, those blue eyes hard sapphires. "Do you have an itch, Brydie? Is that what this is all about?"

I gasped as if he'd physically struck me. "I'm not a fucking dog, Gage!" Rage roiled, explosive and turbulent, and my magic responded, eagerly licking up my chest, urging me to let loose the power singing for release. I strived to hold onto some level of control as I glared back at my mentor.

Gage didn't seem to notice the edge I stood upon, or that his hands were glowing red with his own power as he blazed back, "Don't act like a bitch in heat then."

Ooohhhh! All sense of control evaporated. "Fuck you, Gage!"

Not caring of the consequences, I launched my power at his chest, releasing everything I was feeling, letting it pour out of me in a vicious attack of agony and lust, anger and despair.

Sparks and snowflakes exploded between us as my ribbon of ice smashed against his flaming shield of fire. My power responded to the challenge, bucking for more, and I recklessly opened the floodgates a little further, allowing it the freedom it hankered for. In response, a shrill wind whistled into the room on a shriek of piercing rage, causing Gage's hair to ripple around his face in a cloud of ebony silk.

At my blatant challenge, his lips peeled back in a vicious snarl. There was no fear on his face, only burning anger and a hardness to his eyes that pierced my own rage. It forced me to acknowledge I might have pushed him too far. I faltered, and the lapse in my attack was an opening for his to advance. A small sliver of his fire splintered through my ice and arrowed straight into my chest. I braced myself for the impact, innately aware that it would hurt more than any punch or kick...but instead of physical pain, what I felt was a dark, twisted plethora of emotions. It took me a moment to understand that it was everything he was feeling: hunger, anger, frustration, desire, lust, and pain—everything *I* was feeling.

I reeled backward, my bare feet sliding on the wooden deck. That breach in my power was another opening, and Gage was a blur of movement as he launched himself at me. His body crashed solidly into mine. I prepared myself for a painful landing, but at the last moment, Gage rolled us in midair so that his back hit the ground instead of mine. I slammed on top of him, my body aligned with every hard inch of his. There was no time to retaliate as one of his hands snaked out to grip the back of my head, the other biting into my waist while he pressed me close and lifted us both back to our feet. My hands were trapped, and no matter how much I struggled, he wouldn't loosen his possessive grip.

Holding my gaze, Gage growled, "You. Are. Mine! If there's anything you desire, it will be me who fulfills it. Not that fae bastard."

I snarled, "You lost that chance a few months back!" and slammed my hands onto his waist as I called upon my power. I felt a measure of satisfaction when I heard his sharp indrawn breath as my hands burned through his shirt.

Gage grunted, releasing me to grab both of my hands. He pushed me backward and pinned me to the glass door leading into my room, wrestling my hands above my head. I writhed against his hard length, kicking and bucking. My hands clenched uselessly above my head, aching to release my magic. A part of me understood that to do so would bring ruin upon us all, upsetting not only Lorcan and the fae, but potentially putting all of us in danger if our lodgings collapsed. I had succumbed to the built-up anger roiling uncontrollably through my blood and was suddenly aware I was at risk of completely losing control of my power.

I forced myself to swallow my pride and ground out, "Let me go!"

"No." Gage's cerulean eyes were scorching as he leaned in close to my ear and ground out, "If I'd known that you would throw yourself at the next man as soon as you had the chance, then I would have taken what you offered back on the mountain."

I froze. First shock, then hurt raged. I wrenched my body from his grip in a move he had taught me countless times before. Then, using the momentum of my swing, I pushed myself sideways and lifted my right leg to kick him in the thigh. Gage moved lightning quick, a hand wrapping around my calf to halt my attack. His face set, he grabbed my waist with his other hand and pushed me ruthlessly through the balcony door and into my room. My back hit the feather mattress. Then Gage was on top of me, his mouth slamming over mine.

He wasn't gentle. My lips ground against my teeth as his tongue thrust inside my mouth, swirling and teasing. His hands were everywhere, hard and insistent, one tangling in my hair as he ruthlessly angled our kiss, the other sliding up my stomach to slip under my singlet and firmly grasp my breast.

As our lips and tongues moved in a tangled dance, I was hit with the sharp redolence of woodsmoke and steel. Gage's scent only heightened my emotions, and I couldn't stop my hands from sliding down his back, or my nails digging through his tee shirt in a raking drag before traveling up to clutch at the back of his head. His body was long and hard, and it fit perfectly against my softer curves. I kissed him back with everything I had, pouring not only my lust, but also my anger into that kiss. Then I bit him—hard.

He cursed, rearing back, his eyes glittering. "Want to play, do we?"

"I don't play games," I forced out between swollen lips, my legs curling around the back of his thighs to pull him even tighter against me. I bucked against his groin to emphasize my response and arched my back, my other breast aching for his touch, the nipple taut with want. He growled and didn't leave me wanting, his head swooping to cover my breast in an open-mouthed kiss. He sucked hard, right through my singlet, and I gasped, my head falling back as I fell into the pleasure.

I moaned as his mouth lifted, but he only pushed the wet material up to expose my flesh. The cool air caused my nipple to bud even tighter. Gage leaned forward and blew softly along my skin. The warm air was a caress in itself, and renewed desire surged through me. Its edge was sharpened by the rage that was slowly diminishing, becoming replaced by the promise of sexual release.

I couldn't help slipping into our internal connection, searching the filaments of our bond to determine what it was that Gage was feeling. His answering anger was the first emotion I felt firing down our internal line before I became aware that he was also drowning in a sexual hunger that matched my own.

Gage reared up suddenly from my breast and bit out, "Get out of my head!" Then he leaned forward and bit my bottom lip in warning before dragging his mouth over my chin, down into the sensitive crook of my neck.

I gasped, my lip burning as I tilted my head back, opening myself to his touch. He trailed a series of open-mouthed kisses over my throat before nipping the shell of my ear. Then, once again, he withdrew.

"Gage." His name fell from my lips in a guttural plea. I reached for his shoulders in an attempt to drag his face back to mine.

He eluded me, his tone hoarse. "No, not yet."

His hand left my breast to slip under the waistband of my sleep shorts. My breath hitched, anticipation causing a renewed rush of desire to surge between my legs. His hand cupped me, and when he felt the dampness of my panties, he froze, his head lifting to capture my gaze. His eyes burned into mine. "Do you feel that, Brydie? That reaction is for me. Not Lorcan—me."

His face was stark, and without breaking our gaze, he pulled aside the lace and thrust a finger inside me. I gasped, my back arching off the bed. "More," I panted.

A low rumbling sound came from his throat as he continued to stroke me internally. Then he ground out in a low voice, "I am the one who makes you feel like this, Brydie. Not that fae bastard. Remember that when you are next alone with him. "

Then his lips were back on my neck, his finger mercilessly thrusting inside me as he bit the soft, sensitive curve between my neck and shoulder. I cried out, my skin trembling as hurt and desire slammed into me.

A small part of me was mindful we teetered on the edge of madness, a careful balance between lust and anger. It was a reminder that what was between us was more than just attraction. There was a magnetism, a pull that couldn't be denied, and one that Gage's ironclad will couldn't repel. I could feel myself slipping away, all sense of reason vanishing. I wanted him. I'd made no secret of it before, and I made no secret of it now. "Then give me something I cannot forget," I forced out in husky demand.

His eyes narrowed, and the finger inside me stilled. "You are a goddamn witch," he ground out tightly.

His cerulean eyes were ablaze with lust, their blue depths swirling with inner fire. I wanted that fire along my skin, plunging into my mouth and inside my body. I wanted everything he had to give. "I told you before that I don't play games. I want you, Gage. If you want me, too, then don't tease me anymore. Either succumb or leave me be. But choose now."

The skin was stretched tight across his cheekbones, and

his jaw was hard as he bit out, "Who. Said. I. Was. Teasing?" His finger thrust inside me, in unison with every word.

I shuddered, my body blooming in a torrent of lust as my mind shrieked with satisfied conviction that I had won. He was no longer fighting whatever it was between us, what he felt, what I felt. A burning part of me wanted to know what had made him finally yield. "Why now, Gage?"

His thumb pushed against the hard nub between my thighs, and I gasped as my insides clenched at the burst of pleasure. He held my gaze, watching me with a lazy, self-satisfied smile, as if he had all the time in the world. He said in a low voice, "No more questions, Brydie. Just feel."

I knew it was jealousy that had brought him in here. Jealousy of Lorcan. But in that moment, as his fingers twirled and teased inside me, as his mouth suckled my breasts and his teeth tugged at my nipples in an addictive mix of pleasure and pain, I didn't care what had forced him into this room or how we had fallen together—just that we had.

Gage was a drug I'd craved for too long, an addiction I was afraid could never be sated. I didn't know or care if it was prophecy guiding us; I only cared about here, now, and being on this bed. Because in this intimate moment was passion, fire, angst, anger, hope, and desire. I felt full to bursting and I felt alive. There was no room for fear or tension, no room for the impending threat that always hovered above us, nor was there any fear for Chloe. I felt nothing but Gage, smelt nothing but Gage, saw nothing but Gage. He enveloped me in every way possible and instead of feeling trapped, I felt complete. Whole. Where I was meant to be.

Except, I needed more. Much more.

It was as if he'd heard my thoughts for his face darkened, and he paused in his ministrations, his fingers withdrawing. I gasped, reaching for him to guide his hand back between my legs.

His face tightened, but he allowed me the movement, moving up beside me in the bed to lie next to me. He slipped another finger inside, curling and stroking, and I moaned in response.

"I want you, Gage. All of you." I rotated my hips and squeezed my inner thighs.

He cursed, his jaw clenching. I felt the hard length of him against my thigh, his jeans straining, and I reached down to stroke him through the stiff material. My hands cupped the outline of his taut erection. He cursed and jerked backward. "Not yet," he ground out. "Before we go any further, we need to establish an understanding."

"What understanding?" I managed to gasp out as he stretched me even wider. I felt the pressure building, the precipice of pleasure looming.

The timbre of his voice was low and husky, an indication that he was not as unaffected as he portrayed. "I am not an easy lover. I do not share. There will only ever be you and me. No one else. Is that understood?"

I didn't know what I'd expected, but it hadn't been this. A thrill shot through me because I understood the possession, craved it in turn. "Just you and me," I agreed.

His answering growl told me everything. Then he was gone, his body no longer on mine. "Take off your clothes," he ordered roughly.

I pushed myself up to sitting, and without taking my eyes off his, I lifted the ribbed singlet over my head. His eyes were ravenous as they dropped to my breasts, the tips peaked in the soft golden glow of the bedside lamp. Feeling emboldened by his response and the fierce lust I could feel arrowing down our shared line, I lifted my hips and shimmied out of my shorts and panties. Naked, I lay back on the bed and stared back at him.

His eyes devoured me, lingering on my breasts before moving his gaze between my thighs. "You are fucking beautiful."

The words were raw and open, and I reveled in my feminine power, now confident that the lust he felt for me was mirrored by my own. "Your turn," I urged breathlessly.

Without taking his eyes off mine, he pulled his tee shirt over his head and threw it to the ground. My gaze drank in the muscles and dips and hollows of his chest, his tapered stomach defined by hours of training. I dropped my gaze lower, below the waistband of his jeans to find the bulge in his pants straining.

"All of you," I whispered huskily. "I need to see all of you."

His eyes were hooded, predatory, but there was a sense of male satisfaction down our shared line as he undid the top button of his jeans and slid them down his hips. He was naked underneath, and his cock sprang forth, long and hard. I saw the glistening moisture at the end of the tip, and I almost purred in response.

He prowled over to the bed, confident and sinfully sexy, his hair a dark cloud around his face. His cerulean eyes glittering with intent, he crawled on top of me, his movements slow and deliberate. I made no move to stop him, urging him with my eyes to come closer. This was what I craved. He was what I craved.

Grabbing my hips, Gage held them firmly between his hands as he settled himself between my legs. My face flamed as I anticipated his next movement, his eyes gleaming as he dropped his head between my legs. I moaned as his tongue laved the folds of my opening before plunging into my heat. I gasped, and my head fell back as I became lost to sensation. My body arched off the bed, my hands clenching the bed sheets tightly between my fingers as my heart pounded to a racing rhythm.

"Gage..."

Even with my eyes closed, I could see his face, smell his scent, feel his thoughts. He was everywhere, inside me, around me, consuming me. The feeling was intense, overwhelming; a power that could fracture me apart. My head thrashed against the bed as I felt the draw to the top, sensed the tip of the cliff I now stood upon. I cried out, "Gage, please!"

He left my damp folds to slide up my body, his face taut above mine. His tone was raw, and I could feel the tight control he was reining in. "Tell me what you need, Brydie."

There was no question. "You. I need you. Inside me."

His face darkened, his cheekbones awash in a flush of red. "After this, there is no going back. Is that what you want?"

"Yes," I breathed without hesitation.

But he held back, his hands now grasping my ass as he forced me to hold his gaze. "I do not share, Brydie. I will tolerate no teasing, no touching, or even thoughts of another to come between us."

I held his gaze in a fierce grip of my own. "That goes both ways, Gage."

He stared at me for a moment before a grim satisfaction glinted in his eyes. Then I watched his face as he finally allowed lust to overrule all reason. "Good, because you will be begging for me to stop before this night is out."

And with that dark promise, his mouth dropped to mine in a plundering kiss. I moved against him, feeling his hot, hard length against my inner thigh. I rubbed against him, needing him inside me. He growled against my lips before dragging his own down my throat and taking one of my breasts in his mouth, sucking hard. I bucked again, passion overruling all reason.

He stilled above me. "Open your eyes."

The demand in his tone had me instantly obeying. He captured my gaze with his cerulean fire. I had just enough time to grab hold of his shoulders before he thrust powerfully inside me. I cried out at his entrance, feeling every sensation of our joining. His jaw was firm as he held me close, his sapphire gaze never faltering from my face as his hips drove a rhythm that matched my own, as if he innately knew the tone and intensity I desired. Then it occurred to me that he did, that he was listening closely not only to my body, but also to my mind. We were linked as one, our movements synced.

There was an intimacy in the moment. Raw, wild, and intense. I felt vulnerable and open. After spending what felt like an eon hiding how I felt about him—what he made me feel—in this moment, there were no checks and no hiding. Here, there was only an honest truth. And as I felt the crescendo of his desire peaking, I understood that he was just as vulnerable, just as open. The knowledge gave me the courage to finally let go, and I fell into the rhythm of our joining, meeting each of his thrusts with my own.

The heat between us rose, building to a pinnacle, and this time, I hurtled toward that edge of bliss with no checks. Not wanting to fall alone, I reached out and grabbed his face in my hands, gasping out, "Come with me."

The words had barely left my lips before I fractured,

shattering into a thousand pieces. But as I succumbed to an overwhelming pleasure that threatened to obliterate everything in this world, I felt him stiffen above me just before he roared his release and did what he'd always done and followed right behind me.

CHAPTER 21
GIROM

3RD CENTURY BC, ANCIENT SCOTLAND

Fina knew immediately why Girom had come to her door on dawn. Indeed, she'd known what he would ask of her before the words even crossed his lips. There was no hesitation as she agreed to help the Winter Goddess and her child.

Together, they approached Talorgan's brother, Drust, who they found on the path outside his dwelling, a bedroll and supplies strapped to his back. There was a wild, urgent look to his features when they suddenly appeared in his path.

"What is it? I don't have time to waste on trivial matters," Drust ground out sharply, his hands clenched at his sides as if to prevent himself from throwing them out of his way.

Girom held up a hand. "Hold, warrior. This matter is of an urgency that deserves more than a moment of your time."

Drust hissed and cocked his head to the side. "I beg to differ, Master. The day wanes."

Anger flared at his disrespect. "Is that how you would

address one of the Wise Ones? A Master of the Druidic Code?"

Drust didn't relax his stance. "I'm sorry," he said shortly. "I have pressing matters to attend. Please accept my apology, Master." Then he suddenly seemed to notice who it was that stood beside the Master of Herbs, her face hidden under the nondescript brown robe with the blue stripe around the hood. "Fìna, what are you doing here? Does this matter also concern you?"

Fìna's face was grave as she pushed the hood back. "It concerns all of us, brother. Even Talorgan."

Her tone cracked Drust's veneer. His words were loaded. "What does Talorgan have to do with this?"

"Going by your response, I assume you already know of the dark path your brother has set himself upon?" Girom asked sharply.

Drust blinked. "I don't know what you mean."

Fìna snorted. "Liar. Of course, you know, brother. Your connection to him will have told you that he's changed. I don't need my dreams to confirm how you have always responded to him."

"What are you saying, Fìna?"

"That I, like many in the village, are all aware that you two have fallen out." She gave him a look. "When was the last time you supped together?"

Drust looked away, adjusting the strap of his pack, which hung laden and heavy over his shoulder.

"And when was the last time you felt an open connection to Talorgan?" Fìna pressed.

Drust cut his gaze back to hers. "That's none of your business, little sister."

"I beg to differ, especially when his actions plague my dreams."

Drust narrowed his eyes on his sister's face, then switched his gaze to Girom, looking from one to the other. "I am wondering why my relationship with my twin brother is suddenly garnering this level of interest. I've had enough of these games, and I have somewhere else to be. Please tell me the reason for your visit so I can be on my way."

"Not out here," Girom replied, inclining his head toward Drust's dwelling. "Inside; out of prying eyes and ears."

"No. I don't have the time for a prolonged visit. I have somewhere I need to be."

Sick of Drust's resistance and aware that time was trickling through his fingers, Girom whispered fiercely, "I know about Cailleach and Tritus!"

Drust flinched, his face draining of color. "Are you here to tell me of his crime in lying with a goddess? Because I want no part in it. The man is my friend."

"Good," Girom replied simply. "Then you will be willing to talk further—*inside.*"

Drust pressed his lips together, but stiffly turned and led the way.

Inside Drust's cottage, Girom spent precious time outlining what had happened the previous night between Cailleach, Talorgan, and Tritus. He also went to great pains to stack the evidence for the changes he'd witnessed in Drust's twin brother, and when he mentioned the Dark God's name, Drust's eyes went slightly wild.

Drust couldn't believe Tritus had died at the hands of his brother. He was willing to confront Talorgan then and there, but Fìna halted him with an imperious lift of her hand. "You are a gifted warrior, but your skills are no match for our brother—not alone, anyway. And have you been listening to what Master Girom has been saying? Talorgan has lost his path; the light has dimmed, and he has fallen to the dark.

His actions have created grave consequences. War is coming, brother, I've seen it."

Drust looked incredulous, his voice thin. "War? With the Dark God?"

"It's inevitable," she confirmed. "And it will commence within a matter of days."

He blanched. "If what you say is true, then we need a unified front. An army capable of addressing not only the physical nature of a battle, but one also versed in the druidic arts."

"Yes, brother, we do," Fìna agreed. "For this shall be a war that will determine the fate of our people, now and forever."

Drust was quiet before a moment, then he asked, "How can there be a war when there are many gods to help our cause? If Cailleach has lost her lover, she will want revenge. She has such power that nothing and no one can stop her. What point is there in forming an army? We will only get between the gods and gamble our lives."

Fìna shook her head. "No, she needs us. Arawn has become powerful. His relationship with Talorgan has opened the floodgates, allowing strength to flow out of this world from our brother's veins and into his. Every disciple our brother turns on Arawn's behalf only increases the Dark God's power on this plane. Already, he builds his army."

Girom's stomach twisted. "He builds an army?" he forced out between stiff lips.

"Yes, with the help of our brother." Fìna started to pace. The dawning sun was now filtering through the cracks in the curtains, cutting the murky darkness with blades of light, and her movements had dust motes bobbing in the still air.

Drust and Girom silently waited on her to continue, and

after circling the room, she stopped and looked at them again. "I have seen many things—not only the pivotal actions of the past, but also our future and what we will become. I will not shield my words, for you both need to hear this. You need to hear what Talorgan has started...." She looked past them, her eyes unseeing of what was in front of her as she focused on the memories of her visions. "The future in my dreams is filled with violence, death, and destruction. Our people are no longer druids, not in the real sense that we are now. The world as we know it no longer exists; Arawn and his creatures free to plunder as they see fit."

"It sounds like a replica of the Dark God's domain," Girom said under his breath.

"Yes, and knowing Arawn craves depravity and power, there's no doubt he will pursue the Other thereafter. No place will ever be safe from his reach, not unless we stop him from encroaching on this world any further than he already has."

There was a ring of truth in Fìna's words. Girom heard it and so did Drust, for when he glanced at the warrior, Girom saw profound grief eclipse the man's skepticism. The severity of what they faced weighed heavy. Their people turning away from the light was hard enough to contemplate, but to destroy this world and the Other? Inconceivable!

From Drust's expression, Girom could see the knowledge of his brother's fall had made its mark. If Drust had been secretly harboring the thought that Talorgan could be redeemed, he wasn't now. Girom took this as his cue to admit he was harboring the Winter Goddess and her child at his summer shieling in the mountains to the north.

He explained he had purposely chosen the location because of the season. It was the cusp of winter, and no one in their right mind would think to visit the mountains now, especially with an infant in tow.

On his annual summer jaunts, Girom had always made sure to keep the location of his shieling a secret. He craved isolation after many moons spent tutoring others, and it was a blessing to have a private sanctuary where he could connect in peace and solitude with the world around him. In hindsight, he now wondered if he had built that sanctuary not for his own needs, but for this one moment in time when he would house Cailleach and her infant.

"Her child survived?" Drust said incredulously.

Girom nodded. "Just barely. We were pursued by one of Arawn's pets." At Drust's lifted brow, he explained, "One of his dragons."

Drust's face paled, the blue tattoo on his left cheek standing out in stark contrast. "A dragon? I thought they were a myth."

"Indeed," Girom admitted, "but we are young, and all of the old stories hold an element of truth. To see this creature in the flesh is enough to loosen your bowels. If Fìna hadn't warned me about exactly what I would come across, I'm not sure I could have saved the goddess and her child."

Drust looked at his sister again, a touch of awe in his eyes. "You knew about the dragon and what was to come?"

Fìna rolled her eyes skyward. "When will you begin to believe in me? I left your dwelling two summers ago. Surely you are aware by now that I am capable of not only living independently, but also of controlling my gift?"

He considered her for a moment, his brow furrowed, then he dipped his head. "I apologize. Forgive me, sister. You are more than capable, and I will not disrespect the power you command again, nor will I risk losing the only family I have left."

Girom felt uncomfortable as tears misted Fìna's eyes. "You will never lose me. We are family and family sticks together."

Drust reached out and squeezed her shoulder before turning back to Girom. "I am sorry for my rude greeting. It appears we are on the same path as I was on my way to see Cailleach."

Girom started. "You were already on your way to see the Winter Goddess?"

Drust nodded. "She called to me in my dreams, and when I awoke, I had the urge to pack my bags and visit her. I had no idea what had transpired, but the urgency in her call was unmistakable."

At Drust's admission, Girom felt even more at rest. It was another confirmation he was on the right path. "Circles within circles," he murmured aloud. Catching Fìna's eyes, he saw recognition there; a knowledge of what he referred to—that they were tied, the three of them together.

Drust interrupted his thoughts. "You said the child survived. What was it? A son? A daughter?"

Girom stared at him blankly. "I did not check."

For a moment, he felt silly, given he'd held the naked infant in his arms. But as he dwelt on the circumstances of that moment, and the evil that had stalked them, he had to admit this wasn't a failing. It was a wonder they had managed to escape Falin with their lives. His left shoulder twinged at the memory of the lancing, red-hot, sliver of dragon's fire Falin had sent through the portal just before it closed. If he had been any slower, Falin would have incinerated him and the child altogether.

The healing of that wound had cost him his power for a few hours after, a few hours that felt long and filled with anxiety due to their vulnerability. He'd been conscious it was the ideal time for Falin or Talorgan to attack. Thankfully, they hadn't, and he'd used the time to formulate a plan to seek help before leaving the goddess alone with her child.

"It is of no matter," Drust dismissed. "However, if I make one request in this world, it is this: I would see my friend's child lead a long life. A child does not deserve to pay the price of the decisions of its parents. I know things would have been simpler if they'd never bonded, but if you'd seen Tritus and Cailleach together, you would have understood that it is hard to ever imagine them apart."

Girom nodded. Yes, he'd seen them together with his own eyes. They'd been a blending of souls, impossible to see one and not the other; a union that was both powerful and undeniable. He shifted uncomfortably. He had never experienced a love such as they had, and given his advanced age, he probably never would.

His body chose that moment to ache, little off-shoots of pain firing from nerve endings that hadn't been activated in a long time. His trek across the countryside to follow Talorgan, and then his mad dash after the Winter Goddess and their escape from the dragon had aggravated the discomfort that came with old age. Noticing a small table and bench seat in the corner of the room, he asked the warrior, "Do you mind if I take a seat?"

"Of course."

Girom slowly lowered himself onto the bench, but just as he sat down, Fìna suddenly gasped aloud and wilted like a flower. He cried out and lunged to grab her; but Drust, with his quick warrior reflexes, caught her just before she hit the ground. He snatched his sister against his chest, face stricken at her sudden loss of consciousness. "Fìna? Fìna!"

When she didn't respond, he started to shake her, his white-knuckled hands clenching her tunic.

Girom reached out and touched his arm. "Cease, warrior. She's alright. Can't you see she's having a vision?"

Eyes wide, Drust stared at him over Fìna's head, and Girom realized the warrior had never witnessed his sister— or any other Dream Walker for that matter—experience a vision before. Aware that he must take charge, Girom barked out sharply, "Lay her on the bed, man. All we can do is leave her to do the gods' work."

Drust released a breath of relief and swiftly carried her to his bed. Once she was lying in comfortable repose, Drust faced Girom again, his features tense. "I didn't think Dream Walkers had visions when they were awake. I thought visions only came in their dreams."

Ignoring his aching bones, Girom pushed himself to his feet and shuffled closer to the young woman, where her brother hovered protectively. "Not necessarily. If the call is strong, a Dream Walker can be receptive to visions at any time." A thought crossed his mind, one that made perfect sense, and one that Drust needed to hear. "It's no surprise this is happening now. Fìna is the strongest Dream Walker in our clan. This is not the first time she has had a vision during the day. Given current events, I have no doubt that whatever she is now witnessing is pivotal to our next steps."

Drust pursed his lips but silently sat beside his sister on the bed, taking one of her hands in his. The silence lengthened between them as they waited for Fìna to regain consciousness. It was a matter of minutes before her eyelids began to flutter and her azure-blue eyes stared back at them.

"How are you?" Drust demanded, leaning closer.

Fìna ignored her brother and started to push herself into a sitting position, but then she winced, lifting a hand to her brow before falling back down against the pillows. "Too soon," she murmured.

"What? What's too soon?" Drust demanded. "Are you alright?"

Fìna waved her other hand dismissively in the air. "Yes, yes, I'm fine, Drust. I just sat up too soon. The vision merely lingered."

"I'll get you some water."

As Drust turned away to fill a cup from his water supply, Girom came closer and leaned over the bed, one hand supporting his lower back. "What did you see, Fìna?"

Fìna cut her gaze to his, her eyes clear and determined. "I saw our path and what it is we have to do."

"Shh, not yet. Drink first," Drust insisted, bringing the cup of water to his sister's lips and supporting her as she sipped.

Surprisingly, Fìna let him tend to her. She silently drank her fill before pushing the glass away. After a huge sigh, she said in a small voice, "There is no escaping what I saw."

They both stood there, waiting, and Fìna's next words fell into the heavy silence. "Death. Death was everywhere."

Girom felt his heart stop, and Drust became as still as stone. "Death?" he repeated. "Whose death, sister?"

"Ours! Our people, the humans, the druids, the fae, the dwarves—everyone who resides on this world!" She said with a lowered voice, "I saw war. Talorgan was there—a disciple still, but no longer to the light. He had embraced his calling, falling completely into the dark. Under Arawn's command, he led an army against us—against those who still held to the light." She swallowed hard. "But what chills my blood was not that I saw war, it was that Talorgan's army weren't strangers. They were friends, family, and comrades."

She raised her head to look at them directly, and the glint of tears shone in her eyes. "How does that happen? What power does Arawn or Talorgan hold that could possibly convert those of us who hold to the light? It was a future of darkness, death being only one mis-step away, one roll of the dice, a stray arrow—it seemed inescapable. And there was poverty...so much hunger, not to mention the loss of hope."

In the silence that ensued, Drust asked evenly, "So, war is inevitable?"

"Yes."

Girom didn't need Fìna to confirm that war was what she had seen in her dreams. He saw it in the shadow of her eyes and in the cant of her features. And given the powers he'd seen Talorgan wield, including the dragon at his back, Girom knew it would be a war that could decimate thousands.

A dark movement, greater than any they'd ever seen before, would soon arise. Girom knew there was a reason why Arawn resided in the Underworld. The Dark God was unable to sustain balance, unable to be two sides of a coin like his other siblings, and if he obtained a permanent foothold on this plane, they would all be lost—their people and this world.

Girom could see Drust's warrior instincts settling upon his shoulders like a cloak. He, on the other hand, did not feel so confident. His stomach roiled. How were they to rally their people against this coming war? A war that would turn comrades into enemies? How were they to know who was susceptible to the dark and who wasn't? What would become of them? What would become of all the people?

His voice was hoarse. "Did you see a way to prevent it from happening?"

"No," Fìna responded, her lips bloodless. "Not the war. There is no way to stop it from coming. Even now, Arawn gathers his army as our brother conscripts them. With the powers the Dark God has bestowed on him, and with Falin at his side, Talorgan has grown all-powerful. He appeared invincible in my dream, as if he were immortal himself." She looked down at her hands, twisting them together in her lap as she whispered, "My visions did not show me a path to stop him, either."

Girom's heart thundered. "There's no hope, then? If our death is inevitable, how are we to rally others to fight against the dark tide coming?"

Fìna looked up sharply, capturing his gaze. "No, Master, not everything is lost. There was a sliver of hope, a flash of fire among the darkness...but it came from an unlikely source."

"What was it?" Drust demanded.

"Not what, but who," she whispered. "I saw a bird, its plumage bright and effervescent, as if it were living, breathing fire. At first, I thought it was one of Arawn's creatures, but it appeared removed from my visions, not a part of his dark army."

Girom felt his heart lurch. It could be only one thing. "You saw the Phoenix?"

"The Phoenix?" Fìna's face filled with wonder. "Yes, you're right."

"Who is the Phoenix?" Drust demanded.

"The Custodian of Creation," Girom responded quietly. "He who rules this world and all others. It can be no other." He grasped Fìna's hand. "What did he say?"

She swallowed. "His message was unmistakable. I saw a babe—an infant, and upon that child's skin lay a mark."

"An infant?" Drust questioned incredulously. "How can an infant change this future?"

"It wasn't just any babe, brother. I knew it immediately for who it was—the vision was clear. It was newly born, fresh and bawling, and it lay in a wooden crib in a stone cottage on the side of a mountain. In that same room, there sat a woman. She was dressed in a white dress, and there was an amber pendant around her neck. Her skin was pale, her ash-blonde hair twisted into a long braid. But it was her eyes that cemented my suspicions; they swirled with a silver fire, sparkling like droplets in the sun."

Girom felt physically ill. He'd left a woman in his shieling who fit such a description. "You saw Cailleach?" he croaked, knowing even as he asked the question that this was so. A shiver of unease ran over his skin at the knowledge of how deep Fìna's gift ran.

Her eyes were grave. "Yes. The vision was delivered with a sense of urgency and great importance. It told me that the child is the key to end this war, that it holds the power to prevent the future I have seen."

Girom thought of the defenseless creature he'd left alone with a mother who was not yet aware of its existence. His stomach roiled at his next thought: What if Cailleach had noticed it in his absence? The goddess was dangerous and unpredictable after losing her lover. Would she be receptive to the infant, or irrationally angry that she'd fled from her lover in order to save it?

He took a breath, trying to calm his turbulent thoughts, and asked, "And when will the child of Cailleach and Tritus save us?"

"I'm not sure. All I had was a sense of urgency and

protection, that and a feeling of importance about the mark on its skin." Fìna frowned, no doubt wondering as they all were, how long it would take the child to grow into its legacy. Was the war to continue for years before it could save them?

"What mark?" asked Girom.

"The mark of love."

Her admission stopped him. Love? Then Girom recalled the child's parents and what they were to each other, what they had felt for each other. But was the child's mark in recognition of its heritage or the legacy that was to come?

"The visions do not show me why, just what will be," Fìna continued. "All I know is that we must protect the child at all costs, as it is the key to ending the war. The vision has made it obvious this task is ours. We must protect it. Knowledge of the babe's legacy will only place the child in danger. There are many who follow the light, but to dangle this sin in front of our people will skew their allegiance. The child is as likely to be killed just as much by our people as by Talorgan. We must keep it safe for whatever task lies ahead."

Drust blanched. He shook his head and stepped back from the bed. "No, Fìna. I will not spend my efforts protecting a child when war beckons, and if what you are saying is true, this war will go on for an undetermined number of years. Our people will need every able fighting warrior they have. Besides, its mother is all-powerful. Cailleach will be more than capable of protecting her child. I am needed to lead our people. I—"

"No, you are not!" Fìna exclaimed sharply, cutting him off. "Nor can Cailleach protect the child while also fighting the coming war. The child will be at risk no matter how powerful its mother is." Her voice was firm. "There is a reason you are in this room, brother—that we are all here together. You were part of this from the beginning. You cannot digress from the path laid before you. Earlier, you were the one who claimed that you wanted the child to live, regardless of its parents' sins. That was more than you talking—that was fate, brother. This is the role you must fulfil."

"No, Fìna," Drust repeated, still shaking his head. "I am a warrior, not a babysitter."

"That is true, and I recognize this path is not your usual one, but it has been foretold."

Drust growled, his hands clenching at his sides. "I cannot stand by and do nothing in this war!" he spat between clenched teeth. "Do not force me, Fìna, for I will not follow your decree, visions or not!"

Fìna studied her brother, her features just as tight. Finally, she conceded, "Alright, I am willing to barter. I will give you leave to fight in this war but only *after* we have saved the child. You have just told me that you would not doubt my power again, yet here you are, questioning it once more." She paused before pointedly adding, "Sometimes our paths are not the ones we would choose, brother."

Drust jaw locked as he stared at his sister, not one inch of him relenting. But on witnessing the determined fire in his sister's gaze, he blew out a breath. "Alright, I will help to protect the child by finding it a safe haven before the war. But I have to warn the chieftain first. If what you say is coming, we must begin preparing for this war now."

Fìna held up a hand. "I will allow you to warn the chieftain, but it must not be done by you personally; a missive from another messenger will do. The Wise Ones will demand that you stay for questioning, and I do not need you distracted from your true path. We do not have time for that just now, as we need to set our next step in motion. And have you forgotten Cailleach is expecting you? We must adhere to her call as soon as possible."

Girom silently watched as Drust considered his sister's points. Eventually, he ground out, "Fine, but as soon as I've seen to the child's safety, I will be returning to serve my role in this war."

Fina nodded, no doubt aware she couldn't hold her brother back, no more than he could hold her back from her chosen path.

Returning to the issue at hand, Girom thought about how Talorgan had known Cailleach was pregnant. Ignoring his churning stomach and the nerves threatening to jeopardize his calm exterior, he mused aloud, "Keeping the child safe might prove to be a difficult task. Talorgan knew the Winter Goddess was with child. How are we to hide its existence from him? Given the extent of his hate and jealousies, Talorgan will hunt it down, especially because its existence will prove a blatant reminder of the union between Cailleach and Tritus."

Fina asked, "Did Talorgan see Cailleach give birth?"

"Not the birth. She delivered the baby after she fled from him." Girom thought about those crucial moments. "But Falin saw the babe. There was no way he didn't, not when I carried it in my arms as we went through the portal. He would have also scented the birthing fluids."

Fina frowned. "Could we claim it died during birth?"

Girom remembered when the dragon had landed. Even though their altercation had lasted mere seconds, that moment had felt like the crawl of a snail, every detail etched in his memory. He remembered the child had cried on being released from its mother's womb, and then again when it had lain bereft and forgotten on the detritus of the forest floor. It had continued to wail until that moment he'd picked it up in his arms. The baby hadn't made a sound as he backed through the portal while facing Falin, nor could he recall a noise when he'd closed it, sealing their escape from the devil's own creature. In fact, he recalled it hadn't been until he'd placed the child in the crib that it had made another noise.

To Fìna, he said, "It's possible Falin did not hear the baby cry."

Hope shone in her eyes. "Then this path has merit."

"But even if we could get away with claiming the babe died in childbirth, how are we to hide it?" Drust cut in. "And how many more people know of Cailleach and Tritus's union? How many others would we need to lie to?"

Girom and Fìna looked at each other, both clearly hoping the other had the answer to Drust's question.

In the silence, Drust added softly, "And are you both aware of the crime that would be committed in supporting the child? I am surprised, Master Girom. You are one of the Masters. How is it that you don't see the child's existence as heinous? Is it not a sin for a mortal to mate with a deity? Is it not an imbalance of nature? Why would you support this child's life?"

Girom narrowed his gaze on the warrior, feeling the wrinkles at the corner of his eyes deepen. "I am aware of this sin," he admitted grudgingly, "but I have been guided these last few months. An otherworldly presence has pushed me onward toward my fate. What that fate is, I admit I don't yet know, but I do know with utmost certainty that the story of Cailleach and Tritus is more than that of a mere mortal and a goddess. There are other hands at play, a greater force is pushing us onward."

"The Phoenix," Fìna murmured.

"Yes, and for that reason, among others, I do not believe the child is sin. My faith in the gods will not allow it, not when I held the babe in my arms. It did not feel wrong, it felt innocent."

"That's because it is," Fìna insisted. "Regardless of who its parents are."

Drust pressed his lips together and nodded tightly. "I had to know where your loyalties lie." Then he shook his head dazedly, and a look of unease crossed his face. "I have no idea where that urge to question your motives came from," he admitted.

But then he caught his sister's knowing gaze, along with her message. He sighed. "Fìna's right. This is my path. I can't deny that I feel compelled to protect the child."

"What do you suggest then, brother?" Fìna asked, her words carrying a tone of triumph.

"We must not voice the child's legacy to anyone outside of this group, no matter whether we win this war or not, or we may well end up fighting our own people. Secondly, how will we keep the child a secret, especially if it shows power like its mother?"

Girom stroked his beard, considering the problem. "If the child is half mortal, it won't show any power for another few years yet. There is time to hide its legacy. Getting it to safety is the priority."

"And that raises the question—where shall we take it?" the warrior returned.

A solution popped into Girom's mind, almost as if it had been thrust there by another—and going by what Fìna had seen, it probably had. A feeling of surety accompanied the thought, and he shared, "Not where but to *whom*, warrior. The child will only survive if it is raised by another." Even as he said the words, Girom felt a prickle run over his skin, the same prickle of awareness that had pushed him to follow his disciple three days earlier. He looked at Fìna, wondering if she felt it, too, and saw the same conviction shining in her eyes that no doubt was mirrored in his own.

"Yes," she breathed. "It is the perfect solution to keeping its lineage a secret. But who shall raise it?"

"Cailleach should make that decision," Girom replied. Again, that level of certainty followed. *Yes. Circles within circles.*

Drust cleared his throat and asked, "Aside from finding someone to raise the child, there's an even bigger problem to address—what if Cailleach doesn't give us the bairn?"

Fìna shot Drust a look under her brows. It was clear she felt no hesitation with this plan. Fìna had seen and accepted her path, and although she was younger than Talorgan and Drust, she carried a level of maturity that belied her age. Girom knew her confidence was due to the level of trust she had in her gift, the knowledge that she carried an unparalleled amount of skill and power. He felt a momentary twinge of jealousy, not only at her freedom to explore the paths before her, but also at her wealth of knowledge.

"She will realize that she has no choice," he replied. "It is obvious Talorgan will not be content to let Cailleach go. He's gone too far to back down. By now, my disciple will understand he's lost everything—his brother and his sister, Cailleach, his place in the clan, even his call to the light. He'll be desperate and will soon realize the only option he has available is to continue what he's started."

"And that is?" Drust asked.

Girom looked at him, wondering at the question. Had the man not known what his twin most desired? Had they really grown that far apart in the last few years? He said quietly, "Your brother seeks to obtain the one true desire that first pushed him down this path: Cailleach."

Drust's eyes widened with shock. He darted a look at his sister. Fìna nodded, confirming Girom's statement. Girom saw no surprise on her face; it was clear she'd known all along.

"I don't understand," he stuttered. "Talorgan is a druid, not a god. Why would he curse and persecute Tritus for the same sin that he himself seeks to commit?"

"Do you doubt what we have told you?" Fìna asked, holding her brother's stare. "Do you doubt Talorgan wouldn't have such lofty goals? That he wouldn't think so highly of himself and his power? He was always conceited. His swift rise among the initiates only amplified his thoughts of superiority."

Drust's gaze skittered away as he admitted softly, "You're right. The statement does not shock me, not when I recall his eagerness to return to the mountain for his annual punishment."

"Yes, his infatuation with her began then. I have seen it all unfold these seven days past."

"You saw his past?" Girom questioned, again in awe of Fìna's power.

"I saw every step he's taken on this journey."

Dream Walkers were not usually receptive to receiving visions of an individual's journey, rather, they saw what affected the clan as a whole. Fìna's gift was rare, a skill that had only been awarded to one other Master in their history. Ligach was one of the first descendants of Cerridwen, the goddess of prophecy, and therefore, his visions of an individual's path were accepted. No other until Fìna could claim the skill.

Her voice was soft as she added, "There is no hope for his return, Drust. Not of the brother we once knew."

Drust flinched, and his words when they came were quiet. "I do not envy you this power, sister, especially when it concerns those you love."

The words were an ignition, for Fìna suddenly snarled, "Talorgan is not one I love!"

Drust stared at her. "No longer, I see."

It was Fìna's turn to look away.

Girom cleared his throat and asked, "Broaching this plan with Cailleach will be our biggest challenge."

"Any ideas?" the warrior asked.

"Just one." As Fìna turned back to face them, her features tight, he continued, "Given she's just had the bairn, she'll be weak and defenseless, still without her full power. Although, with the child's birth, her well will be slowly refilling over the coming days. Talorgan will know there is no better time to come for her than now, and no doubt he plans to take her while Arawn builds his army. Given she won't reach the crux of her power for a few days yet, Cailleach will have no choice but to go into hiding. We could argue that taking the bairn with her is too risky, as it will only slow her down, but if the babe has mortal blood, then the child is in even more danger. We could offer our support to mind the babe while the war rages. I'm sure she'll come to see this as the truth; maybe not right away, but not before too long."

"But Talorgan may still come after the child, no matter whomever we give it to," Drust pointed out. "What of that threat?"

Fìna shook her head. "No, he won't. Not right away. He will be too tied up with conscripting Arawn's army and then participating in the war to come. So will Falin. I doubt

Arawn would be happy to forego one of his greatest assets on a hunt for an infant that can wait until later. We would have time to secret it away."

Drust's lips were a thin line as he gave a decisive nod of agreement. "Then I say we stop talking about it and approach the Winter Goddess. Time wanes."

Girom studied him, suddenly aware of what this would cost the warrior. "So, you would see your brother killed then?" he asked softly.

Drust froze, and Girom watched his features turn into grim determination. "He is no longer my brother. He chose the dark. There is no saving him now."

Girom studied him for a moment, his heart breaking for the young man. He gave a tight nod and turned to Fìna. "And you?"

Her eyes were clear, her voice steady, as she replied, "I follow my brother's decree. The Dark God does not belong here, and Talorgan lost my loyalty when he gave his soul in exchange for dark power. Then he lost my love when he murdered Tritus. Alone, we are no match for him, and if left unchecked, his reach will only grow. I do not wish to see our world subjected to such darkness."

Girom could not deny that he was called, and by the Phoenix no less. And even though the idea of approaching the goddess turned his bowels, there was no one else to hand the task to. He had considered what effect Talorgan's fall to the dark path would have on his people. Druids were human, flawed by fickle desires, and he knew many of them already stood upon a knife's edge, carefully balancing on that line between good and evil. Some fell almost by accident to the dark, but some craved it.

He saw now that Talorgan had walked that line for too long, balancing precariously between the two. In the end, it was his ambition and greed that had been his undoing. Talorgan had thought he was destined for greater things and was unwilling to accept his lot in life. Girom wondered if his fall had always been inevitable, even from the moment of his birth.

Heart pounding at the gravity of the situation, he said aloud, "It is decided. If we can convince Cailleach, the child will be under our protection before the dawn."

CHAPTER 22
GAGE
PRESENT DAY, IRELAND

Brydie was fast asleep, her even breathing the only sound in the room. Her naked body was nestled against my side, with a leg thrown over my thigh. Her face was turned into the crook of my neck, and I was enjoying the closeness. It had been a long time since I'd held a woman for anything more than base needs.

Her fresh pine and frost scent invaded my senses, teasing me softly. My hand drifted down her naked skin to stroke over the rounded curve of her ass. Brydie murmured against my neck, and my groin jerked to attention. I grit my teeth, fighting a desire that never seemed to bank. "Shh, go back to sleep," I murmured.

I felt her lips curve against my neck as she nuzzled closer, resettling against my side. As her breathing once again evened out, I forced my hands to remain where they were. Touching her would only fan the flames; it wouldn't get me to sleep. For a moment, I contemplated returning to my room, but leaving her wasn't an option, and I doubted sleep would come to me even if there was physical distance between us. Not now.

It was now obvious that withholding myself from Brydie had been a goddamn waste of time. Ever since I'd first laid eyes on her, there was a strong desire to be close to her, to touch her, to claim her, to be more than what we were. She was a flame that had burned ever brighter.

I'd denied it from day one, shoving that relentless desire to the back of my mind, striving not to acknowledge how my body jerked to life or how my pulse hammered with need. It was a battle I'd fought for almost five long months, exhausting in and of itself. Through all the training and all the physical contact, watching her interact first with Ian and then my brother—it had been a long, hard road of denial that had damn near killed me.

I admitted to myself in the quiet of the room that it had been a relief to give in to my desire and finally claim her. There had been no holding back, no worrying that what we were doing was wrong. I'd fallen into our joining with my eyes wide open, my chest burning with emotion. I'd hoped it would be the end of this relentless longing, this thorn in my side, this *need* to consume her. I'd hoped that after taking this last step, that desire would begin to bank and then decline upon its natural path—as it had with every other woman.

But that hadn't happened. I hadn't immediately returned to my room. I'd stayed. Next to her. Holding her. Relishing the closeness. And what I hadn't counted on was how that burning desire had increased tenfold. Brydie was just like my fire, a flaming conflagration of a thousand embers that never stopped smoldering, constantly increasing in heat... and I was the paper, waiting to be burned.

Trapped. I was goddamn trapped...but it didn't upset me as much as it should. And here was the problem.

My jaw clenched as I thought of the power Brydie unknowingly wielded over me. She had me by the balls. After our explosive joining, I was invested, physically and emotionally. This feeling of hope, of happiness, and what felt like completeness, fucking scared the crap out of me. These emotions were new and foreign. I'd only ever attributed them to my brother and my son before. And now for the first time, I had feelings for a woman—and not just any woman, but the goddamned Daughter of Winter! The woman I'd tried to deny from the first moment we met. I could well understand that if the Guardians before me had felt a small measure of what I did at this moment for their own Daughter's, nothing could have prevented their final culmination.

Just as nothing could have prevented their final sacrifice to keep their Daughter safe.

My heart thumped against my ribcage as an image of Talorgan appeared in my mind's eye. Our final altercation was eight months away. Samhain drew ever nearer, and even though there was power in this world, there was never enough to stop the sun. Their meeting was inevitable.

I tightened my hold, pulling Brydie even closer to my side, aware that this moment, though initiated by a fire of jealousy, was precious in itself. We were on limited time. Come Samhain, one or both of us might no longer be here.

Tap. Tap. Tap.

The sound was soft, yet insistent, breaking that quiet hush before dawn broke. The skin at my neck tingled, and I turned to stare out the glass doors, my lips peeling back as I caught the sharp gaze of a black corvid. The crow cocked its head to the side as it blatantly turned its attention to the naked woman lying wrapped around my body.

I bit off the curse that threatened to awake Brydie and carefully slid out from underneath her. She protested in her sleep, hands clenching in the space I'd been. I ran a hand down her back, murmuring softly as I pulled the covers up, using my body to block Lorcan's view. There was no way in hell that man was seeing any more of what was mine.

With the comforter pulled up to her chin and Brydie now resettled back into slumber, I shoved into my jeans before stepping onto the balcony. As I gently closed the door behind me, the crow launched into the air, its wings rustling. There was a flash of light, followed by a barrage of black smoke. Seconds later, Lorcan stood before me.

He flashed me a smile. "Aren't you going to thank me?"

I was still on edge; still pissed he'd touched my woman. "Why the fuck would I thank you, Lorcan?"

He raised a brow. "Oh, come on, Gage. Don't pretend to be naïve. You know as well as I do that if I hadn't gone preying on your territory, you would still be stuck in an agonizing gridlock of indecision."

A cold, hard burn of anger licked down my spine, and my voice was deadly. "Are you telling me that you purposely came onto her just to get a rise out of me?"

"It worked, didn't it?"

I didn't even blink. I lunged. My fist connected with his jaw in a stinging blow. I felt my knuckles tear as they grazed against his teeth, and I relished the burn, knowing as he reeled backward and raised a hand to his face that the pain was worth it. "Don't you ever fucking play games like that again," I growled. "Brydie is not a pawn, and I refuse to be manipulated."

Lorcan had gone still, and the other hand held at his side had curled into a fist. "I'll let you have that, Guardian," he bit out in a low voice, all the more menacing because he did not roar. "But if you ever touch me again, not only will my offer of sanctuary be revoked, but so will the support of my people in this coming war. You'll be on your own, whether she is the descendant of Cailleach or not."

He was dead serious. "Descendant of Carman or not?" I returned in a hard voice.

A muscle jerked in his jaw. "Touché," he acknowledged on a snarl.

I smiled then, but I had to acknowledge it was bittersweet—I'd been played whether I liked it or not. Yet Lorcan's actions gave me pause, because he never did anything without gain. I watched him carefully, weighing every nuance of his expression. "What do you want, Lorcan? Regardless of what you say, there was a reason you orchestrated that meeting with Brydie tonight. And given you're back here again, there's clearly something else you need."

Lorcan fingered his jaw as he carefully watched me in turn. "You're wrong. I just wanted you to know you owe me." His teeth flashed in the semblance of a smile. "After all, just think about how you'd be feeling if you were sleeping in your room, alone, torn, and frustrated right now."

Fuck! He'd used my emotions for Brydie to elevate his own position. He thought he'd done me a favor? That his actions warranted repayment? I snarled, "There is no debt."

Lorcan cocked his head to the side. "No? Well, I can revoke my gift quite easily. It's not a chore to call Brydie to my bed, whether you've been with her first or not."

I snarled again, the sound torn from my chest, and my next words were quiet but said with deadly conviction. "Leave her alone. She's mine."

"Well, well," Lorcan murmured, that smile not slipping. "Then it appears you are in my debt; but don't worry, I won't be calling in that favor just yet."

I clenched my fists, urging myself to hold it together. I could taste the smoke curling on my tongue, knew I was close to bursting. *Control. You need to regain control.* I took a breath and finally said, "We'll see about that. You're lucky you managed to leave here with dignity."

He simply smiled wider. "Good thing Brydie likes me."

I grit my teeth, holding back the instinctual urge to smash him in the jaw again. Forcing my fists to relax, I used the moment to look him up and down, eying his brown leather pants and naked chest. Why did he persist in wearing no clothes and get around half-naked? Conceited asshole.

There was a glint in his eye as I cut my gaze back to his face, as if he knew my thoughts. I asked bluntly, "What did you talk about with Brydie, anyway?"

"Wouldn't you like to know?" he returned softly.

I was in no state for games. "Tell me."

"Or you'll what?" he smirked. "Make a fool out of yourself by asking Brydie?"

I bit my tongue. *Don't overreact.*

At my silence, Lorcan's smile grew wider. "I thought so. Well, for the moment, it will be my little secret with Brydie."

My chest burned at the implied closeness. "Just get on with it," I ground out. "What do you want, Lorcan? As you can see, I'm busy."

His eyes flicked back into the room, landing on Brydie. "Yes, aren't you just."

I hissed through my teeth, possession writhing to the surface, and felt rather than saw my palms burn, coming alight with a red flame. Lorcan's eyes dropped to my hands.

"My, we are lacking patience tonight, I see. And even after the release you've no doubt enjoyed."

I growled, my body locked tight as my control teetered. "Last chance, Lorcan. Tell me why you're here and then goddamn leave!"

He inclined his head, and with a mocking smile, murmured, "As you wish."

I didn't relax until he turned to lean against the wooden balcony, looking out into the dark forest beyond. When he again spoke, his voice had lost all sense of mirth, the tone now serious. "Initial discussions with my people have confirmed they are willing to support your mission to rescue the fifth descendant."

I came to a stop a few feet away from him, but instead of looking out into the forest, I watched his profile. "In what way?"

"By offering a diversion when you enter the Institute." Lorcan cut his gaze to mine, and I saw how his green irises had narrowed into slits. It was an indication that he could also see in the dark, a blessing of his corvid form.

I considered his response, not denying that I was disappointed. "And that's all?"

Lorcan's tone was firm. "I won't push them to offer more than they are willing. Not after one of your own stole the Dagda's cauldron."

The dig rankled. Callum was a fucking thorn in my side everywhere I turned. "Callum is not our people, Lorcan. I promise you that not all The Oaken Tree are your enemy, and I can guarantee that at least half of them won't even know what Callum has in his possession."

Lorcan merely looked at me. "We shall see."

It was useless to push the issue, not when I wasn't sure how far Callum's stain had spread among our people.

Ignoring the foreboding prickle at the back of my neck, I let the insult rest and focused on Lorcan's message. "We greatly appreciate whatever help your people are willing to offer."

He inclined his head. "When you have your plan firmed up, come and see me, and I will relay any messages you require."

"Thank you."

Lorcan turned, and I felt his gaze move beyond me. Ire flared anew at the knowledge that he was once again looking at my woman. A woman we both knew was naked under those blankets. I shifted, moving to intercept his line of vision with my body.

He cut his eyes to mine, that irritating smile back on his lips. "Easy tiger, you have nothing to fear. Even though I offered her solace, she refused me."

I tensed as the words rolled over me. *The bastard!* My lips peeled back to expose my teeth. "You fucking stay away from her, or I will not be responsible for what happens next."

Lorcan lifted his hands, palms up. "Jealousy does not become you, Gage. Just be thankful you've managed to reel in the prize you most desire."

I shot him a dark look, finally aware of the game he was playing, aware of what he was doing to me. The asshole liked to rile me up, liked to push my buttons. I could understand that living in Faerie didn't offer much in the way of entertainment, but he'd pushed me too damn far. "Piss off, Lorcan. You're not needed or wanted here."

"No, it appears not." His amused gaze returned to Brydie, and I could have sworn there was a softening to his features as he gazed at her one last time. Before I had a chance to consider that look, he turned back to face me. "Just don't screw this up, Gage."

And with that, he once again became the crow. But as I watched Lorcan wing his way through the dark forest, I wasn't sure if his last statement had been in reference to rescuing Chloe or the new relationship I'd just started with Brydie.

CHAPTER 23

BRYDIE

PRESENT DAY, IRELAND

I awoke when I was tugged against a hard, unyielding body. Even before I opened my eyes, I knew who lay beside me. His scent enveloped me, an overwhelming aroma of woodsmoke and forged steel. It was everything that Gage was, everything he imbued. A sharp scent that could protect as well as kill. And he was all mine.

I breathed in his scent and kept my eyes closed for a while longer. I acknowledged how my body felt sore, the skin sensitive, my internal muscles aching. It reminded me of the night I'd just spent, and a smile tipped my lips as I relived the moments of our explosive union.

"You're awake."

The voice was soft, but the tone held enough sexual promise that my toes curled. Desire instantly flared, relentless and all-consuming, and I opened my eyes, instantly captured by his cerulean gaze. There was that usual sharpness to it, an ever-present awareness of everything around him while also being wholly focused on me. But this morning there was also something different, something that hadn't been there before—a softening acceptance, and a returning thirst that couldn't be slaked.

"Good morning," I whispered, reaching out to tug him down for a kiss.

He came willingly, and I sighed as his lips touched mine. I felt the scratch of stubble against my chin as our tongues met in a slow, suggestive duel. My fingers tightened in his hair as I felt my body ignite, sleep forgotten.

His hands snaked around my back and he rolled, pulling me on top of him. I relished the contact of our naked flesh and moaned softly as he deepened our kiss, conscious of the hand that ran down my back to cup my ass with a possessiveness that made my chest tight. I was ready for him after just one kiss.

I pushed myself into a sitting position and rubbed myself against him as I hovered on my knees above him. Capturing his eyes, I deliberately placed my hands on his chest and began to slide downward.

He growled as I took him inside me. "Christ!"

As I sank down on him, I asked huskily, "Are you objecting?"

"Hell no!" His hands possessively gripped each of my thighs. "But you're mistaken if you think you'll be leading this race."

Before I had a chance to understand what he meant, he'd twisted me sideways and we rolled, still joined together. Our positions now reversed, he lifted one of my legs over his shoulder. "Alright?" he murmured, his cerulean eyes intent on my face as he moved his hips in a teasing thrust.

My breath hitched as the movement angled his penetration even deeper, igniting a flood of pleasure. "Yes," I breathed.

"Good." His features changed into an expression I now

recognized; a slash of red staining his cheekbones as he succumbed to the pleasure of our bodies. "Stay with me."

It was the only warning I had before he opened his mind and allowed everything he was feeling to flood down our shared internal line. I was immediately overwhelmed with sensation, feeling every movement he felt, experiencing the ebb and flow of the pleasure growing between us. This connection between us went both ways; I knew he felt my own pleasure, my own emotions. What we shared was more than just a joining of our bodies; it was raw, it was honest, and it was deep, with nowhere to hide.

His eyes held mine as they had last night, and in the light of the new dawn, I met each of his movements with a returning thrust of my own. That pinnacle of pleasure was upon me before I was even aware of its presence, and I sailed over it in a pool of golden light with the knowledge that Gage went with me.

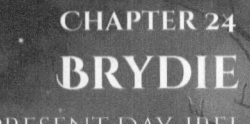

CHAPTER 24
BRYDIE
PRESENT DAY, IRELAND

I sat down at the breakfast table to a weighted silence. Gage was eating a steaming plate of bacon and eggs without any indication that he'd had no sleep last night. Logan sat on the opposite side of the table, a fork poised halfway to his mouth. His bloodshot eyes cut to mine as soon as I sat down. "Nice of you to join us on this glorious morning, Brydie. You look refreshed."

His tone was mocking, in complete contrast to the sour look on his face. I felt the blush creep up my neck. It was inevitable Logan would know of what had happened between me and Gage last night. He would have felt it, which explained the dark circles under his eyes and his surly disposition.

"Good morning," I replied in as normal a voice as I could muster, reaching for some toast and spreads.

I glanced at him out of the corner of my eye to find there was a faint smile tipping his lips. "I would like—" he began.

"Leave her alone," Gage cut in sharply before taking a swig of his coffee.

Logan's smile stretched across his face. "Oh, come on,

brother, I've been waiting too long for this. The girl deserves a fucking medal to have taken you on."

There was a scuffle under the table.

"That was uncalled for," Logan muttered as he reached down under the table.

"It's none of your business," Gage growled.

"Oh, I beg to differ, brother, especially when I could feel *everything* that was going on last night...and again this morning. Suffice to say, I've had no bloody sleep."

My cheeks flamed. "I'm sorry."

"Oh, no need to be sorry," Logan returned swiftly. "I should be thanking you. I've been sick and tired of the bear my brother has become these last few months. I'm hoping he'll now be more even keeled. If Lorcan will allow me to sleep elsewhere, this will all work out much better than before."

Something settled in my stomach at his acceptance. I swallowed this knowledge, feeling a warmth spread throughout my chest.

"No," Gage said bluntly. "You're not sleeping elsewhere, Logan."

Logan frowned at his brother. Then he shrugged and muttered, "Guess I'll have to look into finding myself a woman of my own then. It's either that, or I'll have to employ mindfulness techniques."

"The latter, or you're leaving."

Logan's brow rose. "You drive a hard bargain, and so thoughtfully too, brother. I'm beginning to believe you're suffering my presence." He smirked.

"Like I've said many times before, Logan, it's your choice to stay, but if you do, you have to follow my rules."

Logan lifted both of his hands. "Alright, fine. Mindfulness techniques it is."

"It's not a silly request, Logan. With Samhain approaching, you'll need the exercise. I don't want you falling prey to Talorgan's coercion because you were too lazy to practice. Block me out."

Logan's brow rose. "Block you out? You're like a fucking billboard, man. I can feel everything!"

I squirmed as images of what Gage and I had done together replayed in my mind.

"Besides," Logan continued with a mischievous smile, "I think I'm going to enjoy the reprieve throughout the day; your usual angst is gone."

Gage grunted and aimed another kick under the table.

Logan winced just as Ian walked into the room. His brown hair was rumpled and he was dressed in his usual slacks and shirt. "Morning," he mumbled as he beelined for the coffee pot.

I murmured a response as he helped himself to a cup of steaming black coffee and took a seat next to Logan. Ian took a few gulps of the burning liquid as if his life depended on it before asking, "What's on the agenda today?"

Gage placed his knife and fork on his empty plate and pushed it away. "Lorcan has confirmed the fae will help us enter the Institute by providing a diversion. We're leaving in three days. "

Ian paused, his coffee cup partway to his lips. "So soon? Do we know how we're getting in?"

"Alison has confirmed Callum will be away that evening. It's our best opportunity. I know a way in. Our only task now is to find enough power to portal there. As we're in Ireland, the obvious choice would be through Slieve na Calliagh."

Ian considered Gage's response. "I agree; the tombs are powerful conduits. They'll have sufficient power to create a portal both in and out. I assume you want me to determine the hours of operation and the best way to get inside Hag's Cairn?"

"We should use the power of the spring equinox stone," Gage replied. "It's the only object with enough energy anywhere near here. We need to ensure we don't lead Callum or Talorgan back here, and being at County Meath will throw off our trail."

Ian nodded. "I'll get onto it." He took a sip of his coffee, his eyes flicking to mine briefly as he asked Gage, "What are you two doing today?"

"Resuming Brydie's training. We'll be out all day."

His brows rose. "All day?"

"It's time to work on her other skills." Gage shot me a look as he added, "I haven't forgotten the story you shared about the sapling."

I swallowed. He was talking about that moment in the bush with my father—when I'd shown Dad what I could do. I now knew that had led him to contact the fae in the hopes of suppressing my memory. It was ironic we'd come full circle and I was now in their territory. But the thought of trying to use that part of my power had my stomach roiling.

Gage must have felt my discomfort for he twisted in his seat to face me directly. "It's imperative we know how deep that thread of power runs. We're going to need all your skills to best our enemies." He reached out and placed a hand over mine. "It will be alright. Trust me."

Forcing everything down, I said with no hesitation, "I do."

Logan held a soft smile as he looked from me to Gage before returning to his breakfast, but Ian's brown eyes were narrowed on our hands. To where Gage's thumb was caressing my knuckles.

Ian looked between us, and a dawning conclusion came

over his features. Gage's hand stilled on mine, and I knew without looking that he, too, was watching Ian, waiting on his response.

"I see you two are getting along much better now." Ian's words were clipped, the tone carefully neutral.

Gage squeezed my hand before lifting it to pick up his coffee. "Yes."

At Gage's non-committal response, Ian's face went tight. I looked at him with an apology in my eyes. There was nothing else to say. His lips twisted. "No need to worry, Brydie. There is life after loss as I very well know."

"I'm sorry, Ian."

But the apology wasn't what he'd wanted. His brown eyes widened behind his glasses, turning hard. "Oh, don't get me wrong, I'm happy for you both. Ecstatic even. But it's not every day that your best friend takes your woman."

I felt Gage tense beside me as I tried to reign in my anger. "I was never your woman, Ian," I said firmly.

He didn't even flinch. "Yes, you made that clear on Beinn na Caillich."

My words were soft. "I made a mistake, and I'm sorry. I thought we'd moved on from this."

He stared at me, his lips in a tight line. "Oh, we have. Don't worry about my tender constitution, Brydie. I've suffered greater losses than your supposed affection."

Like the murder of his ex-wife and unborn child. My stomach turned.

Gage growled, "Lay off."

The warning was clear, but Ian didn't heed it. "Why? Do you speak for her now? It's clear you two have finally addressed the attraction simmering between you like a fucking red flag. I'm relieved you've tackled the goddamn elephant in the room, but I'm also wondering what consequences this will have for our party. You've been adamant from the beginning there is no room for relationships in this game, Gage. Your double standards make me question your leadership—it makes me wonder if you're already compromised."

Logan swore. "Ian, you don't mean that. Stop it. You're being a fucking idiot."

But Ian and Gage weren't listening.

Gage shoved his chair back from the table, his hands clenching. I jumped up and grabbed his arm before he did something he'd regret. "Gage, stop."

He didn't look at me, his body bristling as he faced Ian. "Don't say another fucking word or you'll regret it," he ground out.

"Or what? You'll try to beat some sense into me?" Ian returned softly as he deliberately placed his mug on the table and pushed to his feet. He stood a foot taller than Gage, but his presence didn't elicit a modicum of the danger lurking under my Guardian's skin. "You'll win this fight, Gage, but will it make you believe the line you've stepped over was worth it?" he sneered. "I don't see how when it's your own logic you're fighting."

Ian looked unfamiliar. No longer friendly, no longer someone I could rely on.

"I was wrong," Gage bit out. "I tried to fight what's between me and Brydie, I really did, but it's goddamn impossible." His hands clenched by his sides, the knuckles white, as he said, "I don't expect you to understand, Ian."

Ian bristled. "I—"

Logan, who had been quiet to this point, stood up with his cup and plate in hand and interrupted, "Well, as much as I'd like to argue the merits of fate and whether any of you can change what's happening here, I'm not going to waste the morning. I'm out of here because this conversation is pointless."

As Logan turned to put his dishes in the sink, Ian let out a mirthless laugh. "Is that what you think, Logan? That your brother is caught in a trap of fate? That he has no choice in how he feels and acts around Brydie?"

Logan turned to face him, his features carefully blank. "Don't you?" He lifted his chin in our direction. "Can't you see they are tied together; that their paths are aligned? It's more than a push of fate between them. There's a joining of souls. Anyone can see they both want this, whether they're guided by fate or not. I can feel a sense of rightness in their union, and if you let yourself, you will too."

Ian's jaw clenched, and he turned to spear us with his gaze again. At that moment, McKenzie and Aidan walked into the room.

McKenzie halted just inside the door, immediately sensing the hostile atmosphere. "What's going on?" she demanded in way of greeting, pulling Aidan protectively close to her side. Jack let out a little yip.

"Ian and I were having a...discussion," Gage replied carefully. "But I think we've settled our disagreement, haven't we, Ian?"

Ian's face remained tight, but his tone held a touch of sarcasm. "It appears that fate led us to have this confrontation."

McKenzie looked between us, understanding dawning in her expression as it flicked between me and Gage. "Oh, I see," she murmured. She gave Aidan a little push toward the kitchen. "Go and get some breakfast, son."

Aidan looked a little confused as he looked up at his mom. "What's going on, Mom? What was that all about?"

She smiled gently. "Nothing, sweetheart. Everything's fine."

He looked between us before he shrugged and moved for the toaster.

Logan ruffled the boy's head as he moved past him and turned back to Gage. "I'm off to check out this joint. I'm hoping to get some new ideas for a future condo. I think a tree house resort will go down well with romantic couples." He didn't smile, but he sent me a wink over his shoulder as he exited the room, adding, "Good luck training today, Brydie."

I stuck my tongue out at him and turned back to Gage. "Come on, let's make a start. I have a feeling we won't be coming back until I've made progress."

Gage shot me a look under his brows. "Am I that predictable?"

McKenzie snorted behind me. "Hell yes."

Gage let me pull him from the room, but as we passed through the door, I couldn't help looking over my shoulder back to Ian. When I caught the expression on his face, there was no denying the foreboding flutter in my stomach as we left the room.

"Again!" Gage demanded.

I grit my teeth, trying to focus on the sapling before me. Yet, no matter how hard I tried, it did not lengthen or sprout more leaves. "It's no use," I panted. "There's nothing there."

I looked up at him as he stood beside me. There was a predatory watchfulness in his gaze, a blatant possessiveness that hadn't been there before. And my body responded to it. His eyes glittered. I knew he could feel my emotions down our shared internal line, just like I could feel his returning lust. The difference was that Gage's mind was on the task at hand whereas mine wasn't.

"You're not looking in the right place. Think of your magic as being compartmentalized. Weather magic will utilize different energy reserves and require a heavier hand given the various elements you are required to control. Earth magic responds to a gentler touch. Use mindfulness to connect to the plants, the insects, and the soil. Be still and calm. Focus."

"It's not as simple as that," I protested, rocking back on my heels.

"It is," he insisted. "And if you don't keep your mind on the job, you'll be here all night."

I considered him for a moment. "What's in it for me?"

"Mastering another skill, for one."

"You misread my intention, Guardian." I trailed my eyes down his body, which was in his usual black jeans, black leather jacket, and black boots. His hair glinted blue-black in the afternoon sun, offsetting his brilliant cerulean eyes. I met that intense blue gaze as I asked huskily, "I was thinking of other...rewards."

His eyes darkened as he returned, "I can think of a few."

At that illicit promise, I dropped my gaze to find he was thinking the same thoughts I was. *Finally.* I pushed to my feet and took a step toward him.

Gage immediately stepped back. "If we start that, we won't get anywhere," he warned.

I put a hand on my hip, giving him my best smile. "But we've been going for hours; I need a break."

His features remained firm, unswayed. "No. If you think that moving into our new relationship would mean we would no longer need to train and master your skills, you were wrong. I am even more motivated than I was before to keep you safe."

I paused, sensing the layers of truth in his response. He was firm in his position, the emotions arrowing down our shared line confirming he wouldn't budge on this. I should be just as focused, but the change in our relationship had created an emotion I hadn't felt in a very long time. I was happy. Truly happy.

But I knew Gage was right. Learning to master my earth magic would grant me more of a chance to secure a future past Samhain. One with my Guardian, where more of these moments could occur. With the promise of that future in mind, I sighed and turned back to the sapling.

Gage's voice was quiet beside me. "You must want to take action, Brydie. You must want the magic to come forth."

"Do I need to be driven by anger to do so?" I asked, thinking about how he'd pushed me in all our previous trainings; how I'd automatically responded to the threat Garret had posed.

Gage shook his head. "Anger; no. Emotion; yes. It is emotion that drives all power, but before that comes willpower and a belief in yourself to wield it. "

That made sense. Anger had worked for me in the past because it was Gage who I'd been angry at. But since angst wasn't between us any longer, I needed another emotion to drive that need. An image of Chloe came to mind, and I imagined her with Callum, imagined all the things he could have done to her—could still be doing to her. Within moments, I felt the emotion roil inside me—fear, anger, rage.

Holding those emotions tight to my chest, I focused on the inner core of power, willing my earth magic to come to the fore. I imagined the sensation of running my fingers through a cool pool, of feeling the damp earth between my toes, the pungent scent of the bush, and visualized a forest scene back in New Zealand, the fronds of the palm trees and the forest canopy cool and inviting above my head. Holding those senses, I closed my eyes and spread my hands upon the earth, fueling them with the anger I carried about Chloe's situation.

I felt the damp soil and the soft, springy moss between my fingers. I heard the trill of a jay bird, then the soft whirring noise of another bird flying overhead. Inhaling deeply, I smelled the musty damp scent of the detritus of the forest floor and listened closely to the rustle of the leaves as a small breeze carried past me. I breathed in and out, once, twice, three times. On the fourth inhale, I visualized the sapling at my feet, imagined it lengthening, a plethora of leaves bursting forth.

I heard a grunt, and my eyes flew open. Hardly daring to breathe, I looked at the sapling. It was no longer thin and spindly but bursting with fresh, new growth, its previously thin trunk now straight and tall. "It worked!" I crowed.

"So it did," Gage replied, his eyes gleaming with pride.

My heart leapt at the raw emotion. I pushed to my feet and prowled toward him, my mind no longer on the sapling, but on him and how he made me feel. Gage watched me come, his cerulean eyes roving possessively down my body. "Come to claim your reward?" he asked softly.

"I think I deserve it," I replied, stepping into his arms.

They tightened around my back like iron bands, then his head was moving, swooping down to take my lips. My hands thrust into his hair, grasping the silky strands as I pushed up on tiptoe and planted an open-mouthed kiss into the side of his neck.

A soft growl escaped his lips.

"You're sensitive there," I murmured against his skin, now feathering kisses along his jaw.

"And you're sensitive here," he returned, one hand reaching for my breast. I couldn't deny it as he massaged it skillfully, the nipple hardening. "But as much as I'd love to fulfill my promise here and now, I told you that I don't share." In the next moment, his hand was gone from my breast.

I jerked back. "What?"

He nodded toward the trees. "We're not alone. No one is seeing my woman."

His possessive tone had a flush running over my body, and I felt a similar possession bloom inside me as I remembered the male and female sentries. "Nor are they seeing my man."

His eyes gleamed, his lips lifting in a devilish smile as he held out a hand. "Let's go then."

Not hesitating, I took his hand.

CHAPTER 26

GIROM

3RD CENTURY BC, ANCIENT SCOTLAND

I t took Girom a matter of moments to relocate the warrior and his sister to the mountain where the shieling lay. But as they stepped through his portal in direct view of the stone cottage, he felt his resolve begin to waver. He wasn't so sure the goddess would simply pass over her child. What if she'd bonded with it while he'd been away... or worse—killed it?

The sun was now lowering over the horizon, casting a purple haze over the mountains. It was confirmation he'd been gone the whole day, which was a long time to spend in isolation with a baby that would remind its mother of her recently murdered lover.

The others halted beside him, no doubt conscious of his indecision but also aware of who awaited them inside the stone building. Because, for all their discussion, if the Winter Goddess did not agree with their plan, everything was for naught.

It had been a struggle for Girom to use his magic again. Opening portals was draining, and never in his sixty odd years had he opened so many in the span of a few days. He was exhausted and very, very cold.

The thin mountain air was on the cusp of winter. It bit through his green robe, a reminder of the coming festival. Samhain was a joyous occasion, a chance for his people to give thanks and celebrate the bounty they'd gathered over the summer before they embraced the darker half of the year. And because the veils between the worlds were at their thinnest, it was also a time to commune with loved ones who had crossed over to the Other. It was often a time of peace. But not this year. This year, Girom had no doubt Samhain would be marked by the clash of weapons and the pungent stench of death.

Fìna had confirmed the war would begin on the eve of Samhain, two nights hence. Girom felt lost, because what could they possibly achieve in three days? Not much. Still, a missive had already been sent to their chieftain, requesting that he contact their cousins across the salty sea to the west for their aid in the coming war. They did so knowing that even if their cousins decided to aid them, their support would be delayed because many were not gifted in the art of portaling; the majority would have to journey across the sea in a vessel… which meant their people would start this war alone.

Girom's body audibly creaked as he took the first step toward the cottage. The loose shingle skittered under his feet, causing his heart to pound. He half-expected the Winter Goddess to come rushing out to attack them, but all remained silent inside the shieling.

With Fìna and Drust at his heels, he pulled aside the hide door and stepped inside. The soft, flickering firelight cast long shadows, and he paused as the others entered behind him, allowing his eyes to adjust to the dim interior.

"So, the green druid has returned, and with visitors, no less." The slurred, gnarled speech was filled with rasping snorts and gnashing teeth and was coming from the shadows in the far corner of the room.

Girom squinted, but he couldn't discern her form in the shadows. Raising his hands in peace, he held steadily to his nerve and said softly, "One of these visitors is someone you requested, my lady. I found him on my return to the shieling."

The atmosphere suddenly chilled when an icy breeze entered the cottage and rippled around the room. Girom shivered as it found the small crevices in his green robe, stabbing his skin with glacial needles.

Cailleach snarled in a voice laced with menace, "And how do you know that, druid?" There came a whispered shuffling, and a giant figure loomed before them, exposed by the flickering firelight.

Girom gasped. No longer stood the breathtakingly beautiful goddess of before, the one who had been broken and in shock when he left the shieling. Instead, before him now stood a giant crone, withered and aged by a thousand suns. Gone also was the stunning, iridescent white gown that glittered like innocence. In its place was a black wolf pelt. It stretched across her shoulders, covering the drab gray plaid underneath while the head of the beast stared back at them with a threat that belied its death.

His eyes rose to her face, and he found he couldn't shift them. Fixated with a horror that robbed his mind of thought, all he could do was stare at the bulging gray face in front of him. His eyes traced her blackened lips before moving to the two large tusks protruding between them. His mouth parted on a croak, and he stumbled backward into Fìna. She let out a small cry and dropped to her knees, head bowed in supplication. At the same time, Drust fell into a similar position on the other side of him. Their movements jolted him from his shock, causing him to become blatantly aware that he was the only one not giving the goddess her due. Swallowing, he immediately followed suit, his old bones audibly popping in the weighted silence.

Girom's body trembled with terror. He knew her visage would be forever imprinted on his memory, regardless of whether he survived this encounter or not. It was the first time he'd laid eyes on the winter crone. He'd heard stories, yes, but hadn't known whether to believe them, especially after he'd seen Cailleach as a beautiful woman. *Where had that woman gone?*

Above them, there came a series of snuffling snorts, and it took Girom a moment to realize the goddess was laughing. He raised his head to stare in horrified awe as the giant crone took a step closer. With spittle flying from her mouth, she drawled around her tusks, "I see my presence is not as pleasing as before. Along with the mantle of winter, it was a gift bestowed upon me by my brother's bride for a crime *he* committed. However, it suits the purpose before me, just as your presence does, because I find I have need of all three of you in the coming war."

Girom swallowed hard, fighting the erratic beat of his heart and the chilling fear traveling down his spine. To hear her confirm that the war approached was the final puzzle piece slotting into place—a resignation that what they were experiencing was in fact, truth. But what of the child? Where was it? Had this beast killed it?

As if in answer, there came a cry, piercingly sweet and innocent from the shadows where Cailleach had been standing. Girom heard Fìna's relief in the audible release of her breath. The action also seemed to propel Drust into motion. The warrior was the first to come to his feet.

As Girom and Fìna followed suit, Drust said with a bowed head, "I have come as you requested, my lady. On my travels I was intercepted by Master Girom and my sister, Fìna. They told me what had befallen you and Tritus, including Arawn's arising." He halted, and his next words were thick. "I am sorry to hear of Tritus's passing, my lady. He was my friend, and my heart grieves that he is gone. I am also sorry for the part my brother played in his death. Please understand I do not condone his actions, and I am yours to command in this war."

The crone seemed to wither at the stark reminder of the loss of her lover, and Girom tensed as he waited on the Winter Goddess to lash out at what had surely opened a fresh wound. But her words were almost distant, as if she'd removed herself from all emotion.

"And command you I will, warrior. However, you are misinformed. I did not ask you here to participate in the coming war. There is a treasure I need you to protect at all cost—something more important than anything else on this earth."

Drust, with head still bowed, lifted his eyes to the goddess' face and asked the question they were all thinking. "And what is it that you need me to protect, my lady?"

Girom was thankful the young warrior had remembered to focus his gaze away from her eyes, for to hold the Winter Goddess's gaze was to court death. The power of her stare was all-consuming, able to entrap the mind and raze all memories to the ground. Girom himself ensured his own regard did not waver from the bridge of her hooked nose.

The words were soft, layered with an emotion that even her grotesque tusks could not mask. "My child."

Drust didn't hesitate. "Of course, my lady. It would be my honor."

Girom felt Fìna wilt beside him, and he suddenly wondered if their task was going to be easier than they'd thought. Why then, did he feel a prickle of foreboding run down his spine?

"Good," Cailleach said, drawing out the word in a rumbling snarl. "Now, you must listen, because we do not have much time. You need to take her west, across the salty sea to the land of my sister's people. They are located on the western-most shores, their world accessed through the mounds on a series of cliff faces. Do not concern yourself with the direction as you will instinctively know the way— trust the gentle nudge on your senses. Morrígan has promised to smooth the way for you so that when you reach her people, no questions will be asked when you arrive with the child. The fate of this world rests on my daughter's shoulders. She must live, and her lineage must remain unknown."

Girom watched as Drust's hands clenched. He knew what the warrior was thinking; it was a question of whether he was brave enough to say it. In the next moment he had his answer because Drust asked, "And with whom shall I leave the child?"

The goddess stared at him, and the air was suddenly squeezed with an oppressive menace. "Leave?" she rasped. "Leave? She is not to be left there alone! You will remain with her."

Girom felt his heart lurch. Cailleach had chosen Drust to care for the child? Her words confirmed Fìna's vision, another puzzle piece clicking into place.

Drust's face was tight. His displeasure at the task he'd been given was obvious. Clearing his throat, the warrior said carefully, "I do not believe I am suited for this task, my lady. I am a warrior—a leader of our clan. As such, I am expected to lead battles in the coming war." He gestured to Girom and Fìna. "Would not the learned Master of Herbs, or my sister, Fìna, be a more appropriate companion for the child? I am happy to accompany them to the coastline and see to their safe passage over the sea to the land of our cousins, but I do not think my presence will aid them past that given the coming threat to this land."

Cailleach snarled, her silver irises swirling with power. "No! You will not be returning!" Her voice ricocheted around the room in a thunderous roar. "You will remain at my daughter's side as her personal guard. You talk of fighting in this war as if being on the front lines is the most important place to be. It is not. Being by my daughter's side is! Her line will ensure the successful outcome of this battle between light and dark. It has been foretold. With the help of my siblings, a prophecy has been constructed, and on the last day of Samhain, it will become immutable. My daughter is the key to everything. She must remain alive, regardless of the consequences. The war will begin in three days, and she must be far away from here by the time it begins."

Girom felt his ears roar. Again, there came a tingling across his skin, a confirmation that what Cailleach had said was true—that the fight wasn't winning this war; the real fight was ensuring her daughter's survival.

The warrior swallowed. "I apologize for my impertinence but I must ask you, my lady, that if she is so important, wouldn't leaving her in your care be the best option?"

Girom's chest squeezed, and he heard Fìna whimper behind him. But rather than obliterating Drust on the spot as he suspected she would, Cailleach ran a hand down her ugly, twisted body. "Because I am the crone," she replied in a small voice. "As a result of the deal I have made, I am unable to be who I once was. This is my form now; one unsuited to caring for a child."

Girom blinked. It was not the answer he had been expecting, and even though it was riddled with unknowns, he could read between the lines. The goddess had been subjected to a tithe in return for whatever it was she'd requested. And given what he'd just heard, Girom had the feeling that whatever she'd bargained for was related to her child's safety. "Circles within circles," he murmured aloud.

At his observation, Cailleach narrowed her eyes and cut her gaze in his direction. Girom cringed under the weight of her assessment.

"You are an anomaly," she slurred around her tusks. "I have yet to determine your place in this, but it is clear by your actions that you support me in my plight—that, or you choose to fight the spreading perversion of my dark brother's influence. Regardless, you saved both me and my child, and for that, I thank you. It is those actions that make you a candidate for this task. You, the warrior, and this Dream Walker you have brought with you, will all carry my child to safety and stay by her side as she grows into womanhood. Yes, you will all be bound to this task."

Girom started, his mouth agape. "No! I would be a poor candidate for this role, my lady. I am old, nearing the end of my time, and with no experience raising a child." Then suddenly aware of who he'd spoken to and what he'd said, Girom fell to his knees and pressed his palms together in supplication.

Cailleach peeled her lips back in a menacing snarl and took a step forward. The tangled, unkempt length of her dirty blonde hair fairly rippled with her wrath. "You would gamble my daughter's life over the outcome of this war?"

The words were measured, but he knew they stood upon a cliff's edge, on that fine line between life and death. He knew words would only increase her wrath.

At his silence, she said slowly, "If all of you do not accept this command, your lives will be no further use to me. The world as we know it will come to an end. Is that what you want, druid?"

Fìna stepped in front of him and spoke for the first time. "I will happily take the child, my lady. I accept my path." She lifted her chin, gaze fixed carefully on the goddess' nose. "I am the obvious choice. I am young but old enough to have dallied with men, which means having a child in tow will not be unusual. And as a Dream Walker, I am able to see the past as well as the future. If a threat arises, I will have sufficient time to protect your daughter."

The crone considered Fìna, her black tongue slipping out of her mouth to curl around a tusk. "You have made the right decision, but the others must join you. My daughter will need a warrior and a healer over the course of her life, especially if she is to live with the Tuatha Dé Dannan. My sister's people are of a different race; their medicine, like their magic, is different to ours." She looked pointedly at Girom.

Resigned, he cleared his throat. "There is no need to convince me, my lady. I am committed to sharing this burden for as long as I shall live."

"Burden?" Cailleach roared. The wind suddenly shrieked outside the shieling, and fingers of a chill wind whistled into the cottage, peeling back the leather hide across the door as if someone had flung it open in a fit of rage. The icy draughts lanced the three of them, jabbing painfully against their exposed skin.

Girom felt his chest constrict as the ice traveled into his body and began to freeze his organs. He felt his blood become sluggish and heavy, the air squeezing tightly in his lungs. He grappled at his neck.

"Cailleach," Fìna rasped through clenched teeth. "Stop! We have accepted this path."

But the goddess didn't stop. Her feelings had been spurned to the edge of no return. She stormed over to the cradle by the fire and reached down to the bundle inside. With her daughter clasped against her chest, she turned back to face them while raising one hand. She squeezing her huge, gnarled fingers into a fist, and her voice was heavy with feeling as she replied, "I will not stop. Did Talorgan stop when he killed Tritus? Did Falin stop when he came for my child? Did Morrígan's jealous machinations stop, even though I'd lost everything? No! My enemies will not curb their instincts to kill my child. I have sacrificed everything— even the love of my daughter—to prevent what will happen. You do not get to choose this path. Either you accept the way laid before you, or I find others who will."

"No—please!" Fìna cried again. "Girom accepts! All three of us accept!"

Cailleach looked at him again, and even in his frantic state, he recognized the need to confirm Fìna's words. His eyes burned as he gasped his words of acceptance—but the plea was undelivered as no sound left his lips.

He watched the goddess' face crumple into a snarl of contempt. Her bulging gray jowls shook as she opened her mouth and bellowed her rage. The babe in her arms jerked and screamed aloud, the innocent cries more piercing than its mother's roar.

Girom blinked, trying to focus on the babe, but he could no longer see anything clearly. His vision was fading, the flickering colors in the room replaced with varying shades of gray. Girom understood that the goddess was too blinded by her anger, too enraged to listen to the voice of reason.

He tried to hold his panic at bay. If this was his time, then he would go mindfully, with as much peace as he could muster. A chilling calm began to descend, and in that moment of quiet, a myriad of thoughts flooded into his consciousness, along with an overwhelming jumble of images. For a moment, they made no sense, but just as his chest became excruciatingly tight, he understood.

Aware he had but a moment to save them, he used the last ounce of his power to weave an image upon the air—a powerful bird with blazing orange, red, and gold plumage.

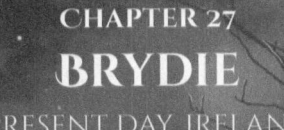

CHAPTER 27
BRYDIE
PRESENT DAY, IRELAND

Two Days Later

G age stopped the four wheel drive in front of a nondescript concrete building on the edge of Oldcastle, County Meath. He killed the engine, flicked the headlights off, and raised a hand. "Quiet."

Blessed with excellent sight in the dark, my Guardian was able to distinguish movement near and far. My lower back tingled as I felt him extend his senses, trying to locate any sense of a threat. After a moment, he muttered, "All clear. Let's get inside so I can ward the building. We have two hours before we meet Alison at Hag's Cairn. Use the time to rest if you can."

Gage alighted from the vehicle and walked up to the front door, key in hand.

McKenzie wrapped an arm around Aidan's shoulders and shook him awake. "We're here, son. Come on, let's get you into bed."

Aidan mumbled something unintelligible, but he groggily followed his mother into the house, Jack dutifully following behind. Ian flung Aidan's seat forward and unraveled himself from his seat in the back. Without a word, he entered the building. I felt the frosty silence between us; whatever chance we'd had to reconnect was long gone.

Logan turned around to face me. We were the only two people left in the car. "You've been quiet this whole trip."

I couldn't deny it. During the three-hour drive from the Cliffs of Moher, I'd spent it thinking about the task ahead. It would be the first time I would use my powers in a defined setting, the first time I would be truly tested. The altercation with Garret and Talorgan didn't count. Gage had taken over with Garret, and I'd had no access to my power while facing Talorgan. This mission would be my first real test...and a mission that would involve retrieving my best friend. My heart raced just thinking about what was at stake. "I'm just thinking about how tomorrow will play out," I admitted.

Logan's eyes softened. "You have nothing to worry about, Brydie. Gage will be with you, and he's trained you well. But it's understandable to be nervous."

Indeed. Gage had mentioned more than once that nerves were what gave you the edge you needed to make it out of situations alive. But it wasn't just my life that was at stake, it was Chloe's too. I was terrified I'd screw something up, that I'd lose her. But Logan didn't need to hear that, nor would he accept it. "You're right. I'm sure everything will go as planned."

"It will." He reached out and squeezed my arm. "Come on, we should get inside. Tomorrow will be a long night."

Gage came out of the building and met us on the doorstep. "Everything's warded. You're in the guest bedroom on the right," he said to his brother.

Logan inclined his head and, heaving his Louis Vuitton bag over his shoulder, left us on the doorstep.

Gage's eyes landed on mine. "Stop it."

"Stop what?"

"Stop second guessing yourself. It's natural to be nervous, but you need to know I believe in you. We'll get her back."

He could feel my emotions, yes, and at times, sense my thoughts, but he couldn't feel my power, didn't know what it was that I felt every time I used it. Didn't know of the darkness that simmered under my skin, the shadows that appeared when I'd attacked Garret, the shadows that appeared every time I'd used my power since. But I knew them for what they were—a warning. A message that my power still maintained a desire to control me. That the battle we'd had was still ongoing.

"She's my best friend," I whispered. "It's hard to separate the emotion from the fear."

His eyes softened. "I know, but you need to try. You're strong, Brydie. Powerful, too, and you've done all the hard work. You're ready for this. It is a good trial for what is coming. Samhain will not be easy for any of us."

"You're right." I reminded myself that tomorrow's mission was a small stepping stone. We weren't intending to fight Callum, only rescue Chloe. In and out. Silently and stealthily. No quarrels, no brawls. But there were so many unknowns, so many—

Gage reached out and grasped my shoulder, interrupting my spiraling thoughts. "Let's go inside," he said softly.

I felt the tug of desire along our shared bond and lifted my head to see the message in his eyes. We both knew we had only two hours left of what I'd come to see as our short period of freedom—two hours to pretend we had no burdens, that our lives weren't marked by fate. It was a distraction I craved.

I reached up to cup the back of his neck, tugging his ear down to my lips. "What are you waiting for then?" I said in a low voice, before nipping his ear and striding away.

His low growl had my lips lifting as I entered the master bedroom.

GAGE WAS PUTTING on his boots when his cell phone beeped. He tapped the screen and read the message before turning his eyes to mine. "We need to leave now."

My stomach dipped at the knowledge that we'd soon see Alison again. She was the key to finding Chloe.

I jumped out of bed and quickly pulled on my clothes as Gage finished tying his shoelaces and came to his feet. I could feel his watchful gaze as I smoothed down my warm sweater, aware he was thinking about what he'd just done to my body.

Ducking my head to hide the flush riding up my cheeks, I pulled on my own boots, then snagged the hair tie off the floor and coiled my hair into a loose ponytail. Gage had ripped it out of its customary braid as soon as he'd closed the door.

We left the bedroom, and Gage rapped on all the doors, ordering everyone to the vehicle. McKenzie came out carrying Aidan, trussed up in a blanket and looking groggy. No questions were asked as we got in the vehicle and began the drive to Slieve na Calliagh.

For my benefit, Ian explained Slieve na Calliagh was a series of four hills and a well-known archaeological site containing megalithic tombs that dated as far back as the fourth millennium BC. Each hill contained passage graves, but the largest hill and the largest tomb was named Hag's Cairn, after Cailleach. And inside Hag's Cairn were two large stones; one in the middle of the tomb and the other on the ceiling, both of which were illuminated by the sun at the dawn of the spring equinox.

"There is power there, not just in the site itself, but in the stones themselves during the equinox," he now explained.

"Are they like the carlin stone?" I asked.

"Yes, with a few differences. The carlin stone always holds power, but these ones are a lot smaller and only powerful during the spring equinox."

"Hag's Cairn has been chosen as an entry and exit point into the Institute because, during spring, the stones will contain enough power to mask our magical signatures when we portal in and out," Gage explained.

I turned to McKenzie. "Have you seen the stones before?"

She shook her head. "No, but I've been meaning to. I heard some of the symbols on the stones belong to Cailleach."

"What symbols?"

McKenzie gestured to her arm. "The same ones tattooed on our bodies."

My eyes flew open. "What? That's..."

"Prophetic?" McKenzie offered with a small smile. "Yes, I suppose it is."

Each of the descendants affected by Cailleach's prophecy carried a tattoo. Gage had one at the back of his neck. It meant 'guardian'. Ian's was on his right forearm and meant 'knowledge'; McKenzie's was on her left bicep and read 'hope', and mine was at my lower back. It meant 'love', in reference to the extent Cailleach had gone to protect her daughter, the very first Daughter of Winter. "Does that mean Chloe has a tattoo?" I now asked McKenzie.

But it was Gage who had answered as he navigated a bend. "Yes, on her right ankle. I saw it at the airport."

Okay then. Which meant he really had known who she was back then. Swallowing, I asked, "What does it mean?"

"Trust," he said softly.

Of course, Chloe would be associated with trust. She was the only one I'd trusted enough to open up to during my childhood; my first and only real friend.

Gage pulled into the car park soon after that, and we exited the vehicle for the short walk up to Hag's Cairn. After tucking a blanket under his chin and kissing him softly on the forehead, McKenzie left Aidan in the car with Jack before warding it from view, then we began the walk up to Hag's Cairn.

The moonlight illuminated the open, winding trail, and a chill breeze blew gently around us as we trudged up the hill. The peaks of the four hills loomed ahead, their silhouettes stark against the starry night, while numerous rock cairns glinted under the moonlight.

No one said a word as Gage led us toward the highest peak, a soft mist beginning to permeate the air. Ian had said Hag's Cairn stood at two-hundred and seventy-six meters above sea level, and that became true the higher we climbed.

At the top, the atmosphere was quiet; still. There was a feeling of anticipation here, a weighted silence, as if a hundred eyes were watching. My lower back tingled, telling me I hadn't needed Ian's stories to understand Cailleach had once been here. I could feel the residue of her power just as I had at the tarn and on Beinn na Caillich.

Gage led us around the large mound of rocks to a small stone entranceway. The gap looked narrow, barely wide enough to accommodate us, and I couldn't see anything past the entrance but inky darkness. "Is that the entrance to the tombs?" I asked quietly.

Ian nodded. There was a touch of awe in his tone as he said softly, "Can you believe it was constructed over six millennia ago?"

On this dark, starry night, with the breeze blowing secrets around us, I could. It felt ageless here; these mounds of rocks had seen many lifetimes, and it was not hard to believe that buried under these hillsides were the skeletal remains of the first settlers to this land. "Are we going in?"

"No, there's enough power to enable us to portal from here," Gage answered.

As soon as the words left his lips, the air shimmered and whined and a portal rent the air. Alison stepped through and the portal snapped shut behind her. She faced us, her black cloak swirling around her ankles. Her hood was down, her black hair framing her bright blue eyes and perfect bow lips. "I'm on the clock," she said by way of greeting. "I can only spare thirty minutes before Callum becomes suspicious."

I narrowed my eyes at her, while McKenzie elicited a snort and said, "Well hello to you too."

Gage raised a hand. "That's enough. We all need to respect the risk Alison's taking in meeting us here. Let's not waste her time."

He was right, I had to think of Chloe. No matter what I felt about Alison, right now she was our only way in and out of the Institute. I said in as neutral a tone as I could manage, "Alison."

"Descendant," she returned with a smirk.

I grit my teeth. *Think of Chloe.*

"Thank you for coming, Alison," Ian forced out next. "I appreciate it's difficult to leave."

He was another one in our party who wasn't overly fond of her, and I'd worked out the rivalry between them was because Alison had taken his position as Lore Keeper for the clan.

"Any time is difficult these days," she purred, flicking her long hair over a shoulder. There was an awareness of her physical charms in the way she held her body, the cant of her head, the sway of her hips; every movement calculated. "Callum is suspicious of everyone. It seems that having an ancient artefact in your possession can make you even more paranoid than most."

"Is he aware that something is going on between us?" McKenzie asked in a tight voice, always conscious of the safety of her son.

"I've no doubt Callum is aware that something is up," Alison returned. "But I'm certain he has no idea of our liaison, or what it is you intend to do tomorrow night."

"Good," Gage said.

"What's the plan?" I demanded.

"That's what we're here to clarify," he returned, looking to the Lore Keeper. "Alison has the details."

Alison turned her blue gaze to mine. "Which I will not share right now. Given Callum's skills as a Dream Walker and what he holds in his possession, it's not wise to confirm plans until we are about to execute them."

I couldn't argue with her logic, but the way she delivered this news in her smug fashion had my body locking in anger. I bit my tongue to halt my curse.

"No comeback then? Well then, this may work after all," she said, looking at me with a smug smile on her face. Then her gaze moved behind me. "But there's someone here I haven't met. You're clearly Gage's twin."

Logan stepped up beside me. "The name's Logan."

She pursed her lips as her eyes traveled the length of his body. "It's obvious you don't contain any magic, but you're not completely powerless either."

Logan turned to me and said plaintively, "Why does everyone say that?"

Gage said brusquely, "This is Logan, but that's all you need to know, because he won't be involved in the mission."

Everyone could hear the warning to back off, but Alison was an exception to the rule. Her smile widened. "Touchy," she replied softly. "And I suppose you'll neither confirm nor deny he's your brother, even though you look alike?"

Gage's voice was cold. "We all have people we must protect, Alison."

"And secrets we like to keep," she returned coolly. Ignoring him, she held out a hand to Logan. "A pleasure to meet you. I'm Alison, and I'm sure you would have worked out I'm one of Callum's Lore Keeper's."

Logan inclined his head, accepting her hand without hesitation. "On the contrary, I disagree. From what I'd seen and heard about you, I think you're your own Lore Keeper."

A flicker of surprise passed over her face before she released his hand and turned back to Gage. "Do you have a diversion planned on this end?"

He nodded. "A third party has agreed to aid us tomorrow night. We've been promised a sufficient distraction when we portal in."

She quirked a brow. "And who is this third party? Can they be trusted?"

"Yes, and that's all you need to know," Gage said shortly.

Alison considered him, her lips in a thin line. "Fine. But it's on your head if things go wrong."

"I wouldn't expect anything less, Alison." He crossed his arms over his chest. "Let's get into the details. What time are we to arrive, and how long will we have?" Gage asked.

"Briana claims that Callum usually leaves around nine and returns in the wee hours of the night. I wouldn't take longer than three hours; anymore and you're gambling."

I recalled Briana was one of the women forced to keep Callum's bed warm at night. She was also feeding Alison information.

Gage nodded. "Thank you. Did you find out where the descendant has been situated?"

"One of the men believes she's in the dungeons."

My heart clenched. McKenzie had been right.

"Where in the dungeons?" McKenzie asked. "That area is a rabbit warren of hidden cells."

Her face was pallid in the moonlight, her eyes wide, and I couldn't help but feel she spoke from experience. Not for the first time, I wondered what had befallen her at the Institute.

"Callum likes to make a fuss when someone is being held captive," Alison was saying. "But the descendant's capture has been hushed. It means he's invested. There are areas in the dungeons that are hidden away for special prisoners. They're heavily warded, and only one prison warden can access them. Egan's cells are on the south side. Are you familiar with the layout of the dungeon?"

McKenzie gave a stilted nod, her features tense.

Gage cleared his throat, drawing the attention back to him. "We'll map it out tomorrow. Thank you for all the risks you've taken to get us this far, Alison."

She eyed him closely. "Finding her is one thing, Gage, but have you thought about what will happen when it's found she's gone? There will be an uproar, and the alarm will be raised. Finding her is the easy part, getting her out won't be."

"That's where you come in," Gage returned.

Alison's brow rose. "Me?"

Gage's eyes narrowed. "Who else would I be asking? Isn't that why you're here tonight? To aid us, and in return, we'll help you get rid of Callum."

She lifted a hand, palm out. "Not so fast. Removing Callum is a common goal, but requiring our aid to retrieve the descendant is a different deal altogether. I would have thought we'd helped you enough by confirming where she is and the day and time to enter."

"But don't you hold a pact with Cailleach?" I demanded. "I know Callum doesn't give a shit about it, but surely not everyone thinks that way."

"What pact?" she shot back. "It's not a priority right now, not when the path Callum has forced us upon will result in harsher retribution. We have more to fear from him than we do of an ancient pact between the gods."

"So, what are you saying?" McKenzie asked. "That your aid for tomorrow will come at a price?"

"That's exactly what I'm saying," Alison said bluntly. "You know how this goes—we can help you, but only if you're willing to do something for us in return."

I withheld a curse. "And what would that be?"

"I want Jake," she said simply.

"Jake?" I repeated.

"He's one of Callum's personal guards."

McKenzie and Ian swore, but Gage didn't seem surprised.

"What do you mean you want Jake?" I asked. "Do you want us to kill him?"

"Not kill, you stupid bitch," she sneered. "I want you to *save* him."

The insult had my hands clenching, and I took a step forward, but before I could say anything, Gage snarled, "Talk to her with respect or all deals are off."

Alison cocked her head to the side. "I will not apologize," she said softly. "You owe me for helping you regain her magic. Without my assistance, she would still be powerless." Her eyes dropped pointedly to my hands, and I looked down, suddenly aware they were glowing. I hadn't even noticed.

I lifted my head and held her gaze. "For that, I'll let the insult pass, but if you speak to me like that again, I won't be responsible for the consequences, no matter what rides on our union."

She arched a brow. "Big words. I doubt you have the ability to match them."

Gage flung out a hand at Alison while reaching out with his other to grab one of mine. Squeezing it tightly, he said, "Look, let's just take a step back. Emotions are riding high, but we can help each other. How exactly do you expect us to save Jake? Hasn't he drunk from the cauldron?"

Alison's face tightened. "He has, but we've been working on a way to reverse the curse. We think we've found a way to release him from Callum's binding."

"Have you found something in the lore?" Ian demanded, his eyes alight with curiosity.

She nodded. "Aine found something in Morrígan's Lore Book."

"But they're written in fae," Ian said, a frown feathering his brow. "How could she read it?"

But I'd worked it out already. "Because she's a descendant of Aine." Aine was a goddess who was said to have many human lovers, which meant a druidic descendant within our clan was highly possible.

Alison cut her eyes to mine. "Clever. It appears there is something in that blonde head of yours after all."

Bitch! Was she purposely trying to initiate a fight between us? Feeling my fists clench at my sides, I released a breath and saw a puff of white release from my lips. Gage squeezed my hand again, his unspoken message to hold it together traveling down our shared line.

Logan's voice was smooth, urbane. "I must say, my first introduction to a female Lore Keeper has been insightful. Are you all this rude?"

Alison simply smiled. "Thank you for the compliment."

Logan gave her an incredulous look, but the interlude had broken the tension and given me time enough to get myself back under control.

Alison's gaze was back on mine, focused and intent. "You know the descendant Callum is holding prisoner, don't you?"

There was no use denying it. She had already seen enough evidence of my emotional involvement tonight. Releasing another breath, I let go of Gage's hand and said quietly, "Yes. Her name is Chloe, and she's my best friend."

I waited for the coy smile to spread across her face, but instead her voice was low, strained. "Then you understand what it's like when Callum has someone you love."

Jake. She loved Jake.

Holding that cold, blue gaze, I said, "Yes."

"Then why do you not agree to my tithe? I want to rescue Jake just as much as you want to rescue your friend."

I considered this, realizing that if what we'd been told

was true, Jake was just as much of a prisoner as Chloe, having been also taken against his will and tied to Callum through the cauldron. That must be hard for Alison to watch, day in and day out. Was it a lesser cruelty to have been apart from Chloe all this time? Not having to be in the same building as her, knowing she was a prisoner? Yes, it was. And I doubt I would have been able to unreservedly fall into Gage's arms if I'd been reminded of that fact every day.

I looked at Alison with new eyes, saw the coldness in her gaze, the rudeness, the carefully timed lift of her lips, the sway of her hips not as a threat but as armor...a shield that was similar to my Guardian's. Just like Gage, she, too, felt deeply. My gut churned at the truth of it.

Alison was oblivious to my revelation, her mouth tightening as she looked down at her watch. "I only have another ten minutes. If you aren't willing to rescue Jake, there'll be no support our end, and this visit has been a waste of time for both of us."

Gage's face shuttered. "Our people swore an oath to Cailleach that they would help her descendant, giving aid in the war against Talorgan. You know it's not right to dangle another tithe over our heads."

"Not right?" Alison repeated, eyes glittering. "What about what happened to our people? About what Callum has done to them? What about those who have turned away from the light? Those who are falling into the darkness? Many of us will not recover—hell, many are already lost! Is that fair, Gage? Is it fair that we aid you and you don't aid us, your own people?!" Her eyes shifted, coming to rest on Gage's brother. "Even you, Logan. Even if you have no druidic magic, you have ties by blood to our people. I refuse to believe you would turn your back on us."

Gage snarled, "It is not our fault Jake was subjected to the cauldron or that Callum now rules our people. We have been outed from the clan because we've had no choice but to follow the path fate has in store for us. We are not at fault for those who chose to elect Callum, or for those that chose to slide into the darkness." He stepped toward her, leaning in close. "The question should be why didn't the *clan* band together and oppose Callum's rule?"

Her face hardened. "Because of the cauldron. Because he was a snake who waited, biding his time, for the right moment to strike. His poison spread throughout our people, his promises, his threats. Too many were swayed. Too many did not understand his motives. And those of us who had the power to do anything were cut off at the head before we even had a chance to." Alison's throat bobbed, her hands rising to rake through her hair. Her next words were slower, quieter. "Jake held a lot of power, almost on par with your own," she said to Gage. She laughed, the sound mirthless. "He did well during his initiation, showed too much promise. His power attracted Callum like a moth to a flame, and he approached Jake with an offer he couldn't resist. Aside from me, the only person who held any sway against the offer was his father. Ike was against the promotion; he's never trusted Callum, even before we lost Fergus. But Jake didn't listen."

"Jake is Ike's son?" Gage demanded.

Her face softened. "Yes, he told me you'd remember him. Ike has been a prominent leader of our group since Fergus's death. Ike did his best to steer Jake away from the position, but Jake wouldn't have it." She grimaced. "He craved the power and status the position would bring him."

"Someone else should have been looking out for him."

Alison's eyes were accusing as she stared at my

Guardian. "Everyone else was either dead or gone. With the Wise Ones and Fergus dead, the only law that counts is Callum's. Ike tried to stand against him, but he was one person, and Callum took his actions personally. He demoted Ike to looking after the waterways."

"Why would he do that? Ike holds powerful water magic," McKenzie said.

Alison turned to her. "Which is the reason why Callum demoted him. Catching onto a pattern here?"

Ian cleared his throat. "If we agree to this, how will Gage and Brydie extract both Chloe and Jake?"

Alison released a breath. "Ike has a few ideas. They're plausible, especially since he has a way to get you in and out of the Institute unseen."

"How?" Gage demanded.

"The water outlet to the sea."

"Won't that be protected by wards?"

Alison shook her head. "We've found a loophole— Callum has only warded the outside of the castle walls, but he conveniently missed off the gray water pipe that runs underground to the coast. Ike found it a few months ago, and it's only known to a select few of us who have a penchant for freedom. Telling you this puts a lot of us at risk, but Ike told me I could trust you. Was he wrong?"

"He's not wrong." Gage ran a hand through his hair, admitting softly, "Ike and I have an understanding. He helped me out when I left the Institute."

"He said as much," Alison said. "He didn't share the details, but I understand enough to know he stuck his neck out for you. I would have thought you owed him for that."

Gage's face darkened. "I do, but this is a lot more than you think. Jake chose his own path. Submitting to the dark arts is the same process as submitting to the light—he freely chose that path. He can't be helped until he desires the change back, which may never occur."

Alison's entire frame tensed. "I know the odds I'm up against," she hissed, "but I refuse to give up hope. Your agreement to rescue Jake tells us these words between us aren't just empty intentions." Turning to me, she added, "And it gives us good reason to follow Cailleach's descendant come Samhain."

I knew the comment for what it was—dominance. But that right was mine to claim. I was the descendant of the Winter Goddess, and it was time to claim the legacy I was born into, including my place in this clan. One that wouldn't be beneath Alison or any others who sought to subdue me or use me for their own means.

I placed a hand on my hip, my stance causally deceptive, my words anything but as I said slowly and firmly in a voice that held no hesitation, "I'm well aware I will not win this fight on my own. Cailleach tied The Oaken Tree to an agreement that has held for centuries, and regardless of what Callum dictates, it's time to cash it in. The clan owes my family, and make no mistake I am calling in that debt to be paid. But I also see a need to prove myself, and I have no problem in illustrating I am here to support our people. I promise you we will get Jake out. If we don't, let it be known The Oaken Tree has every right to rescind their support." I held out my hand, ignoring the sharp curse from my Guardian, and asked bluntly, "So, Alison, do we have a deal?"

Her hand reached out and clasped mine, her lips curving into her first genuine smile. "We have a deal."

A s soon as Alison left through the portal, I rounded on Brydie. But she was ready for my attack, her words flying from her lips.

"It was clear you weren't going to agree, Gage, and I couldn't let the chance to rescue Chloe go."

"But Jake is compromised! Don't you understand what that means? Even if we rescue him, it may be a wasted effort. He may never recover and be who he once was."

There was sadness in her eyes, but her face and her voice remained firm. "That is Alison's fight, not ours. All she was asking for is that we get him out."

"And how the hell would we do that when we already have to retrieve Chloe, and later on Ingrid?"

Ian sent me a look of gratitude, but my eyes were on Brydie. She was smiling smugly now. "She didn't specify *when*, just after we had rescued the descendant. I thought we could tackle this next step once Chloe was safe."

Ian snorted. "She's right. A time wasn't specified."

My gaze sharpened on Brydie's face, tracing the outline

of her features, the cool caress of the wisps of hair across her cheek. My hand itched to reach out and tuck them behind her ear. I met her eyes and smiled, making sure she could feel my raw pride. "Alison was right; there's more inside that blonde head of yours than you let on." It was another indication of how far she'd come—how much she'd changed.

"We should get going," McKenzie cut in. "I'd like to check on Aidan."

The sharpness in her tone caught my attention. Her face was pinched, and there was a hollowness in her eyes, as if reliving the past had slashed her self-confidence. I nodded. "Let's head back."

Turning, I led them back down the hill to our vehicle. A heavy silence fell on the open grasslands...until a stone skittered, cutting through the still night air.

I halted, turning slowly and peering into the darkness. I could see nothing, but there was a faint presence tickling the air currents. The scent was subtle, a blend of the environment around us—moist earth after a soft rain, and the hollow, heavy moisture of clinging mist. The acknowledgement of those two scents stopped me cold. They were weak, but they'd been cleverly camouflaged, and I knew the movement of the stone had not been a mistake. My neck hadn't tickled in warning, meaning whoever was out there wasn't an immediate threat.

"Show yourselves," I demanded.

A voice called out to our left, "We come in peace, Guardian."

Friend or not, I tensed, reaching for my power. I lifted one of my hands, my palm alight. "I won't ask again."

The air shimmered to the left, and two figures appeared at the bottom of the barrow over Hag's Cairn. I narrowed my eyes, my suspicions confirmed when I saw the peaked ears among their dark, flowing tresses. Fae.

The tallest one broke the silence. "Lorcan told us where to find you. We've been waiting here since nightfall."

The confession threw me. They would have heard everything we'd just discussed. How had I missed their presence? "Why did you not announce yourselves when we first arrived?"

The fae male looked to his companion. "We were about to when your visitor arrived." His face twisted with distaste. "We did not want to announce our presence in front of her. To all intents and purposes, the fae have disappeared from this world, and we'd like to keep it that way."

"Understood." I could appreciate their need for secrecy. "Does your presence mean you are willing to help us enter the Institute?"

The male nodded. "Lorcan advised we are at your disposal."

"And you are welcome. Please, come closer, I can assure you we are all trustworthy."

The others were silent behind me, but I could feel their tension as we watched the two fae males walk down the hill toward us. As they came closer, the moonlight illuminated their features. Both were dark haired, with coal black eyes and tanned complexions. Combined with their scents, I knew them for what they were: Lorcan's spies; his eyes and ears in this world.

The tall one stopped in front of me and gave a slight bow. "My name is Mahon, and this is my brother, Padriac," he said, gesturing at his companion. "It is good to make your acquaintance. Padriac and I were willing to offer aid in return for your help in locating Carman's descendant."

"Well met." I clasped their hands in greeting before

gesturing at the others. "I am Gage, and this is Brydie, Logan, McKenzie, and Ian; all of us are descendants of Cailleach's prophecy. This meeting is of mutual benefit to us all in attaining what we both need."

"Indeed," Mahon replied, his dark eyes serious. "I came to confirm we have a diversion planned for tomorrow night, but we need you to tell us what time it will be required."

I appreciated Mahon's direct manner. "Three hours before dawn. Will that work?"

Mahon bowed. "It will be done."

"And what exactly do you have planned?"

His brother spoke up this time. "Something our goddess once did. The significance will not be lost on the leader of The Oaken Tree, or any other druidic clan for that matter."

"A tsunami?" Ian guessed.

Padriac shifted his dark gaze to Ian. "Just so. Morrígan's power eradicated most of the Fomorian army in one hit. I've no doubt the gravitational pull associated with our magic will create a level of interest near and afar."

It was a fitting diversion and impressive. "You both hold that level of power to move the tides?"

Mahon shook his head. "Not alone. We will have help."

He didn't elaborate, and I didn't push him. We all had secrets.

"And where will this tsunami fall?" Brydie cut in. "Should we be worried about the effects on people, land, and crops?"

Mahon shifted his gaze to her face and bowed his head, his eyes dipping in respect. "No, the tsunami will not hit land. We will hold it steady before turning the tide."

"Thank you," she murmured. "Your help will be most welcome."

Mahon bowed once again. As he straightened, he flicked

a glance at his brother, before saying, "If that will be all, we have Lorcan's bidding to attend to for what is left of the night. If we do not see you prior, we wish you every success on your mission."

I clapped a hand on his back. "Thank you. We appreciate your assistance more than you know."

Mahon bowed again. "Pleasure."

Padriac voice was gravel as he intoned, "May the goddess light your way."

"And may your people be at rest," I returned.

A look of approval glinted in his dark eyes before the shadows around their bodies lengthened, eclipsing their forms, and he and his brother vanished.

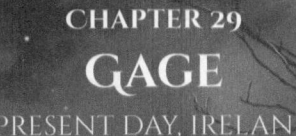

CHAPTER 29

GAGE

PRESENT DAY, IRELAND

Close to midnight the next evening, McKenzie and Aidan entered the living area, where Brydie and I were cataloguing the range of weapons we would take into the Institute.

McKenzie eyed the gun and set of knives on the table before taking hold of Aidan's shoulder, halting him just inside the door. "No touching the weapons," she said firmly.

Aidan would be involved in what was to come tonight. We could no longer hide what was happening from him, and the kid needed to know the truth of what Brydie and I were about to do. He was looking down at the carpet, hands in his pockets. He looked tired and anxious. He was also unnerved. He knew damn well the meaning of the weapons laid out on the table, which meant it was best he channeled his anxieties into worthwhile work.

"Aidan, come here, son."

The kid left his mother's side and came to me, not reluctantly, but not with his usual jauntiness either. I clapped a hand on his shoulder and pulled him close, bending down to meet him at eye level. "Your mother is going to need you tonight, Aidan. In fact, we're all going to need you."

Aidan looked at his mother, then back to me. His eyes were as round as saucers. "What's happening, Gage? Is Talorgan coming?" His voice almost broke on the last word.

I gripped his shoulder hard, confirming with my touch that he was here, that he was safe. "No, Aidan, he's not coming. Brydie and I are leaving, though—just temporarily. All you need to know is that we are retrieving the last descendant missing from our party. We will be gone for a few hours, but during some of that time, your mother is going to check up on Talorgan and see what he's doing. But because we won't be here, and Logan and Ian will be otherwise occupied watching the house, your mother's going to need *your* help."

McKenzie made a small noise of distress. I refused to look at her as I continued, "Your mom needs an anchor to this world, Aidan, and I think you'd be the best person for the job."

"What does it involve?" Aidan breathed, his face pinched.

"Your mom will need to be watched over while she's dream walking. We'd normally entrust this job to another adult, but we're short on the ground, and we all think you're old enough to help." I stared deep into his eyes, imparting the importance behind the task. "What do you say? Are you up for this, kid?"

McKenzie's shoulders had loosened at the revelation of the task I'd set for the boy.

Aidan swallowed. "I'm up for it."

His voice wasn't strong, but the conviction in his eyes was enough to convince me. "That's good, Aidan. Because after tonight's mission, I think it's time we begin your druidic training."

Aidan's mouth dropped. "Really? Even though I haven't shown any promise of power?"

Aidan was at least four years older than I'd been when I was initiated, but then, I'd shown promise at five years old. Whether Aidan's magic manifested or not, he needed to learn our ways, not only to understand our history and values, but also to acquire knowledge to keep himself safe. He wasn't my kid, but as the only male role model living with them, I should have addressed this a long time ago. I was ashamed I hadn't realized this until now.

"It doesn't matter," I assured him. "The first lesson in Druidry is to learn about the balance in nature, and if you aren't touched by one of our codes, you'll still carry other skill sets that will help our people. Besides, it's time; you're almost of age."

There was no hesitation as Aidan nodded. "Yes! And I'll prove it by watching Mom, Gage. I promise I won't let anything happen to her."

"Good man, because there's no other job more important." I reached out to ruffle the top of his head and was surprised when two thin arms wrapped around my middle. My eyes caught McKenzie's, gratitude shining in hers.

"Thanks, Gage," Aidan whispered, before peeling away and walking back to his mother.

McKenzie squeezed him tightly. "Why don't you head off to your room for a bit, son? I need to work out some details with Gage and Brydie before they head off tonight."

"Okay, Mom."

As Aidan left the room, Brydie, who had been quietly

observing the interlude, asked McKenzie, "Where will you dream walk?"

"Here in the house given Gage has imposed some wards around it for another forty-eight hours."

"And Ian and Logan?" Brydie asked me. "What will they be doing?"

"They'll be doing what they're doing now—guarding the house. After what happened at Hag's Cairn last night, I'm not taking any chances with the fae. Mahon and Padriac came with good intentions, but if there are any others like them who don't, we had no warning to prepare."

Brydie's face tightened, and it was enough to tell me that she, too, had been perturbed by the silence of their approach and how none of us had picked up any warning of their presence, not even through our tattoos or the pendant.

On that train of thought, I turned back to McKenzie. "Anything could happen tonight, and we need a contingency plan in case we don't return on time. It's risky to stay here alone, so if we're not back by an hour past sunrise, you are all to leave. Head back to the Cliffs of Moher and stay under cover until sunset. Lorcan's people will take you in without question when the portal reopens."

She opened her mouth to argue, but I cut her off. "Think of Aidan, McKenzie."

She shut her mouth. "Fine. But don't be late."

"We'll do our best," I replied, once again conscious of the sliver of fear I could feel from my protégé. I brushed her hand lightly in passing as I reached out and sheathed another blade behind my heel, adding, "But I'm confident we'll get out in time."

My phone beeped. I reached out and swiped the screen open. Alison. Her text was short and to the point:

Co-ordinates: 57.0366859, -5.7165919

They were coordinates for the outlet pipe on the coast. The Institute wasn't noted on any map and was well-warded, invisible to everyone, even other members of The Oaken Tree. But the outlet pipe that Ike had found could be traced.

After sending her a thumbs up, I entered the coordinates into my phone. Google spat out the location: Inverie, Mallaig, Scotland. So, that was where the Institute was these days. Far enough away to be out of sight of prying eyes and remote enough to remain inconspicuous. But what made my blood run cold was that it wasn't far from Beinn na Caillich. Callum had only been twenty-six kilometers away from us.

"What is it?" Brydie asked.

"The coordinates to the outlet pipe. We're good to go." I put my phone back on the table. "Let's finish loading up, then have something to eat. We'll be moving out to Hag's Cairn in two hours."

When I looked up, McKenzie's face had paled, but Brydie's held both grim acceptance and an urgency to proceed.

THE NIGHT WAS COLD, the air weighted. It was as if Cailleach's spirit was here and knew what we were about to do. I turned to Brydie, who was trailing behind me up the path to Hag's Cairn, her leather jacket pulled tightly around her body. "Stay close," I murmured.

She simply nodded. I knew she was mentally preparing for what we were about to do. I'd explained quite ruthlessly that it was likely people would die tonight, whether that be by her or my own hand. I would shield her from the violence as much as I could, but we both knew I could not guarantee her innocence.

She hadn't flinched but her lips were bloodless she'd replied, "I understand."

There were no excuses, no backing out or second thoughts, just straight determination. I'd felt nothing but fierce pride. Being mentally prepared was the biggest battle of any fight, and Brydie already had a tenacious grip on that hurdle.

I kept the goodbyes short with Ian, Logan, McKenzie, and Aidan, brusquely reminding them to be on their guard and to leave for the Cliffs of Moher if we weren't back at the designated time. They knew better than to argue with me, although I'd felt Logan champing at the bit and knew he was displeased at our separation. Too bad. This wasn't his fight, it was mine.

We reached the narrow entrance leading into the tomb of Hag's Cairn. I glanced down at my watch. One-fifty-five a.m. We had five minutes. We'd left the timing down to the wire, not willing to wait out here longer than necessary.

Brydie's features were tense, and I felt the need to establish the ground rules again before the portal opened. "Remember, I'm in charge. You listen to everything I say. You only move when I say to move. You only speak when I say to speak. And you never leave my side."

I then went over the plan again, repeating the directions Alison had texted through moments before. "We'll be portaled in next to the outlet pipe. It will be large enough for us to enter, but it will be dark. We'll use a flashlight for light—no magic until necessary. We'll follow the tunnel for fifty meters uphill. At the next bend in the pipe, there's a narrow fissure on the northern side of the wall, wide enough for us to slip into. We'll enter an open cavern, which is the bathing chamber for the prisoners. The guards patrol the dungeons in twenty minute shifts, repositioning clockwise. We'll have to wait for a fresh guard change before moving into the cells. We'll have fifteen minutes to get into the lower section of the dungeon. We'll do this by following the main tunnel to the end of the passageway, then turning left. This should take us to Egan's area. He'll be on the door and won't be subject to a change in guard for another twelve hours. We'll have no choice but to take him out."

Brydie was nodding, mentally digesting the directions I was running through for the tenth time.

"After that," I continued, "we find Chloe and get the hell out of there. The whole operation should take us two hours, leaving us an hour to return to the bathing chamber and back into the tunnel. If we get separated, wait there until dawn, or if the alarm sounds on your watch, then you portal out of there, even if I'm not with you. Understand?"

Features set in grim acceptance, she held my gaze, her silver eyes swirling with power in the light of the moon. "Yes."

"Good." Satisfied, I looked down at my watch once again. One-fifty-nine. "Get ready."

I watched the seconds count down. When they reached fifty, I pulled in the power from the equinox stones behind us. It punched me in the gut, a strong dose of old, ancient strength. Gritting my teeth, I held onto the coordinates in my mind as I watched the seconds tick by. Fifty-seven...fifty-eight...fifty-nine...

I flung out a hand, opening a portal. The air whined and screamed, my hair billowing behind me. I reached out to clasp Brydie's hand. "Let's go."

We stepped through and my boots touched wet sand. There was the sound of waves crashing against the coastline. I knew the outline of the Isle of Skye well enough to know we'd arrived where we should. I released Brydie's hand and looked around, spying a narrow tunnel about ten feet away. Most assuring was the trickle of dark, muddied water gushing out of it and into the sea, along with the smell on the air, which was unmistakable over the salty brine: gray water and sewage.

I squeezed my fist closed and the portal vanished.

The air was still and heavy, and I could smell the faint residue of my magical signature hanging in the air. I wove a rune on the air and flicked my fingers seaward, creating a light breeze to disperse the remnants of my power. We didn't need a tail.

I turned to look at Brydie then, taking in her quiet, focused manner. Knowing she was as ready as she'd ever be, I grabbed her hand again and tugged her toward the tunnel entrance.

CHAPTER 30
BRYDIE
PRESENT DAY, SCOTLAND

The smell was unbearable. I didn't want to think of what manner of things were inside the water as we slowly waded, bent over, through the narrow tunnel. It rose at a steady uphill incline, the surface beneath our feet slippery.

Gage held the flashlight. The weak, yellow light only pierced the gloom for a few feet. I stayed close behind him and willed my breathing to stay normal. In and out. Focused and calm.

I could feel my Guardian's tension, the only constant in this shadowy void. He'd honed himself to a fine edge of self-control, and the tingle along my skin told me he'd gathered his power. Every step brought us one step closer to Chloe, and I kept my mind busy by counting them as we walked.

Gage suddenly stopped and turned to face me, the flashlight aimed at our feet. He leaned in close to my ear and whispered, "This is it."

There was a new sulphuric scent in the air. We'd reached the bathing chambers.

But instead of searching the wall for the narrow fissure

that would gain us entry into the bathing chamber beyond, Gage wrapped a hand around my braid and yanked me forward. He slammed his mouth on mine in a kiss that could only be described as fierce. I took as much as he gave, tasting him on my tongue—woodsmoke and forged steel...a honed blade. The kiss was a reminder of what was at stake, that we were in this together, and that he was by my side.

Gage pulled back, a smile tugging at those sensuous lips, and passed me the flashlight before turning back to the tunnel wall to look for the narrow opening Alison had described. A few minutes later, he beckoned me closer.

Naming it a fissure had been apt. The gap was barely wide enough to accommodate me, let alone Gage. On the other side, there was a loud hiss, and a waft of suffocating, sulphur-laden air hit us in the face.

Gage gestured at me to pass him the flashlight, which he wedged into the tunnel wall. Then, with one last look at me, he began to squeeze his body through the gap, and I followed. Every scrape of our boots, every rustle of our clothing against the rock was inordinately loud. We took it slowly and carefully, and I refused to think about what would happen if we had to move quickly on our return journey.

We exited the small gap and entered a cavernous room where three large pools were submerged into the floor. Natural hot springs. The air was wet and heavy, the room hushed. The light came from numerous candles encased in wall sconces, their flickering flames creating a foreboding mix of light and shadow. The atmosphere was further enhanced by the rising steam, which incessantly seethed and curled above the pools to roil against the ceiling above.

Gage had inched his way around the cavern and now stood at the entrance. He looked down at his watch then beckoned to me. I crept up quietly, melting behind his back. He pointed out the entrance and held a finger to his lips while tapping his ear.

I listened and could just discern a murmur: guards. I distinguished several voices. Based on their short conversation, I realized they were changing over.

Gage lifted a hand, signaling we wait. I heard footsteps walking away. Moments later, Gage began moving his hands. There was a faint stirring of magic on the air before a muffled voice cried out, "Berit! The bathing—"

There came a muffled thump, followed quickly by a second.

Gage grabbed my hand and tugged me into the corridor. Just ahead, slumped on the ground, were two men, both dressed in brown robes, the glint of steel at their waists. I refused to look at their faces as Gage pulled me further down the passage. We had twenty minutes to reach the dungeons before the next change of guards.

Our footsteps were hurried, and I tried to quell my panting breath. At the end of the corridor, we came to an intersection. The path forked, one way leading up a winding staircase to the right, the left one leading downward. Cold air wafted down the staircase, but the passage to the left was dank and putrid, flickering with faint light.

Gage tugged me down the left passage, and we hurried through the shadows cast by the wall sconces. When we reached a blind corner, Gage came to a halt and held a finger to his lips. Quiet. He then raised two fingers. Two guards. Then he pointed those fingers at my chest.

What? I stared at him. He narrowed his eyes and pointed once again at my chest. I knew what he was saying: your turn.

I swallowed, heart racing. This was my chance. Willing

my mind to focus on the task at hand, I thought of what was riding on this mission, of my best friend, trapped and alone as Callum's prisoner. I thought about how she'd be feeling, how lost and scared. I felt my rage build at the unfairness of it all, and my magic responded, a roiling mass of power surging against my chest. I flexed my fingers into fists as I felt that energy coursing through my veins. A corresponding icy burn licked across my skin, and I knew without looking down that my palms were alight with power.

Gage had moved to stand beside me, shoulder to shoulder. One of his hands rested on the wickedly curved dagger he always wore at his waist, the other in front of him, a lick of fire steadily burning along his skin.

The muffle of the guard's footsteps came closer, and the pair rounded the corner. Our eyes met, and they halted, one hand instantly reaching for the swords at their belts while they lifted the other in in a parody of Gage's stance. One of their palms glowed a muddy green, the other light blue.

"Who are you?" the guard on the left demanded, his voice gruff, his hair balding and near-white.

Gage didn't respond and I couldn't. Conversing with them hadn't been part of the plan. Besides, my throat was locked tight as I concentrated on containing the power bucking against my chest.

The silence lengthened, and the younger of the two men, his hand suffused in blue light and trembling, threw back his head and screamed, "Intruders!" just as he let loose an ice arrow.

I vaguely heard Gage swear as he released a bolt of fire, obliterating the guard's shard of ice. At the same time, I released my power, slamming both of my hands at the guards. Vicious, driving wind smashed into their chests, lifting them off their feet and throwing them backward, where they crashed into the wall of the corridor behind. There was a groan and then a low moan, before they slumped forward and fell to the ground.

"Come on!" Gage urged, continuing to race down the passage.

Just behind us, I could hear the murmur of voices, the clang of steel, and the muffle of racing feet. It was my fault. I'd hesitated, which had allowed the guard to raise the alarm, and now they were coming.

We ran down the corridor, which opened into another large chamber. If the smell hadn't alerted us, the numerous cells lining the walls were evidence enough that we'd finally reached the dungeons. I didn't dare look too closely inside the cages. The emaciated figures inside were mere shadows, some laying slumped on the floor, some leaning dejectedly against the bars. Their eyes were initially curious, but as they spied our racing forms, some of them began to murmur, then cry with hope.

"Save us!"

"Help me!"

Gage ignored them all as he relentlessly led me further into despair and depravity. The space between us was suddenly filled with a ribbon of flame. It streamed between us, blasting into one of the cells. A scream erupted from within as I turned to face who or what had done that. I felt my blood freeze when I saw not two, but six guards sprinting after us. One of them released another stream of fire, this one aimed directly at my Guardian.

He jumped to the side, narrowly missing the fire that hit the wall beside us. "Keep going!" he cried. "We're almost there."

Ignoring my screaming limbs and aching chest, I followed him around the corner. A blast of rock sounded behind me, then the earth began to tremble beneath my feet. Dust and debris fell from the ceiling as both Gage and I were flung into the wall. My shoulder took the impact and pain bloomed. Gasping, I clutched my arm as I turned back to face the guards who grimly approached. They'd slowed to a walk, their eyes on mine.

"Don't attack," one of them called. "Or we'll be forced to subdue you with no amount of force."

Gage, having pushed back to his feet, snarled, "On the contrary, don't come any closer or you'll find yourselves dead. We don't wish death on any of you."

The guard who'd spoken assessed Gage with narrowed eyes, fingering the sword at his belt while his other hand swirled with fire. "We also wish you no permanent harm. We've had orders to ensure your safety. If we fight down here, there is a very real threat the ceiling will cave in. There will be no winners. Is that a risk you're willing to take?"

"Are you?" Gage returned coolly.

I looked between them, my shoulder throbbing.

"You are surrounded," the guard menaced, his eyes and those of his companions narrowed on Gage. "Drop your weapons and stay your hands."

No! This was not how it was meant to happen. Not how it would be. We had come for Chloe and we were leaving with Chloe. She would not rest down here a moment longer, and these guards would not stop us. Sending Gage an internal message, I threw my hands up in the air. My power hurtled from my palms, smashing into the ceiling. There was a loud boom as it hit the roof, then a split second later, gravel, rock, stone, and dust obliterated everything in sight.

The ricochet of the blast threw me backward, but this time my back thumped into a familiar form. Debris fell from the ceiling, and a high-pitched ringing whined in my ears.

The light had vanished, the candles in the wall sconces blown out with the force of the explosion.

"Brydie." Gage's voice was guttural, scratchy, his fingers digging into my arms.

"I'm okay."

A light suddenly pierced the gloom, not torchlight, but red flames. They licked around one of Gage's hands, pushing back the oppressive darkness. I blinked and caught sight of the large pile of rubble a few feet from where we lay. Rock and other debris now blocked the corridor. The ceiling had caved in, right where I'd aimed my power. On the other side of the rubble, I could hear coughing, shouting, and groaning. I refused to consider what I'd done, who could have been injured, who may have died.

"Are you alright?" Gage demanded as he pulled himself out from under me and pushed gingerly to his feet.

I wasn't sure; I was too scared to move. "I—I think so."

He moved toward me and reached down to offer me a hand. I grasped it, and he hauled me to my feet. I watched his face turn into a grimace as he caught sight of my left wrist which I cradled against my chest. It wasn't broken but it felt sprained.

"Can you hold light?" he asked, meeting my gaze.

I knew he could feel the pain my wrist was causing me. I nodded and turned my mind inward, focusing on my power. I coaxed a small tendril forward. My right hand immediately rippled with blue-white light.

Gage snapped his fingers, and the flames vanished from his hand. He cupped the elbow of my injured arm and urged me onward. "Come on, Chloe's cell should be just ahead."

She was close. It was all the motivation I needed. Steeling my mind to ignore the pain, I staggered along beside him. Gage appeared unharmed and moved as fluidly as he always did. I, on the other hand, was limping, my right knee swollen and stiff.

A few moments later, the passageway began to narrow, and the end became visible, terminating at a single cage. Gage paused, then began to turn around, eyes narrowed.

"What is it?" I breathed.

"Egan isn't here."

The prison warden. A shiver racked my spine. Where was he? Gage was tense, and the tingle at my lower back illustrated he was using his senses. After a moment, he relaxed. "There's no one here, save whoever is in that cage."

"Is it safe to approach?"

He held my gaze, his features soft. "Yes, but I'm warning you now that she's unconscious."

I swallowed. "Let's get her out of here."

His eyes glittered like sapphires. "More than willing to oblige."

Still cupping my elbow, he walked me up to the cage. The light from my hand illuminated the small space, illustrating a female form lying prone on the floor. Her face was in shadow, angled toward the far wall, but I could see that familiar long, black hair trailing in the dirt, no longer glossy and perfectly straight, but tangled and snarled. My heart clenched, and it broke the final chord on my carefully controlled emotions.

"Is..." I swallowed and tried again. "Is she okay?"

"I'm not sure."

Gage never lied to me, but right then, I wished he had.

His closed his eyes and then opened them, his face tight as he admitted, "The dungeon's themselves are warded but the cage isn't. It's just locked."

The expression on his face and the rising anxiety I could

feel along our shared line had me asking, "Why is that a problem?"

"It means we can't portal out of here. It means Callum has ensured that no prisoners and no visitors can enter or exit the dungeon through their own means. The only way out is the way we came."

My stomach dropped, nausea rising. *No! This was not how it would end!* I stared at him, the unfairness of it all threatening to overwhelm me. Behind us, I heard the clang of metal on stone—the unmistakable sound of rubble being cleared. Then a thought hit me, and I sent him a flash of teeth as I shared, "I guess that means we'll need to destroy more walls so we can get out and make that portal."

Gage eye's gleamed. "Right."

He shoved his hand in his leather jacket and pulled out a pocketknife, flicking one of the pins open to release a skinny, narrow hook. I held my breath as Gage inserted it into the lock on the cell door. He jiggled it around a few times, and I heard a snick. Gage paused, and I knew he was thinking the same thing I was. It felt too easy. The sound of shouting came again, then more rubble was being scraped away.

"Quickly," I urged.

Gage pushed the door, and it swung open without a sound. "Stay here," he ordered before walking in. He stood over the still form for a moment, face tightening, before looking back to me. "It's her."

Relief hit me at the same moment the pendant flared, and an ominous stabbing pain was felt at my lower back. Gage cursed, his eyes shooting behind me, and I whirled.

The air was shimmering directly behind me. As I watched, the form solidified into a hooded figure, razor thin and slightly stooped. The head lifted, and the face under the hood was thrown into relief, illuminating a vision of nightmare.

The skin was ravaged, pocked with numerous holes, the flesh stripped from bone. But it wasn't the gaping wounds that caused me to freeze in my position, or the rising fear that was a piercing dagger in my heart—it was the eyes. The right one was a burning cerulean blue, almost identical in color to my Guardian's, but the other...it was a fractured starburst of color, the blue iris flecked with yellow, red, and turquoise. It was at once uniquely beautiful but at the same time deathly cold, for within that fractured gaze burned a hatred so intense I felt myself shrivel under its heat.

I recognized that stare, recognized the depth of that hatred. Yet this time, instead of accommodating another human vessel, there was an innate understanding that this was his real form. And regardless of how shockingly thin he was, the wave of power that emanated from his body was incredible, like nothing else in this world.

My emotions were in turmoil, my mind a scrambled mess, and there was a burgeoning pressure squeezing inside my head. I was frozen, unable to form a single thought or move my limbs.

A hiss of sound came from between lips that were half formed, the tone laced with savage violence. "We meet again...Daughter."

With horrid fascination, I realized his speech was disabled because he struggled to formulate sound without the full use of his lips, and the wheezing that pierced the air was his breath as it whistled in and out of nostrils that were more bone than skin.

I swallowed, my mouth achingly dry, as I stared back, frozen in terror at the specter before me. I tried. I tried to turn, to call out to Gage, but my body—my mind—it refused to listen. I reached for my power, but all that awaited was a banked fire. My fingers flexed at my sides, empty, quiet. What was wrong? Why wasn't my magic responding? Now was the time to be unleashed, now was the time to be given the will to destroy as it pleased!

"Trapped," the voice hissed.

I met that startling, deformed gaze, saw those lips lift in a hideous semblance of a smile. The word repeated in my mind as if he'd willed it: Trapped. *What was trapped?*

A bony finger lifted and tapped against the hooded skull. "I can read thoughts...descendant. ...You're unable to move.... Trapped."

Talorgan flicked his fingers, a dismissive gesture, and a small amount of the pressure pushing against my mind lifted. This time, when I tried to glance back at my Guardian, my body moved as I willed it to.

Gage was still leaning over Chloe, but he was eerily still, as motionless as her prone form on the floor. Talorgan had said I was trapped, but was he referring to Gage or me?

A snuffling chuckle erupted from the wraith in front of me. "Bothhh of you..." he slurred.

It was true—he could read my mind. Chilled, I gasped out, "How are you here?"

The specter smiled. "My newfound alliance...with druid...and you."

"Me?"

Those mismatched eyes wandered, tracing my features before traveling down my neck where they stopped, fixating on the pulse I could feel throbbing wildly in my throat. "Your...blood."

That revelation was immediately drowned out by a huge blast behind us, causing me to stumble backward. Moments later, I heard pounding footsteps.

Talorgan hadn't moved, his form still flickering in and out, a confirmation that he was here in essence alone. What would have happened if he'd been here physically? What power would I have faced? Would he be stronger? What chance would I have had?

The figure snarled, "None." His face burned, twisting into a sweeping hunger. "Lucky...not Samhain. Lucky... power limited."

The message was loud and clear, because at Samhain, his reckoning would come. Whatever Callum had done, whatever lore he'd created by using *my* blood meant that Talorgan could escape the prison he'd been sent to. He could now leave at will, whether within a host or as a specter of his form. My head whirled, and my gut churned; I felt like I was going to be sick.

Gage had warned us all; many times. He'd even warned the jeweler at Aviemore, as well as Lorcan in Faerie, that things were changing, that the playing field had been skewed. He was the only one who'd had the insight to understand a tide of darkness was building, and it was about to break over us all. But this...this was more than I'd expected. This was more than Gage had probably expected.

A familiar voice broke through the horrified trail of my thoughts. "Thank you, Master. I can take her from here."

I shifted my attention from the wraith to the man who had approached unawares. Callum now faced Talorgan. His demeanor was respectful, almost reverent, as he gave a short bow.

Talorgan's heavy gaze shifted from my face, their burdened power now falling on Callum. "Contain the descendant...but don't break her.... She's mine."

The possessiveness in that tone caused my heart to stutter.

"Of course," Callum replied. He turned and gestured to the cell behind me. "And what of the Guardian and the other woman?"

"Kill them," Talorgan hissed, eyes flaring with violence.

Callum bent his head in compliance and moved beyond my sight.

Talorgan pinned me once again with that dreadful, deadly stare and whispered, "Now my plans...fulfilled...time to leave. ...Until Samhain, descendant."

And with that parting shot, his form wavered once more and faded from sight.

I immediately felt my mind be released and, without a second thought, I dug deep down into my well of power and whirled to face Callum.

But he wasn't where he'd been moments earlier, instead, he was inside the cell, a wickedly curved dagger held against Gage's throat. And Chloe; she remained as she'd been before—still and motionless on the ground at their feet.

I hesitated, staring at Callum, my hands alight with power, the magic writhing for release in my chest.

Callum smiled. "I wouldn't do that if I were you, or your Guardian dies."

For emphasis, he pressed the knife against Gage's neck, and the slight wince on my Guardian's face had my heart stuttering. Why wasn't he fighting back?

As if he could read my confusion, Callum sneered, "Your blood has come in handy these past few weeks. The sample you gave us enabled a lot of experiments, one which has successfully allowed me to trap your Guardian's power within this cell. You've also proven neither of you can scent the new lore. It makes me wonder if you're too close to the source." His smile widened. "I must say I'm pleased with the results."

My heart was pounding so loud I could barely breathe. The cell had been warded with new lore using my blood? Lore that wasn't recognizable to either of us? Lore that had trapped Gage's powers...and possibly caused Chloe to remain unconscious?

It was suddenly too hard to breathe. Too hard to think straight. My mind was a mess of thoughts. *Think, goddammit, think!*

Callum hadn't killed Gage. Not yet. And he didn't do things without reason. He had to have a stake in all this, a motivation...

I forced out between clenched teeth, "Why? You're going to kill him anyway."

"On the contrary," he drawled. "Regardless of what Talorgan ordered, I have other plans for your Guardian."

"What plans?" I breathed, any pretense of hiding my fear now gone.

Panic began to claw at my throat, and my power bucked, craving release. But Callum, as if noticing the call of my power, pushed the tip of his dagger further into Gage's neck, and a trickle of blood trailed down his olive skin.

I met Gage's eyes, pleading with him, silently asking him what I should do.

He opened his mouth, grunting, "Do it!" Then his body was flying forward as Callum violently kneed him in the back.

"Shut up!" Callum spat, reaffirming his hold by yanking on Gage's hair. The leader of The Oaken Tree stared back at me, his beady eyes swirling with triumph. "As much as she wants to kill me, I know she won't risk hurting her precious Guardian." Gage hissed in denial, but Callum continued, "And as it so happens, I have need of another guard with particular skills. You would be the perfect candidate. I would be remiss to waste such an opportunity through the simple act of death."

My stomach clenched, my nails biting into my palms. Trapped. I was trapped again, this time by the dagger held at Gage's throat. Callum knew I wouldn't do it, knew I couldn't risk it. Could likely see I didn't trust the power that throbbed through my veins or that internal flicker of darkness craving freedom. My control was tenuous, and unleashing my power on Callum, that close to Gage, was a gamble I wasn't willing to take. Especially when I wasn't certain the dagger held against his throat would kill him first.

But the alternative was just as bad. Using my Guardian as one of his guards! How was that possible? The answer was immediate: *The cauldron.* He would make Gage drink from the Dagda's cauldron.

"Ah, yes," Callum drawled. "You've come to see the full picture, and I see the notion doesn't please you. Is it the fact that he'll be working for me, or the fact that he'll forget all about you once he drinks from it?"

I pressed my lips together, fear twisting inside me.

Callum laughed. "Oh, this is priceless! I'm honestly intrigued at what will happen when he drinks from the cauldron now. I wonder if it will permanently severe the bond you share." Callum cocked his head to the side, not relenting his grip on the hilt of the dagger or Gage's hair. "The thought that your emotions still remain tied intrigues me. That level of torture would be unprecedented."

I remained silent. Gage's eyes burned into mine. His voice was roaring in my head. *Do it! Do it now! Run!* He was screaming so loudly that I couldn't think, couldn't breathe. All I could do was stare stupidly at them both, frozen in position, undecided. Unwilling to take the risk and attack, and unwilling to leave him.

Callum sighed at my lack of response. "You're no fun. Given you haven't attacked, it's safe to assume you've decided to submit and save the life of your Guardian. How very boring of you. I admit, it's not much fun when my plans go as expected. However, no matter, not when I have a prize worth exploring." He smiled down at Gage, who glared back.

"To guarantee your continued support," Callum continued, "I've prepared in advance of your arrival. If you would like to see Gage live another day, you'll not fight the gifts I'm about to bestow upon you."

Callum smiled as he nodded his head at the guards who had gathered in a group behind me. One approached, carrying an object that felt alien, wrong. I dropped my gaze to what was in the guard's hand.

They were round circlets of iron, encased in glowing runes. Bracelets. Their very presence made my skin crawl. Inside, my magic bucked against my chest, not clawing for release, but pounding in fear now. "What are those?" I forced out.

Callum smiled. "Your concession to allow your Guardian to live."

I looked back at Gage. He remained motionless, the dagger still pressed against his throat. I knew that if I denied the imposition of these shackles—because bracelets they were not—that dagger would plunge into my Guardian's throat and his lifeblood would drain away.

"Well? What will it be, descendant?" Callum drawled.

I turned back to the leader of our people, rage and fear spiraling up my throat. Staring into his hateful face, I firmly clamped down on the magic that bucked and writhed inside me, my skin burning from the inside out. Sweat broke out across my forehead. Both of my choices were no choices at all, but I had to choose, and I had to choose *now*. There was no question of the route I'd take, not with what Gage and I had shared...not when I loved him.

Loved him. With everything I had.

Given the choice, I chose love.

I chose him.

I held out my arms, baring my wrists to the guard.

Callum smiled triumphantly. "Bind her. Tie her wrists together for added security to stop any ideas she may have of getting free, then have her delivered to my chamber."

Gage made a noise, a guttural sound of such pain. As soon as our eyes met, I felt sick. The defeat and searing pain in his gaze was too much. Guilt ate away at me. I knew my decision to choose him was what he'd feared all along, what he'd fought so hard against. He'd been so strong until recently, right up until that first night in Faerie when he'd denied every chance to be more than a Daughter and her Guardian. My heart clenched at his pain, at his disappointment, but it was a decision I would make every time.

The guard didn't hesitate to do Callum's bidding. He tore the watch off and slammed the bracelets over my wrists. As soon as those iron bands were locked into place, my body felt trapped, strung tight. My eyes burned, my head throbbed, and the magic in my chest suddenly vanished, coiling within itself into a tiny, threatened ball. I was burning, a fever racing through my veins.

What the hell were these bracelets? What had they done to me? But I couldn't voice the question aloud; my mouth was now dry, my mind a swirl of muddied fragments.

I barely saw another guard move forward, barely felt him pull my arms behind my back and tie them together with a thick rope, nor did I feel the rope being lashed tightly around my wrists. I moved as if in a dream as I was pulled down that long, dark passageway, now cleared of rubble.

I didn't once look back to the man I left behind; I was unable. But inside, I was screaming. Past the pounding pain in my head, all I could see was the everlasting vision of my Guardian's panicked cerulean gaze.

CHAPTER 31

TALORGAN

3RD CENTURY BC, ANCIENT SCOTLAND

Talorgan herded the virgins into the hastily erected wooden structure. He ignored their whimpers, their looks of fear, the stench of sweat and urine. They would find no mercy here, not from him or any of the Otherworld creatures or dark druids slowly filling their camp under the cover of the trees.

After the last woman had entered the shieling, he dropped the hide into place and turned to the two sirens who stood respectfully beside him.

"Stay here. Guard the shieling," he said firmly. "No one goes in or out, including you."

He emphasized the warning with a flick of his wrist, allowing red and black smoke to curl around his hand in a sinuous implication of the death they could otherwise expect.

Instead of flinching, the beautiful, naked sirens sent him a chilling smile, their perfectly gorgeous features transformed into faces of nightmare as their razor-sharp teeth glistened in the shards of moonlight.

"We do not fear you, druid," the siren on his left drawled, her voice husky and wanton.

"You have no need to worry about their escape," said the other. "We only enjoy the taste of men." Her eyes dipped to run pointedly down his body, lingering at the place where his groin was hidden from view under his blood-red robe.

Talorgan wondered why he did not feel a crawling whisper of disgust at her lewd suggestion—not even a touch of fear. His emotions were becoming wooden, empty. Was this another reaction to the power now coursing through his veins? He shied away from what that might mean when he found Cailleach. He refused to believe his feelings for her could change, especially when he still felt a hunger to claim her as his own—to claim her as was his due.

He decided that the best way to proceed was to ignore the siren's suggestion. "Good, then I will not hear any reports of *accidents* in the night. Do not leave your posts until I return."

Without giving them a chance to reply, he turned on his heel to search out his Dark God, more than aware Arawn was waiting to hear his report on how many virgins he had rounded up for the impending ceremony. His missive would please his master. Arawn had asked for thirteen, and on the first day thirteen had been found.

It had been no easy feat to return to his village and ignore what had happened on the mountain last night. He'd hungered to show everyone his power, but Talorgan had known his people weren't ready to learn the full extent of what he had become in the past six months; he had to start slowly in order to win over those who hovered on the line between light and dark.

Dawn had been breaking across the horizon as Talorgan entered the village through a portal at the edge of their settlement. He sent a signal out to those druids whom he knew favored the dark arts, his invitation encouraging them to bring others to the meeting who would be equally interested or curious.

Arawn had tasked him with building an army, knowing he would need more than just creatures of the Underworld to win this war. The Underworld creatures were all vicious and horrific, led by their base instincts, and when exposed to violence or lust, they lost all sense of control and became rabid animals. For Arawn to win this war, the Dark God needed generals who could lead with their heads, not with their selfish desires. So, Talorgan had come back to his village not only to entrap thirteen virgins, but also in the hope of converting some of his own people to the cause.

The act was a double-edged sword; a carefully contrived battle tactic that would break the spirit of even the most stalwart druid they would face on the battlefield, because no one wanted to kill their closest friend. No one wanted to kill their own father, let alone their child. Yes, his plan held merit, one which may well see him win this war for Arawn.

Talorgan had been surprised at the sheer number of druids who answered his call. It was nigh on a third of the village. He only gave them a glimpse of his power—enough to elicit their support in rounding up the thirteen virgins Arawn requested. They were taken throughout the day, herded to a spot in the woods he'd camouflaged from prying eyes with the use of his newfound power. And after the last of the thirteen had been caught, he'd turned to the group and given them a choice—to join him and earn a share of their own power, or die. Not one of them had balked at his offer, so he'd given them instructions to go home and pack their things, then meet him at the encampment on the Cairngorm Mountains. One asked where exactly it was, and his reply had been short: "You don't need directions. The call of power will lead the way."

Not one of them had asked about the Winter Goddess, or her sister, Brighid. They'd either forgotten about both of them with the promise of dark power, or they'd blindly accepted he had the goddesses' permission to establish his camp on the mountain.

Accomplishment was what he now felt as he'd returned with not only the virgins Arawn requested, but also a number of druidic soldiers now being added to the Dark God's ranks.

As Talorgan walked to Arawn's tent, he tried to block out the sound of the portal that permanently remained in place at the edge of their encampment. The portal was large, having been stretched to its fullest capacity, and Talorgan had seen all manner of beings walk through it. He'd also caught sight of the world that beckoned beyond; an arid, burning wasteland of sand and rock with dark, monstrous beings salivating at its opening. Arawn's people.

Talorgan had sensed their hunger, knew they ached to rake their claws into this soft, rich land and plunder everything it offered. Unfortunately, they had to bide their time, because with the amount of power required to maintain the portal, Arawn could only bring them through one at a time.

Their entrance into this world was painful. Their agonized screams cut through the air, reverberating around the mountain range as if time and matter itself was against their entrance into this world—as if nature itself knew they brought disruption to the tenuous balance.

He still remembered the first arrival. Shock and revulsion were twin swords in his chest as he witnessed the creature come through the portal. It was a dullahan, its head missing from its sturdy body as it silently rode through upon its black war horse which let loose a roar of pain and rage. A sluagh had followed—a dead, malevolent ghost; and after that was a beautiful, naked maiden, her body curvy and ripe, her long, red hair like rippling fire down her back.

Talorgan had shifted next to his new master then, his interest piquing as a slim hope radiated from his chest. Maybe the Underworld didn't just contain creatures of the night? Maybe it was also home to creatures of beauty and light?

The maiden had sidled up to him, her form swaying with silent invitation. He hadn't been able to stop himself from reaching out a hand in welcome. She'd walked straight into his arms, rubbing her body against his as her hands wandered to his groin. His swollen member had stiffened further, desire shooting through his veins as he cupped her rear and palmed one of her breasts. He was overwhelmed by a compulsion to take her there and then, regardless of whether his master watched them. The thought had his head rising to meet Arawn's gaze.

The Dark God had been standing there, watching them with an arrogant smirk on his face. That expression hadn't made sense until the naked maiden looked up at him and smiled. Talorgan froze as he was met with razor sharp teeth that gleamed with deadly menace. Upon her breath was the smell of carrion, fresh and ripe, the putrid stench attacking his senses. His member had instantly softened with the awareness that danger lurked within her desirable shell.

She opened her full, luscious lips and purred, "I love the taste of men. It's been an age since I tasted anything but the vile creatures in our world. You, my love, will be a tasty treat...one I will savor."

Talorgan had attempted to lurch back at her blatant threat, but his body had been leaden and unresponsive.

The siren chuckled. "You've been ensnared, my sweet. You can't escape."

Talorgan looked to his master. "Arawn, tell her who I am," he pleaded, wondering if his newfound god would let this woman enjoy her sport or whether he would extend a measure of gratitude and release him from her spell.

Arawn had merely raised a brow. "I think not. I am intrigued to see how this will all play out. Look on it as an opportunity to test your newfound power."

Incredulous, Talorgan was speechless for a moment. Then, understanding that no help would be forthcoming, he'd turned back to the waiting siren. Deciding hesitation could have no place here, he sucked in a breath and released it, wincing at the odor as he did so. "Remove me from these bonds, or you will never get the chance to sate your hunger in this world."

The siren had looked from one to the other, her face curious. Talorgan had taken the moment to call forth his power. It responded instantly, a conflagration of rage, a living, breathing inferno which exemplified his hate and desire for retribution. He felt his hand warm, and the scent of his power wafted on the cool breeze.

The siren caught whiff of the new odor, and this time it was her who froze, the smug look on her face slackening. She'd taken a step back from him, her hands falling away from his groin, and snarled, "You hold dark power. Power like the Master. How did a creature such as you attain this gift?"

Talorgan spoke the truth. "I awakened Arawn and offered him my soul in return for power. In doing so, I also allowed him entry onto this world, and in turn, you and all the others to come." He waved a hand at the arid, smoking world through the portal behind her.

"You?" She cut off a snort when Arawn offered no rebuttal. Her eyes moved restlessly between them, and she suddenly had the look of a caged rabbit. She nervously licked her lips and asked, "What power did the Master give you?"

"Immortality."

She blanched. "I see." Stepping sideways, away from the portal and further out of his reach, she added, "Then this little tryst between us is misfounded. I apologize for my ignorance of your position; I will not forget again."

Talorgan hid the swell of pride at her deference to his position. "For that, I will allow your actions to be forgiven. But know this, woman, if you ever put me in that position again, then there will be a reckoning."

Her lips curled into a saccharine smile. "Do not give me reason to, druid. Your position may be strong now, but at some stage you will make a mistake, and Arawn and his people do not suffer fools lightly." She inclined her head and turned away.

Talorgan hissed but let her go when he caught sight of Arawn's amused visage.

"She is right, you know," the Dark God murmured. "I will not tolerate insubordination or stupidity. And any gifts I have bestowed upon you can easily be taken back if you do not prove worthy of them."

Talorgan's heart had lurched. Would Arawn cast him aside that easily? Where was the Dark God's sense of loyalty? He cleared his throat. "In that case, I will not give you reason to."

Arawn stared at him, and it had felt as though he saw

right into Talorgan's very soul to all the desires and fears he secretly harbored. "See that you do."

The afternoon had dragged on as one creature after another had entered their world. And after observing a number of them, all hideous and vile, Talorgan no longer flinched. After a time, the darkness that leached out from under their skin was no longer abhorrent, and in fact, seemed to call to the darkness in him. He realized he understood these beings, understood their pain at being outcast for how they felt and the emotions they gravitated toward, because after all, he felt the same. Rage, lust, jealousy, vengeance—all vied for a foothold in his mind.

So now, tonight, Talorgan did not look inside the portal as he went past, and even though he could not see the latest army contingents walk through, he heard them. Their screams were unmistakable, and he knew without looking at them that the beautiful, soulful women would be wearing long, white cloaks. Banshees. With their piercing wails dogging him, Talorgan walked to his master's tent in the middle of the encampment.

The two sentries positioned in front of the entrance were enough to freeze anyone's blood, and even with his dulled emotions, Talorgan felt a kernel of real fear. It didn't matter how many times he came across the cù-sìth; these hounds commanded a deep respect that could only be forged by age and power.

The two Underworld hounds had shaggy, dark green fur. They were the largest Talorgan had ever seen, and in their short time on this world, he had learned there were three of them, all loyal to Arawn. They were his hellhounds, favored disciples whom he allowed at his side. Of course, Arawn also had dragons, but no creature was as loyal as a hound, and going by their size, their strength, and the lethal intelligence that lurked inside their glowing green eyes, Talorgan knew Arawn had chosen his personal guards well.

At his approach, both hounds turned their full attention on him, and the closest one spoke. The voice, when it came, was a dark serration of sound, gravelly, low, and menacing. "The druid has returned. Have you adhered to our master's wishes?"

Talorgan tried not to focus on the beast's large jaw that was the size of both his palms, or on the rancid flesh clinging to those pointed canines. But the waft of the creature's breath could not be ignored, putrid and carrying nothing but death. "The master will be well-pleased with my tidings," Talorgan returned in as firm a voice as he could manage.

The hound closest to him peeled its muzzle back in a garish parody of a smile. That this creature was capable of such intelligent communication had a chill whispering over his skin.

Its tongue rolled out of its mouth to lave the side of his jaw as the hound said with a pointed stare, "Ahh, a shame. I have waited a long time to taste druid blood once more. You may have thwarted my plans today, but I'm sure the opportunity will arise again."

Talorgan felt his anger rise at the insubordination. He was not Arawn, no, but his pact with the Dark God had granted the hellhounds and the other creatures of the Underworld entry to this world. He was owed a level of respect for those actions, and he was done not being recognized for them.

Between clenched teeth, he growled, "I would not push, hound. I appreciate your role is to protect our master, but to insult me is to barter for your life. Are you that unintelligent that you do not understand how much power our master has gifted me? Who and what he has also bound me to? Falin is my subject, as I am Arawn's. Therefore, if you insult me, you also insult him. So, hound, choose your words wisely, because I never forget an insult, and one too many may cause my wrath to raze you to the ground."

The hellhound snarled in response, hackles rising. Its massive paws scoured the ground, long claws dragging in the earth. Its companion also snarled, turning glowing, green eyes to his face.

Talorgan clenched his hands at his sides, summoning that dark, sinuous pool of energy deep within his core, and waited. He was terrified of an attack from these creatures, but at the same time, he craved the release a fight would bring.

As if an unspoken message had passed between the two hounds, they launched as one at his form. Their large bodies obliterated the light of the moon, and all Talorgan could see was two large, dark green shadows hurling themselves toward him. He raised his hands and released the energy he'd been building, aiming his magic at the beasts' bodies. Just as their front paws slammed into his chest, he heard their howl of agonized pain as his magic seared them.

The smell of burnt fur was overwhelming as he was thrust backward onto the cold, hard ground. The hounds slammed on top of him, their combined weight crushing two of his ribs with an audible crack. They used their momentum to lunge forward, gaping maws snapping at his face and neck. Talorgan twisted his head from side to side, desperately trying to escape their lethal teeth. Frustrated at their lack of purchase, the two hounds again reared as one, this time to rake their paws down the length of his body.

Talorgan felt their long claws rend his skin, slashing his blood-red robe into tatters.

Without the breath to cry out, Talorgan cut off the emotion, severing the tie to his nerve endings with a practiced mindfulness that only one with endless drills could master. He could feel the potent, hot, flood of power that now simmered under his skin. With it, there also came an awareness of his immortality—a gift from his god. It reminded him that the hounds could do their worst and he would still survive. However, that didn't mean that he would give them the satisfaction.

He didn't want to become their sport—their plaything—and he didn't want to concede any of his power and position to these two creatures as he had the siren. They needed to know he was Arawn's preferred disciple—his first and only disciple. And that anyone who came after him had to get in line.

Fortified by his desires and his all-consuming need to win this power play, Talorgan focused on his attack. His hands were trapped, hanging uselessly by his sides, but his mouth remained open, offering a release for the magic that sang in his veins. A hound, frustrated by its lack of purchase, latched sharp teeth onto his arm, readying itself to pull it from his body. At that moment, Talorgan released a drawn-out sigh.

From his mouth came a coiled rope of red and black smoke. It arrowed straight at the hound, whose jaws were wrapped around his upper arm. The smoke pierced the hound's left eye, and it reared backward, its jaws releasing his upper arm as it yelped and shook its head.

The disruption caused the other hound to jerk its head up from Talorgan's neck and look in surprise at his brother. It was the moment Talorgan needed. He raised his free arm and grated out harshly, "Fire!" before slamming his hand into the hound's side.

The hound on top of him flinched as the fireball singed its fur. Then, as if in slow motion, it turned to strike him with its eerie gaze. Hatred blazed within its green eyes, hot and potent, before excruciating pain caused the hound to lurch off him in a frenzied scramble. As both hounds howled and snarled and threw themselves to the ground in a rabid exhibition of agony and rage, Talorgan came slowly to his feet, a hand clasped to his middle as he studiously tried to ignore the pull of sinew and torn muscle. Blood coated his robe, and the smell of iron overwhelmed his senses. His own blood was what he smelt, and it made his resolve unwavering.

Talorgan had made sure his answering attack couldn't be escaped. His magic had been deadly and sure, with the intent to do permanent damage. He would not allow these creatures to undermine his position in this new army—not ever again. Aware that time was of the essence, he lifted his hand, ready to end their time on this earth when the tent flap lifted, and a figure *flowed* rather than moved out of the entrance, another large shadow padding at his heels.

"Halt! What is the meaning of this? Why do you disgrace me and my position by fighting like rabid dogs?"

The voice was a whiplash of power, a discordant melody that pierced Talorgan's mind with a blow that was at once lethal and a soul-searing melody. It was enough to check his response, for in the haze of retribution, he recognized who and what now demanded his attention—Arawn, the Dark God. His perfect, gorgeous face was twisted into a scowl of displeasure that did nothing to detract from his deadly beauty, and at his side stood a third hellhound, even bigger than his injured brothers.

Cold reason hit Talorgan starkly in the belly as he realized how close he'd been to killing two of his master's favored subjects. He immediately stilled his instinctive reaction to kill the hounds. With the withdrawal of his magic, they collapsed to the ground, their large tongues lolling from their gaping maws as they whimpered in deference to their master.

Aware that he, too, must appease his riled god, Talorgan dropped his hands to his sides and bowed his head in deference. "I am sorry, my lord. We were merely settling a disagreement."

The hellhounds snarled in unison, and the one on the left, now with only one glowing green eye, added in his growling, guttural voice, "We were merely testing his allegiance, sire. We thought to determine his right to stand beside you."

Arawn had his head cocked to the side in an impression of consideration, but Talorgan was not fooled. The Dark God did nothing by chance. Every move, every stance was an act of precision, bringing him one step closer to his ultimate goal—establishing himself on this plane. "It appears this test of yours has been successful given the mess of your right eye, Uren." Arawn flicked his gaze at the other injured hellhound. "And you, Lonc, appear to have a nasty burn on your side. Tell me, hounds, what do you think the outcome of this *test* would have been had I not interfered?"

Both hounds dropped their muzzles to their front paws and whimpered again, this time at the hidden threat so cleverly interlaced within Arawn's question.

It was Lonc who answered between clenched teeth, his voice a low, snarling growl of anger, "The druid surprised us, but we would not have succumbed. Uren and I were about to put him in his place."

"Lies!" Talorgan hissed, clutching at his ragged stomach which now throbbed with a viciousness that had him yearning to fall down and heal the wounds in peace. "I was about to administer the killing blow when you walked out, Master."

Arawn cut his carmine eyes to his disciple. "Indeed," he murmured in a silky tone. "And then where would I be without my two hounds, druid? They do me a service, guarding my quarters day and night, often running errands for me. If you had killed two of them, I would have two vacancies to fill, both of which I am very particular about."

Talorgan immediately bowed his head in apology. "I am sorry, my lord, but I had no choice but to prove my worth. I'm sure you would have done the same."

The smile vanished from Arawn's face. "Do not presume anything of me, druid!" he grated out in a low voice, his tone no less deadly than if he had shouted. "Know this: You may kill any of my subjects, save my favored. That alone includes my three dragons and my three hounds. And no matter what disputes arise between you, there will be no life taken by your hands. Is. That. Understood?"

Although the tone was clearly a threat, Talorgan didn't feel as he once had. The Dark God's request felt weaker, whether that was because he was gradually losing his sense of strong emotion, or whether he had come to the understanding that he had lost more than he would ever know, he wasn't sure. But what he did know was that this promise could not be one-sided. If he was to survive in this new hierarchy of power, alongside his dark master, then his position had to be established right at the outset, without any question of his ability.

So, he raised his head and forced himself to look into those carmine eyes, not flinching when Arawn afforded him a chilling smile, those sharp, serrated teeth like lethal daggers in his gorgeous face. "I will make that promise if the hounds and the dragons make their own promises. I will become no one's victim, nor will I disadvantage myself by agreeing to this on my own. Besides, I tire of these power plays. They have become boring and predictable. I would rather use my energy to forward our cause and take what is rightfully ours."

Talorgan caught a fleeting glimpse of what looked like surprise cross Arawn's features before it was erased by a look of cunning. Arawn turned to his three hounds. "What say you, hounds? Will you agree to this?"

Lonc and Uren snarled, but Brude, the third hellhound who stood stoically at Arawn's side, pawed the ground and rumbled between clenched teeth in a voice deeper than his brothers, "We accept, Master."

Arawn cut his gaze back to Talorgan. "And you, druid? Do we have your promise to end this fighting and save it for those who deserve our wrath?"

Talorgan inclined his head. "You have my word that I will not kill your hellhounds."

Arawn smiled, a show of teeth. Talorgan knew the Dark God had noticed his carefully chosen words, was aware he had neither promised not to hurt them again, nor made mention of the dragons. "Good, then let us get onto the rightful matters at hand. Come, Talorgan, we have an attack to plan." Confirming the discussion had ended, Arawn turned smoothly and flowed back into his tent.

But before following his master, Talorgan stared at each of the hounds in turn. Uren stared back at him with one ruined eye, hatred gleaming from the depths of the other; Lonc's long, shaggy, green coat was bristling, no doubt from the pain emanating from the burn in the shape of a handprint at his side; and Brude merely stared back at him, a measured look on his canine face, as if weighing his worth and the risk he posed to them all.

Ignoring the injured hellhounds, Talorgan took one step forward, toward the tent. Brude peeled his lips back from his muzzle and stood taller, his hackles raised.

Talorgan eyed him, his words calm. "I wouldn't do that if I were you, Brude. Your master is waiting."

The hound didn't blink as he stared back at him, his focus deadly and absolute. And while they were locked in visual combat, a voice, harsh and grating, seared Talorgan's mind. It was undeniably Brude's, and the fact that the beast could communicate with him this way checked his steps.

"Do not underestimate who we are, druid. Do not underestimate where we come from, and do not underestimate the relationship we have with our master. You would do well to not come between us again, especially if Arawn is not in sight."

Talorgan didn't allow a hint of fear to cross his features. To meet all three of them alone would change the odds he'd just faced, and judging by Brude's muscular build, much larger than that of his brothers, not to mention the intelligence that lurked in his eyes, he understood their fight here tonight could have ended very differently.

Talorgan recognized false bravado was the only way forward. "I accept the warning, however, given the agreement that was just conceded, I doubt either of us will be fighting to the death again—not unless you wish to sign your death warrant before your allotted time."

"Trust me, druid," Brude replied in his mind with a snarl, *"if the time is right, we will take it. There is a different freedom in death, especially when all hope is lost."*

The words checked Talorgan's next step. Hope? The hound had hope? What hope? What did they desire? Did all creatures that followed the Dark God have their own ambitions, their own desires? Was that what had aligned their path to Arawn? It was a concept so profound that Talorgan could feel the very truth of it in his bones.

Of course, Arawn was a master at playing on desire. He understood the power in wanting something so badly that you forgot all sense of reason and committed yourself to deeds you wouldn't have been able to contemplate before. The Dark God had chosen well, feeding on sinful cravings and the urge to possess something that could not otherwise be had. That led to the question: What was it that the hellhounds desired?

Aware that discovering the answer would take time, Talorgan chose to ignore Brude's comment and took another step forward. He clenched his teeth together as the cut sinew along his chest and abdomen pulled, blood oozing between the fingers pressed to his side.

Smelling the iron on the air, Brude's lips quivered, saliva dripping from his jaw, but Talorgan didn't stop his deliberate, measured pace toward the tent flap. As he passed Brude, he felt the back of his neck whisper with the knowledge that he was within killing range.

Talorgan held his breath as he drew alongside him. But Brude didn't respond to the provocation, and as Talorgan took another step forward, the bristling hound allowed him to enter Arawn's tent, unmolested.

He didn't have time to release a breath of relief, not when he now faced a greater threat. The Dark God was standing before his war table, a gold goblet in his hands. As the tent flap swished into place behind him, Arawn looked up from the statues he was contemplating on a crude map etched into the table.

For all its drawling sweetness, Arawn's tone was deadly

as his carmine eyes pierced Talorgan. "I trust the news you bring is positive?"

He bowed his head. "All thirteen virgins have been captured. They are sequestered in the shieling. I have two sirens standing guard."

"Good." A cruel smile flitted across the Dark God's face. "Now that we have the virgins, everything is in place. We must now prepare for the sacrifice."

The sacrificial ceremony that would enable Arawn to channel his power and open the portal even wider to allow more of his people to enter this world and swell their ranks.

A surge of excitement swelled in Talorgan's chest. The next phase of his plan would soon begin—war would ensue, and it wouldn't be long until he had what it was he most desired: the Winter Goddess. "When will we begin the ceremony?"

"Tsk, tsk, druid," Arawn taunted as he lifted the goblet to his lips and took a sip. "You must have patience. Have you forgotten where power lies and what event is drawing nigh? I have not been on this world in an eon, but I can still remember when Samhain falls and what the moon can offer when it is at its fullest. In less than three days, the new moon will be rising with Samhain's birth, and we would do well to wait. The veils between the worlds will be at their thinnest; it is the ideal time to open the portal further so all my people can enter."

Talorgan felt his skin crawl at the reminder of who and what those people outside the tent were. Since his fateful meeting with Arawn, Talorgan had seen many things he hadn't believed to be real, and he understood that the old tales of his masters were true. For not only were there dragons and hellhounds, but also banshees, sirens, wulvers, sluaghs, and fairies. All of them with a cant toward the dark, all of them reveling in cruelty and malice. And with that came desire, jealousy, and greed. Even now, as he stood before his Dark God, he could hear them squabbling outside the tent; snarls, howls, and shrieks of anger and defiance penetrated the still night air.

"As you wish," he responded with a slight bow.

"Oh, I do wish," Arawn returned with a glint in his eye. "Nothing and no one will prevent me from getting what I desire. I am done with overseeing that hell hole. This world has been denied me too long, and given the circumstances of my awakening, it appears my siblings have not been balancing the scales as they should. My coming is a blessing, and the people will welcome it." Arawn cocked his head. "Isn't that right, druid?"

At the question, a tiny whisper of doubt slewed through Talorgan's mind. This altercation with the Dark God had gained unexpected momentum far beyond him simply claiming Cailleach for himself...but he'd come too far down this path to return now. He squashed all hesitation and replied, "I have a wealth of power I never had before, Master. For that, I am extremely thankful."

Arawn considered him. "Yes, you do hold immense power. May it act as a reminder that I favor those who join me. There will be more of those gifts in future should you succeed in the rites we will be performing at Samhain. I need that army, and now that I am here to guarantee my people's safety, they will come." He put the goblet down on the table and looked carefully at Talorgan. "You're aware my siblings will fight me on this? That they will do whatever they can to prevent my transition to this world?"

Talorgan nodded. Of that, he was sure.

"Then the steps here are simple. If we don't carry out the sacrifice, we won't have an army, and if we don't have an army, we will lose the war before it's already begun. For all my power, I am still only one god against many. It is imperative the virgins remain virgins until two nights hence, or the magic we wield will not be enough to stop my siblings. Do not fail me on this, druid."

Talorgan felt the weight of those words as if they were a dagger in his heart, knew that failure wouldn't be countenanced—not only because it would appease his master, but also because it meant he would lose that which he most wanted. That which was his entire reason for being on this path: Cailleach.

"I will not fail you, Master."

"See that you don't."

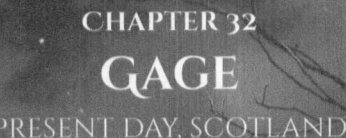

CHAPTER 32
GAGE
PRESENT DAY, SCOTLAND

I watched as Brydie was led away by two of Callum's guards. My blood hammered with the need to follow her and wrench her from their grasp, to take her and run and leave this godforsaken nightmare. But I was trapped, caught like a spider in a web, my magic chained, my body captive.

Callum's voice was soft, almost solicitous, and it cut right through my panicked thoughts. "Thank you for bringing her to me, Gage. I wasn't sure if you'd fall for the dream I planted in McKenzie's head."

I froze. "What did you say?"

"You heard me." Callum widened his stance and clasped his hands in front of him, his new blood-red robe swirling around his ankles. "I planted a dream in McKenzie's head. I made her believe the fifth descendant was in the dungeons, beaten and tortured. If it hadn't been for our close connection, I'm not sure it would have worked."

"Your close connection?" I repeated.

"Oh, you didn't know our history?" Callum smiled smoothly. "McKenzie and I spent some time together about ten years ago. If she'd been open to experimenting, we would still be together."

I couldn't stomach this any further. "I know what you did to her," I said between clenched teeth. "I know all about your jealousies, your insecurities, and your need to dominate."

He stared at me, the slight widening of his eyes illustrating his surprise. Then he shrugged. "I suppose it makes no difference to me whether you knew or not."

"You should care," I bit out, "because retribution is coming, and it won't be by my hand."

He lifted a brow, bald head shining in the torchlight. "Oh, so it will be delivered by her, then, is that it?" He laughed. "I don't think so. I know how scared McKenzie is, how she can't even bring herself to come to the Institute. She ran away with her tail between her legs. I doubt she will have the courage to face me again."

"You'd be surprised by the motivation revenge can bring."

He clasped his hands behind his back, considering me. "Hmm, well I'll relish the challenge. McKenzie was always true to form—just like all redheads, she has a vicious temper when she lets it loose."

Sickened, I looked away. My eyes fell on Chloe, still silent and unmoving on the floor. "From what I can see, it looks as though you didn't plant anything in McKenzie's head. The fifth descendant doesn't look well cared for."

Callum snorted. "Oh, this is priceless. You really have no idea, do you? Do you not understand that it was all a ruse, a careful plan to make you attempt this rescue mission? Planting that vision of the fifth descendant provided the perfect opportunity to get the Daughter of Winter within these walls. All it required was some added motivation on Alison's part to do as I ordered."

What the fuck did he just say?

Callum was watching me closely, and he smiled at my expression. "Oh, you didn't know about Alison, either? It's a time for revelations then, isn't it?"

Fuck! I'd trusted Alison. My instincts had told me she was sound, that she had the right motivation to get rid of this bastard—this evil spreading stain that was bringing our clan to ruin. I stared at him, my eyes burning, head pounding. That pressure was only exacerbated by Callum's next words.

"Alison told me all about your little meeting when you failed to get Cailleach's Lore Book, as well as your plans to overturn me. I can't say I was shocked to hear that, but I was most surprised that you contemplated doing it prior to Samhain. I'm actually flattered I have created this much of a problem." His smile was deceptively beatific.

"How does it feel to be a failure, Gage? To understand you failed to protect the Daughter of Winter? To accept that you're homeless? And that an attempt to overturn me has been thwarted by a woman you trusted?" He shook his head. "I must say I'm disappointed. You're not the worthwhile opponent I'd thought you'd be. How did you ever come to receive the role of Guardian? The title is lost on you."

I tasted ashes as Callum threw those words like knives into my chest. My head was splitting, and I felt sweat break across my forehead. Had my instincts failed? Alison's motivations were genuine, not to mention she hated Callum; I'd been convinced she remained true.

But I'd been wrong.

It was my fault Brydie had been captured, my fault the

future of our people was at risk. There came a roaring in my ears, along with an overwhelming urge to obliterate everything around me. Except there was no outlet available. My magic roiled inside me, unable to be released. My breath burned in my chest and my skin felt thinly stretched. Whatever lore Callum had placed on this cell was strong; a cruel, agonized binding. Had this new lore been created from Brydie's blood? And why couldn't I scent a magical signature on the air?

I fisted my hands and forced out the question I needed an answer to. "What are you going to do to her?"

He knew exactly who I meant. "I'm nothing if not self-serving. I will give her to Talorgan eventually. But until then, I see no problem in using Brydie for my own means."

Rage whispered across my skin, my body burning with it. "You bastard! The answer to this prophecy does not lie in using her blood to create more lore! Cailleach did everything she could to protect her daughter and those who came thereafter. Why would she do all this only for the prophecy to culminate in killing them for their blood?"

"Oh, Gage. You are a little confused," Callum said, his smile widening. "I don't need to kill Brydie. Not when I can blood-let her regularly. If managed right, we could siphon enough of her blood to create new lore for many years to come. There are others in the clan who understand her potential. New lore provides a chance to escape this shit show of a prophecy we're tied to. Especially when it's obvious Talorgan will win this fight. After all, how can a Daughter of Winter—and one who's been sequestered from her legacy all her life—have a chance of overcoming an all-powerful nemesis? Talorgan is stronger than any of us, and history doesn't lie. Not once in all this time has a Daughter defeated him. Why should this woman be any different?"

"You forget the prophecy," I growled. "You forget the pact our clan made with Cailleach."

Callum shook his head. "I haven't forgotten, I just choose not to follow such whimsy. Regardless of whether The Oaken Tree provides support or not, Brydie won't win. Nora, though, she was another story. In her prime, she should have beaten Talorgan. But she, too, failed to protect us. She, too, failed to reverse the curse that affects us all. I saw her move—or lack thereof—for what it was; for what all Daughters before her have done."

"And what is that?" I rasped.

"They failed us. They chose to follow their own paths, to live their lives rather than sacrifice themselves for the good of our people. They chose not to attack Talorgan, not to see an end to his presence or the dark shadow he creates. I chose not to place my hope in the Daughter to end this prophecy, because I refuse to let yet another claim my future."

"And I suppose you think you've got the answer? Will you sacrifice yourself to save our people?"

Callum smiled again, but his eyes remained cold. "I'm a pragmatist, Gage. It's obvious Talorgan will eventually win this war. After centuries of our people fighting him, it became clear the path to success lies in joining him. I also see the benefit of reaping the power the Dark God offers. Our relationship, based on a mutual need, has created a level playing field, especially now I have the cauldron in my hands."

I felt ill. "You're a traitor to our people and unworthy of your position."

Rather than snarl in anger, Callum's brows lifted. "I beg to differ. You cannot see reason because you're too close to the problem. I saw a way out of this mess, and I took it. I grant it's not conventional, but it has merit, especially because my first experiment proved Brydie's blood is capable of making new lore."

"In which you burned down an ancient castle that could have provided safety for our people come Samhain!" I roared back at him.

He was fucking insane! Couldn't he see the damage he'd done? Couldn't he hear himself? He'd lost the light, and he didn't even know it. "You will damn us all with this path. Talorgan is not the ultimate enemy, Arawn is! Did you forget why he was sent to the Underworld? It was because of his depravity and unbalanced nature. Creating his rise on this world will kill us all as surely as if you'd plunged a knife into each person's heart." Not breaking his gaze, I said harshly, "Have you not noticed how dark lore changes us? Look to your guards—look at Jake, Mary, and Samuel. They are not themselves. They are shells of who they used to be. Dark lore changes us; it makes us something else. This is not the Druidic way!"

Callum merely shook his head, calm and collected. "I'm beginning to think I will have no use for you in this new regime, Gage. I'd thought to retain your services and use your gifts to help our people, but your apparent lack of support and your blindness to the cause is irksome. I admit, using the blood of Cailleach's descendant is a gamble, but a solid one since the lore was originally created by the gods. And what better descendant to overrule the lore affecting us all than Cailleach's own? There's some symmetry in that, you have to agree."

I ground my teeth. It was pointless to argue further. Anything I said would be deflected. Callum was convinced. There was no changing his path, whether it led to the ruin of our people or not.

At my lack of response, Callum said softly, "You would do best to forget Brydie, who she is, what she is. Your revolution has failed; Alison betrayed you. I have the Daughter, Cailleach's last living descendant, and Talorgan's ultimate revenge will soon be upon us." Callum's gaze was unwavering as he drove home his next words. "I have never bet on the underdog. It's a risky business that rarely succeeds, and it became obvious fairly quickly that a Daughter of Winter sequestered from her legacy all her life was doomed to fail from day zero. Therefore, I had to look out for our people, and I needed strength to do that. Talorgan and Arawn are formidable, but if we all bind our collective strengths together, we would have a chance of overcoming them."

He gestured to Mary, Jake, and Samuel and continued, "I have three powerful guards, but none of them are leaders. You are. You're someone who can rally the clan, instill a sense of security." His face was earnest as he looked me in the eye. "You have those skills, Gage. Regardless of your failures, you know how to convince others to fall into line. If we are to succeed, I need people like you to keep them on the straight and narrow, someone they can count on. You left this clan ten years ago, yet they still remember you and what you stand for. They'll follow you without question. Your job will be to convince them that this is the path, that control of the future is in our hands, not in passing it over to a Daughter of Winter."

Disbelief at his spiel had me snorting. "You think to offer me this position after how I've failed? After trusting Alison? After being captured, and now, losing Brydie?"

Callum grunted. "Don't be fucking stupid! I'm not asking you to lead our clan; that will be my job. You'll simply be following my orders and rallying the crowd. There will be no room for failure with my vision guiding the ship; I won't countenance it." He swept a hand out. "The deal is on the table, so what do you say?"

Join Callum of my own free will? Ignore the machinations, the murders, and the countless betrayals he was guilty of in reaching his current position? Ignore the growing stain of dark magic that overshadowed our people? He had to be joking. "Go fuck yourself, Callum."

Callum blinked, a clear sign he hadn't expected the rejection. Before I could add to the burn, he lashed out, his right arm swinging. A burst of pain coincided with the sound of my nose breaking. "Wrong answer," Callum bit out.

I hadn't been able to defend myself, whatever magic had locked me immobile on my knees in this cell also extended to my physical abilities. My head flew back as his fist viciously jabbed my nose. The attack was sudden and quick, just shy of the required force to break it. I wasn't sure if that had been his intention or not, but the tang of defeat was still heavy. The hopelessness of my situation burned.

Ignoring the pain in my nose and the warm blood now gushing down my chin, I looked Callum in the eye and forced out a cruel smile. "Not the answer you were expecting, I take it?"

Callum's lips firmed, the only warning I had before he pulled his fist back, dropped to a knee, and slammed it into my stomach.

The air whooshed out of my mouth, and I coughed, then inhaled, a rush of blood collecting in my throat. From a distance, I heard a murmur from outside the cell, the shuffle of the guard's feet. Was there a glimmer of recognition there? Awareness of who and what Callum was? What I stood for? But as I waited, bent over, trying to catch my breath, I soon realized that Mary, Samuel, and Jake weren't going to help. The power of the cauldron was too strong. I was on my own.

Enraged at that reality, I did the only thing I could. Deliberately, slowly, I cleared my throat and spat at Callum's feet. The bloody phlegm hit the bottom of his red robe.

Again, Callum didn't hesitate. This time he aimed a fist at my right eye. My head was again flung backward as starbursts of light flashed behind my eyes. Blinking against the pain, eyes watering, I jerked my head back to Callum and tried to focus on his face, but the leader of The Oaken Tree had come to his feet and was now lashing out with an open-palmed slap across my cheek, again and again and again, lost in a fit of rage. The civilized mask had gone. His face was red, his bald head sweating, his lips twisted in a vicious snarl.

I could do nothing but take it. Silence was my only defense. Pain exploded everywhere, the rippling fire in my body adding to the sensation. Eventually, his attack stopped, and swollen and hurting, I opened my eyes to find the leader of The Oaken Tree half bent in front of me, his hands on his knees as he gulped in air.

"That was stupid," he panted. "You needlessly angered me. I was prepared to have a civilized conversation." He pushed himself to his full height, walked a few steps closer, and grabbed my hair, tugging my head up so our eyes met. "You underestimate my reach, Guardian," he sneered. "You think you're untouchable, a true rebel for the cause, but there's something I learned from a very young age. And that's that everyone has secrets...and I've taken the time to find out yours."

My heart lurched. *No...*

Callum was watching me closely. He smiled and, in a

replica of a lover's caress, he rubbed his knuckles down the side of my swollen, burning cheek. "I can see your fear," he whispered. "I can see you're wondering if I know all about the boy who is no longer your best-kept secret."

I sucked in a breath. "I have no idea what you're talking about," I forced out between lips that had gone completely numb. The words were slurred, barely recognizable.

Callum lifted a brow. "Oh? Do you not? Should I show you, then?" He turned to Samuel and snapped a finger. "Get me a bowl of water."

Samuel sent him a cool nod, his face unmoving, and turned toward the prison warden's lodgings that were visible at the end of the corridor. Callum's hold on my head was brutal, and I lost sight of Samuel almost immediately. I could feel my face swelling as my mind raced with scenarios of what Callum might know, whether he really had found Saul.

Those moments felt like an eternity when Samuel returned, his feet echoing on the stone floor. He neither hurried nor dawdled, just walked to a steady beat. The movements of all Callum's guards, their actions, their scent —it was unnatural, wrong. Was this what the cauldron did when used with dark lore?

Callum gestured a few feet to his left, and Samuel entered the cell and silently deposited a bowl of water on the floor next to us before retreating. My skin crawled at the pungent signature that trailed behind him, the potent smell of rot.

Callum flashed me another wide smile as he tugged on my hair, drawing it over the bowl. "Come and see what you deny."

My heart thundered in my ears as he held his hands above the bowl. He muttered under his breath, and a trail of red and black smoke released from his palms, arrowing straight into the water and disappearing under the mirrored surface. I watched closely, my unmarred eye fixated on the sudden ripple of movement across the water. Images swirled in a riot of color, as though spinning through the fabric of time. I felt my heart beat faster as the colors solidified into a picture, into a form I thought I recognized. I sucked in a breath as that lens zoomed in to focus on a child's face. Was it...?

I immediately tensed, barely containing the sigh of relief that threatened to whoosh out in a loud exhale. I concentrated on keeping my face and body tight while inside, all I felt was exaltation. Callum had fallen for the red herring—the boy in the picture wasn't Saul, but rather his doppelgänger; this Saul had brown eyes just like Catriona did.

I jerked back from the bowl and roared with every emotion I could muster, "If you touch him, I'll kill you!"

Callum whipped his head to his guards and snapped out, "Hold him!"

Jake, Mary, and Samuel remained impassive, their expressions neutral as they followed Callum's demands. Their hands glowed with power as they squeezed their fists into tight balls. I felt invisible bonds curl around my wrists, my biceps, my calves, even my waist, until I was locked, frozen in place and unable to move anything but my head.

Callum watched me, once again sporting a congenial smile. "Kill me, would you, Guardian? I'd like to see you try."

I snarled, rearing back. "You fucking bastard!"

"Yes, yes, I know. I've heard it all before." Callum turned and began to pace the small cell, his hands clasped behind his back. "You know how this goes, Gage. You know how useless your threats are, and now I have my sights on the boy, I'm sure you understand the significance of your decision. As I said before, if you were to die, it would be a great loss to our clan. On the other hand, I have a position here for you if you're willing to take it. And in return for your service, I can guarantee wealth, women, or whatever it is you desire—you need only ask." He stopped his pacing and turned to face me, adding quietly, "Or the boy dies. It's as simple as that."

I grit my teeth, aware that I was still stuck in a quandary, for even though my son was safe, if I didn't say yes to Callum's offer, I'd be allowing this other boy to be murdered, which was a travesty and would, in effect, be admitting to Callum that this boy wasn't my son. Which meant Saul would be hunted.

I couldn't do that—Saul meant everything to me. But the alternative—saying yes to Callum and agreeing to his offer —would mean losing Brydie. And not just Brydie, but everything. Our people, the world. We would all lose.

Callum wasn't stupid. He would keep Brydie prisoner, draining her blood day in and day out for his own needs in the hope that he could create new lore that would save us all from ultimate damnation and the shadow of Talorgan and Falin. But he was walking a fine line, a dangerous line, and every day was a step further into irrevocable darkness. I knew that, come Samhain, he intended to let Brydie go, but that didn't mean he would release her whole or healthy. Talorgan would still get his revenge—that ultimate final blow—but only after Callum had taken what he desired.

Right then, it became clear to me there was only one path left, and I prayed it was the right one as I held Callum's gaze and said firmly, "You can rot in hell. If Talorgan kills

Brydie, the world as we know it will be over, and my son will die regardless."

The cool confidence on Callum's face twisted, his eyes narrowing as he assessed me. "You surprise me. That decision goes against your nature." He bent down on one knee, his face close to mine as he asked softly, "What are you hiding from me?"

I bit the inside of my mouth and stared back at him.

He turned and looked once more into the bowl of water, then back at me. "This boy, he isn't your son, is he?" he demanded, his voice once again flavored with a slash of confidence. "It's so damn obvious now. I have to say I'm impressed by your ability to think ahead, and that you even had the nous to establish a false identity. This is good; this shows me you have the skills for the tasks you'll be required to undertake."

My blood chilled at the thought of following Callum's commands, but still I held my tongue.

Callum pushed back to his feet and continued looking thoughtfully down at me. "You know," he continued, "if the chalice didn't require its victims to drink of their own free will, I'd have you tied to me already. However, as it doesn't work that way, you're a challenge, and one I find interesting enough to meet. So, Guardian, I accept. I *will* find your son, and you *will* drink from the chalice of your own accord. After all, with a knife held against his throat, it will be hard not to do so. And in payment of your sins, the first act I'll request of you will be to kill McKenzie, and possibly my son."

My heart lurched, my gorge rising, as Callum's verdict sank in. He would make me kill McKenzie? Kill Aidan—his own son? Cold fear slid down my back, even as I refused to accept his words. "Aidan was never your son."

Callum's voice was almost congenial. "I totally agree with you, because I never asked for the whelp. McKenzie was fool enough to get herself pregnant."

My blood boiled, and I clenched my fists, biting my cheek hard to contain the emotional response that roared for release. I buried the protective surge, buried the rage now blooming in my chest and gritted out, "And now you want me to kill them both."

He clasped his hands together in front of him. "I find the proposal has a fair amount of justice to it, don't you? It will also be sufficient payment for your sins given you've taken in the boy and nurtured him these last nine years."

There would be no coming back from that deed, even if I wanted to. Because, regardless of being demanded by the chalice, it would still be a sin, one I'd still have committed by my own hand, coerced or not.

The demand was vicious. I was to either betray Brydie and my people or kill two people whom I looked upon as my own. Callum's leering face did nothing to calm the riot of thoughts firing through my mind.

"So, what will it be, Gage?" Callum's voice was velvet smooth.

I went rigid, wanting time, wanting out of this godforsaken mess. I remained silent, considering every alternative as I tried to find a way out.

Callum shifted, a sound of impatience. "I said, what will it be? I am waiting. You must decide now!"

If Callum had found my son, he would have shown me. He was too conceited not to pass up the opportunity. That meant Callum hadn't found Saul yet. There were also the shields, the numerous silent shadows I employed to keep Saul safe. Those men were still in place, and they'd remain that way until I pulled them back. It was obvious Callum wanted me, otherwise I would be dead. That meant I had time, and time was all I needed.

But there was risk involved. There was no knowing what Callum would do to Brydie or how much she could endure. Would she survive imprisonment and the reins of Callum's influence? I thought of my Daughter of Winter, of what she had survived so far, of what challenges she had faced. Not once had she balked, not once had she failed me, and I was certain she wouldn't fail me now.

I refused to consider what Callum would do to her. How she might change, who she might become. Because, no matter what happened, I had made a promise to myself that I would get her back. If we survived Callum and his machinations, if we got out of here alive, I would damn well get her back.

"Well?" Callum prompted, a sardonic glint in his eye. As if he knew that I had no choice, that I had to say yes.

I enjoyed watching the self-satisfied glint erased from his eyes as I said firmly, "The answer is no. I will not drink from the chalice."

His voice was low, hard. "Are you telling me that you are willing to barter the life of your son and everyone else you hold dear for the lives of two people who are not of your blood?"

The comment sickened me. "McKenzie and Aidan are my family, regardless of blood. I will sacrifice no one for your cause, not when the future you offer is full of death and darkness."

Callum snarled, "You're making a huge mistake. Can't you see this is the only way out of this mess?"

"Can't you see that Brydie is the answer?" I returned. "She has potential. You just need to believe it."

"I think not, Guardian. And you have just signed your

death warrant over a woman who has yet to prove herself. A woman who is currently trapped from now until Samhain. A woman whose days are numbered."

The truth of those words arrowed into my chest, and my mind and body instantly rebelling against them. No! I would not lose her! I would find a way out of this mess. We would survive this. We would survive Callum and whatever Talorgan threw at us.

Holding onto that hope, I held Callum's gaze. "So be it."

His upper lip curled, and he snarled in return, "So be it."

CHAPTER 33
BRYDIE
PRESENT DAY, SCOTLAND

The trip to Callum's rooms was a blur of twisting corridors, torchlight, and shadowed faces, the bindings on my wrists heavy. The passageways were a rabbit warren of tunnels and doors. I was reeling with what had just happened and was in no state to mark corridors or directions, no way of remembering how to get back to the dungeon and out.

Gage.

Chloe.

I'd left both of them trapped inside that cell. With Callum. Callum, who had plans to make Gage one of his guards by forcing him to drink from the cauldron. And Chloe; I still had no idea what he intended to do with her... probably follow Talorgan's bidding and have her killed. I'd lost everything. How had everything gone so wrong?

My guards finally came to a halt outside a set of double doors made of heavy oak. An iron bar was drawn across them. Numb, I watched as each guard held a palm to the door. A red glow appeared around their hands, and the bar effortlessly slid upward before the doors swung open. I caught a glimpse of the large, luxurious bed in the middle of the room, the ornate fireplace flickering with flames, and the heavy, red brocade curtains lining the walls from floor to ceiling before I was thrown inside the room.

I scrambled into a sitting position and watched the guards enter the room. The doors swung silently closed behind them. One of them bared his teeth at me, his brown robes swirling around his ankles, and barked, "On your feet. Get into the other room." He gestured at the doorway to the left.

I didn't move.

His companion snarled and lashed out with a kick to my stomach. I groaned and curled into a fetal position. My skin was still screaming, my head still pounding; I could barely register what it was they wanted.

The guard beside me dropped to his haunches, his brown eyes narrowed as he bit out, "We'll only ask you once more, bitch. Get on your feet and move your ass into that chamber!" He stabbed a finger at a black door to the left.

Withholding another groan, I pushed to my feet and forced my body to move. My body was screaming with agony, each move sluggish. The guards watched me, the leers on their faces making my stomach turn.

As I walked past them, a hand reached out and slapped my ass. I flinched, my skin burning through my jeans, but still I looked ahead at that black door and took another step.

"Oh, he's going to have fun with you. Lots of fun." The words were soft, almost tender. "And if I'm lucky, I'll get to watch."

The other guard growled in approval as he moved to open the black door. All I could see was a dark room and a stone floor. I refused to show the horror building inside of me. My body was screaming, my mind too, and my fists clenched uselessly at my sides.

The first guard laughed. "Can't reach your power?" he sneered, reaching out to grope my breast and squeeze it painfully.

Not thinking of the consequences, I halted in front of the door and turned my head to spit in his face.

The guard's hard brown eyes closed, but instead of lashing out, a cruel smile crossed his face. "Oh yes, you're going to be a fine challenge. One he'll enjoy."

He raised his boot and kicked me hard in the back. I lurched into the room, sprawling across the stone floor. Behind me, the guards chuckled. Then the door slammed, and a lock audibly snicked into place.

It was dark, oppressive, the air heavy with the stale scent of iron. There were no stimulants, no distractions, nothing but my memories.

I thought about the events leading up to this moment. I thought about Gage, the dagger against his throat, the plans Callum had in store for him. I thought about Chloe, unconscious on the floor, of the fate that awaited her. I thought about Ian, Logan, Aidan, and McKenzie, whether they were safe or if Callum had claimed them too.

The panic clawed its way up my throat, building upon itself exponentially, and within moments, I was gasping for breath, my body rigid, my mind screaming with uncontrollable terror.

IT COULD HAVE BEEN minutes or it could have been hours before that door opened again.

Torchlight illuminated the room, pushing the shadows

to the corners. Its soft glow hurt after the suffocating darkness, and I narrowed my eyes at the two silhouettes standing in the doorway—Callum, his blood-red robe almost black, and one of his guards.

"Lying in supplication already, I see," Callum drawled.

I didn't answer as he stepped inside, the guard following to stand just inside the room, his attention focused on me. The action was almost laughable given I hadn't moved since he'd kicked me into the room. I hadn't been able to.

Callum dropped to his haunches in front of me. "Come now, don't be scared, my dear. You know this day was always going to come. It was inevitable you would fall into my hands. Your powers are weak, your mind even weaker; add to that the strong enemy at your back, and it was obvious it was always going to end this way."

So, this had been his plan all along. *Traitor!* I forced myself onto an elbow and forced out hoarsely, "I feel sorry for you. You have lost your freedom, and you don't even know it. Rather than make a stand and fight, you have condemned yourself to become another man's puppet. You're nothing but a coward."

He snarled, moving so quickly I didn't see the vicious backhand he sent to my face.

My head flung sideways, pain exploding like a cacophony of vultures lifting into the sky, as tears flooded my eyes. I bit my lip hard, trying to halt the whimper that threatened to release. Then, without understanding why, I began to laugh.

Callum went still. "What's so funny?" he growled.

My head lifted, my cheek burning, and as my eyes met his, I spat in his face.

His beady eyes glittered. "I'm going to enjoy breaking you."

My skin crawled at his soft tone. "Talorgan told you not to break me."

"There are many interpretations as to what it means to break someone, my dear."

My heart lurched.

"What? No smart comeback this time? Pity, I'd hoped you'd keep that fire for a few more days yet." Callum pushed to his feet, the red robe shifting like ripples of blood as he began to pace around the chamber, snapping his fingers as he went. At every snap of those fingers, a wall sconce came alight, illuminating the room.

"We have many months to whittle away before Samhain, and it would be a waste to not use your gifts before we deliver you to Talorgan," he continued. "After all, we'll need to feed and clothe you, and offering some kind of payment in return for our hospitality is more than fair. You see, Brydie, we need more lore. Not the same lore—different lore. We've realized the drop you gave us a few months back didn't have the strength it required. The lore we created with that drop had a use by date, which isn't very useful, wouldn't you agree?"

Callum stopped walking and tapped a finger against his chin as he pinned me with his dark stare. "I've thought about this over the past few weeks, and I have an idea that the problem isn't with the source but the quality of your blood. You gave us the vial willingly, were likely helped to attain it. But with dark lore, there's always a price—a tithe for a tithe. So I've a theory, Brydie. I think we need to take your blood under different circumstances—when you're terrified, scared, and alone. When all hope is lost, when all you feel is pain and darkness." He smiled, and it was all teeth and no warmth. "Thankfully, I'm an expert at that."

A chill crept over my skin, a coldness that went bone

deep. I strived to maintain my indifference, but it was a front, and he knew it.

Callum turned to his guard. "Julian, shut the door, then come and hold her."

The guard—Julian—did Callum's bidding with an anticipatory gleam in his eyes. He hauled me to my feet and turned me around to face Callum. Then I felt his hands reach down and grope my ass. I snarled a warning. In return, one of his hands slipped between my legs and pinched my sex.

I twisted my head, yanking against his hold, and spat, "You fucking perverted bastard!"

Julian smiled, a row of rotted teeth glinting in the torchlight. He looked over my head to Callum and drawled, "Well, well, the kitten has claws."

I trembled, rage slithering down my spine as his hands wandered back over my ass. "I'll kill you if you touch me like that again," I rasped.

Julian only laughed. "And how are you to do that, kitten, when your magic is trapped?"

But Callum's voice, silky and quiet, added, "Do as she says or I'll kill you first. I will only say this once, Julian: Leave her alone, she's mine."

Julian froze, and his hands immediately snapped to my upper arms. His response was stilted, formal. "Yes, Master."

Callum's pace was measured as he came closer, stopping within a few feet of me. "You know how this works, Brydie. You have a choice."

"What choice?" I forced out, another chill settling over my body.

"There's always a choice; haven't you been told this? However, that choice isn't necessarily fair, I must admit. But

I'm a betting man; I always bet on the course with the highest odds. So I'll offer you the choice of the win first." He slid his hands into his robe and rocked on his heels, calm and controlled, as he delivered, "I want you to join me. Together, we would be stronger, and even more powerful than Talorgan. We would triumph at Samhain and eradicate the threat of who and what he is once and for all."

"Are you saying you want us to be allies?" This wasn't what I'd been expecting. It didn't make any sense, not when he was already aligned with Talorgan.

"That's exactly what I'm saying. Join me, Brydie. Of your own free will, I ask you to embrace the dark arts. Together, we will be a united force with unimaginable power, able to stop any who stand against us." His gaze was unwavering, the intensity of his stare hot and heavy.

"And I would be your partner and a co-leader of our people?"

"Of course. We would be a united front." His eyes lowered, running down my body to linger at my breasts, then between my thighs. "Being with you wouldn't be a chore."

My skin crawled, and I swallowed the bile at the back of my throat. The proposition was unexpected. Was this really the path I was meant to travel? Was this what the prophecy had had in store for me all along? Was this the reason why I'd been captured?

There was no doubt darkness resided inside me. I'd become aware of it before that day at the Claymore, when my instinctive reaction had been to kill Garett. It was part of my legacy, an insidious essence that was like oil, slippery and toxic, unable to assimilate. It had taken me a while to understand it was a part of my power. It was the dark to the light, death to birth, the moon to the sun. A part of a whole that made up the balance. And it was a side of me I fought every day. To take up Callum's offer would mean allowing the darkness to take full reign, to stop flirting with the shadows but instead fully eclipse the light.

This world didn't need any more darkness, not with what already stained the horizon....

I met Callum's gaze. "No."

A cruel smile blemished his lips. "I can't say I'm surprised at your answer. I knew it was too soon to offer you the win first, but it always pays to be honest with your captives, don't you think? Just as I should share that as you've chosen to stay in your current position, you'll be providing us with tonight's entertainment. Of course, if you change your mind, this evening's activities can always be rescheduled. You need only accept my offer."

My heart pounded at the promise of the pain to come. I wanted to scream and yell at the unfairness of it all. At how helpless I was. At the choices he offered not being any choice at all. But I said nothing, thankful the training Gage put me through had prepared me for the position I was now in. Whether I would remain stoic in my decision in the days to come was another story, but I would cross that bridge when I came to it. *One day at a time, Brydie.*

Callum waited, but when my lips remained shut, he turned to his guard and ordered, "Hold her still, Julian. Your job is to ensure she remains conscious."

My body went rigid as Callum turned away to pace the chamber and look up the walls. In the shadows of the torchlight, I could just make out the objects hanging in neat array—a macabre range of whips and blades and other weapons I'd never seen before. Behind me, Julian reasserted his hold, his fingers digging into my arms and reminding me I was trapped in this nightmare.

I dropped my eyes to the floor, and it was then I noticed the trailing dark stain on the stone beneath my feet. I followed the red-brown trail to a flat stone table situated to my right and noticed the manacles hanging from the wall behind it. It was evidence enough. I knew exactly what this place was used for.

After circling the room, Callum looked over his shoulder and caught my eye before he reached up and pulled something down from the wall. I couldn't see what he held. He walked along the wall a few steps and reached up to grab another object, this one long and coiled. It wasn't until he moved closer to the torches that I saw what he held. It was a whip, but instead of a leather tail, there were strings and strings of knuckle bones. Callum held it loosely as he tested its weight, flicking it casually upon the floor. The ominous clacking of the bone knuckles hitting the stone was the only sound in the room.

Realizing he had my full attention, Callum dragged the bone tail over the palm of his other hand. "This weapon is a favorite of mine. Most come begging for what it offers, but I have a feeling this won't apply in your case." Holding my gaze, he slowly raised the bones to his nose and inhaled. I felt a wave of dizziness wash over me as his eyes rolled closed, a look of ecstasy crossing his face.

Lowering the bones, he gave me a wolfish grin. "Before we begin, there's something I should tell you: This room is sealed, meaning no noise comes in, and no noise goes out. No one knows where you are either, Brydie, which means no one is coming to save you. I've routed out all the traitors within the nest, Alison being the first among them. I promise you that any other lingering rodents will soon be destroyed."

My heart stopped beating. Alison...? Was he saying that even after all our careful schemes, he'd got wind of our plans? It was another confirmation this had all been a trap, a carefully constructed spider's web.

Callum tilted his head to the side as he digested my reaction. "Why are you so surprised? You should never have underestimated me. I always know what goes on in this Institute, who comes, who goes, and that's because Jake has a special skill many don't know about. Not only is he the most skilled in fire, but he's a tracker. He can trace magical signatures all over the world, no matter the distance. He's routed out more traitors than I could ever have hoped to discover on my own. But his past ties to Alison have always been a threat to my position, not to mention her role as Lore Keeper gives her more power than I'm willing to offer, so I've had her watched right from the start."

I felt the blood drain from my face. He'd known everything. Every single movement. When we'd met, where we'd been. All the deception and secret meetings had been for naught. I couldn't spare a thought for what had happened to Alison, and I clung to the fact that Gage had made the rest of our party promise to leave if we hadn't returned by dawn.

Swallowing hard, I forced my racing thoughts to halt. To think. I had to find a way to escape. But how? I had no magic, and my body, my mind...I felt ill, consumed with a fever, exhaustion tearing me down. And without magic or the full use of my body, the only weapon I had was my words—words that could either goad, or encourage, but at times...maim. So be it.

Forcing the panic down, I held his gaze and used the

only weapon I had. " Everyone knows what path you have taken to claim your position as leader of this clan. Perversion is a crime that does not go unpunished, Callum. Jake and everyone else you've forced into submission will seek compensation for what you've made them do, who you've made them hurt. So, instead of worrying about what will happen to me, I think it only fair to warn you to prepare for the reckoning to come."

Callum snarled, his cool mask slipping. "You forget yourself if you think you can threaten me! You also forget I have three personal guards who relish their positions. They willingly agreed to the role without any coercion."

"Was that before or after you tricked them into drinking from the cauldron?" I returned.

Callum's face tightened. "I can't decide if you genuinely think you can threaten me or if you're the most stupid bitch I've ever come across."

"I guess you'll have to find out." I smirked, hiding the fear, and reminded myself that hope still lived. It lived in the manner of Callum's response, in the way his face now flamed and his hands clenched. All I had to do was hold on and look for an opportunity.

Callum's face reddened even further, and he prowled closer, the knuckle bones sliding along the floor in a crawling whisper. "After I've whipped you to within the last shred of your humanity, I'll collect every drop of blood that your body releases. Then I'll give you time to heal. You'll think it's all over, that the worst has come." He stepped in close, his breath hot on my face as he added with a soft whisper, "But I'll be back. Again, and again, and again."

My skin crawled, the hairs rising on back of my neck, but I forced myself to stand still. Behind me, Julian's breathing quickened, his hands tightening around my arms.

"Let me guess, no comment?" Callum enquired with a cocked brow.

I bit the inside of my cheek, tasting blood. I was tempted to spit it in his face, but that was another reaction I wouldn't give him the benefit of seeing.

"I thought so." Callum chuckled darkly, then he stepped back and flicked the whip on the stone. There was a sharp crack, the sound poignant in the weighted silence. "In that case, let's get on with it. Julian, turn her around."

Julian turned me around until I was facing him. My nose instantly filled with his body odor, and my skin crawled as his gaze fixated on my chest. I closed my eyes to block out the sight of him at the same time I heard a light whistle on the air.

The first lash was a nightmare of fire.

The second lash caused my knees to buckle.

The third lash had me screaming.

I was lost, adrift in a sea of agony as Callum's whip fell again and again, a nightmare of cracks and tearing flesh that was complimented by the sounds of my raw screams. I wasn't aware of the blood running down my ruined back, pooling upon the stone floor. Not until Julian cursed and stepped sideways, narrowly missing one of Callum's misguided lashes. His foot slipped in the blood, and he fell, tugging me down. I slammed onto the stone, whimpering; my thoughts as shattered as my ruined back.

I'd promised myself not to show weakness. I'd failed. I was no savior, no Daughter of Winter. I was a weak, pitiless fool. A woman with no right to the legacy I'd inherited. Tried, tested, and found wanting.

I was barely conscious of Julian scrambling away, my blood coating his robes, the scent of iron now overpowering

Callum's rancid signature. I lay there, my cheek resting against the stone floor, my eyes struggling to remain open.

Callum's grinning face descended, his dark eyes flashing with triumph. It was the last thing I saw before his fist drove my chin back in a vicious uppercut.

Darkness began to descend, and I reached for it.

I awoke to darkness, cloying and thick, my body curled into a fetal position on the cold, stone floor. My body was screaming with pain, my back on fire, and my head pounded to a blinding tempo. I slid a hand over the stone, my palm trailing in something sticky before I pressed it to my forehead.

The movement had nausea rising, and I inhaled sharply, smelling the sharp scent of iron. Like a gunshot, the memories flooded in.... Callum's proposition. My response. The beating. Bile hit the back of my throat as I remembered the bone whip slashing across my back, at first bruising, then splitting the skin.

Blood. There was so much blood. Blood that Julian had slipped in, bringing me crashing down with him. Blood that I was lying in.... My heart rate sped up, and my stomach heaved, vomit splattering onto the stone. Soon I was panting, my breath coming in short gasps as I began to lose control.

This was all part of Callum's plan. He wanted me weak and submissive. Wanted me to feel desperate and alone.

How long had I been lying here on this floor, alone in the dark?

Suddenly frantic, I fumbled into a sitting position, surprised my body could move so fluidly. The skin and muscles felt tender, as if the ghost of injury hovered over my body. I slowly reached around to touch my back and found my leather jacket was now in shreds, but the skin underneath my tee shirt was smooth and unmarred. At first, I was confused. But as I inhaled again and smelled the signature on the air, I knew. Callum had healed me. There was no denying that rancid, unnatural scent. Like a buildup of toxic chemicals, it overrode the more subtle scent of Julian, who'd smelled like a stagnant pond on a hot day.

It didn't take long to understand why Callum had healed me. He had made it quite clear he wanted my blood to create new lore. That from now until Samhain, he would take it with or without my permission. When my fingers touched the skin inside my left arm, the area felt bruised. Callum had fulfilled his promise; he'd delivered on his threat and taken my blood. Which meant it was highly likely he would deliver on his other one—*"After I've whipped you to within the last shred of your humanity, I'll collect every drop of blood your body releases. Then I'll give you time to heal. You'll think it's all over, that the worst has come. But I'll be back. Again, and again, and again."*

Ice slid down my spine. A roaring reverberated in my ears. This sense of peace—it was no reprieve; it was the calm before the storm.

CALLUM KEPT HIS PROMISE. He returned; again, and again, and again.

During his second visit, I was tied to a chair. Julian had reached down and wrenched my boots, then my socks off, and then slowly, painfully, he'd pulled my toenails off, one by one. The agony was inexplicable, my screams resonating around the stone chamber, and throughout it all, Callum had calmly smiled, remaining the refined leader, polite and well-mannered as he used the moment as a training exercise.

"When you remove their toenails," he said to Julian, "you should always do it slow and steady. The longer you prolong the torture, the more their minds will break, and the faster we receive the intel we need."

Only when every toenail had been removed, only when I slumped forward in my chair, broken and utterly destroyed, had Callum pulled a wickedly curved dagger from his belt and sliced a shallow cut across the vein in my wrist. I'd been oblivious as my blood dripped into the bowl on the floor.

I lost all awareness of time until Julian stepped forward and bound my wrist, clotting the wound. As he untied my bonds, Callum dropped to his haunches in front of me. "Not so tough anymore, are you?" he murmured softly, reaching out to lay a soft caress over my hair.

I smelt his signature flood my senses, the rancid chemical buildup stealing the oxygen in the air. I grit my teeth as he ran his hands over my feet, healing the bleeding stumps on my toes, then growing new toenails. Barely holding on, I'd locked my jaw tight, refusing to give away one more piece of me in another ragged scream.

Seeing my expression, Callum laughed, a hand reaching out to cup my cheek. The motion was poignant, symbolic of a lover's caress. "Oh, this is going to be too easy. I'd hoped for more fire, but your reaction confirms I've bet on the right horse. You don't have what it takes to best Talorgan." His fingers drifted down to my chin and tightened, pulling my face closer to his so we were eye to eye. "There is another way, Brydie. An open door just waiting for you to step through. Join me, and this will all be over."

The words were indistinguishable, and there was a loud buzzing in the air. I felt nothing but a strange emptiness. I closed my eyes; it was answer enough.

His fingers dug into my chin. "Well, it appears you have some fight left in you yet. Good; I'm pleased. I find you are a welcome release at the end of the day, and I'm not ready to give up on this entertainment just yet." I felt him lean in, and his voice was soft against my ear, full of that dark promise I'd come to fear as he whispered on a soft caress, "Until tomorrow, Daughter of Winter."

His fingers were gone, and my chin fell to my chest. I heard them leave the room, the door shutting behind them. Even then, I refused to open my eyes, not when they had taken the light with them. I slid off the chair to the stone floor and crawled to the corner of the room where a thin blanket lay. It offered meagre protection against the cold draughts that slipped through the cracks in the stone walls, but I wouldn't have wanted it any other way. The air flow was a blessing given the pan I used for toileting needs was infrequently changed. It helped reduce the pungent, shaming scent that screamed of my helpless position. Not that I had a chance to forget I was Callum's prisoner.

After his first visit, a pattern was established. Once Callum had left, Julian would arrive. His arrival was marked with an offering—a tray of food and a lone candle. He'd place the items on the floor, just inside the door, and with a sneer in my direction, he would leave.

At first, I was thankful for that small light. It pushed the shadows away, the darkness no longer crowding against my senses. But by the fifth day, I resented that light. Resented what it illuminated—the stone room, the stone table, the chair, the ropes, the manacles, the weapons on the wall, and most damning of all, the increasing dark stains on the floor. They were a reminder of what I had endured, what I still endured, and how helpless I was.

That first night, I didn't eat. When Julian returned and found I hadn't touched my meal, he forced it down my throat. "Boss's orders," he grunted.

After the meal was done and the candle had sputtered out, I was left to sit in the dark...until the door was unlocked. Callum would be standing there, silhouetted by the torchlight, and Julian at his back; a prelude to the horror that would follow.

Yet those hours spent alone in the dark were torturous themselves. I was plagued with questions, playing out different scenarios and almost making myself sick at the unknown. Where was Chloe? Where was Gage, and why couldn't we feel each other along our shared bond? Was he coming for me—could he? Were McKenzie, Aidan, Ian, and Logan alright, and had they safely returned to The Rowan Tree? Where was Talorgan? Did he know what Callum was doing?

The questions revolved in my mind, an endless cycle of anxiety and fear, tempered by the beast growing inside of me. I could feel my legacy crawling under my feverish skin, angry that it couldn't be released. My head pounded incessantly, a fever racking my body. Every day, every hour —every minute—became an ongoing battle until my body and mind was forced to succumb to sleep.

My dreams were fitful, nightmares of fire and flesh as I

relived every moment in this room. And when I awoke, screaming and gasping, I would reach under my tee shirt and grasp the pendant. But instead of feeling its usual warmth or a gentle humming vibration, there was nothing. It was now just a simple adornment. Just like Nora, it had abandoned me, as had everyone and everything else....

CHAPTER 35
ARAWN
3RD CENTURY BC, ANCIENT SCOTLAND

Arawn's lips peeled back in a feral smile as he stood in the shadows and watched the women in the shieling. His cock jerked at the look of terror on their faces, and he thought of taking one before her time of sacrifice. But why stop at one? Not when he had a veritable feast in front of him.

His lust magnified, his blood heating at the thought of sinking his member into one of the women—a human woman, and a virgin at that. It had been an eon since he'd lain with a woman, an eon since he'd touched this world, since he'd felt anything but the acrid, burning dust that lined the back of his throat day in and day out. He still struggled to believe he was standing on this plane and in this world—not in a dream state, but in his *real* form.

He reveled in the change in light, for here, the sun was allowed to move. It was able to give homage to the rise of the moon, and even though his powers were presently restricted on this plane, there was still power to be found in the night. For with the night came the dark, and darkness shrouded dark deeds, enabling depravity, violence, and lust.

Arawn shifted his gaze from the captured virgins, his carmine eyes piercing the darkness to survey his people. They could not see him; he had masked his form in magic. Magic that had been denied him in the Underworld. But here, he had freedom. Here, he could hide.

He flexed his fingers at his sides, reveling in the response that surged through his body. It felt good to feel his strength returning, to acknowledge he once again held a significant measure of power. When Talorgan had given him his soul, it had been the first step to freedom, establishing a desired connection to this world. It had been easy too. All he'd had to do was feed the druid's depravity. Talorgan hadn't needed any encouragement. In fact, the druid had fallen down the rabbit hole he'd cleverly crafted far too easily. All he'd needed to do was dangle his whore of a sister in front of the man, and the druid had responded.

When Talorgan, of his own volition, had offered his first sacrifice, Arawn felt an answering thrust of power. The druid's dark deeds had strengthened their connection to one another, regardless of the fact they resided in different worlds. Arawn hadn't hesitated to test his newfound power and had opened the veil between the Underworld and this one. The fabric between the worlds had split easily, without any effort, and when he'd put one foot forward and felt it breach this plane for the first time since being banished to his hellish domain, elation had consumed him.

He'd spent the subsequent days that followed as weak as a lamb, realizing that even though he'd been able to cross over, his power hadn't. And after following his intuition and feeding the druid with his desires, Arawn had finally felt his power begin to build with every passing day.

Soon, it would be limitless. Soon, he would be all-powerful. All he needed to do was ensure the success of the coming sacrificial ceremony. It had been cleverly planned to coincide with Samhain, at a time when the veils between the worlds were at their thinnest. His offerings would not only enable the full return of his power, but they would also widen the portal, providing entry for even more of his people.

Arawn was aware the return of his powers would not guarantee his permanent return to this world, not when several of his siblings would take great pains to see him removed. Which meant there was a need to build an army; a deadly, destructive force that would obliterate not only lives but also hope. And as he now looked upon his people, he acknowledged with no conceit that their appearance alone was enough to make any enemy balk before they'd even attacked.

A movement to his left cut through his thoughts, and Arawn narrowed his eyes when he caught the flicker of a sinuous dark shadow. He tracked its movements, conscious that it leeched a veritable amount of power. He inhaled, scenting the air, and on recognizing the familiar taint of his own signature entwined within the notes of that new scent, he knew who that shadow was—Talorgan.

When Talorgan had approached him in Bull Sleep, the druid had been half the man he was now. But since Arawn had bestowed gifts upon him—immortality and an unrelenting, all-encompassing power, not to mention the dragon at his back—the man had become more than a druid, he'd become his disciple. A disciple who would lead him even further to power.

His eyes now on the druid, Arawn watched Talorgan morph into his true form, his blood-red robes swirling around his ankles as he walked toward the shieling. His pace was measured and controlled, confidence and purpose in his gait. The druid stopped to question the sirens before opening the door to the shieling to check on the captive virgins. Minutes later, he was shutting the door and walking away.

Arawn scrutinized his disciple closely, searching for any weaknesses. It was a test Talorgan passed without question, for the druid showed no intention of rescuing the virgins or reneging on the coming sacrifice, and for the first time, Arawn let himself believe that with this man at his side, he had a real chance at retaining a permanent foothold on this plane. Especially after Talorgan had killed his nemesis, Tritus.

At that death, Arawn felt the first stirrings of true power returning. Strength had flowed through his veins, his powers becoming stronger with each passing moment. But with his power had come his desire. He'd been denied life's pleasures for too long in the Underworld, teased by memories of his time on this plane. But now he was here, he was no longer restricted by duties. No longer subject to the chains of his prison. Here on this plane, there was a wealth of opportunity. Here, he could do and act as he pleased. And all he wanted now was to rape and pillage that which had been denied him. It had been an age since he'd felt his cock thrust between a woman's thighs, an age since he'd wanted to.

No!

The word reverberated in his mind—and with it came the vision he had been trying to halt all these years. A vision that brought a piercing pain to his heart and an unbearable longing that threatened to destroy him.

Clenching his teeth, he pushed those memories down and forced himself to walk away from the shieling. He melted into the shadows, embracing the ebony night like a beloved cloak. His thoughts kept him company, fueling his determination.

Soon. You can have whomever and whatever you want, soon. Because when this world is finally yours, nothing and no one can stop you.

CHAPTER 36

GAGE

The cage stank. By my count, I'd been in this cell for two weeks. Two goddamn weeks where the only people I'd seen were Egan, my prison guard, and Callum.

The bars of the cell were warded; every time I touched them, crippling pain ricocheted through my body. My captors were careful—I was served water and a meagre bowl of slop without any utensils. I had no means of escape and no access to my magic. No means of releasing the building tension that ached to be released.

I was going fucking insane.

All I could think about was Brydie, where she was, what she was doing, whether she was okay. The only thing containing the lid on my panic was that I knew she was alive. The bracelets Callum secured to her wrists had not only restricted her power, but they had also weakened our internal connection. It hadn't snapped completely, though. A thin gossamer thread remained, the only thing confirming she was alive.

Callum came every afternoon, to gloat and to taunt. A

week after I'd been imprisoned, he leered, "She's a fiery little thing, isn't she? Her body is a little small for my liking, but I do enjoy being able to touch her whenever I feel like it."

Rage had blanketed my vision, and I'd grit my teeth to remain silent, knowing he wanted a reaction—a reaction I would not goddamn give him. I had little power here, but I would fucking use what I had.

But he hadn't stopped.

"Did you know she enjoys pain?" he continued. "I think she's now beginning to crave our sessions together. There's a darkness inside her she can't hide from." He considered me through the bars, that smile playing on his lips.

I withheld a flinch and reminded myself there was a fine line between light and dark. A line I'd crossed more than a few times myself.

At my continued silence, Callum laughed. "Even those you are destined to protect seek the darkness, don't they, Guardian?" He crouched down outside my cell, peering at me through the bars. "And I'd hazard a guess that even if we'd never caught her, you wouldn't have been able to control her. That part of her is wild; it can't be caged. Exposing her to pain has benefited my research greatly. Her blood is compatible with the lore and has created new avenues to explore. Why, even now, you're being tested with it." He flicked his gaze around my cell—the cage I couldn't escape from—and that smirk played on his lips. "It appears I was right. My plans will finally be implemented, and we'll soon be looking at a whole new world."

A cold sweat slid down my spine as I recalled that conversation. Another week had passed since then. What would happen to Brydie if she was tortured for weeks?

Would she still be capable of the task before her? Would she be the same woman I had come to know and love? Unease settled in the pit of my stomach, because with each passing day, I could feel the woman I used to know slipping away.

CHAPTER 37

BRYDIE

PRESENT DAY, SCOTLAND

I was roused by the sound of the key in the lock. Moments later, the door to my prison opened to reveal five robed figures silhouetted in the doorway. Their faces were shrouded in darkness, their hoods covering their heads, but Callum's blood-red robe, his stature, and his smell, were unmistakable.

Trepidation licked along my skin. This was no ordinary visit.

With a wave of Callum's hand, one of the hooded figures lit a torch in the wall sconce. The eerie glow threw the hooded face into relief, and my breath caught as I realized it was Jake. The man Alison loved.

He stared back, his features impassive, not a nuance of emotion crossing his expression.

Lost. He was lost.

I cut my gaze to the others, realizing Callum had brought all three of his personal guards to my cell, now able to distinguish the older man and the hunched figure of the crone. But I didn't know who the remaining tall, slim figure was. It was hard to determine if the body underneath the robe was male or female.

While Jake shut the door, Callum laid a proprietary hand on the figure's arm and stepped forward, lazily lifting the hood of his robe back with his other hand. His bald head shone in the torchlight as the three guards fanned out behind him in a protective formation—as though I was still a threat.

I felt like laughing—manic, uncontrollable laughter, but there was nothing left inside me, nothing that could harness even an ounce of energy.

He frowned. "You're weaker than usual," Callum said, observing me closely.

I bit my tongue to stop my response. It was a wasted exercise; Callum only heard what he wanted to hear.

"It appears my timing is opportune because I can't have that, Brydie, not when I have lore that needs to be written and tested before Samhain. If your state of mind fails, your blood is not fit for use."

Again, I said nothing, my hands clenching and unclenching at my sides. *What did he want? Why were they all here?* My heart was pounding, screaming for answers to my questions—questions I didn't want to voice aloud.

But the leader of The Oaken Tree answered them anyway. "So in order to sweeten our continued partnership, I have brought you a bargaining chip."

What was he talking about? But it soon became apparent when he pulled the tall form next to him into the torchlight. At his gesture, the hooded figure silently lifted a hand and pulled back the hood.

My heart stopped beating as everything around me came to a screaming halt. I stared in shocked silence at that face. A face I hadn't seen in months, a face I'd come to rescue....

Chloe.

I gazed at Chloe, drinking her in. I couldn't see much behind her robes, but she looked frail, almost skeletal. Her face was so pale, her hair matted and unkempt.

"Chloe?" I asked again.

Her gaze remained blank.

Callum's voice was smooth. "I wouldn't expect her to respond to you, my dear."

What had he done to her? She was so close, yet untouchable. "Why is she here?" I asked slowly, my heart breaking.

Callum turned to face Chloe, his eyes roving down her slim form. "She has important lineage. My family has always had an interest in ancestry. My great-great-grandfather used to maintain the records of our clan's genealogy. It was a hobby he enjoyed, and he was good at it. He made meticulous recordings of everyone's lineage, but he focused on certain bloodlines, specifically those families affected by Cailleach's prophecy. Of them all, he paid particular attention to Talorgan's line. There were not many people who had bothered to remember who he was before he followed Arawn, but my grandfather found descendants of those who did."

As he talked, my gaze drifted back to my best friend, who just stood there, a still, silent doll, her eyes fixed on the wall behind me. Not once had they shifted down to meet mine, not once. Telling myself not to panic, I turned my gaze back to Callum and tried to focus on what he was now saying.

"My ancestor's life's work was rewarded, for he unearthed a very valuable piece of information," he continued, hands now clasped behind his back and that damning sly smile back on his lips. "It appears that in a moment of rage, Talorgan raped a woman from the village. That woman only told one other person—a relation of my soon to be great-great-grandmother many generations back. By the time my grandfather looked into her history, it was too late. It was said she'd fled the village as soon as her pregnancy became noticeable, and there her history supposedly ended. But when this information was passed onto me, I knew how valuable it was, for if Talorgan's descendant was ever found, there's no denying they would become a very valuable asset, one I could use as security."

No....

Callum leered. "Yes, I can see you've worked it out, my dear. And your assumptions are correct—Chloe is the descendant of that woman, and in effect, a descendant of Talorgan." He cocked his head, eyes glinting. "Ironic, isn't it, given that you're best friends? Or is *frenemies* the appropriate term here?"

I couldn't respond, couldn't even find my voice to do so. How was that possible? How had we gravitated toward each other and been in the same country, let alone the same school together, without being aware of our connection? But then a comment from Alison reverberated through my mind: *Like attracts like.*

My gaze flew back to Chloe, and as I looked at the familiar face that had been my rock since my parents death, I questioned our bond. Did we gravitate toward each other because of the prophecy and our link to the past? Did that mean our friendship wasn't formed on love and affection, but rather on an ingrained, fated need?

I desperately searched her face for some kind of emotion, some kind of indication that she knew it was me in front of her—her best friend. But she remained frozen, a blank doll.

Feeling Callum's gaze on my face, I cut my eyes back to his. "I still don't understand why she's your prisoner," I said in a low voice, urging it not to break, to not show him how much this news affected me.

There was a cunning glint in his eyes. "Because, my dear, just like you, Talorgan doesn't know of her existence. He has no knowledge he got that woman with child all those centuries ago. Have you not realized how meticulous I plan? I envision all scenarios, and even though I may be allied with Talorgan, you must never doubt that I have my own agenda. I play my own game, descendant, as you should have done."

I swallowed. We had underestimated him in more ways than one. "And what is that game?" I forced out past the lump in my throat.

Callum smiled, as if pleased I'd questioned him, pleased he could share his genius with me. "You, my dear, are an enigma. The only Daughter of Winter to have been kept a secret. I find it fascinating that not even the Guardians knew of your existence. And neither did Nora, your own grandmother who came to visit you. Why couldn't she feel a connection to your legacy, hmm? I believe it is because your blood will create new lore that could turn the tide of power. Power that will be in *our* favor, not yours or other descendants of Cailleach, and certainly not Talorgan's. So, my dear Brydie, for all intents and purposes, I support Talorgan's cause, yes, but I refuse to tie my destiny to his."

Callum turned on his heel and began to pace. "I have often wondered how it was possible to keep your existence a secret, so I tasked Alison with going over the Lore Book again. I asked her to decipher every nuance and detail. She found a passage about like attracting like—a passage we have interpreted to read that all players eventually find their way back to each other. And once we heard of your existence and your location, I knew the time had come to use the information my great-great-grandfather had unearthed, so I tasked my people to search not only for you, but also for Talorgan's descendant. It's unbelievable how easy it was to find her." He stopped pacing and turned to face me. "She was your best friend. Like did indeed attract like, wouldn't you say?"

His smile was as sharp as a knife, and it sliced a deep cut into my heart. I swallowed again, refusing to drop my gaze; refusing to see how much this hurt as he unearthed how he had found Chloe.

"We watched you both for days before we made our move," he continued, face now darkening. "Except one of my men made a mistake and tried to take you instead. The silly fool was intercepted by your Guardian and only got so far as drugging you. If he'd just waited and done what he was supposed to and taken Chloe as planned, I would have had you both long ago. He wasted my time."

My heart stuttered at the memory of that evening in the nightclub back in New Zealand. How I'd met that man on the dance floor, then accepted the drink he'd bought me. I remembered the sickness that had come over me, then how I'd blanked out at the bar. *That...that had been one of Callum's men—not Talorgan?*

My pulse raced at what this meant. Callum had been involved from the very beginning—from the exact same moment Gage had entered my life. Callum had been watching me—*watching us all*—this whole time. He'd known about me, about Chloe's impending trip, about our relationship—everything. I felt ill.

"Yes, I can see that you remember," Callum continued softly. "It was a near miss on our part, and I'm thankful Gage did not recognize Bevan's signature that night. After his failed attempt, poor Bevan was forced to apprehend our initial target, and because I held insurance over him, he did as I bade, watching as Chloe boarded that airplane, leaving you and your Guardian in New Zealand. He boarded that same plane, and as soon as she stepped onto the tarmac in London, she was ours. We have you to thank for that, Brydie. Without you, we'd never have found her."

My stomach roiled. I felt my jaw lock with the effort of keeping my mouth closed, but the urge to lash back at him was too strong. "You're a traitor to your people! You disgust me."

That glint came back into Callum's eyes, and my skin crawled as he ran his dark, beady eyes down my form. "You offer an enticing challenge. I've been wondering what it would be like to have you in my bed—cleaned up, of course. Every taunt that passes your lips just excites me into anticipating that moment even more. Ian's sister is not the wife I desired. She's too malleable and soft for my liking, without any steel to her soul. Not like you. Look at you, beaten and miserable, yet you still carry fire."

I snarled, "I will never lie with you."

That smile played on his lips again. "We shall see," he murmured, his eyes now shifting to Chloe as he added pointedly, "You just need the right motivation."

Horror slid down my spine. If he threatened Chloe, I would do it. I would do *anything* to ensure her safety.

I looked at her again, silently begging her to respond to my silent call. And this time, by some miracle, her gaze dropped and finally met mine. Those eyes, so familiar, stared back at me as if I was a stranger.

"Chloe?" I pleaded, not caring that Callum was watching, listening. That my attempts only added more fuel to the fire.

Callum laughed. "Don't you ever listen? There's no point, my dear. She doesn't even know you anymore."

"What have you done to her?" I cried, unable to keep the façade up any longer. Every moment she stared back at me without any sense of recognition was another crack in my heart I was unable to hold back. I whirled back to Callum. "What is the point of taking her captive? Once Talorgan knows who she is, he'll kill you."

He cocked a brow. "You have no idea, do you? She was your best friend, yet you felt nothing in her presence." He looked at Chloe, his eyes containing more than nominal interest as he said, "Aside from her obvious physical attributes, there is power in her blood, and I'm thinking of experimenting on hers next."

I froze as fear whispered down my spine. "No. You will not touch her."

"And what do you intend on doing to stop me?" he asked silkily, gesturing at the bracelets around my wrists. "You're effectively powerless, my dear, not to mention you're trapped inside this room. How do you have a hope of preventing me from doing whatever I please?"

The smooth reply had the effect he intended. The anger roiling in my veins was snuffed out like a candle in the wind. The utter hopelessness of my situation returned with a devastation that rendered me speechless. He was right, I was powerless. There was nothing I could do to save Chloe or myself.

A soft chuckle broke the weighted silence. "Well, this little interlude has gone on for long enough. It's been very successful too. I can taste your despair in the air, so poignant and heartfelt." He gave me a toothy smile. "It means we can forgo the exertion of our normal activities and get straight into the blood-letting. I must admit I'm pleased about that because I've been exhausted as of late." He turned to the tallest of his personal guards and ordered, "Take her blood, Jake."

Panic arose as Jake immediately snapped his fingers, and a wooden bowl appeared in his upturned palm. He walked purposefully toward me, his movements smooth and controlled. I could feel the vibrations of his magic. He felt powerful, strong, and the signature he emanated reeked upon the air—a curling insinuation of choking smoke.

He gestured at the chair to my left. I hesitated, not wanting to meekly fulfil Callum's wishes, but one look at Callum and his pointed nod toward Chloe was enough to have me seating myself without question.

Jake knelt before me and placed the bowl on the ground, then wasted no time in lashing my legs to the chair. My gut churned as I anticipated what was to come. My head buzzed, a ringing sound piercing my ears. Feeling desperate, I reached out and grabbed Jake's arm. His gaze met mine, and this close, I could see his eyes were hazel, a wonderful mix of green and brown, yet unfeeling and cold as ice.

Knowing I had mere seconds, I said urgently under my breath, "Fight it, Jake! Fight *him!*"

Those detached hazel eyes merely stared back at me with not a spark of interest.

I squeezed his arm tight and hissed, "Think of your father!"

He blinked, and his movements stilled.

Callum swore. "Leave him," he growled "Or you will reap the consequences."

But, encouraged by Jake's response, I pushed away the fear of his threat. "Jake, your father loves you," I pushed. "He needs you."

Jake, blinked again, his body still unmoving, but this time his eyes changed. As if a veil had lifted, he looked at me —truly looked at me.

I pushed again. "Jake. Please, help me."

He suddenly turned to take in the room, and at that exact moment, Callum snarled, the sound feral and full of such profound anger that I shrank back into my seat. He rushed forward and sent a vicious kick to my chest. The chair, with me in it, was flung backward onto the stone floor. My head hit the ground with a sickening thud, and white lights flickered at the edge of my vision. With bile traveling up my throat, I turned my head, trying to find Jake.

But Callum was there, a hand on either side of the young man's face. He was chanting softly under his breath. The air squeezed around them, expanding and then shrinking. I felt the hairs on my arms raise just before there came an explosive snap and that tell-tale sizzle at the back of my neck.

Callum stopped chanting and stepped back. He ordered

in an authoritative voice, "Jake, ignore this worthless bitch and take her blood as I requested."

Jake inclined his head in a sharp nod and turned to face me, a wicked, sharp looking blade emerging from amidst the folds of his robe. He reached down and grabbed my left arm, hauling the chair and me back upright. His fingers were tight, bruising, and he refused to make eye contact, that glassy, frozen expression back in place.

"Don't do this, Jake. Fight him!" I rasped. But my protest was weak; I knew it was pointless. Whatever chance I'd had of reaching him before had vanished after what Callum had just done.

Ignoring me, Jake silently tied me to the chair, then yanked on my left arm again, pulling it taut. He swiftly ran the blade of his dagger down the inside of my elbow to my wrist. I couldn't help crying out. The cut was deep—deeper than any made before. Blood instantly welled, a vivid crimson that poured over the side of my arm and splashed into the bowl conveniently placed below.

Jake's grip was unrelenting. I sat there gasping, now singularly focused on keeping down the contents of my stomach. Time slowed down, and my vision began to fade. My eyes drifted closed.

From a distance, a voice, calculating and cold, broke through the haze. "That's enough for now, Jake. Heal her."

With that voice came the grim realization that I was still trapped in this nightmare. I blinked, opening my eyes to see that smirking face, with the bald head and the malicious gaze, right as there came a vicious pain along the inside of my arm. I knew without looking down that Jake had staunched the flow from the wound and was now healing my arm.

Once healed, the young man reached down to pick up

the bowl and carried it over to Callum. I blearily watched as
Callum dipped an index finger into the bowl and brought it
to his lips. He sucked and swallowed, his eyes closing as a
look of ecstasy traveled across his face. My stomach turned,
and I felt pressure at the back of my throat.

"You're a sick fuck," I murmured, too far gone to realize
I'd said the words aloud, too tired to care about the
repercussions.

But Callum heard me. His eyes flew open, and his face
was a cold mask as he stepped up to my chair. Without any
warning, he lashed out with a vicious backhand. Pain
exploded in a miasma of burning heat as my head whipped
backward with the force of the blow. For a moment, the
chair teetered on two legs, then crashed to the floor. Before I
had a chance to breathe, Callum was kneeling on my chest,
driving his fist into my face again and again. I couldn't move,
couldn't even lift a hand to prevent the blows given my
hands and legs were still tied to the chair.

After a while, I felt nothing. It was as if the blood-letting
and the pain I'd endured to this point had exhausted all
emotion and feeling in my body. But the sound of Callum's
fists was a monotonous drumbeat, a reality I couldn't escape
from. All I could do was lie there, staring up at the dark
ceiling through swollen eyes, watching the torchlight flicker
among the shadows chasing each other across the roof.

I was removed. Void. Stripped of all my shields. In that
moment of quiet, I realized something. I realized hope was a
fool's errand. The tiny flame of hope I'd been nurturing
inside me was not strong enough in the face of who and
what Callum was. He was too powerful, too cunning. He'd
allied himself with Talorgan, and he held a fae vessel of
unimaginable power. How was I to beat that? Beat *him*?

Each blow pushed me further over the edge, closer to

the oblivion I craved—but not fast enough. *Why was I holding on?* Why was there a part of me still trying to fight him, still hoping for escape?

There was no escape. If I ever managed to leave this hell hole, I wouldn't go far; either Callum's personal guards would find me or Talorgan would.

I heard my jawbone crack. The sound pierced the argument in my mind, a cruel statement that proclaimed holding onto hope was a fool's errand. That tiny flame inside me trembled and flickered dangerously, hovering on the cusp of being snuffed out. I screamed at it to die. Yet it refused to go out.

Unwilling to fight anymore, I allowed my eyelids to flutter closed...only to fling them open again when a crazed scream pierced the void.

CHAPTER 39

BRYDIE

C allum stopped suddenly, mid-swing, and roared as he jumped off me, "She's fighting the binding. Hold her!"

Dazed, I lay there in shock as I forced myself to focus on the scene before me. Chloe was caught between Samuel and Mary, her face twisted into a grimace as she kicked and struggled against their hold. It took me a moment to understand what I was seeing. She was awake!

I opened my mouth to tell her that it was okay, that I was here, but my jaw wouldn't work.

As if she'd heard my silent cry, Chloe's eyes caught mine. I saw the moment recognition hit her—that it was me she was seeing, her best friend. Her voice was thick with emotion as she cried, "Brydie!"

I could only stare hopelessly back at her, barely holding on but trying to convey in our shared gaze that she wasn't alone in this nightmare.

Callum came to stand in front of her, his movements stiff. He'd always been so careful up to this point, never losing the fine edge of his control. But I'd snapped that thread today, and I felt the harsh consequences of what I'd goaded him to do, for the pain in my body was returning, the numbness I'd reveled in only moments before dwindling with every passing second. Every breath was like a thousand shards of glass in my lungs, every minuscule movement a burning lance against my face, in my chest, even in my heart.

Chloe locked her gaze on Callum, instantly recognizing the biggest threat in the room. "You fucking bastard!" she screamed, continuing to fight Samuel and Mary's hold. "Let us go!" Once again poised, Callum said smoothly, "I'm afraid that's not possible, my dear."

"What are you talking about?" she cried. "All you have to do is let us go. People will miss us. Let us go now before you regret it."

Callum ignored her, instead turning to Samuel and ordering, "Heal the blows I've dealt to the descendant, then get me another chair."

Samuel nodded and came toward me. I was barely conscious of what he did to me, my eyes locked on my friend, but when I felt a sharp excruciating pain in my jaw, I knew it was no longer broken. The whole time, my eyes remained trained on Chloe. I wasn't aware Samuel had entered Callum's adjoining chambers and returned with a chair in his hands until Callum gestured at Chloe and ordered, "Tie her to it."

"No!" I cried, the sound broken and weak.

But Callum heard me. He glanced idly back at me, that small, taunting smile back on his lips. "Haven't had enough yet?" he purred in a low caress. "I'll be happy to oblige after I've dealt with your friend."

I inhaled sharply, and the action crippled me, sharp stabbing pains in my ribs robbing me of breath. It appeared

Samuel had only healed the superficial wounds on my face and body; time would heal the rest.

Helpless, I watched as Chloe was forced into the chair. At a sharp command, rope suddenly appeared in Samuel's hands, the strands glowing green and pulsating with unnatural energy. I smelled the signature on the air, the notes rancid and pungent as if a field of vegetables were rotting in the sun.

When the ropes touched Chloe's skin, she screamed and writhed in agony. Callum moved in and swiftly backhanded her. As Chloe's head snapped backward, her cry cut off mid-scream, and I felt the impact of his assault more than I had when those fists had been aimed at me.

"Chloe!" I screamed, but what came out was a mere whisper of sound. My throat was hoarse, ragged, my voice box destroyed.

I watched her blink dazedly, blood running freely from her nose to drip onto the brown robe she wore—clothing I'd come to hate with a vengeance. Her head turned toward mine, her brown eyes huge in her pale face. The stench of her fear was palpable.

Callum smiled. "I'm glad to see you have changed your attitude, my dear, although I admit I am disappointed. Given your lineage, I thought you'd have more fight."

Chloe began to tremble at his congenial smile, so at odds to the violence he unleashed. "I have no idea what you're talking about; I'm adopted," she said in a shaking voice. "This is all a huge mistake. Please, let us go."

Callum smiled benignly. "Oh, my dear, I'm not mistaken. You have the mark of Talorgan."

"What mark?" Chloe cried, her voice rising into a shriek. "Who is Talorgan?"

Callum bent down and pulled her brown robe up to

expose her calves. He pointed to her ankle. "This is the mark of Talorgan," he explained. "Every descendant is said to carry it."

The shadows in the room hid the detail of what he was gesturing at, but I could discern a dark smudge on the inside of her right ankle. It was Chloe's tattoo, the one she told me she'd had done just before we met at high school. She'd said it used to be a phoenix in flight. She had had it done on a day she bunked school.

"That's my tattoo," Chloe whispered, her voice a thin thread of sound. "I had it done when I was eleven."

"No," Callum replied softly. "You had a tattoo put *over* the mark. It doesn't escape the fact it was there in the first place, or that it's hiding under the ink."

"I don't understand," she said, her voice now panicked. "What's so important about it?"

Callum looked down at her, and there was a small pause before his next words. "Because you are the descendant of an immortal. A being so powerful, he can reach through the veils between worlds and command others to do his bidding."

Chloe's face went sheet-white, her mouth opening in an O of shock. Her eyes darted over Callum's face, then, realizing he believed what he'd just shared, she swallowed. "Immortality? Prophecy?" she gasped out. "This is crazy. You've got the wrong person. Please, let me go." She caught my eyes and added, "Let us both go!"

Callum ran a hand down her long, black hair in a soft caress. "Shh, my pretty. Don't get all worked up. Things will go easier if you just stay calm. All I have for you is some questions."

Chloe trembled and visibly shrank from his touch, carrying an ingrown awareness that Callum had no boundaries, no lines he wouldn't cross. I bit my lip, striving to prevent my fear from drowning out all else. I couldn't bear to see Chloe hurt. I just couldn't. It would be the final thread holding me together.

"Alright," she said, her voice a thin thread. "What do you want to know?"

Callum smiled again, the effect serpentine. "That's my girl. I knew you'd come around." He clasped his hands behind his back and rocked on his heels, looking for all intents and purposes as if we were discussing the weather. "Now that you're willing to work with me, the answers I need are quite simple. The first thing I'd like to know is what's your specialty?"

Chloe's brow furrowed. "Specialty? I'm an architect."

Callum sighed, and his voice was lacking patience when he retorted, "I don't fucking care what your career is, you dumb bitch! I'm talking about your magic. What element or power do you gravitate toward?"

Chloe's eyes flew to mine. I could see the bewilderment on her face. Her lips trembled. "I don't have any magic," she forced out shakily.

Callum's lips thinned. "Oh, that's where you're wrong, my pretty. There's something inside you, I can feel it." He turned away from her, his fists clenching, then he whipped back around to face her again. The action made Chloe jump, her eyes widening with fear. "Can you feel him, then? Your father?" he asked her.

If it was possible, Chloe's face went even paler. "My father?"

"Well?"

"No," she whispered, her face crumpling. "I can't feel my father. Please—just let us go!"

"Christ! You're fucking useless!" Callum threw his hands

into the air, then turned to face Samuel, his eyes narrowed. "I need answers and I need them now."

Samuel gave Callum his unblinking gaze. "What do you propose, sir?"

"Anything that gets the answers I need."

Samuel inclined his head, then snapped out a command. Branches, slender and strong, shot out of his palms and wrapped around Chloe, twining around her and the chair in a vicious stranglehold. They wrapped around her torso, her legs, her arms, her neck. It happened so quickly, she barely had time to release a shriek. The sound was so agonizingly fearful that my blood chilled at the sound.

She was struggling ineffectually as the branches squeezed around her body tighter and tighter, unrelenting in their pressure. I watched in utter helplessness as they wrapped around her neck. Her breath wheezed, an avalanche of sound in the quiet room, then suddenly, it was abruptly cut off, her breath caught in mid-exhale. In horror, I watched her face change from white to red, then to shades of purple. It happened so quickly I could barely process that I was watching her being strangled in front of my eyes.

"Noooooo!" I screamed.

I felt something tremble violently against my chest, then my eyes were suddenly blinded by a brilliant, bright arrow of pure white light. The pendant!

Hope blossomed, fragile like a hothouse flower, but in the next moment, my world rocked as I was shoved violently to the side, my kidneys delivered a sickening series of brutal kicks. The chair legs underneath me shattered, and my arms and legs came free of my bonds. I tried to move away to escape the pain and ended up rolling onto my stomach. The kicking stopped. Gasping, trembling, I lay there, my cheek pressed against the cold, rough surface, nausea wracking my body.

"I'd forgotten you wear that pendant around your neck," a cool, cultured voice said above me with a slight pant to it. "Jake, do me the honor of retrieving it for me, please."

I was roughly rolled onto my back, then Jake was there, his hand sliding under my tee shirt. When I felt his hands latch onto the pendant just below my breasts, he hissed and pulled back so suddenly he stumbled.

"What is it?" Callum demanded, his brows drawn in question.

"I cannot touch it," Jake replied. "It denied me."

Callum turned his head, considering me. "We shall see about that."

I froze at his tone. I knew the only way someone could take the pendant from me was if I was dead. That thought alone was enough to push the stubborn refusal of my fate once again to the surface—a death wish I couldn't curb. "The pendant is mine. Touch it and I will kill you the first chance I get," I rasped.

Callum laughed. "Another wasted threat? I struggle to see how that would be possible given your current position. Do you have any idea what it is you carry about your neck?"

I stared at him, hatred roiling in my chest. "Of course, I do. It's a family heirloom."

He sneered, "Oh, my dear, quite the contrary. You carry a sliver of a fae vessel."

His revelation was another kick to my gut, just as powerful, just as deadly. "What?"

Callum's eyes dropped to my chest, where the pendant had dimmed, its white light now flickering, its low hum almost non-existent. "That pendant around your neck is a small piece of the Stone of Destiny. I assume you've heard of it?"

I had, from one of my father's childhood bedtime stories. The Stone of Destiny came with the Tuatha Dé Danann when they left their world for this one. It was said to have the power to confirm who the real kings of Scotland and Ireland would be—loudly crying out in joy if the Rightful High King sat upon it.

"Yes, I've heard of it," I finally said. "But there is no significance to its power other than proclaiming a true heir."

Callum smiled. "Which is exactly what it has done, my dear. That pendant confirms you are of Cailleach's bloodline, and its acceptance of you is a proclamation that you are a true Daughter."

Gage had said as much, but he'd also said he believed the pendant did more than that. He'd warned me to keep it secret, hidden under my clothing at all times. I'd hoped it would turn into something of value, something that would aid us in the coming war with Talorgan. But here, in this moment with Callum, I'd just found out it wasn't a weapon, but an object with no other power than to proclaim my birthright.

But yet, it was still a significant part of my ancestry. Countless Daughters before me had worn it around their necks, as had Cailleach. It was not Callum's, and I was adamant he would never have it. "Good luck getting it off me because it will stay here until my last breath."

His smile widened. "Oh, there are many ways to skin a cat, my dear. And little do you know that I have been looking for leverage to hold a certain meeting for a long time. This reminder of what you wear around your neck is opportune."

"What are you talking about?"

He smirked. "Soon enough, you shall see."

The glib comment did nothing to settle my nerves; it was an indication Callum had yet more plans in store for me.

...It was then I realized the enemy wasn't Talorgan—Callum had been the real evil all along. We should have been focusing our efforts on him instead; the cobra who was waiting for the right moment to strike.

The taste of defeat was poignant, as was the anger. It had me pushing myself onto my knees, biting off a groan as I faced Callum. Very slowly, I clearly enunciated, "Fuck you!"

Callum's jaw clenched. It was the last thing I saw before there was a blur of movement and he punched me in the stomach. Chloe screamed as I toppled to the floor.

From a distance I heard Callum snarl, "Silence her!"

Blinking, my face and body on fire, I could barely make out Jake as he came into view. He waved a hand over my face. The effect of his action was immediate. I felt myself robbed of sound, my mouth and throat working, yet no noise erupting—not even the gasp of my breathing was audible.

"I tire of this game," Callum said to Jake. "We need to move onto the next phase of testing to see whose blood we can mix with Brydie's. As Gage is contemplating his options, the obvious choice is Talorgan's descendant. However, I'm in a quandary here, because in order to do that, I need to confirm where her abilities lie."

"What do you suggest, sir?" Jake asked.

The words fell into the ominous quiet like a gunshot in the night. "Get me the cauldron."

My heart stopped beating. If Chloe drank from the cauldron, she would forget everything—who she was, who I was, where she belonged, her parents. No!

Jake's voice cut through my rising panic. "What of the Daughter?"

Callum grunted, "Let the bitch watch."

An intensity of emotions twisted into an ugly knot inside my stomach. Fear. Wrath. Loathing. And the biggest one— hate. I hated Callum with a vengeance I hadn't known existed. My eyes burned as I stared at his face, fixing on that hateful smile, that gleaming bald head.

I heard the door of the chamber open and close. Moments later, it opened again, but this time there was a marked change. I felt it right to my bones—an undeniable charge of energy that hummed incessantly and screamed of power. There was a familiarity to it I couldn't deny. I recognized the same vibrations and energy patterns in the pendant around my neck. *Like attracts like.* It confirmed my pendant was indeed a sliver from another fae vessel, because what had entered the chamber couldn't be anything other than the Dagda's cauldron.

I slowly turned my head and caught sight of Jake who, with leather gloves on his hands, was carrying a tarnished silver cup. It looked like an old sports trophy, unremarkable and stained by time. He carried it carefully, almost gingerly, and upon the air was a melody, pure and unadulterated that was increasing in volume with every passing second. A melody that was so beautiful it was undeniably lethal.

Callum accepted the cup and pulled a knife from inside the folds of his robe. Holding his left hand over the cauldron, he cut deep into his palm. He winced as he squeezed his fist, and I watched as thick, red blood flowed inside the tarnished rim.

When the steady trickle turned into a drip, Jake silently handed Callum a bandage. Callum wrapped his hand before taking the cauldron from Jake with his bare hands.

Was that because he was the owner of the vessel? Was it that only one person could lay claim to its power at a time, just like the pendant around my neck?

I saw how the cup now glowed, the silver no longer tarnished but bright and polished, as if the blood had transformed it to new glory.

I shuddered as a new sound now rode upon the air. It's symphony was no longer a pure melody but a discordant chime now building to a crescendo.

Callum reached out and touched Jake's shoulder, and together they turned their backs to me and faced Chloe, their broad shoulders shielding her form from view. I heard Callum's voice begin to chant with a mixture of guttural sounds before Jake's younger voice began to weave in; a lilting dance of two different tones. As if in response, that incessant dark melody that could only be coming from the cauldron grew, pounding to a rhythmic beat.

My heart raced in time to its devastating pulse. Each beat reminded me that there was nothing I could do to help Chloe.

The men's chanting suddenly stopped, and the discordant chiming also ended. The forms in front of me moved, and I was greeted with the vision of Chloe swallowing and intermittently choking as she drank every drop of blood in the cauldron.

Then, more frightening than any sound, was the utter silence that followed.

I whimpered, fear squeezing my throat and cutting off my airway as Callum and Jake stepped back, the cauldron back in Jake's leather-clad hand. Chloe's face was slack and her eyes closed as she sat slumped sideways in her chair. A few drops of blood were running down her chin. Utterly transfixed, I stared at that dark trail. My mind tried to shy away from the truth those red lines told as I waited on Chloe to open her eyes and look at me.

Moments later, her eyelids fluttered. She blinked, once, twice, then her head swiveled, looking around the room. When her eyes found mine, her expression was neutral, her demeanor remote,...and the light within those brown eyes had gone cold. There was no recognition, no emotion, no warmth. There was nothing.

The truth of that stare broke through my consciousness, and the dam broke. I threw my head back, releasing the ghost of a hoarse, gut-wrenching scream—

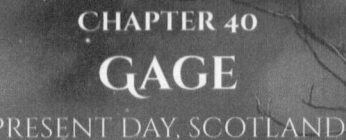

CHAPTER 40

GAGE

PRESENT DAY, SCOTLAND

I tensed when I heard footsteps coming down the long corridor that led to my cell. I didn't need to see who it was that came; I would recognize that distinctive shuffling walk anywhere. And going by the growl of my stomach, Egan was bringing my supper.

Tensing in anticipation of the altercation to come, I remained seated on the stone floor and leaned my back against the rear end of the cell, as far away as I could get from the enchanted bars. *Show no weakness.*

The steps came closer, and my hunched guard came into view. Egan's eyes were recessed under thick black brows, and they unerringly found mine through the gloom.

"Dinner m'lord," he announced with a mocking bow, the torchlight in the corridor highlighting the sneer permanently etched upon his long, narrow face.

He bent and placed the tray on the ground, just outside the cell bars. The water in the mug sloshed over the rim, losing half its contents. I eyed the bread, a pathetic dry and blackened lump, and my stomach growled again, cutting through the silence.

Egan snickered. "Hungry, are you? Well, eat up, m'lord, or I won't be responsible if the rats get it."

I could easily snag the mug and the bread by simply walking over and reaching through the cell bars, but I'd played this game before; I knew what that move would cost me.

When I remained where I was, the sneer on Egan's face became a snarl. "Don't tempt me, m'lord. You know the boss doesn't like his pets to waste away."

Oh, I knew exactly what Callum's motives were when it came to keeping his prisoners alive. For his proclivities, he enjoyed them weak. Torture wasn't any fun when your victims were unconscious, and blood didn't flow so well either. It was another reason why I didn't reach for my supper tray.

The taunting smile on Egan's lips disappeared. "Maybe it needs some condiments to make it tasty," he suggested softly.

I tensed at the tone. Egan held my gaze as he fumbled for his zipper. His cock tumbled into his hands, and he palmed it while he stared at me. I held that gaze, hatred twisting in my gut. I could do nothing as, with cruel intent, he took aim and pissed over the bread and water.

The stench of his urine was overpowering, and a killing rage sprang to the surface. I refused to look down at my ruined supper and strived to keep my face expressionless, knowing the bastard wanted a reaction. Retaliating only spurred him on, and that only resulted in more pain and humiliation on my end.

Egan shoved his cock back into his pants, and with a huge smile on his face, he nudged the tray closer to the bars of my cell. "Eat it," he said softly, a hard edge to his tone.

Still I didn't move.

In the ensuing seconds, Egan snarled, all pretense at patience now gone, "Is it going to be like that then, is it?"

With one hand, he pulled a key off the ring he kept in his pocket and reached for the whip on his belt with the other. He lazily flicked it onto the floor, the movement illustrating his experience with the weapon.

I was unable to mask my reaction, my muscles locking at the memory of the pain that whip had already imposed. The festering wounds across my back remembered the vicious barbed tails that had bitten into my skin. But it wasn't the whip that made my heart beat faster or render my hands slick with sweat as I squeezed them into fists by my side. It was that Egan had perversions he was allowed to pursue at his leisure down here, and on the first day of my imprisonment I'd found out exactly what excited my prison guard.

And it would be his downfall.

I'd been watching and listening, searching for a way out, and I'd soon realized Egan was the loophole in this dungeon—the path of his depravity the only escape route available.

He flicked the whip through the cell bars, the barbed tail expertly latching onto the skin of my left leg through my jeans. I bit off a cry of pain and leaned down to pull the curved blades from my skin. Seeing my reaction, Egan yanked on the whip's handle, embedding the barbs even deeper, and said with a low laugh, "It appears you're caught, m'lord. I suggest you stand up, or you'll find the kiss of my whip on your nipples next."

He yanked on the whip, and the barbs ripped through my flesh as he tugged them loose. I bit my tongue as I felt blood flow down my shin bone. "Fuck you," I ground out.

Egan grinned. "Now, now, m'lord. You should know

better than to taunt me after your last beating. With your powers gone, you know you're not as fast as I am."

I growled; the bastard was right. I hated this feeling. Hated feeling so worthless. So hopeless. *Keep your head. Look for the opportunities.* And for now, that meant obeying this fucker. Gritting my teeth, I fought the dizziness in my head and used the indents in the stone wall to pull myself to my feet.

Right on cue, as soon as my back hit the wall, Egan flicked the whip again, and this time the barbs sliced through my black tee shirt and into my abdomen. I bit my tongue again, and this time I tasted blood. I closed my eyes as the world whirled in front of me. I was too weak to escape the agony; my mind too sluggish to focus.

Egan used the distraction to his advantage, yanking once again on the whip. I cried out as the barbs ripped through my skin, sagging against the wall and falling to my knees. My breath was coming out in gasps as I strived to maintain consciousness. *Hold on. This is your moment. Just hold on.*

Lifting my head, I watched Egan use the reprieve to unlock the door of my cell and swiftly enter. The heavy iron door ominously slammed shut behind him. *That's it, Egan. Come on in.*

I didn't dare divert my gaze to the key still inserted in the lock, nor did I question my position, or the fact that my body was weak and my magic was gone. This was the moment I'd been waiting for. Possibly the only moment I had left.

My prison guard took two steps toward me, the whip grating across the stone floor with a menace that had an ominous shiver chasing down my spine. "On your feet," Egan ordered softly, cracking the whip once again.

The barbs hit my left forearm this time, slicing through

my leather jacket. I swallowed a moan as they entered my skin.

Egan growled again. "I said on your feet. Now!" When I didn't move, he flicked the whip a third time, and the barbs latched into my chest. Just as quickly, they were pulled out of my skin.

As my head swam with the pain, I smelt it: a rancid, putrid smell floating on the air between us. I choked as it invaded my nostrils and understood then why I was so badly affected, why mindfulness wasn't working. Egan's whip had been enhanced with druidic magic, and not just any magic but with dark lore, imbibed to impart pain at an exponential level.

I looked up at my prison guard. Even through the pain, I could see the evidence in his eyes. Just like Callum, an inky blackness swallowed his brown irises—confirmation that Egan had dabbled more than once, that he'd lost the light.

"My patience is running thin," Egan growled. "This is your last chance before I deliver on my promise."

I knew it too. Holding my breath, I pushed my back against the cell wall and used my legs to heave myself back to standing. My body felt incredibly heavy, the muscles straining to hold my weight. Another wave of dizziness rolled over me as I staggered drunkenly along the wall of the cell, just catching myself from sprawling at Egan's feet.

Egan snickered. "Oh, how far the mighty has fallen. You're no match for anyone."

My chest burned at the taunt, more so because it was true. I was as weak as a fucking newborn babe! Even though I was a foot taller than my hunched prison guard, I could feel the shift in power—and I didn't hold the reins. My heart pounded anew. *Think, dammit! Use this to your advantage. Remember Brydie.*

"Turn around," Egan ordered. "Hold onto the bars."

I tensed at the command, unwilling to turn my back on the man. "No."

The whip cracked again, this time slicing into my right cheek. I failed to bite back a shout. Blood welled, flowing down my chest, and I had nothing, absolutely nothing to fight him with. Aware that only more pain would follow, that weakness would soon cause me to lose any chance I had, I slowly turned and faced the wall.

"Good," Egan murmured from behind me. "Now the pants. Drop them."

I froze. The first time Egan had entered my cell with the whip, he'd lashed my back. He reached out at one point, running his hand down my spine, and I'd arched instinctively, biting off a scream. But I'd heard his indrawn breath, and on glancing over my shoulder, I'd seen him palm himself.

The whip cracked again, interrupting my thoughts, and this time it sliced through my leather jacket and into the waistband of my jeans. I cried out, knees buckling.

"Pants—now!" Egan ground out.

Gasping, I groped for the buckle of my jeans, squeezing my eyes shut as the pain rolled through my body like a wave. The fly dragged loudly as I pulled my zipper down, and in the weighted silence I heard Egan's indrawn breath. Gritting my teeth, I forced my jeans down my hips. They slid down easily; my body thinner than it had been two weeks ago.

Egan shifted on his feet behind me. "Don't stop there," he rasped. "Take them off completely."

"Fuck you!" I returned in a snarl, unable to hold the protest back.

Another lash followed. I crumpled as the metal barbs cut into the backs of my thighs. My lacerated cheek slammed into the stone wall. I breathed heavily, fighting the darkness begging to descend. *Hold on, dammit! Hold on!* I couldn't give into the pain, this was my only chance; I knew exactly what would happen if I fell unconscious.

Egan crept closer, and his voice was soft and sinuous as he bent down to my ear. "You know how this is going to end, druid. Everyone pretends they don't like it, but they do, and this is happening whether you're conscious or not." He paused again, and this time there was no room for patience in his tone as he demanded, "Naked—now!"

He was standing less than a foot away, the rancid stench emanating from his body stronger than the smell of defecation coming from the corner of my cell.

This is your moment—your only moment. And there was no fucking way this was happening!

Using every ounce of energy I'd hounded in reserve, I bent down and snatched my jeans up with both hands, while using the momentum to swing my right leg up in a powerful roundhouse. My foot connected with Egan's chin, and he went flying backward. But even as he fell, instinct had him flinging his whip in motion. I dodged the lash, falling on him in a desperate tackle.

I heard the end of the whip's tail connect with the stone wall behind me right as my body collided with his. The perverted bastard kept his wits, the heel of his palm slamming into my chin. My head jerked back, my teeth snapping together. Stars exploded, my vision darkening. Its call was almost cathartic, a temporary escape from this madness, but an image of Brydie, of us entangled in bed, pushed me to keep going, to *fight* for our survival.

Dodging Egan's next blow, I managed to raise one of my arms to send a hard jab squarely on his nose. His head hit the stone floor with a sharp crack. Blood splattered across my face and Egan moaned, his eyes closing.

I didn't hesitate. My fist was a bullet, smashing again and again into his face. All I could feel was white-hot rage, all sense of exhaustion, dizziness, and weakness now gone. The magic that clamored for release hammered against my senses in a pounding conflagration, another reminder of the torture I'd endured, the things they'd done to me. They would all pay, and the man beneath my fists who had humiliated, tortured, and taunted me—he would be the first.

Images of the last two weeks replayed in my mind. I saw Egan smirking at me, defecating in my food, touching himself. I saw Callum, his sneer, that cruel smile on his face, the manic light in his eyes. I heard his threat—to kill my son, to touch Brydie. *No! Mine! They were mine!* Again and again, my fist hammered into Egan's face, not seeing his features, not seeing anything as I was consumed with rage.

"Gage!" The voice was a shriek, a buzz of sound.

It came again, and this time hands touched my back. I didn't hesitate. I whipped around and sent my fist flying. There was a grunt, and a shadowed form crumpled to the ground. I didn't deign to look, didn't care who or what had interrupted me; I was owed payment. I turned back to Egan, but I didn't see his pulpy face, now unrecognizable, or that he no longer breathed. I was too intent on delivering a punishment long overdue.

I raised my fist again, but this time a hand caught my wrist, stopping me mid-swing. I snarled, turned, and sent another fist flying. It failed to connect, and I saw, too late, a shadow fly through the air. The breath whooshed out of my lungs as a heavy weight crashed into me. I fell sideways, toppling off Egan to slam against the floor of my cell.

The shadow didn't give me time to respond, clambering on top of my body and effectively pinning me to the ground. I blinked up at the ceiling as a voice layered with an undercurrent of fear ground out, "You have to stop, Gage!"

I knew that voice. I turned my head and snarled, the sound more animal than human. I now had a new prey—one who also owed me blood. Eyes locked on hers, I violently bucked, twisted, and rolled, losing her in a fluid roll. Violence, anger, hatred—they all drove me onward.

Coming to my feet, I ground out in a hard voice, "You're dead."

Alison's face blanched parchment white, her black hair in stark contrast to the purity of her skin. She shook her head from side to side, her hands held up in front of her. "Please, Gage, you've got it all wrong. Let me explain."

Ignoring the shadows that had entered my cell, I ground my teeth together and took a step toward her. "I'm done with your explanations. You betrayed us."

"No, I didn't!" she bit out urgently. "Please, listen to me!"

I didn't want to. I took another step closer, but before I could take a third, my body was once again restrained. My head whipped left and right as I realized that the shadows were druids, their forms draped in hooded brown robes. Incensed, I said, "There's nothing to explain. You double-crossed us for your own gain. I'm only going to tell you once —let me go now or you'll live to regret it."

Alison's features tightened at my deathly tone. "There's a lot you don't know, Gage, but you can trust in the fact that I'm still loyal to the cause. I still want Callum dead."

"Then why the hell did you double-cross us?" I growled, wrenching my hands against the invisible bonds. One of the guards grunted, stumbling back a few steps. I sent him a sneer. Let them see how long these bonds will hold. I was done with being held captive!

"Stop! Just let me explain," Alison cried, her hands again lifting to act as a buffer between us. "After our meeting in Aviemore, I returned to the Institute to find Callum had been watching me. He told me to keep him informed of your actions. He held insurance for my continued loyalty."

"Insurance?" I spat the word out. "What is more important than everyone's lives?"

Sorrow was in her eyes. "He had my brother."

With those words, she had my attention. If she'd said anyone else, I would have disregarded it, but I understood the need to protect family, the need to protect a brother. I'd do anything to keep Logan safe, even if it meant gambling with the lives of others. "Had?"

Her face turned bleak. "Callum coerced Ryan to follow his path by offering a position of power. All Ryan had to do was test Callum's new lore." Her gaze shifted then, traveling past mine to look beyond the cell walls, into a memory. "Ryan agreed to be his guinea pig, but it didn't go as planned. The new lore changed my brother. Ryan became something...other, not himself. But Callum still insisted he continue the experiments, that he hold to his end of the bargain. I tried to argue but Callum wouldn't listen, and when he found out I'd met with you at Aviemore, Callum promised me that if I delivered both you and Brydie to the Institute, then he would release Ryan from the testing."

"What happened?" I asked, although I had already guessed the answer.

"Callum didn't keep his promise." She shifted her gaze, her eyes again meeting mine. "Ryan was forced to wield more new lore and it killed him the day after you were captured."

For a moment, I just stared at her, my mind churning. I could taste her grief, knew she spoke the truth, but I didn't trust my instincts any longer where she was concerned. I couldn't afford to. Every second was another one in which someone, maybe Callum, would come. Every second in which Brydie was suffering. "Why are you here? Why haven't you escaped?"

Her mouth tightened. "Because he still has others I care about." She gestured at the four shadows standing quietly, listening and watching our exchange. "We are all in the same position. We didn't know the extent of Callum's machinations until a few days ago. Since securing Brydie, he's pushed his experiments to a new level, and those of us who've been subjected to his whims and made to use the dark arts can feel its effect. I...I have used them." She looked away, her hands clenching. "And the more I've used them, the more they've changed me. I feel different, less connected to the world and my senses...and I am now unable to read Cailleach's Lore Book."

I blinked. "What? You're the Lore Keeper. How is that possible?"

"I can only assume it's because I've turned from the light."

I digested that, my gaze narrowed on hers. I witnessed the tight, pale tone of her face, the tense stance. "Are these changes true of everyone who wields Callum's new lore?"

Alison nodded. "All of us have experienced weakened ties to nature. Our gifts have diminished."

My blood ran cold. The web of intrigue surrounding Callum's proclivities had widened as a result of Alison's revelations, but the urging in my gut to rescue Brydie and get the hell out of here couldn't be denied any longer. I felt torn, wanting to run for her now but knowing I should obtain the full story from Alison first. I had to know exactly what we were dealing with, because if we managed to escape this hell hole, I would be burying us underground, allowing us the time to recuperate what would surely be both physical and mental wounds.

"How long did it take for you to notice the change?" I asked her.

"Almost immediately, but it wasn't until we were forced to use the new lore a third time that we began to see changes in our gifts. For me, the words in the Lore Book became blurred, and by the fourth time, I found I could no longer read it."

Alison glanced at a tall, thin, brown-robed figure to her left, who inclined his head at her unspoken question. His scent was filled with the smell of wildflowers and fresh loam, like a cool breeze on a spring day. Yet there was an underlying scent tainting the freshness of that signature— the faint smell of slow-forming rot.

Alison waved a hand at the man. "Jason can no longer call forth growth in our botanical garden. Anything that requires nurturing now withers and dies at his touch. And Frederick, Carrick, and Liam,"—she gestured to the other forms surrounding us in turn—"all have similar stories. Our gifts no longer nurture."

Her words were poignant because this sounded very similar to the fae curse, except instead of being cursed by another, we had done this to ourselves—some willingly but most unwillingly, and all due to Callum. Rage licked up my spine at the fate our people now faced. My tone was harsh. "I still don't understand how you let him take power like this."

"We could do nothing! Not when he holds all the power —the cauldron has seen to that."

Yes, the fucking cauldron—the fae vessel that gave him all the power he needed to give effect to his plans. Plans he'd no doubt had for years. I clenched my jaw. "We have underestimated Callum. His ambition will cost our people their future."

There was a round of muttered agreement, and Jason growled, "He needs to pay for his sins. He must die."

Similar sentiments echoed.

"We all want that," I said in a firm voice, "and I have said many times before that I will help you see to his end, but now is not the time. I am leaving tonight with the Daughter of Winter, because I firmly believe she is the only way out of this mess. If her blood can create lore that changes the future of our people, imagine what the full power of her legacy can do if given the chance. There is a possibility we can reverse the lore, but only if we rescue Brydie and the fifth descendant."

"That is why we are here," Alison said softly. "We are here to help you escape." She looked down at Egan and added quietly, "Although, it appears you didn't need our help."

I didn't bother to look at Egan. His stain on this world had come to a welcome end. All my attention, all my focus was now on rescuing Brydie. And Alison owed me. "I will need everything you can spare to get her out of here."

To her credit, Alison didn't hesitate. "You have the five of us, and there are others ready above to help in any way they can."

Adrenaline surged through my body. "Good. Take me to Brydie."

CHAPTER 41
BRYDIE
PRESENT DAY, SCOTLAND

Chloe was gone.

Those words repeated in my mind on a constant loop. Our eyes met. Her blank, disinterested gaze moved on almost immediately to rest on Callum—another one of his puppets.

Unable to make a sound, I was only vaguely aware of Callum questioning Chloe. I heard enough to understand she wasn't aware of any druidic power she might hold, nor did she have any clue about her ancestry.

I closed my eyes, feeling exhausted. My body was numb, my soul bruised, my emotions in shreds; I craved the oblivion of sleep. But Callum's voice was an insistent distraction, becoming louder with every passing moment as his frustration grew over Chloe's responses, and I had no choice but to listen.

"It's obvious Talorgan's descendant knows nothing," Jake was saying.

Callum snarled, "She is no asset if we don't know her strengths. I thought enslaving her would open any blocked memories she might have."

There was a pause before Jake asked, "What other avenue would you like to explore, sir?"

"What we have been preparing for all this time— summon the Phoenix."

The Phoenix? Was the Phoenix a pseudonym for another druid, and what was he being summoned for? Aware this could be a new threat, I forced myself to focus on the men in the room.

Jake's tone was neutral, but his words were a warning. "He is unpredictable."

"But he is all-knowing," Callum snapped back. "As the Custodian of Creation, he can see everything. We are under time constraints. He is the obvious choice."

"He will request a tithe."

Callum smiled, his gaze straying to mine. "Yes, and Brydie's presence here is opportune."

Jake flicked his gaze to mine, and understanding crossed his face. I had no idea what conclusion he'd come to, but that cold pit in my belly only deepened.

"The benefits of summoning the Phoenix will outweigh the risks, and he holds the answers we need," Callum announced firmly. "I am tired of being Talorgan's puppet. If we can determine what talent Chloe holds, we will have an idea of his weaknesses and be able to exploit them through new lore."

Even in my numb state, I could appreciate the logic behind this course of action. Callum had tenacity. If only he was working with us toward a common cause against our enemy rather than using it to pursue a personal vendetta for power.

Jake acknowledged his master's decision and pulled a dagger from the folds of his robe. In a parody of the same cut he'd given me earlier, he slashed his arm from wrist to inner elbow. The blood welled, and as soon as it began dripping onto the floor, he began to chant, his eyes burning in his thin face. The words were guttural and ancient, and Jake's young voice was soon joined by those of Mary and Samuel, all three of them falling into a natural rhythm. Callum silently looked on, his demeanor tense, his eyes focused.

The chanting went on, a monotonous lilting that kept repeating itself, until suddenly, Jake raised his bleeding arm to draw a rune upon the air and commanded in an authoritative voice, "Arise!"

The air immediately began to hum, the atmosphere taut and expectant, and the shiver that ran down my spine tingled ominously at my lower back. A pocket of air in the middle of the chamber began to shimmer, oscillating and contorting with an amalgam of shadow and color. There was an explosive *pop,* and the space was rent by a violent deluge of heat and flame.

I blinked at the bright symphony of orange, red, and gold, lifting a hand to shade my eyes, and as my vision sharpened, I felt my mouth drop open. Before me was a creature I'd only read about in myth—a phoenix.

The large bird hovered above us, a burning conflagration of power. It swallowed all available space in the room, its fiery plumage mesmerizing and dangerously beautiful. The heat from its body burned with an unearthly intensity that had me shielding my face with my arm. My lungs burned, the heat suffocating, and I tasted ashes on my tongue.

In the shocked silence, the Phoenix flapped its wings, creating a backdraft of fire and flame that coalesced into a myriad of embers and twinkling fireflies. It's head cocked to the side, and it turned its red and golden eyes singularly on Jake.

"Why have you summoned me?"

The otherworldly voice roared through my mind. The sound was both feminine and masculine, reverberating with two different layers, one sweet, the other discordant. Yet, I would have been a fool not to recognize the dangerous impatience explicit in that tone.

Jake flicked his eyes at Callum in a silent request to take the reins. Noting the movement, the Phoenix swiveled its head to the leader of The Oaken Tree, who dipped his chin in a gesture of respect toward the bird. "I summoned you, Magnificent One, because I seek answers."

The Phoenix cocked his head to the side, the movement so unnatural it acted as a sharp reminder that he was a natural predator. I felt unrelenting fear slide down my back as the beast replied, *"Your machinations are beneath me. I live outside the realm of the human world. Why would you deign to awaken me for answers to your questions?"*

His last words ended on a deafening roar, the impatience at such impertinence unmistakable.

Callum, his face red and a fine sheen of sweat coating his bald head, replied evenly, "There was no disrespect intended. We merely acknowledge you hold the answers we seek—answers that have been lost over the ages."

With its glowing golden eyes, the beast surveyed Callum. *"You have mistaken me for a common lackey. I do not share my knowledge with just anyone, and I have no interest in learning what occurs here. I tire of this conversation. Release me from the summoning spell, or I will invoke death upon everything in this room."* The response was deadly calm, but there was no denying the dark edge of truth in the tone.

Callum held up a hand. "Wait. I appreciate my request will require a tithe, and I am happy to make an exchange."

The Phoenix's eyes blinked, and the unerring change in his focused stare was so predatory that I stifled a gasp. I prayed Callum would screw up, that the Phoenix would end his miserable life.

"You try my patience in more ways than one, human. What could you possibly have that would intrigue me?"

"There are two things in this room that I believe you may be interested in," Callum replied calmly.

"Two? You are so sure of yourself that you believe I would have interest in two things?" The Phoenix's plumage blazed with his words. His eyes roved the room, alighting on each of us in turn.

I could feel the hum of power and knew the beast was using his senses to determine what it was the druid alluded to. The Phoenix's gaze turned to me, and at the searing burn of his attention, I knew this magnificent creature could destroy me with a single thought.

"This one has something which was once mine."

I was caught, trapped in his gaze, unable to speak, unable to move. My mind whirled, wondering what it was I had that he recognized. It took seconds to realize it was the pendant around my neck. Was the world this beast hailed from the same world in which the stone had originated? They both exuded a discordant otherworldly melody and carried a strange, intoxicating power. *Like attracts like.*

Callum interrupted my thoughts, his voice smooth like butter. "It can be yours in exchange for the information I require."

The Phoenix's eyes glinted, his feathers reshuffling in a whisper of flame as he said very carefully, *"Yet it is not yours to command for it has claimed another in this room."* His writhing, red-gold eyes perused my form.

Callum cleared his throat. "The woman is my prisoner, and as such, the object is mine to give."

I withheld a shiver, knowing the pendant could only be removed on my death.

The Phoenix's eyes never left mine. *"May I see that which we discuss?"*

"Of course," Callum replied, jerking his head at Jake.

Jake leaned down and yanked the neck of my tee shirt, ripping it from the collar to halfway down my chest to expose the pendant. I glared at Callum as his eyes lingered on my breasts. Sickened, I turned my attention to the Phoenix, whose full attention was on the stone lying under my breasts.

His irises burned with eternal flame as he raised them to meet mine. *"Even though it is a mere sliver, there is no denying it is from the Stone of Destiny. It's very presence is familiar...."* Something flickered in the bird's gaze, but it was gone before I could put an emotion to it.

"Do you agree to the terms of this transaction then?" Callum pushed. "Will you answer five of my questions in return for this stone?"

The Phoenix cut his gaze to Callum, assessing the druid's body language and the sneer scrawled across his face. *"I will answer three questions in return for that which this woman holds."*

Callum's brow furrowed, and for a moment, it looked as though he was going to argue, but then he said, "I accept."

The bird inclined his head. *"So be it. Name your first."*

Callum took a steadying breath and asked, "Who will win the war between Talorgan and Cailleach's descendant?"

The Phoenix glanced from Callum to me, and his

glowing eyes were bottomless pools of knowledge. *"That question cannot be answered with certainty. The path changes daily."*

My blood chilled at the level of his confidence.

Callum released a breath. "But you can see the future. Surely the route is clear?"

"There are too many variables to confirm the future at any one time. The scales are often tipped by an outside force that can manipulate the fabric of time." The Phoenix paused, then said deliberately, *"Your second question."*

Callum's lips thinned, but he bit out, "What power does Talorgan's descendant hold?"

The Phoenix unerringly turned his gaze to Chloe, and the act itself caused my throat to tighten. Was there nothing he didn't know? And why wasn't he helping us? As the Custodian of Creation, couldn't he see the balance was skewed and we needed his assistance?

Unaware of my torment, the Phoenix responded, *"Talorgan's descendant has a rare ability. She is able to repel druidic magic. The lore will not work on her."*

Callum froze, his face slackening. "What?" He turned to look at Chloe, taking in her position on the chair and her disinterested expression. "But she has responded to the cauldron."

The Phoenix flapped his wings, a buffer of hot embers and ash singeing the skin of my face. *"The cauldron is not druidic lore; it is a fae vessel."*

Callum's face paled. "Is her father also exempt from the lore—future or present?"

The Phoenix blinked, those incandescent eyes blazing with absolute power and confidence. *"Yes."*

"Then how can we kill him?" Callum cried, his voice

losing it's cool confidence, the edge of panic creeping into his tone.

The Phoenix merely responded, *"The tithe is now owed."*

Callum stepped back. "What? No! You have yet to answer my last question."

"On the contrary," the Phoenix responded smoothly with a voice ravaged by an eternal number of sunrises, that melody in his tone now darkening to a rising crescendo. *"I have answered three as was promised. This one goes above our agreement. The tithe is now due."*

Callum stared at the bird, a sheen of sweat on his face. I knew how he felt, the Phoenix's response that Talorgan and Chloe did not respond to druidic lore had all but obliterated my mind. But how had Gage attacked him on Beinn na Caillich then?

As soon as I considered the question, the answer became obvious—for Talorgan had not been in his true form, he'd been in another. He was hosted by mortals, their bodies and genetic codes susceptible to power. But in his own body, in his own form—and immortal at that—the Phoenix claimed Talorgan was incapable of being affected by druidic lore. And by extension...so was Chloe. Which also explained why she'd fought the bonds of whatever lore Callum had used to keep her malleable.

One look at Callum and I knew he was now reflecting on the path he'd chosen. He'd believed the answer to removing Talorgan was the creation of more lore—new lore that was founded in the blood of the descendant of the Winter Goddess. Only he'd now found out he was wrong. He'd led our people down a tunnel of darkness and ruin. into a future without light all for naught.

The Phoenix's plumage suddenly flared in orange, red, and gold flames as he flung his head back and screeched. He looked at Callum with deadly intent, as if the leader of The Oaken Tree were now prey, and demanded, *"The tithe is now due!"*

The energy in the air was different now, dark and dangerous. Yet Callum seemed oblivious to the harm the Phoenix could do. He appeared to be in denial of what he had just learned for he said softly, "I think not. You have not shared anything of consequence that will aid my cause. The reason for this meeting was to ascertain how we can kill Talorgan. You have not provided any means to do so. As such, *you* have forfeited the right to your tithe unless you answer my last question!"

The Phoenix's voice was deathly quiet, more frightening than any roar. *"You have broken the bonds of hospitality. I will give you one final chance: Make the payment now or retribution is due."*

Callum laughed in the face of his threat, not a whisper of fear in his demeanor. "I beg you to do your worst. I have the cauldron. It is time to test its power."

Callum held up his right hand, the cauldron clenched in his fist. The Phoenix screeched in his piercing otherworldly tone, and his plumage became a blazing inferno. His beak opened wide and wildfire spewed forth.

It happened so quickly I didn't have time to think. All I could do was watch that plume of fire launch at Callum. Yet, it never reached him. Callum stood behind a shield of silver that shone with such otherworldly incandescence I knew it came from the cauldron in his hands. The Phoenix's fire ricocheted off the shield and hit the wall of the chamber in a shower of sparks. Smoke filled the room.

I scrambled backward, sliding on the stone floor as I sought to escape the heat. I glanced at the Phoenix to see his curved beak opening once again, his eyes on Callum as he was now rushing to the door. But instead of hitting Callum in the back as he pulled on the doorknob, Samuel stepped in front of his master, and the Phoenix's fire hit the man squarely in the chest. I watched, horrified, as Samuel stumbled backward, flames licking his robe.

At first he was silent, but then the chamber was filled with an inhuman screech that soon became a babble of terror. In that moment, I understood the Phoenix's fire had destroyed the cauldron's grip on Samuel's mind, that whatever cap had been on his emotions was now released.

Time slowed to a crawl, and what followed was utter chaos. Samuel's cries turned to screams of agony as the fire traveled over his body. The smell of burning flesh and hair consumed the room.

I watched in open-mouthed horror as he stumbled blindly toward Chloe, who still sat in the chair, bound and tied, completely oblivious to the danger in the room. Forgetting I didn't have a voice, I tried to scream in warning. It was pointless. There was nothing I could do as Samuel smashed into her side.

They fell together in a flaming heap upon the floor. The flames trembled as if on the cusp of extinguishing, and I held my breath, but then they flared with renewed energy, catching onto Chloe's clothing. Seconds later, her piercing shrieks of agony filled the chamber.

That cry of such terror and suffering pierced me right in the heart. *Not Chloe—no, no, no, no!*

The world tilted, and a burn of desperate fear curled inside my chest. I felt something inside me respond; a rumbling tableau that ached for release. Without questioning it, without denying it, I opened my mind to my power and flung both of my hands out in front of me as I screamed in utter denial of Chloe's death.

There came a sharp, piercing burn at my wrists and then a stream of blue-white light erupted from my hands and violently smashed into the Phoenix's flames. The was a deafening boom, and the scene in front of me was eclipsed in a flash of bright white light before an all-consuming darkness fell.

BRYDIE

PRESENT DAY, SCOTLAND

The sudden onslaught of silence was deafening.

I released a breath, the sound inordinately loud in the eerie, black silence. My heart pounded in time with the relentless energy inside my chest. My legacy, now free and unfettered, craved further release. I lifted my hand, and at a single thought, a ball of blue-white light appeared, cleaving the darkness.

For a moment, I just stared at my hands, disbelieving. For weeks, I'd been powerless, the bracelets on my wrists suffocating my magic. But now, it was back. How...? But the answer was obvious when I looked at my wrists; those vexing bands were no longer there. I gasped, and the sound that escaped my lips also confirmed I'd broken the caveat on my voice.

"No human has ever silenced my fire."

That unearthly tone was unmistakable. I whirled to find the beast behind me. As our eyes met, his plumage came alight, and he blazed once again, bright and wholly magnificent. I raised a hand to my eyes, gasping against his brilliance.

The Phoenix's voice was commanding. *"Who are you?"*

For a moment, I didn't know how to respond. Surely he already knew who I was? But in the face of his resplendence, the answer was obvious. "I'm nobody." Even as I answered, my legacy fizzled to a low murmur, as if paying homage to the creature in front of me, aware that his power was more than mine would ever be.

The bird's eyes seared mine, and in that discordant melody that was at once masculine and feminine, he said carefully, *"That is where you are wrong. A nobody couldn't have repelled my fire."*

I swallowed. Is that what I had done—extinguished his otherworldly fire? Thoughts of the fire reminded me of Chloe. I whirled, searching the darkness. Where was she? In the light of the Phoenix's flames I found Mary and Jake first, both of them slumped against the far wall. I saw Samuel's charred body next but couldn't see the lump lying just behind him in the shadows. *Chloe.*

I turned back to face the Phoenix, numb with loss. "I just wanted to save my friend," I whispered.

The Phoenix looked at Chloe. *"I have seen such motivation before in a few of my children. And with that pendant around your neck, the family history is unmistakable."*

"You...you know Cailleach?"

"She is my daughter."

My heart stopped at the matter-of-fact response, my voice a reed thin. "You are the All Father?"

The Phoenix inclined his head. *"And you are each my children's creations."*

I couldn't comprehend what that meant. All I could think about was my best friend; my heart was breaking. "Why did you grant me the privilege of being the only one to survive in this room?"

"*On the contrary, final privileges have not yet been granted. The future of all those in this room is uncertain, for I have stopped time so that we may talk.*"

"St-stopped time?" I stuttered.

His burning stare was unflinching. "*I am curious. Your power was enough to halt my own, enough to make me reconsider my decision.*"

My heart leapt. "She still lives?" I breathed, hope a thin thread.

"*At the moment, and only because of what you wear around your neck and the promise I made to your mother.*"

The Phoenix was not referring to my biological mother but my first mother—Cailleach. "Why?"

The question was so simple, yet I knew the answer before he replied. There was a *knowing* in my veins, a sense of such utter, overwhelming completion.

"*I promised Cailleach that her firstborn and those of her line would forever be protected. The boon I granted binds me to protect her children...no matter your insolence in cancelling my fire.*"

I gaped at him. He'd been present when Cailleach established the prophecy, had likely directed her on this path! He wasn't just old—he was *the* oldest being in the world. I stared back at those iridescent golden eyes that held such unfathomable power.

His continued in a softer tone, "*I see you, my child. I know you, and I feel the weight of your future stretching before you. Your mother requested a boon in honor of love, and against all reason, I granted it. I have not come to regret it, and in fact, through the passage of time I can now see that she offered me a gift—something I could not see before. Cailleach has shown me love can prevail, that it is an emotion with enough power to tip*" *the scales of nature back into balance. After all, you have just proven this in the move you made to quell my fire."*

I swallowed hard. Chloe. He was talking about my love for Chloe—my best friend. "Thank you," I forced out, feeling like I should say the words but unsure of what exactly I was truly thankful for. After all, this prophecy had been created by him, and the trials and tribulations I'd had to address thus far were not a gift...yet the time with Gage had been. The friendships with Logan, Ian, and even McKenzie were also something I didn't regret.

The Phoenix looked at me, that softening of his features still apparent as he said, *"Our time together has come to a close, my child, but you must understand this is not the end. We will meet again. In return for the sacrifice you were willing to risk, and in honor of what your mother has given me, I leave you with a parting gift. But be quick, my child, for the magic will only last for the space of five hundred heartbeats."*

I stared at him in confusion, but the answer soon became obvious when slowly, deliberately, the Phoenix blinked, and a tear rolled from his eye. It slid down his feathers and hovered upon the air. My heart pounded as that tear floated unerringly toward Chloe's prone form, and I held my breath as hope flared. I'd heard the stories about the power of a phoenix's tear and what it could do.

I counted the seconds: one... four... seven... ten.

Nothing.

I turned back to the Phoenix, hope crumbling. Had the myths been wrong?

He hovered above me, eyes on mine, ever watchful. *"Patience. You must master your doubts, child. A leader does not hesitate in the heat of battle; a leader does not question their abilities. Believe in yourself and what you desire will come to* pass. *And remember what I did for you. Remember, because a tithe will be due.*"

Before I had time to process his message, the Phoenix was eclipsed in wildfire, and then he was gone, the only evidence of his presence a lone red feather drifting lazily to the floor.

The eerie silence was broken by a groan, the sound carrying a wealth of pain.

I froze, hope a fragile bloom in my chest. I knew that tone.

This time, there came a voice, weak and rasping. "Brydie?"

Very slowly, I turned to face where Chloe had been and gasped when I saw she had pulled herself into a sitting position. My voice wobbled. "I'm here. Hold on!"

I inched along the stone wall. My legs were trembling, weak as a newborn filly's. I stumbled and hissed when my shoulder slammed into the wall.

"Are you okay?" Chloe called in a trembling voice.

"I'm fine," I gasped, forcing myself to blink away the red haze.

"Where are you?"

"I'm here, Chloe, I'm coming."

But Chloe began to sob. "I can't see you! I can't see anything!"

I threw my ball of blue-white light higher into the air, hoping it would push back more of the shadows. "It's okay, Chloe, I'm coming."

Her voice came again, thready and breathless. "Where are the others? The man in the blood-red robe? The guards he had with him?"

Could she not see the bodies in front of her? "It's okay," I repeated. "I'm coming."

As I limped closer, my heart broke as I watched her swivel her head left and right, her eyes wide and unfocused. *No....* *Was she...?* But the truth was right in front of me—Chloe was blind.

It was suddenly hard to swallow, and I bit my lip, trying to halt a whimper at the unfairness of it all. *She'll be okay. We'll fix this.* I kept my mind focused on reaching her as I inched slowly toward her.

When I came upon Mary, she was eerily still. She lay on her back, her eyes wide open, her features frozen in a look of horror. It was obvious the Phoenix's flames had touched her, and going by the state of her robe, which only showed burn marks up one side of her left arm, she would live if given the chance.

I stepped over her, and my left foot prodded her arm. I froze when her chest suddenly rose and fell. When she didn't blink or move further, I remembered the Phoenix had said I had five hundred heartbeats. Which meant it was well and truly time to get out of here, and quickly.

In a few more steps, I was there. I bent down and grabbed Chloe's arm, feeling a heartfelt rush of relief when I found her clothes still intact, her skin unblemished.

She jerked at my touch, a sharp cry erupting from her mouth.

"Shh, Chloe, it's alright. It's me."

She didn't hesitate, blindly throwing herself into my arms and hugging me tightly. I gasped at her touch, at the pressure against my bruised body. I gently gripped her arms with both hands and pushed her away. Her face looked up at me, eyes wide, as I said urgently, "We need to leave right now. Can you walk?"

She nodded, her brows drawing together. "I-I think so."

"Good. Let's go. The Phoenix only left us a certain amount of time."

She stumbled as she came to her feet. "The Phoenix?"

Had she no memory of what had happened? "I'll tell you everything later. Let's just get out of here."

She nodded grimly, and with her hand clenched tightly in mine, we began to walk toward the door. I felt the tears roll silently down my face as I steered her around Samuel's prone body. He lay face down on the floor, his body blackened and charred. My power had been too late to save him, but it confirmed the Phoenix had been granted the retribution he was owed, even if it had been directed toward the wrong person. But there was no room for sympathy in my bruised heart. Not after the part he'd played in my capture.

Apart from her quickened breathing, Chloe didn't make a sound as we passed Jake. Like Mary, he was also on his back, eyes wide open, his mouth frozen in a scream. I wondered then, given their open eyes, if he and Mary were also blind like Chloe was. And if they were, was it due to the Phoenix's fire or my own?

It was another thought I squashed immediately. Those questions could wait. We needed to get out of here first.

In the next two steps, we reached the door. For a moment, I just stood there, staring at Callum's bedroom chamber, stunned by the colors, the rich tapestries, the lush furnishings. These past few weeks, I hadn't seen anything but the four stone walls of my chamber, and the scene in front of me was an explosion of color that was at once overwhelming and a blatant reminder of what had been done to me.

Swallowing hard, I gripped Chloe's hand and steered

her toward the large oaken door that led out to the hallway. I was relieved to find it was ajar.

We were two steps away from passing through the doorway when a rush of sound roared in my ears. There came an audible *pop*. A moment later, I heard the clatter of footsteps. The Phoenix's boon of five hundred heartbeats had come to an end.

I lunged for the large oak door and ducked behind it, tugging Chloe against me and slapping a hand over her mouth. "Shh!" I urgently whispered against her ear as I squeezed us as close to the bedroom wall and the door jamb as possible.

She was tense, her whole body trembling, but to her credit, Chloe kept her silence and didn't struggle. I slowly lifted my hand from her face, squeezing her arm for comfort, letting her know with my touch that it was going to be okay. We weren't helpless. Having removed the bracelets from my wrists, my legacy was once again in reach.

The footsteps pounded closer, rushing into Callum's bedroom and heading straight into the adjoining chamber. There came shouted exclamations and sounds of confusion.

"Jesus, they're all out!" one of them cried.

"Where's Callum?" another grunted. "I can't see him."

A calmer voice confirmed, "He's not here."

A pause, then another barked, "Rouse them. Quickly! We need them."

I was loathe to attack and announce our position. If it had just been me, I would have taken the chance and run for it, but I couldn't leave Chloe, and I couldn't take risks. Instead, I stood there, my hand on her arm, silently willing her to remain quiet as we listened to the guards trying to rouse Mary, Samuel, and Jake.

"They're not responding."

"Are they dead?"

"Samuel is but the other two aren't, and their eyes are open." This voice was older, more settled.

"Dead? How?" a high voice squeaked.

"If you were using your brain you'd realize there's a magical signature on the air...and it's not druidic."

A loud exhalation. "What should we do then? Regan needs them at the sewers. The rebels are attacking."

The older voice of reason came again. "Christ! Calm the hell down, man. Don't lose your head. The rebels are few in number. By the time we get everyone down there, the tide will have turned. Come on, we can't leave them here. We'll have to carry them between us and hope they come around on the journey."

The others grunted their agreement, and I listened tensely as between them they gathered Mary and Jake. Grunting and shuffling, they carried them out of the room. By some miracle, they never touched the large oaken door or looked behind it. Their footsteps disappeared, becoming muffled by the commotion I could hear breaking out within the castle.

Chloe hadn't made a sound, but there were silent tears falling down her face. My heart ached at those wide, unseeing eyes. I leaned in close to her ear and whispered, "It's safe to move. Come on, I promise you we're going to get out of here. All you need to do is listen to me and move quickly and quietly. Can you do that?"

She jerked her head in affirmation, but I could sense her fear. Squeezing her arm again in reassurance, I stepped from behind the door to scout the hallway in both directions. But just as I was about to pull Chloe along, I heard the sound of more footsteps hurrying down the corridor.

"Shit!" I pushed Chloe back behind the door again. "Stay quiet!"

She whimpered, her body trembling violently. I knew she hovered on the cusp of shock; whatever threads were holding her together were about to snap. Borrowed time. I was on borrowed time.

The footsteps burst into the room.

"Quick, in his chamber!" a familiar female voice cried.

No. Not her... I bit my lip, hard, and reached for my magic.

Another set of booted feet raced into the chamber.

"She's not here," another familiar voice growled.

My heart stopped.

That feminine voice again. "The Learned Rooms! He often visits the scrying chamber. I think it's where he experiments with the lore. If he has her anywhere, it will be there."

I waited, my pulse racing for the answering reply, the air trapped within my lungs.

That brusque voice came again, sharp and commanding...and familiarly arrogant. "Given the coup, he may be desperate enough to kill her if provoked. Let's move."

It was all the confirmation I needed. "Gage?"

My voice was weak, a mere croak of sound, but going by the sudden silence that fell, I knew they'd heard me. Chloe whimpered beside me, aware our cover had been blown. Her face was frozen in fear. I reached out and squeezed her hand reassuringly. "Shh, it's okay Chloe," I whispered. "Stay here. I'll be back soon."

I stepped out from behind the door and faced the entrance of the dark chamber in which I'd been a prisoner for the past few weeks, and there, in the doorway, appeared a familiar figure. His whipcord lean body was clothed in dirty, black fatigues—the same clothing he'd been wearing when we entered the Institute.

I stared at him, disbelieving. Bruises visibly marred his skin, and his eyes were sunken from lack of sleep, but it was him. Gage.

"Brydie." His voice was hard, but there was something else in his tone, as if he couldn't quite bring himself to believe I stood before him.

"You came for me?" The words were unplanned, but there were fueled by the horror of the last few weeks, the need to believe that hope still lived, that I'd been wrong in that chamber—wrong about everything.

"You believed otherwise?"

We stared at each other for the space of a heartbeat, and I watched a look of such profound relief, grief, and happiness cross his features. That release of emotion caused me to take a hesitating step toward him, and with that move, my world began to crumble.

His body moved fluidly to meet mine, and then I was in his arms, crushed tightly to his chest. The pressure had me flinching, and he immediately pulled back.

"Where does it hurt?" His hands were now running lightly over my body. His face was tense, white lines bracketing his mouth as I felt him use his power, assessing my injuries. He suddenly snarled, and his voice was animalistic. "I'm going to fucking kill him for touching you!"

The emotion in that tone floored me, and I felt the dam inside me begin to crack. I held onto my emotions tightly; not here, not now. We weren't out yet, and I needed Gage to focus on the task at hand, not my injuries. I gently grabbed his hands. "I'm fine, Gage. Now you're here, I'm fine. But how did you find me?"

A muscle ticked in his jaw. "I had some help." He jerked his head to the side, and I followed the action to find a sea of faces now surrounding us...Alison's one of them.

A low growl immediately escaped my lips. "You fucking bi—"

Gage interjected, "No, Brydie, it's okay. They're with us." He squeezed my hands, his gaze intent. "It was all a ruse to distract Callum. He was blackmailing her, but she's here now to help us get out—they all are."

I hadn't taken my eyes off Alison. Her eyes assessed me coolly from head to toe, but her face was unreadable. "Good to see you're alive."

"Did you wish it were otherwise?" I snapped.

One of the men beside her cut in with a sharp look at his watch, "We need to leave right now. Someone will come back soon, and I have no wish to be trapped in this room."

Gage's face tightened, and he pulled me to him in a possessive grip. "I agree. Forget the other descendant. Open a portal to Slieve na Calliagh, and we'll take it from there."

Alison nodded, raising her hands and turning to face the wall. That familiar whirring sound erupted, and the space in front of us began to oscillate and expand.

"No, wait!" I cried, trying to pull away.

He gripped my arm, spinning me to face him. "What is it?"

I pointed to the oak door. "I'm not leaving without her."

As if on cue, a whimper came from behind the door.

Gage's brow furrowed. "You found her?"

I nodded, that tight feeling still in my chest. "Yes, except she's...not okay."

His eyes searched mine.

"We can't wait much longer, Gage," Alison bit out, her

face now shining with a fine sheen of sweat. "The portal won't hold for long."

Holding my gaze, Gage bit out, "Send the others through first."

The others began to file through Alison's portal, one at a time while Gage released me and I moved to the oak door, pulling it back to reveal Chloe. She was still trembling, her face deathly white. My heart squeezed.

"It's okay Chloe, we're getting out of here," I whispered softly, reaching out to grab her hand.

She bit her lip and I saw the blood well as she held on tight to my hand. I carefully guided her toward Alison's portal. I felt Gage's silent perusal and knew he'd instantly comprehended the reason for Chloe's lost, unseeing gaze.

There came the sound of new footsteps pounding down the corridor.

Alison hissed, "Move it! I can't hold this much longer."

Gage didn't hesitate. Grabbing my free hand, he pulled us both through the portal.

CHAPTER 43

TALORGAN

3RD CENTURY BC, ANCIENT SCOTLAND

Twilight leached across the sky, heralding the night's arrival. Talorgan watched it spread its raven colored fingers and mused at how the disappearance of the sun's rays did not create a coldness in his body. It was now obvious that embracing the darkness was changing him. His thoughts and his feelings were all skewed. The only emotions he felt anymore were dark: sinful lust, anger, and hate. No longer were there any feelings of joy, acceptance, or love. He didn't feel regret either.

It was poignant that he'd had this realization today, because today's end was not like any other. Not only did it herald the end of summer, but it also announced the dawn of winter. Samhain had come. Falling between the autumn equinox and the winter solstice, the darker half of the year had been born. And in just a few moments, when the last of the light was extinguished, the veils between the worlds would become thin, and all those who'd fled to the Otherworld would be able to cross into this world if they so desired.

Samhain was a time of offerings. It was also a time to

appease the gods, and the god whom he most sought to appease stood to his left, silent and still as he marked the beginning of his reign on this world.

The last of the light extinguished. Talorgan felt the hairs on his arms lift; he understood the scales of nature were about to shift. The air fairly crackled with electricity, and a breeze lifted, a natural shriek distinguished from the many creatures who waited for the impending battle to begin.

Arawn raised his arms above his head. It was a signal to light the torches. As one, they came ablaze, illuminating the large pyre in front of them. The ring of torches threw the innumerable number of Arawn's followers into garish relief.

Now silent and still, the dark army stood in a large circle facing the pyre, their bodies tense with foreboding. Talorgan caught the glint of steel and the curve of bows. Some of them—mostly those in animal or ghostly form—had no weapons whatsoever. But then, they didn't need them, not when they had claws or jagged, lethal teeth, or ethereal bodies that held powers far more gruesome than a blade's thrust.

The druids he'd managed to recruit were freshly robed, their new blood-red hoods pulled over their heads. They were sporadically situated among Arawn's people, standing comrade to comrade as they anticipated the sacrifice that would herald the new era this war would bring.

...If they won.

The thought brought acid to the back of his throat. These past three days, he'd left no room for self-doubt, believing his purpose to be strong, that this was the path he was meant to be on. Why this chink in his armor now?

Talorgan reminded himself he'd come too far to go back now. Lost too much. He couldn't return to his old life, couldn't return to his brother. By now, Drust would have heard of what had befallen Tritus. The knowledge of his death would upset Drust...and if he also knew that it was his hand who had killed the Gaul, well then, that would break the last tenuous thread of their twin bond.

His throat was tight as he swallowed. This waiting tension was preying on his thoughts, and it did nothing to ease the sour twisting of his stomach. Action was what they needed.

He flicked his eyes to the side, checking to see if the three hellhounds still watched him. Lonc and Uren flanked the Dark God, but Brude stood at his master's back, eyes and ears alert. As if sensing his attention, the beast swung his large head to look directly at him. Talorgan refused to meet his gaze. There would be no powerplay between them. He would bend to no one unless he had to.

Talorgan squeezed his hands into fists and searched for the internal core of his power, to remind himself that he indeed held power—more than anyone could imagine. It eagerly licked at the back of his throat, a rancorous burn that craved release. *Soon*, he soothed against its bucking urge. *Soon we will show everyone what we can do.*

As if on cue, a hand pounded against a drum, a slow, drugging beat. Arawn inclined his curly black head, the horns glinting in the light of the torches. In response, a message was passed up the line of waiting sentinels to the shieling where the two sirens stood vigil out front. At the urging of the army, their demeanors suddenly changed, shifting from still and watchful to predatory. With hissing and rough gestures, they pulled open the hide flap covering the entrance to the shieling and herded the thirteen white-clad virgins from the stone building.

Talorgan watched the women with a clinical detachment. Their tears and wails of fear fell on deaf ears.

The sirens hissed, using sharp sticks to prod them into a line before gesturing at them to walk the small deer trail down to the waiting army encircling the pyre. Talorgan couldn't help narrowing his focus on their movements, his gaze latching onto the feminine outline of their bodies under their sheer white dresses. The luscious sway of their breasts and the curve of their hips elicited burning desire. He had a sudden, overwhelming urge to take one of those women now, regardless of who and what watched.

It was a poignant hunger, one he knew was fed by the need to take the edge off the building anticipation throbbing in his veins. He reined in those instincts, reminding himself this was all part of the ceremony. The real woman he wanted would soon be his.

This message was enough to break the daze he'd fallen into, enough for him to look away and take in the faces of all the gathered men and women who displayed the same desire on their own war-painted features. It was another reminder of the power their master held over them, the power the Dark God could wield with barely a whisper. Because even now, Arawn stood there, his brow clean and dry, no sign of strain anywhere. Indeed, he even looked to be smiling, as if he was enjoying the nefarious thoughts filling everyone's minds.

The procession of the virgins neared the waiting circle, and Talorgan could now see their features. He shied away from their accusing stares and their hatred, and in some cases, their pleading and bewilderment. Some of those women were from his village. Some of those women he'd known his whole life, and even played with when they were children. He shifted his gaze from their faces to focus on their long, unbound hair. It streamed down their backs, lifting in the cool breeze that had suddenly awoken.

The circle parted, opening to allow the procession through, and Talorgan felt the weighted silence—punctuated by whimpering and the occasional sob—as if it hovered over his shoulders. So much rode on tonight's sacrifice. Nothing and nobody could interfere or prohibit it from happening.

He felt a sudden chill on the air and knew the abrupt drop in temperature was more than a natural occurrence. Then, that insinuating breeze began to whisper, attempting to lay claim to his desires.

Look at us. See our beauty. Claim our bounty. Look at us. Look at us.

The voices were persistent, almost as loud as the drums that didn't falter in their steady beat. Arawn had warned them all of what to expect. That this sacrifice would be the most important sacrifice they'd ever have to make. That their own desires would be tempted like they never had been before. Because to receive power, one had to first earn it, then be tested to one's limits. And tonight, they would all be tested with desire.

Samhain held unimaginable power. Not only by lowering the veils between the worlds, but also by awakening dark desires normally crippled by self-control. There was one exception to tonight's sacrifice—the ceremony Arawn had chosen only called for female virgins, meaning those that didn't favor women were exempt from temptation this evening.

Look at us. Take our offering. Cement our union. Become as one. Look at us. Look at us.

Talorgan gritted his teeth against the urging of those whispers. Arawn would not suffer any transgressions. The Dark God had warned them all that death awaited those who succumbed to their desires. The virgins could not be defiled or the ceremony and all they worked toward would be for naught.

Talorgan had personally seen to it that the sirens knew their task tonight. As women intent on devouring men, he knew he'd chosen well, and they'd been tested numerous times already, having to fight to protect the women's virginity. The bandages on the sirens bodies and the fresh limp among the guard on the left were testament to that.

The virgins' steps faltered as the crowd broke apart and they saw the pyre in front of them. It was as if in that moment, they'd collectively understood their fate. As if up to that point they'd held fast to a measure of hope that they would escape the hell they'd been subjected to these last three days.

Not now, though. Not after seeing the pyre.

Their fear was powerful, a sharp, bitter scent that flooded his senses. Talorgan felt his blood stir, a dark excitement thrilling in his veins. It was the first emotion he'd felt in a long time, and it gave him pause. Fear. Their fear was what excited him, and it was obvious this emotion similarly affected the waiting army. An overwhelming wave of dark desire bloomed from the waiting soldiers at his back, heralded by snarls and the restless movement of feet. He glanced at the crowd, noting the lecherous sneers on their faces.

The virgins whimpered in terror and came to a stumbling halt, but the sirens gave them no quarter, instantly prodding them with sticks. The breeze shrieked again, ripping and tugging at the virgins white dresses and flying hair. The sirens snarled for good measure, baring their sharp teeth, and with the wind pressing insistently at their backs, the virgins staggered forward, inexorably toward the pyre.

Another voice spoke above the howling wind, this time low and deadly. It was the unmistakable voice of their master, his power lucid in his ability to touch their minds: *"The time is now. Sirens, make haste!"*

In response to their master's dark demand, the sirens dragged one woman after another onto the pyre, tying them to the posts that were arranged in a circle on top of the meticulously stacked debris. But as the third woman was being secured, the next virgin in line suddenly broke away, racing toward the edge of the army. There came a collective indrawn stillness from the observing soldiers, and Talorgan felt a strong need to chase the virgin and have her for his own. She was the answer to his insatiable desire.

But the hounds beside Arawn snarled long and hard, their harsh, grating warning unmistakable above the shrieking wind. It was enough to check the soldiers who had unconsciously broken ranks around the circle in preparation to give chase. As if it pained them, one by one the soldiers grudgingly took a step back, resuming their position to stand, once again, in an unbroken circle.

Everyone, even the sirens, now turned to watch the virgin run. The air was electric with tension and a ravenous anticipation. No one made a sound.

Unchecked, the virgin raced headlong to the edge of the circle and launched herself at a figure in a blood-red robe. Hands shot out to collect her, pulling her in close. Talorgan jerked, jealousy blooming that his comrade could lay claim to the woman's body. Brude snarled again, this time right by his side, and the warning was enough to halt his instinctive urge to give chase.

Swallowing hard, Talorgan watched the skirmish that followed, now understanding the virgin had run to someone she knew—someone she thought she could depend on for help. Talorgan squinted, his eyes narrowing on the blood-red figure. As his vision sharpened, the blurred features of his comrade became defined, and he recognized Ciniath, a druid from his village. He then turned his attention to the virgin, but his intuition had already told him who she was—Fionnuala. Ciniath's sister.

His breath hitched, understanding that this would be Ciniath's test. No doubt he'd recognized his sister as soon as she'd left the shieling.

In the next moment, his question was answered when Ciniath flung his hysterical, sobbing sister behind him before throwing his arms wide with a mighty bellow that was a war cry of both fear and fury. His body rippled, his robe flying out behind him as he drew on the well of his internal power with a suddenness that had his head jerking back as he shouted, "Lightning!"

The air sizzled, at once deathly still, then the next, electric. The ebony night sky was pierced by a streak of white lightning that split the hallowed sky asunder. It snapped down, forking into two just above Ciniath's head to spear the ground on either side of him.

The earth ricocheted, bodies and debris hurling into the air with an impact that could be felt all the way up to the dais upon which Talorgan stood with Arawn and the hounds. Talorgan flew backward from the force of the impact, landing on his back. Ignoring the pain, ignoring everything but the need to *see* what Ciniath would do next, he rolled, coming to his feet in a rush of tangled robes.

In the deafening silence, Talorgan speared his gaze to Ciniath. He felt his heart thundering as emotion powerfully lanced into his chest. It was as strong as the blast he'd just encountered, a piercing thrust that stole the breath from his body. And without analyzing it, he instinctively knew it for what it was—hope. Because if Ciniath could stand against the full force of a dark army to save his sister, then there was a chance that he, too, could renege on the deal he'd made with the Dark God. There was a chance that he, too, could gain the forgiveness of his brother for the deeds he'd done. A chance that he, too, could regain his place in his village as the next Master of Herbs—a path he had diverted from two years ago and thought lost.

But those seconds of deafening silence were a lie. The dream of a reality he secretly craved only lasted the duration of an indrawn breath, for on its release, Talorgan watched as a dullahan, on his black war horse, leaped over a dead kelpie and lashed out with a lethal swing of his axe. It swung through the air and cut through Ciniath's right leg in a foul swoop.

Ciniath cried out, his other leg giving out from under him. But even as he fell, the druid kept his hands raised, this time to face the crowd of dark soldiers who were now advancing on him with black menace. But before he toppled to the ground, Talorgan saw Arawn step into his line of vision. He'd been almost forgotten in the melee, but now that the Dark God was visible, Talorgan felt his stomach plunge. Arawn, not a wisp of hair or clothing out of place, faced Ciniath with a black snarl etched across his features, and Talorgan watched as he threw his hands in Ciniath's direction with a vigor that made the air pop.

That was it. But it was enough, for when Talorgan's gaze flew back to Ciniath, he saw that the druid was choking, his hands scrabbling for purchase at his throat. As Ciniath crashed to the ground, Talorgan saw a leg—the other now amputated just below the knee—kick out and spasm in a desperate fury.

What had Arawn done?

Using his core of power, Talorgan honed his sight and focused on Ciniath's face. His blood chilled as he saw a rising black miasma travel from under the collar of Ciniath's robe all the way up to his forehead, eclipsing his skin in a shriveled mask of decomposing dust. As he watched, the druid's eyes rolled upward, the veins a starburst of blood-red, and his once childhood friend released his last breath in that final kiss of death.

Talorgan felt the perspiration on his skin chill as the small bloom of hope that had burst from his chest was obliterated on a wave of black despair that tasted like ash at the back of his throat. Frozen, he could do nothing but watch as Ciniath's sister, screaming and slamming her hands upon the ground in a desperate cry for divine help, was dragged away from her dead brother and ruthlessly pulled toward the waiting pyre. With leaden limbs, Talorgan turned to watch as she was tied to a pole, then as the other remaining virgins—either anchored by shock, or lost to the chaos of the violence they'd just witnessed—followed thereafter.

Numb, unable to move, Talorgan could do nothing but stare straight ahead as the army reformed into a circle and his Dark God sacrificed the thirteen virgins in a burning smolder of fire and flame.

CHAPTER 44

LOGAN

PRESENT DAY, AMERICA

I'd been watching him for a few days now. I knew his patterns—what school he attended and what he got up to after it ended. My careful observations told me I had only a short window of time to collect my nephew, from three to three-thirty, straight after the bell rang.

I was ready and waiting at three sharp, trying to act nonchalant, leaning against my rented Porsche as if I belonged with all the other school parents as I waited for Saul to emerge from the school gates. I knew Catriona never picked the kid up. She was a sales assistant in a fashion store in town, and after watching Saul these last few days, I knew he was expected to catch a bus and meet his mother in front of that store by three-thirty.

A shrill, high-pitched ringing sound pierced the air, and a swarm of students began filing out of the school gates. For a moment, all I could see was a sea of blue uniforms, but then I spotted Saul in the throng. His long, gangly body stood at least a head above his classmates, his ebony head gleaming in the sunlight. There were ear buds in his ears and a swagger to his gait as he walked unhurriedly along with his hands shoved into his pockets.

Target in sight, I pushed off the car, took a deep breath, and began to cross the road. My heart was erratically pounding in my chest. Saul looked just like his father had at this age, and knowing who I was about to meet caused a depth of emotion to writhe in my gut.

Saul saw me almost immediately. He came to a sudden halt in the middle of the sidewalk, his face pinching white. Then, as if in a daze, he moved out of the crowd of students onto the grass verge and fixedly watched me approach.

As I came close to my nephew, he pulled his ear buds out. "Who are you?" he demanded.

I considered him for a moment before deciding the best way forward was to share the honest truth...well, as much as I could. "I think you already know the answer to that."

His eyes narrowed. "You look just like my father, but he's dead."

I tried not to flinch at that blunt statement. "Well, I should. We're identical twins."

Saul's lip curled, hostility emanating off him in waves. "Mom told me he had a twin, but I didn't know you were identical. Why are you here?"

The animosity threw me, but I understood it. I'd abandoned him, effectively ignored him for the past nine years. It was time to get this conversation on an even keel. "Look, Saul, let's start again. My name is Logan. I'm your uncle, and I'm very excited to finally meet you."

Saul jerked his head back as I said his name, and as he looked at me accusingly, I saw Gage staring back, not just in the eyes but in the way he held his body. "How do you know my name?"

"Your father told me all about you not long after you were born."

Saul looked away, his eyes on the last, straggling students. A few sent us curious, inquisitive gazes, and I steadfastly ignored the glances of the other parents, concentrating wholly on my nephew.

Saul released a breath and turned back to face me. His tone was hard. "That must have been soon after he died. And seeing that he's been gone for the last nine years, I find it surprising you decided to come into my life now. Why the sudden interest?"

Saul's hostility was rife, leaving a bad taste in my mouth. It hovered between us even without my innate sixth sense, because on seeing him for the first time a few days ago, it had become immediately obvious that the internal connection I held with Gage had expanded to include his son. I was able to feel my nephew's emotions just as I could my brother's. The question was, could Saul feel mine too?

I shoved my hands into my pants pockets and rocked back on my heels, wondering how the hell I was going to tell the kid that he had to come with me. My task was supposed to be simple. As soon as Gage and Brydie had returned to Faerie with Chloe and a few other stragglers in tow, he'd ordered me to get his son on a plane back to Ireland. I'd readily accepted the request; after all, Saul was family. I was also aware there wasn't much I could offer to the prophecy. But this task I could do. Or so I'd thought. Seeing Saul's hostile response, that hope was now dwindling.

Aware the kid was waiting on my response, I opted for a touch of truth again, admitting, "I'm here because you're in danger, and it's time you learned who and what you are."

Saul's eyebrows disappeared under his overlong fringe,

and those azure eyes, so like my brother's, blinked in surprise. "What danger, man?"

"It's hard to discuss out here." I bit back a curse and looked around us again, aware of how vulnerable we were out in the open. I could hear Gage's voice in my ear, shouting at me to move quickly. The students had thinned out, but there were still a few others milling around, and I knew from Gage's experiences and his countless warnings that I couldn't trust anyone. "I can tell you, but you'll need to come with me."

Saul's eyes narrowed on my face. "Why should I come with you? I don't know you."

True. Fuck, this was harder than I'd assumed. I needed something to get him on my side. Something he desired... and maybe shocking him with the truth was what was needed. Holding firm to my path, I dropped a bombshell. "You need to come with me because your father is still alive, Saul."

Saul's voice was barely a whisper. "What?"

"I said, your father is still alive."

The kids face blanched as he stared back at me, acknowledging the conviction in my tone, the knowing in my gaze. "How?"

I spread my hands. "If you want to find out, you'll have to come with me."

Saul's lips thinned, and I witnessed the indecision warring on his face—to come with me or to flip me off. "Did he send you to get me?" he demanded.

I considered him, cocking my head to the side. Saul was almost ten. He knew how to run, he also knew how to think for himself, and was therefore able to see through any subterfuge. "Yes. Do you doubt it, kid?"

His eyes narrowed, and then he did the strangest thing.

He reached out and touched me. I felt a sharp jab where his hand made contact with my arm before a barrage of images arose in my mind's eye. "What—?"

My voice was abruptly cut off as the images rolled to life in quick rewind. I saw Gage and Brydie at the breakfast table at Faerie, then Gage and me at the Claymore as we shared a joke about the waitress who had looked me up and down. The video went in rewind a few more years to stop on an image of me and Gage out to dinner, his face serious as he told me he had a son. My arm burned under Saul's hand. Then, before I could speak, the video rewound again, this time all the way back to the night of that fateful fire. I saw Gage's five-year-old face, withdrawn, shocked, and hostile as he told me the fire was all his fault, and then the image was gone, wrenched from my mind's eye by the kid's hand lifting off my arm.

I blinked, feeling slightly disoriented as I stared at my nephew. "What the hell was that?" I'd never come across it before. I also hadn't heard Gage talk of another druid with that ability.

Saul looked at me, no apology on his face. "I had to know."

"Had to know what?"

"You asked me if I doubted if my father was still alive." He shrugged. "I did. So I verified it."

"Huh." I had meant it rhetorically, but the kid clearly had gifts he could utilize. Just like his father. "And do you believe me now?"

Saul's face was tense, but his eyes swirled with a wealth of emotion, his hands unconsciously clenching and unclenching at his sides. I could almost taste his excitement, offset by frustration and anger. His confirmation when it came was raw. "After what I just saw, I can't deny he's alive," he admitted hoarsely.

Gage's son was more like him than he knew. The kid carried himself with a maturity that made him appear older than what he was. "How do you feel about that? I know it's a lot to take in."

Saul's azure eyes burned. "I'm not sure. Does my mother know he's alive?"

"Yes. She's known all along," I brutally admitted. "In fact, it was her idea that you grow up not knowing the truth." I cocked my head to the side. "Did you ever wonder who has been supporting you all these years?"

The kid's face went parchment white. "The fortnightly payments," he whispered.

I nodded. "Yes, that was your father. He never forgot about you. He didn't want to see you lack for anything— even if he wasn't allowed to see you."

"Wasn't allowed to see me?"

"Your mother saw to that."

Saul pressed his lips together, and without tapping into our inner connection, I felt the hurt and the anger that he suddenly held toward his mother. He'd just realized she'd lied to him. I understood hurt, knew what it felt like. Gage had locked me out for most of our childhood, only allowing me back into his life at sixteen. The nine years we'd been apart had been crippling, and as I looked at my nephew and felt his reaction to his mother's betrayal, it was clear this blow was just as heavy.

I reminded myself it had been necessary to get the kid on board. I ignored the fact there was no need to throw Catriona under the bus, and I felt not a twinge of remorse at telling the kid his father was alive. Far from it. Because, like

Gage, I'd missed out on knowing his son, my nephew. Nine years bloody wasted due to Catriona's spitefulness.

Conscious the kid was stewing and trying valiantly to contain his reaction, to distract him, I pointed to his hands and asked, "How did you learn to do that?"

"I've always been able to do it." He shrugged and ran a hand through his thick swatch of hair. I ignored the fact that it trembled.

"And I bet you've kept it a secret," I guessed.

Those azure eyes widened and black hair flopped over his forehead in the slight breeze. "You're not going to tell anyone, are you? I thought I could trust you seeing that you know things too."

I raised a brow, repeating, "I know things?"

He snorted. "Oh, come on, man! Don't pretend! I can feel it. There's a vibration around you that's not around others. It feels like mine."

I couldn't deny that I was relieved at this revelation, even though he was misguided. He was most likely referring to our shared internal connection—a connection he still wasn't aware of. Yet, knowledge of his own abilities and his assumption that mine were similar would go some way toward helping him believe who and what he was. "You're right," I admitted. "I do have gifts, but they're not like yours or your father's. I can merely sense people's emotions, specifically your father's...and yours too."

Saul looked at me. "You can feel what I'm feeling? Without touching me?"

I nodded. "Can't you?"

He shook his head, his eyes wide. Well, there was the answer to that question.

The kid demanded, "Prove it. Tell me what I'm feeling right now."

So, this would be my test. I put my hands in my pockets and stared at him for a few moments. As I looked into his eyes, a wave of emotions rolled over me: fear, nervousness, excitement, anticipation, and hope. I shared them.

Saul's eyes widened and then his face paled. He swallowed visibly. "Alright, I believe you."

I smirked. "Any other questions, kid?"

He nodded slowly, then asked, "How long?"

"How long, what?"

"How long am I to be staying with my father before he sends me away again?"

My stomach flipped. There wasn't just resentment in that question but loss and pain. "Kid, your father is one of the most complicated men I know, but one thing is certain: family means everything to him. *You* mean everything to him. And up to this point, he's pushed you away because that was the safest thing he could do for you." I reached out and placed a hand on his shoulder, telling him with everything I had that what I said was the truth. "Your father loves you, Saul. He didn't have a choice when your mother took you and left. He respected her wishes to stay away, but even though he wasn't allowed to see you, he's never once forgotten about you. He's wanted to meet you for a long time."

Saul shot his gaze to mine. "Then, why wait nine years?"

I squeezed his shoulder and bit out quickly, "Two reasons. One, you're of age; and two, it's no longer safe to leave you here with your mother."

His brows drew together. "Why not?"

"Because she can't protect you, Saul. I know that may sound like a bunch of bullshit to a nine-year-old, but I can't explain it any other way, especially when it's not my place to do so. Your father will have all the answers, and if you can wait to talk to him, I know he'll tell you everything." I looked the kid in the eye. "Do you understand what I'm saying, Saul?"

The kid shifted his gaze to look over my shoulder, but I could feel his casual dismissal was in sharp contrast to the emotional turmoil writhing inside him. Another poker face, just like his father. "Sure, I understand."

I wasn't convinced but I let it fly, conscious as I sneaked a glance at my wristwatch that time was running out. Three-fifteen. The kid had missed his bus, but if he didn't leave with me soon, Catriona would come looking. "Anything else?" I asked him softly.

"If what you are saying is true and I'm in danger, what about my mother? What happens to her if I come with you? She'll be expecting me home from school soon."

I'd known this was coming and had expected it to be his first question. "We can't tell her where you're going or who you're meeting right now, Saul. She wouldn't understand, and she doesn't want you to know your father. Telling your mother about this right now will only put us all in jeopardy, including her. If you decide to come with me, I can promise you that she won't be harmed. Your father has also ensured that someone will remain to watch over her." I considered him, noting his skeptical face, and held out my arm. "Here, test me if you don't believe me."

Saul stared at my arm for a moment, then he shook his head. "No, I don't have to. I saw everything I needed to the first time. I believe you, even though you sound crazy."

His conviction gave me pause. "Why, kid?"

"Because I dreamed it," he admitted softly. "I thought I was dreaming about my father, but he was dressed just like you are. I must have been dreaming about you."

I inhaled sharply. "You're a Dream Walker?"

His eyes cut to mine. "What's that?" he returned.

I held up my hands. "It's nothing to be scared of, but you'll find out soon enough after you've met your father."

His face scrunched up, and he blew out a breath. "Fine."

"Does that mean you want to see him, Saul?" I purposely omitted the fact that his father was currently in Ireland. One step at a time.

Saul's eyes widened at the question. "I—I...don't know."

I could feel his hesitation, but it was overridden with a strong desire to meet his father. "You won't be alone, kid. I'll be there, and he's hanging out to meet you."

Saul's eyes locked on mine. "Then why didn't he come himself?"

I tensed. I couldn't very well tell him the full truth, that he and Brydie were recovering from an altercation with the sadistic leader of their druidic clan. Instead, I couched my reply. "He would have come if he could, but he's protecting someone else right now—someone important. I was the next best choice because you're my nephew, and he knows I'll do everything in my power to safely bring you to him."

His eyes narrowed, as if deciding whether or not my response held merit. I silently begged that he wouldn't ask me who and what Gage was protecting. That conversation must be had between father and son, and I was a poor substitute given I hadn't lived with the legacy as Gage had. But instead he asked, "How did you know where to find me?"

I smiled slightly. That was easy. "Your mother may have taken you away, but your father still managed to watch over you. He has always known exactly where you were, Saul."

"And now he thinks I'm in danger? Is it something to do with these gifts?" He lifted his hands.

I nodded; Saul's knowledge of his own druidic gifts only

helped my cause, making my story more believable. "Yes. It has everything to do with that. Your father can tell you all about it. That is, if you want to meet him?"

Saul's jaw locked. I could feel his indecision as he teetered on the edge. Then he exhaled. "Yes, but only because I deserve answers."

"I think you do too, kid." I withheld the triumphant smile that threatened to split my face. I'd celebrate later—when we were on the plane.

His eyes narrowed on mine. I could sense his curiosity, his burning questions, but to his credit Saul held them at bay. Instead, he hoisted his school bag up on his shoulder. "Okay, let's go then."

"That's it? No further questions?"

He shook his head. "Like I said, you've already told me everything I need to know."

"What if I told you we're also leaving the country?"

He nodded. "Yes, I know we're going to Ireland. It doesn't matter."

Huh. For a moment, I was poleaxed. All the careful subterfuge had been for nothing. I suddenly felt unsure; I'd expected more of a fight. Then I remembered that Saul was a part of an ancient prophecy wielded by the gods, that he, too, was most likely touched by fate. Blowing out a breath, I decided to roll with it. "Okay, kid. Let's go. My car's over there." I gestured to the other side of the street.

Saul's eyes popped open when he caught sight of the low-slung sports car. I had to admit that with its compact curves and sleek, black paint, the Porsche looked out of place in this suburb. "That's your ride?" he squeaked, eyebrows shooting into his hairline.

"Yeah. It's just a rental."

He whistled low under his breath. "That's a pretty flash rental!" He shot me a look. "Are you loaded then, Uncle?"

My lips lifted. "I do alright."

As he gave the Porsche another appreciative glance, I reached out and lay an arm across his shoulder. "Come on, kid, the sooner we get on the plane and to Ireland, the sooner you can ask your father as many questions as you like."

INSIDE THE PLANE, I took a seat in one of the leather chairs, then turned back to glance at Saul, who'd paused in the middle of the aisle. The kid's eyes were round as saucers, his mouth gaping.

"Something wrong, kid?"

Saul cut his gaze to mine. "You own this thing?" he asked slowly, his eyes traveling over the flat screen TVs that were bolted on side tables next to each leather chair, the gaming console and hand controller on the other side, the mini bar in the corner, the bathroom to the left, and the huge double bed visible behind a curtain at the rear of the plane.

I nodded. "It's pretty much my second home."

"Wow! Cool!"

I gestured to the leather chair beside me. "Make yourself at home. It's going to be a long flight."

My nephew didn't hesitate to jump into a chair and clip his seat belt on before reaching for the gaming console and a pair of Bluetooth headphones.

At that moment, two pilots entered the cabin, one fair-haired, the other dark, both showing iron gray at their temples. They weren't my usual on-call pilots, but almost a month ago now I'd sent mine on an extended holiday after deciding to stay with Gage. The pilots who'd flown me to the States had returned to Ireland a few days back, and I'd managed to book these two late last night.

The fair one walked forward, hand extended. "Sir, I'm Mark Collins. It's nice to meet you in person. Thank you for employing our services for the return trip to Ireland." As we shook hands, he gestured to the man beside him. "This is Captain Mann, who'll be flying the plane with me. The weather is looking stable for the next twelve hours, however, in case of any turbulence, it's advisable to remain in your seat with the seatbelt fastened."

"Thank you. I appreciate you both coming on board at such short notice." I gestured to Saul. "This is my nephew, Saul. Please don't worry about attending to our needs; I know where everything is, and the boy and I can see to ourselves for the duration of the flight."

Captain Collins looked relieved. He nodded and clasped his hands together. "Great. Well, we'll get back to flight prep then."

I inclined my head.

After a quick salute, they entered the cockpit, shutting the door firmly behind them.

I turned to Saul and gestured to the gaming console in his hand. "I hope you're ready for an ass-whooping, kid. It's been a while since I played a worthy opponent."

Saul's eyes lit up, and without further hesitation, he slammed on his headphones.

CHAPTER 45

TALORGAN

PRESENT DAY

On a plane over the Atlantic Ocean

I blinked. The sun pierced my vision and threw warmth over my skin. I relished the heat, the smells, the tastes on the air. I felt my blood pumping; the oxygen flowing through my body. It felt good to *feel* again, to experience something other than pain and decay. But for all this, I knew I was on limited time. I could already feel my vessel struggling, the brain hemorrhaging. Humans were a poor receptacle for my power, but I would take any chance I had at such freedom.

I glanced down at my new body, noting the crisp, white uniform. The badge on my chest was brassy and bright. Squinting, I read the word 'Captain' upside down before I discreetly looked around me. I sat in the cockpit of a plane, my hands clenched around the controls. A man sat to my left, seemingly dozing with his head tipped back and his eyes closed.

Elation raced through me. I'd done it! For the third time in as little as a few weeks, I'd managed to leave the Nether and enter another vessel. This new alliance with the druid was bringing me a host of benefits previously outside of my reach, and I berated myself for not exploring this avenue before now. But I couldn't dally, not today; I had a plan I needed to set into motion.

I felt the grin split my face, and I flexed my fingers. The plane suddenly nosedived.

"Collins! What the fuck?" the man to my left shouted as he scrambled upright. He was dressed similarly, also with a badge on his chest. Captain Mann. I held a vague memory in my mind of entering the cockpit with him.

"Sorry." I forced the word out of my mouth, curbing the instinctual pull of the vessel. "My fingers slipped."

Mann sent me a dark look as he grabbed for his own set of controls, pulling them back firmly before flicking a switch. His jaw clenched as he forcefully leveled the plane back into a smooth climb. Only then did he whip his head toward me. "What the hell was that, Collins?" he demanded, his eyes conveying a modicum of concern. "You've never lapsed on the job before. Are you feeling okay? Maybe you should take a break."

I cleared my throat, but the words didn't come. Exerting a small amount of pressure on my vessel's brain, I triggered another response. "It might be wise if I take a break. I'll check our passengers."

My voice stumbled on the last two words as I felt the man behind the body trying to break free and take control. I gritted my teeth and exerted more pressure, feeling a few blood vessels burst inside the brain. I bit off a curse, aware that with that action, I would only have a few minutes left in this body.

Mann blinked at me, his eyes wide. "Okay, Collins, take

as long as you need. Have a nap even; I can take it from here."

I jerked my head stiffly and extracted myself from the cramped space. I forced my vessel to exit the cockpit as quickly as possible, aware that time was no longer on my side. On entering the main cabin, I immediately spied my targets seated at a small table in the middle of the plane. They were both dark haired and blue eyed, one a child, the other a man.

The man looked up as I entered, his gaze piercing, and I felt a twinge of awareness. He was a dead ringer for his brother, the only difference being that he was smoother, less rough around the edges, and with an urbane, sophisticated grace to his movements. My eyes traveled over to his companion. The kid looked no more than ten years of age. I smelt his lineage immediately, confirming exactly whose son he was.

I withheld a shout of triumph. I'd done it! I'd located Gage's brother and his son, managing once again to travel into a body that could get close to my targets. The incident on Beinn na Caillich had been my first experiment and was testament that such an action was possible. It had also shown me that there were restrictions in this newfound freedom, time being one of them. The human body wasn't capable of withstanding all that I was. A sense of urgency pushed me forward into the room.

The kid's brow furrowed as he spied me, and I immediately sensed his unease. Gage's twin looked up, as if he'd felt his nephew's emotion. Their actions confirmed they both held potential, an awareness that was higher than the average human. It was another piece to the puzzle, another step in the right direction—if I could achieve what I had set out to do.

It was exhilarating to come close to my prey, to know that in one move I could end their short lives with a final kiss. It was tempting to succumb to this dark urge, which over the years of servitude to my Dark God had only become more entrenched. Gritting my teeth against this insinuating desire, I held my thoughts firm to the ultimate end game, visualizing what it was I most desired, and reminded myself of the larger plan at stake. There would be no killing today.

"What was that?" Logan demanded with an edge to his tone. "Are we running out of fuel?"

"No, just some unforeseen turbulence. I came to check on you both. My colleague, Captain Mann, is still flying the plane."

I'd barely got the words out before my heart thundered hard. I stumbled, one hand instinctively scrabbling at my chest.

"Jesus, are you alright?" Gage's brother immediately moved forward, a hand reaching out for my arm. I accepted his touch, biting back a smile of triumph as he guided me into a seat. In that moment, I took the opportunity that chance afforded me. I clutched his arm and imposed my will on my vessel, forcing the fingernails to extend into claws. They pierced the flesh of the man's arm, and I quickly released the carefully crafted poison. I saw Gage's brother's body stiffen, aware of the exact moment my gift entered his bloodstream.

"Uncle?" the boy asked from behind him.

I sensed rather than saw the kid jump up from his chair and move toward us. Aware I had mere seconds, I leaned in close and hissed in the man's ear, "You are mine!" Then I pulled back, extracting my nails from his arm.

Gage's brother reeled back, his face a dazed mask.

My heart beat sluggishly now, and I was aware of its failing as I silently watched the kid grab hold of his uncle.

"Logan? What is it? What's wrong? Are you ill?" The kid asked, his distrustful gaze flicking back to mine. I kept my face carefully blank even as I felt more blood vessels burst.

Gage's brother blinked at his nephew, focusing on his expression. "I'm fine, kid. I just lost my balance for a moment."

"Well, you should also sit down then."

As my head dropped to the side, I saw the kid guide his uncle to a chair. Elation spear-headed through me, and I felt a smile crest my lips as I celebrated that phase one had been successful. But that final motion was my undoing, and the tether holding me to this world suddenly snapped. No longer able to accommodate the weight of my power, my vessel's brain imploded.

CHAPTER 46
SAUL
PRESENT DAY

On a plane over the Atlantic Ocean

I settled my uncle and turned back to the pilot. His head had rolled to the side, and he was staring back at me with his eyes wide open. His face was gray, and there was a strange, triumphant smile stretched across his lips.

I shivered. There was something odd about him, something I didn't trust. But why wasn't he moving? Why was he staring at me like that?

I slowly moved forward, reluctant to approach but undeniably drawn to the pilot. By the time I stood within touching distance, I confirmed what I already knew to be true—the pilot was dead.

TO BE CONTINUED IN ...

Winter's Vengeance (Daughter of Winter, Book 5)

Uncertain allies, faltering battle plans, and a shocking future. The legacy is no longer what it seemed.

Broken by the horrors she experienced at the hand of their Druidic leader, Brydie and those she loves escape to Faerie. There, shattered by grief and with her spirit fractured, she must begin the road to healing while still forging the path that fate demands of her.

The shadow of war is a burgeoning storm cloud on the horizon, and a series of dangerous assumptions may destroy all chance of victory. The need to secure allies is more pressing than ever, and Brydie must navigate her way through tenuous relationships to reawaken long-dead alliances with distrustful Fae, dwarves, and selkies—even as the weight of a terrible secret threatens to shatter all hope for her future.

Destiny awaits, and so does her final altercation with the Dark One, but first, vengeance must be wrought.

Winter's Vengeance is the fifth book in a dark fantasy romance series based on the myths and legends of the Celtic winter goddess, Cailleach Bheur. Featuring dark magic, druids, fae, selkies, mythical creatures, and a morally grey hero with an enemies-to-lovers romance, it is perfect for fans of From Blood and Ash, A Court of Thorns and Roses, and the Fever series.

WHAT DID YOU THINK?

Thank you for reading the fourth book in the *Daughter of Winter* series. If you enjoyed *Daughter of Winter,* can I ask a big favour? Please, can you take the time to leave a star rating and a short, honest review on Amazon, Bookbub, and/or Goodreads? As an indie author, reviews are our lifeblood as they not only give the author (me) valuable feedback, but they also enable our book to become visible to other readers. Therefore, your review is sincerely appreciated.

Additionally, if you'd like to reach out and provide feedback about this book or simply to say "hi," please don't hesitate to email me at *corina_douglus@live.com* as I'd love to hear from you!

GLOSSARY OF TERMS

All Father (The) — See 'Custodian of Creation' and 'The Phoenix'.

Banshee — A beautiful, wailing woman wearing a long, white dress. Seeing and hearing a banshee would herald your death.

Beinn na Caillich — A mountain in the Isle of Skye, located on the Red Cuillin (see 'The Cuillin' below), also referred to as 'The Hill of the Old Woman' in association with the Cailleach.

Ben Cruachan — The highest summit of a grand range of sharp peaks between Loch Awe and Loch Etive in Argyll and Bute, Scotland. Said to be the home of the Cailleach.

Carlin Stone — A prehistoric standing stone associated with the Cailleach. In *Daughter of Winter*, the stone regenerates Cailleach's power, while also acting as a portal to other worlds.

Children of Winter – Children of Cailleach Bheur i.e., those associated with The Oaken Tree.

Cliffs of Moher — A series of cliffs that tower over the rugged coastline of County Clare, Ireland. They are the focus of much folklore and said to be home to otherworldly beings and mystical creatures. In *Daughter of Winter*, they are the gateway to Faerie, which is the home of the Tuatha Dé Danann.

Cuillins (The) — The most prominent mountain range on the Isle of Skye. The range is broken into two distinct groups, defined by the color of their rocks, one red, the other black, or otherwise known as the Black Cuillin and the Red Cuillin.

Cù-Sìth – A large, dark green, shaggy hellhound. Three of them assist Arawn in his rule of the Underworld. They are said to be a harbinger of death, with paws the size of a man's hand and glowing, green eyes. Their job is to accompany depraved souls to the Underworld.

Custodian of Creation (The) — Also referred to as the 'All Father' or 'The Phoenix'. He created all the Celtic gods and goddesses; they are all his children. His role is to ensure a balance is maintained within this world and others.

Dagda's Cauldron (The) — One of the four treasures of the Tuatha Dé Danann. It is said to leave no one unsatisfied and can bring about your heart's desires. Like all things, it can also be used for evil, and in *Daughter of Winter*, Callum uses it to coerce people to do his bidding.

Dark Arts (The) – Druidic magic that utilizes the darkness rather than the light. Using it comes with consequences, which are often deadly.

Daughter of Winter (A) – A direct descendant of Cailleach Bheur.

Dormant (A) – Someone who possesses no ability to access their magic.

Dream Walker (A) – A druid who can roam alternate planes by way of dreams, ofttimes with the ability to look forward into the future and backward into the past.

Druid (A) – Children of the Celtic gods, and humans who follow pagan lore and/or wield the natural power of the world around us (thus, even those who are Dormant are still considered druids). Every druidic clan in *Daughter of Winter* is associated with one of the Celtic deities i.e., The Oaken Tree, which is Gage and Brydie's clan, is associated with the Cailleach.

Dullahan (A) — A headless man riding a black war horse.

Equinox Stone — Refers to the stone inside 'Hag's Cairn' (see below). It is said that when the spring equinox is in play, the dawn light spears the stone, tracing a mural of prehistoric art that is said to mimic the movement of the rising sun. In *Daughter of Winter*, it is a location of potent power, providing another link to the Cailleach.

Faerie — The underground home of the Tuatha Dé Danann. In *Daughter of Winter*, it can only be accessed through a portal at Hag's Head on the Cliffs of Moher at sundown.

Four treasures of the Tuatha Dé Danann — The Sword of Nuada, the Spear of Lugh, the Cauldron of the Dagda, and the Lia Fáil (Stone of Destiny). Each treasure is said to come from four magical cities: Findias, Gorias, Murias, and Falias, from the original homeland of the Tuatha Dé Danann, up in the stars.

Gauls — Groups of ancient Celtic people who came from a region of Western Europe, encompassing present-day France, Belgium, the Netherlands, Luxembourg, and parts of Switzerland, Germany, and Northern Italy.

Glamaig — The highest peak of Benin na Caillich.

Glamored — A magical disguise, where we blur the lines of our true forms.

Gleann Caillich — A valley in Argyll and Bute, Scotland, again associated with the Cailleach.

Glen Sligachan — A small settlement near the Cuillin mountain range.

Guardian (A) — The man prophesied to protect the Daughter of Winter. In *Daughter of Winter,* this is Gage, and previously his grandfather, Reuben, before him.

Gulf of Corryvreckan — A narrow strait between the islands of Jura and Scarba, located in Argyll and Bute off the west coast of mainland Scotland. It is said the Cailleach used to wash her great plaid in the waters to usher in the turn of the season from autumn to winter.

Hag's Cairn — A chamber inside a megalithic tomb complex at Slieve na Calliagh. It is home to the 'Equinox Stone' and comes alight when the spring equinox is in play. It is also said this is the burial tomb of Ollom Fotla, a past High King of Ireland.

Hag's Head — The name given to the most southerly point of the Cliffs of Moher in County Clare, Ireland.

Hellhound – See 'Cù-Sìth' above.

Isle of Skye — The second largest island in Scotland, located in the Inner Hebrides, on the west coast.

Kyle of Lochalsh — A small village located in the county of Ross & Cromarty that is located on the Lochalsh peninsula. A bridge provides access to the Isle of Skye, which is located on the other side of the peninsula.

Lore Keeper — A druid who knows how to interpret and read the language of the Celtic deity they have formed a connection with. To be a Lore Keeper, one must undergo years of training.

Lore Books — Contains all the runes and enchantments associated with a particular Celtic deity. These books can only be read by Lore Keepers who have formed a connection with a Celtic deity.

Magical Signature — The residue of someone's magic, felt upon the air by using your senses.

Null (A) — Druids who ingest magic. They cannot perform magic themselves but can easily absorb its efforts, making it null and void.

Phoenix (The) — See 'Custodian of Creation' and 'All Father'.

Runes — Runes are ancient alphabets used by early peoples. In *Daughter of Winter,* we refer to these as druidic runes. They are based on the Ogham Script (which is an ancient language associated with trees), but later included its own alphabet. Druids cast runes to conduct magic.

Samhain — A day marking the end of the lighter half of the year (summer) and the beginning of the darker half of the year (winter). On this day, the veil between the living and the dead is especially thin, allowing spirits of the dead and those living on other planes to visit our world.

Sensitive (A) — Someone who holds no druidic power but carries a heightened sixth sense. In *Daughter of Winter,* Logan is a Sensitive, and he can feel Gage's emotions, even from across the other side of the world.

Sgùrr Alasdair — The summit of the Black Cuillin (see The Cuillin).

Shieling — A stone hut.

Siren (A) — A beautiful, naked maiden with razor sharp teeth who likes to devour men.

Slieve na Calliagh (also known as the Loughcrew tombs) — A range of hills containing an ancient burial site near Oldcastle, County Meath, Ireland, which are named after the Cailleach. It is said she created these monuments while striding across the land and dropping large stones from her apron. Slieve na Calliagh contains more than twenty ancient passage tombs and cairns dating back to the 4th millennium BC. The two main tombs on the site are known as Cairn L and Cairn T, the latter of which is also called the 'Tomb of Allah Fodhla' or the 'Hag's Cairn'.

Sluagh (A) — A dead malevolent ghost.

Tarn — A small mountain lake.

The Alder Tree — The druidic clan based in Northern Ireland.

The Oaken Tree — Gage, Ian, and Brydie's druidic clan.

The Other — An alternative reality where people and all living things are reborn (if not cast to the Underworld for misdeeds).

The Rowan Tree — The fae clan based in Faerie, whose sovereign goddess is Morrígan.

The Stone of Destiny — One of the four treasures of the Tuatha Dé Danann (see above).

Tuatha Dé Danann (The) — People of the goddess, Danu. They are a race of supernatural beings who inhabited Ireland before the ancestors of the modern Irish. In *Daughter of Winter* they are referred to as 'the fae.'

The Underworld — The Underworld used to be a rich and mystical place of beauty, youth, health, and joy. However, due to events happening between Arawn and his siblings, it turned into a place of sin, death, and depravity. In *Daughter of Winter,* those who turn to the Dark Arts and exercise dark magic are sent to the Underworld on their death, rather than the Other.

Touched (to be) — To be possessed by Talorgan.

Voice — A technique learned early in druidic training. If done correctly in the right tone and with the right emotion and intention, it can coerce people to do your bidding.

Yule — Yule marks the winter solstice, which is the shortest day/longest night of the year, marking the turning point where the sun begins its long journey back to its midsummer peak.

Watcher (A) — A member of the Tuatha Dé Danann who chooses to watch the Daughter of Winter.

Winter Solstice — The longest night—or when the sun is tilted at its furthest point away from the earth. It was celebrated by the Celts in similar ways to how Christmas is celebrated.

Wulver (A) — A half-wolf, half-man. It has the body of a man with a wolf's head and is covered in short brown fur.

LIST OF CHARACTERS

Airmid — A short, brown-haired fae woman who attends to the needs of Brydie and Gage and the rest of their company while in Faerie.

Andrew MacKay — Brydie's deceased father. He died in a car accident a few years ago with his wife.

Aidan — McKenzie's son.

Aine — A member of The Oaken Tree. She is a descendant of Cerridwen, and the Lore Keeper of Morrígan's Lore Book.

Alison — The current Lore Keeper of Cailleach's Lore Book.

Berit — A guard of The Oaken Tree. He was killed by Gage when he and Brydie infiltrated the Institute to rescue Chloe.

Brydie MacKay — A young, orphaned woman who lives in New Zealand. She is unaware she is the marked by an ancient prophecy wielded by the gods and the Daughter of Winter—the last living female descendant of Cailleach Bheur.

Briana — One of Callum's 'companions,' forced to adhere to his sexual appetite.

Callum — Current leader of The Oaken Tree.

Caroline — Ian's ex-fiancee, murdered by Falin when pregnant with Ian's child.

Carrick — One of The Oaken Tree. Along with Alison and others, he helped Gage and Brydie escape the Institute.

Catriona — The mother of Gage's son, Saul. She lives in America.

Chloe — Brydie's best friend. In Winter's Legion, we find out she is being held captive by Callum at the Institute.

Conall — From The Oaken Tree. A man who approached Gage with Briana, Oona, Mark, and Alison.

The Council — Also known as the Wise Ones. They are learned masters of druidic lore who have earned the right to take a position on the Council. They are the voice of reason and act as a benchmark against the leader of The Oaken Tree's rule, thus preventing totalitarianism.

Cynthia MacKay — Brydie's deceased mother. She died in a car accident a few years ago with her husband.

Darryn & Michael — Two friends who Chloe and Brydie party with at a nightclub in New Zealand.

Duane — A guard of the Tuatha Dé Danann. He helps to guard the gate in and out of Faerie.

Eachna — A guard of the Tuatha Dé Danann. She guards the gate in and out of Faerie.

Egan — A prison warden of The Oaken Tree who took many liberties with his position. He held Gage prisoner when he was captured at the Institute, and for his sins, was later killed by Gage.

Edmund Judd — The owner of a jewelry store in New Zealand.

Fergus — The previous leader of The Oaken Tree. Deceased.

Frederick — One of The Oaken Tree. Along with Alison and others, he helped Gage and Brydie escape the Institute.

Gage Campbell — A druidic bodyguard tasked with protecting the Daughter of Winter.

Garret — A young man touched by Talorgan, who they met at the Claymore pub at Broadford Bay.

Ian — Gage's friend, and one of the descendants marked by prophecy. He is a historian who lives in Perth, Scotland.

Ingrid — Ian's sister, and Callum's new wife.

Jack — Aidan's Jack Russell.

James — Brydie's ex-fiancé.

Jason — One of The Oaken Tree. Along with Alison and others, he helped Gage and Brydie escape the Institute.

Julian — One of Callum's guards. He helped Callum torture Brydie at the Institute.

Liam — One of The Oaken Tree. Along with Alison and others, he helped Gage and Brydie escape the Institute.

Lorcan — The leader of the fae/Tuatha Dé Danann. He is a direct descendant of Morrígan and can shape-shift into the crow, and is therefore ordained to be the one to lift the curse hanging over his people by finding the descendant of Carman.

Logan — Gage's twin brother.

McKenzie — Nora's housekeeper, but also one of the descendants of prophecy. She is an experienced and powerful Dream Walker.

Mahon — Of the Tuatha Dé Danann. He is one of Lorcan's spies.

Margaret — Chloe's adoptive mother.

Mark — From The Oaken Tree. A young lad who approached Gage with Briana, Oona, Conall, and Alison.

Mary – An old crone, who is one of Callum's three personal guards.

Melanie — The woman James works with, and who he slept with while engaged to Brydie.

Nora MacKay — Brydie's grandmother, and the previous Daughter of Winter.

Oona — One of Callum's 'companions,' forced to adhere to his sexual appetite.

Padriac — Of the Tuatha Dé Danann. He is one of Lorcan's spies.

Patrick – Chloe's adoptive father.

Phoenix (The) — Also known as the All Father or The Custodian of Creation. He created all the Celtic gods and goddesses; they are all his children.

Rascal — Brydie's cat in New Zealand.

Regan — One of the guards at the Institute. He led the fight on Callum's behalf against those who were rebelling against Callum's rule *and* providing a diversion to get Brydie and Gage out.

Reuben — Gage's grandfather, and the previous Guardian of Nora.

Ryan — Alison's brother. He was killed by Callum after being forced to delve into the dark arts.

Sandra Morgan — The security guard who tried to run them down on the road to Perth, Scotland.

Saul Campbell — Gage's son.

Simon — A man touched by Talorgan who meets Brydie in a nightclub and drugs her with the intention of kidnapping her. (We find out his real name was Bevan in *Winter's Legion*.)

The Wise Ones — See 'The Council' above.

Past Characters:

Arawn — The Dark God. Ruler of the Underworld and all inhabitants.

Brenna — A druid from The Oaken Tree clan. She is Tritus's mother and Cernunnos's lover.

Bres — Half-Fomoire, half-Tuatha, he was once a leader of the Tuatha Dé Danann. He was a terrible leader and was thus replaced by Nuada of the silver hand.

Brighid — The goddess of light, who ruled over the summer months from Beltane to Samhain.

Brude — One of Arawn's three hellhounds (or Cù-Sìth). Brude is the largest of them all and the leader of the trio.

Cailleach Bheur — The ancient Celtic goddess of winter and the harbinger of death. She is more readily known as the crone but can also appear as a beautiful young woman. She rules over the winter months from Samhain to Beltane, with the mantle then passing over to her sister, Brighid, to rule over the summer months.

Carman — A witch from Athens who moved to Ireland with her three sons after her husband died.

Cernunnos — A horned ancient Celtic deity known as the Wild God of the Forest, who ruled over animals, fertility, and wild places. In *Daughter of Winter,* he used to rule over the winter months prior to Cailleach attaining his role. He is Tritus's father.

Cerridwen — The goddess of prophecy.

Ciniath — A druid from Talorgan and Drust's village who was recruited by Talorgan to fight in Arawn's army. He was killed by Arawn when he tried to save his sister, Fionnuala, who was chosen as one of the thirteen virgin sacrifices at Samhain.

Dagda — Known as the King of the Druids, or the Good God. He is a well-known Celtic deity who ruled over life, death, the seasons, agriculture, fertility, magic, and druidry.

The Dark Master — One of the druidic masters—or one of The Wise Ones—from the Pict village where Drust and Talorgan grew up.

Drust — A Druidic warrior from a Pict village where Tritus's people strike up an uneasy alliance. He is also Talorgan's twin brother (identical).

Falin — One of Arawn's three dragons.

Fionnuala — A woman from Talorgan and Drust's village who was recruited by Talorgan as one of thirteen virgin sacrifices at Samhain. She was burned on a pyre with twelve other women.

Girom — A druidic master of herbal lore and Talorgan's mentor.

Ligach — He was the first descendent of Cerridwen, the goddess of prophecy.

Lonc — One of Arawn's three hellhounds (or Cù-Sìth). Brother to Brude and Uren.

Morrigan — A sovereign goddess of the Tuatha Dé Danann, well known as a great war queen and associated with war, death, and sexual power.

Phoenix (The) — The All Father. The Custodian of Creation. He created all the Celtic gods and goddesses. They are all his children.

Talorgan — A druidic acolyte who lost his way by falling for a woman he couldn't have (Cailleach) and striking a bargain with the Dark God to make her his. This action caused Arawn to form a connection with this world and is what caused everything to unravel. He is also Drust's identical twin brother.

Tritus — A Gaul who came from across the salty sea. He arrives in Scotland with his tribe, who strikes up an uneasy alliance with a Pict village.

Uren — One of Arawn's three hellhounds (or Cù-Sìth). Brother to Lonc and Brude.

About the Author

Corina Douglas lives in New Zealand with her husband and four kids. If she's not running her indie editing business, *Burning Legacies Publishing,* she can be found exploring the forest, doing that stretchy yoga thing, or with her nose in a good book. She writes dark fantasy romance stories based on Celtic mythology, with a special focus on pagan Scottish, Irish, and Welsh folklore.

Corina loves to hear from her readers. Join her on social media and stay up to date with future works by visiting the sites below. You can also join her monthly newsletter and grab a free short story from her website.

www.corinadouglas.com

- amazon.com/author/corina.douglas
- tiktok.com/@corina.douglas.author
- instagram.com/CDouglas_author
- facebook.com/corina.douglas.author
- bookbub.com/authors/corina-douglas
- pinterest.com/CDouglas_author

ACKNOWLEDGMENTS

I would like to thank everyone who has helped me on this journey, most especially my husband, Jonny, who has loaned me the use of his office (and vehicle!) on the odd weekend and dealt with the children and their dinner while I try to write in peace.

Special thanks goes to Maria, my wonderful cover designer, who has breathed visual life into the series with my new rebranded covers.

Thank you also to the numerous people at SPS, who have become my author friends. To name a few, this includes Nola, Linda, Joy, Wendy, Qat, Ally, Jeff, Jess, Astrid, Ashley, Heather, Lauren, Reen, Tasche, etc. I truly treasure your friendships even though we live on opposite sides of the world. Keep on writing!

And finally, most especially thank you to you, Cooper. Life is precious; we must hold onto it with everything we have. Please know I love you so very much.